Fortune's Hostage

RON BURROWS

Published 2009 by arima publishing

www.arimapublishing.com

ISBN 978 1 84549 381 3

Printed and bound in the United Kingdom

Typeset in Garamond 11/14

Swirl is an imprint of arima publishing.

arima publishing
ASK House, Northgate Avenue
Bury St Edmunds, Suffolk IP32 6BB
t: (+44) 01284 700321

www.arimapublishing.com

For Caroline

Chapter One

Portland, England, February 1758. Jack Easton stands at the window of the room that he has made his base of operations since returning from Maryland on his mission of revenge. Before him, through the leaded panes, lies the craggy wooded valley that winds down three hundred feet to Church Ope Cove, scene of the fateful ambush that was the start of all his troubles. His face is still, but his brow is creased as if fretting on some mystifying puzzle. He shakes his head almost imperceptibly and lets out a long reflective sigh. A letter has been delivered from Captain Auld, late of the Rebecca, and it is still clutched in Jack's hand. Its contents have left him a little shaken.

The captain's promise to share the prize money from the captured French brigantine, *L'hermine,* had been on Jack's mind for weeks, but he had never really let himself believe that it would amount to much. With the arrival of the letter, however, he now knew its worth, and his thoughts were already airborne on a wild flight of fancy, flitting from one heady possibility to another. Hopes and aspirations, dreamt and then discarded once as unattainable, were now suddenly within his grasp. As he recalled these half-forgotten dreams, bringing each before his mind's eye like some rediscovered treasure, his gaze wandered down the steep descent that lay before him until coming to rest on the sheltered waters of the Cove. The virtual descent was calming; his view was now of a timeless scene in which a pair of crabbing boats moved about unhurriedly amongst the floats that marked their pots. For the fishermen who sculled the sturdy lerrets, these daily rituals might never change, thought Jack wryly, as he sifted the calamitous events that had snatched him from such humdrum routines. But his gaze did not linger in the Cove for long. A low winter sun laid a shimmering path across the blue expanse of the bay beyond, drawing his eyes upwards to the distant horizon, which lay steel-edged against a watery February sky. Someone less taken by his thoughts might have admired the stunning view, but Jack was almost blind to it. Was he dreaming all this, he wondered, suddenly? No, surely not, the letter in his hand was proof enough, even though he had needed to read it several times to be sure that he had not misunderstood the captain's intent. The frown that had dwelt upon his forehead now melted, and his eyes, caught by reflections of the sunny scene outside, lit up as if he had been struck with some amazing thought. Captain Auld had indeed been true to his word! For Jack's part in the brigantine's capture, his share of the prize money would amount to a staggering one thousand guineas. He was now richer than he could ever have imagined!

Jack placed the letter on the table and stood enjoying the moment, pondering the happy state of things. Everything that he could have hoped for seemed miraculously to have fallen into place: Smyke, his tormentor, had been convicted and would hang; Jack himself had been exonerated and could now return to America as a free man, the stain upon his name removed for good; and his family's Wakeham quarry too had been rescued from certain financial ruin. Jack had every reason to be satisfied with the outcomes of his brave mission, embarked upon from his Maryland exile, admittedly, with such vague and naïve expectations six months before. This monetary reward was breathtaking and very welcome, but it was the icing on a cake of triumph and delight, and it made a very rich mixture indeed!

But Jack was not long in this euphoric state before his mood began to cool, becoming by degree more thoughtful and calculating. Other items of news in Auld's letter had captured Jack's interest too, and one item in particular had caught his eye. No doubt Auld's conversational snippets had been written as incidental background, perhaps by way of filling out the captain's second page, but the reference to his movements after berthing his tobacco ship, *Rebecca,* in Cowes had caused Jack to speculate nevertheless. He picked up the letter and read the page again.

'*...I kept L'hermine in view for a good while after casting you and First Officer Goddard off in the Channel approaches.*' The captain wrote neatly in an educated hand. '*Her jury rig looked most ungainly as you sailed north-east for Portland and I admit to having had a few doubts as to her seaworthiness after the pounding that we gave her. I gather from Goddard, however, that the rig held up well despite being put severely to the test on your helter-skelter ride around the Bill! Another near miss, Jack, from what I hear – that blessed guardian angel of yours continues to watch over you! My Rebecca, by comparison, made more sedate progress to Cowes due to the slack winds – and then, to cap it all, I was forced to fret a night at anchor outside Hurst Castle as the tide had turned against us by the time we approached the narrows. Damned infuriating it was too, for the Cowes approaches were clearly in sight not ten miles up the Solent! Arriving at Cowes somewhat later than I* *had expected the following morning, I thus left the ship and sailed for Portsmouth at once to commence negotiations on the value of our prize; and it was as well I did for I arrived just as Goddard brought L'hermine in and anchored in the Roads. As you will now know from this letter, I was able to extract a most satisfactory sum from their Lordships, but it was not without some adroitness on my part...'*

The Captain went on to mention the French officers and seamen who had been taken captive in the skirmish - men now destined to languish as prisoners of war until arrangements could be made for a satisfactory exchange. Like sacrificial pawns, they would be given up in a game of diplomatic trading with the enemy; it had been their value in this respect that had made the prize so high. However, while Jack had found all this of interest, it was the captain's hasty departure for Portsmouth that had been of the greater significance, and it was this that had therefore drawn his eye.

To understand why this fragment of information was a matter of such intrigue may be worth some explanation. It might be remembered that the boatswain aboard the *Rebecca*, a Mr Judd, was a shifty character who had played a clever sleight of hand with the cargo of tobacco, slipping a portion of it from the main manifest onto another of his own keeping - one from which sales would enrich his own pocket. It was a clever scam that had gone practically undetected during several previous trips; indeed he had employed threats of violence to get the new first officer of the *Rebecca*, Philip Goddard, to cooperate. The captain's early departure was therefore significant in that it would have left Judd in charge of the ship, and he would certainly have capitalised on this lack of supervision - especially since everything, including the re-branding of the hogsheads, had already been set up for his subterfuge.

It may also be remembered that Jack had been given a free passage aboard the *Rebecca* by the shipping agent, Thomas Harding, in Charlestown to keep an eye on the cargo because of his suspicions of skulduggery. But when Jack was caught nosing around the hold inspecting Harding's consignment, Judd had had him thrown into the brig to prevent him finding out too much. Being locked up had not stopped Jack from deducing Judd's game eventually, but it was nearly the end of him, for as an illegally returning exile he would have been hanged if he had been handed over to the authorities.

Then, in a stroke of luck as it was to turn out in the end, the French warship, *L'hermine*, had appeared on the horizon and Captain Auld, providentially, had had Jack released for the ensuing fight. Judd must have thought himself undone with Jack once more on deck, but by then Jack and Philip Goddard had already cooked up a plan to catch Judd in the act so as to ensure his conviction. By electing not to confront him there an then, they made the boatswain believe that he had been let off the hook. Their subsequent departure to sail the prize-ship home without anything further being said on the matter, should have reinforced this impression. And now the captain, by his absence at the unloading, might unknowingly have contributed to the illusion.

As Jack brought all this back to mind, he could not help feeling a certain anticipatory malice at the notion of Judd's thinking himself in the clear. For if the boatswain had proceeded with his planned thievery as had been hoped, he would have fallen straight into the trap that Jack had set with his warning note to the agent in Cowes. The thought of Judd's bewildered face when he was caught red-handed on the quay turned Jack's malice into outright pleasure!

All this said, it was still only wishful thinking on Jack's part that Judd's demise would have been the inevitable outcome of Auld's early departure. But it was at least a distinct possibility that the boatswain would now be behind bars, and his intimidation of the first officer thus ended. If this had indeed come to pass, thought Jack, it would be the happiest possible conclusion to a lamentable episode in his new friend's career. Moreover, Judd would never know who had brought him down, and thus would not be likely to direct his vengeance at Goddard or his family as he had threatened, nor damn him with accusations of complicity. This was what the pair had plotted so carefully to avoid; for if Goddard's hapless entanglement with Judd's activities became public, it would punish the young officer's momentary naivety with lifelong disgrace – a disproportionate sentence, Jack thought.

Eventually tiring of this conjecture, however, Jack's thoughts soon drifted back to the main content of Auld's letter; and he allowed himself again to be taken by the heady fancies of his new wealth. It had not been long since Jack had won his freedom by being acquitted of the cooked-up charges that had ultimately led to his exile. After his years of penal servitude it still felt strange to come and go just as he pleased. But now the prospect of prosperity had shifted the very foundations of his life.

To clear his mind, Jack took a walk across the Island to the west cliffs where he stood for a while gazing down upon the rocks on which he had so nearly met his end in *L'hermine*. The breaking waves were calmer now, but the terrifying images of that early-dawn near-catastrophe as the Portland cliffs sprung out of the darkness, flashed into his mind with startling clarity. With a shudder, he recalled his desperate fight at the helm of the captured French brigantine as he nursed her stalling sails to claw upon the treacherous wind to save the damaged vessel from a splintering demise. In his mind's eye, he saw Goddard and his crew dashing from mast to block and back again in their frantic battle to trim the sails to a new and vital tack. A shiver ran down his spine as he relived the agonising minutes of uncertainty that followed - as fate teetered in a lethal balance between the rocks on one side and the maelstrom of the tidal race on the other.

Dragging his thoughts once more back to the present, he glanced down to the Bill - and beyond, southwards, out into the benign blue vistas of a placid English Channel where full sails of every shape made stately progress on the gentle breeze. There were no whitecaps on the Race now, no threatening skies, none of the vicious over-falls of that grim dawn when the violence of the rip might have torn his jury rig to shreds and left them at the mercy of the unforgiving waves. Behind him sat the squat tower of the lighthouse whose extinguished fire had shone no warning, as if it had meant the course of his life to finish there, his mission of revenge left unconsummated.

But he had succeeded then, just as his good fortune had also prevailed during all the challenges that he had encountered on his long voyage from Maryland, a mission embarked upon with such careless optimism only three short months before. He now realised how lucky he had been to pull it off, for he well knew that he had brought Smyke to justice as much by providence as by any cleverness on his part. It seemed almost as if some guiding hand had steered him and protected him - as if God's light had shined upon a righteous goal. That dreadful episode in his life was now behind him, and he thanked the Lord; but as he gazed across Lyme Bay, with salty air once more upon his face, he found himself suddenly rather restless. Perhaps it was his recollections of these adventures that had fired him: the heady sense of dangers overcome? Perhaps his fibre was beginning to rebel against the lulling sense of ease that had recently set in, the dawning of listlessness after living on the edge of danger for so long? Whatever the reason, he found himself curiously craving some new adventure, some new challenge that would test him again. Was this a young man's restless soul that spoke so bravely into the wind, it might be wondered; or was it tempting providence; or perhaps even a premonition of things to come? We shall soon know the answer.

Jack looked westwards to the horizon, imagining that his extended line of sight over the countless horizons that lay beyond would end at his new farmstead at New Hope, and that the sea below his feet would connect him directly to it like an uninterrupted thoroughfare. He thought longingly of his wife, Rose, waiting for him there, pregnant with their first child; and he recalled his solemn if hopeful promise to be back in time for the birth. He thought fondly of Ned and Sebi, his faithful partners on the farmstead whom he had come to look upon almost as his brothers. And as he thought of them, a smile came to his face at the memory of their unease on the night they had found themselves forced to take sides as Rose had tried to prevent his going. While they had not exactly been fulsome in their endorsement of his reckless mission, neither had they tried to interfere. Jack hoped that they would be pleased with what he brought them, for he intended them all to benefit from his gain.

It was such thoughts as these that beckoned him home, and the gentle landscapes and quiet, verdant creeks of the Potomac formed rosy and alluring pictures in his imagination. The memories of the hardships he had earlier endured as a convict now seemed a distant memory, long since overtaken by events; and the residue of bitterness had subsided now that Smyke had at last been dealt with. And although he still felt the occasional pang of unease about his solemn undertaking to join Sir Michael's militia, this too had been pushed to the back of his mind. Instead, flushed with thoughts of the opportunities that his new wealth would bring, his mood soared; and casting gloomy thoughts of parting from his Portland family aside, he was suddenly impatient to be on his way. He thus resolved at once that as soon as the prize money arrived from Captain Auld, he would find a ship and race home as fast as the winds would carry him. But in the meanwhile, there was one event that Jack would feel compelled to attend - although he anticipated it with strange ambivalence.

The day of Smyke's execution dawned under a clear blue sky in which Saturn still shone brightly in the west, even as the sun's fiery rim first broke the horizon over Weymouth bay. The air was icy cold, and a thick frost lay on the slopes of the Nothe, a craggy peninsular at the mouth of the river Wey, on which an earthwork and palisade fortification had been built, rebuilt, and extended over past centuries. Looking down from its ramparts, the course of the river below was visible only as a ribbon of thin mist which, but for their masts protruding, all but obliterated the many boats that lay to moorings along its banks. Within the fort's earthen enclosures, a hangman's platform had been erected on a patch of level ground on which, despite the freezing breeze that had sprung up with the dawn, a gathering of townsfolk had assembled in anticipation of the coming spectacle. If they looked sullen and miserable, it was because of the cold rather than any sorrow they felt for the prisoner who now approached imprisoned in a sturdy wooden cage mounted on the back of a horse-drawn open cart. As was customary on such occasions, the crowd commenced to hurl abuse and projectiles at its reluctant passenger as it drew near, but on this occasion their shouting was more than usually vehement.

To the many in the crowd who had reason to despise the corrupt former chief of the Dorset Customs service for his arrogant duplicity and bullying self-importance, not to mention his extortion and double-dealing, Smyke's broken appearance must have given a perverse satisfaction. His stature had visibly withered, his shoulders become stooped, his face turned into an ashen and expressionless mask. The time spent in the squalid cells of the Dorchester gaol in the few short weeks since his conviction had clearly extracted its toll, for his red-rimmed eyes now stared unseeingly into the distance, not registering the hostile faces who now taunted him.

The four-wheeled Customs' post-chaise, used so effectively on the night of Smyke's capture, now sat at a discrete distance behind the crowd, its two dappled-grey mares standing motionless like sculptures but for the steamy exhalations from their nostrils in the cold air. Inside the carriage of the rugged vehicle, the shadowy figures of two men could be seen looking out through its side openings. It would have been difficult by casual glance for any outsider to identify the two observers sitting in the relative darkness inside, but closer inspection would have revealed them to be Jack Easton and Captain Andrew White, the new Customs chief promoted to take Smyke's place. The observing pair sat in silence as Smyke was taken from the cart and led, shackled at wrist and ankle, onto the platform where the hangman and a priest waited with studied patience.

From his seat, Jack glanced across the carriage as the noose was placed around Smyke's neck, catching his companion's eye with a meaningful look. He had waited so long for the moment when Smyke would receive retribution for his callous crimes. Not only had two

Customs officers lost their lives by his hand, but the deaths of Elizabeth Dale and Ben Proctor could also be laid squarely at Smyke's door. And in Jack's mind, Smyke was also responsible for the later suicide of his father - the poor man being so filled with self-recrimination for the smuggling debacle that had brought such catastrophe to the Island, that he had thrown himself from the cliffs.

But if Jack had felt anger and bitterness throughout the seven years of his exile, that demon was now being exorcised by the spectacle before him, to be replaced by the soothing balm of retribution to see an end of this corrupt and evil man. Jack now had a new life in Maryland with Rose, herself an unwitting victim of Smyke's murderous plot, and the promise of a family and prosperity at New Hope to look forward to. And while Jack would never forgive, nor forget the terrible suffering of the many who had fallen victim in the sorry tale, he had at least begun to feel a sense of closure on the matter. And in his mind, the souls of the dear departed would soon at last find peace, the crimes against them justly avenged.

Andrew White caught Jack's glance and returned it with an understanding nod. He too had suffered. White had lost his good friend Hayes and his Captain, Middleton, by the hand of Smyke and had been made to look a fool in the eyes of his colleagues. His feelings, as he watched Smyke's futile struggle as the hangman slid tight the knot, were not as measured as those of his companion. No noble sense of justice flowed in his veins. He could only feel the raw pleasure of spite; a thrill that caused his flesh to tingle in anticipation of seeing Smyke suffer and his evil life extinguished. Yet his impassive features would not have given such feelings away, even as the hangman pulled his lever.

The trap door opened and Smyke's body plummeted beneath the platform with a sickening crack that many in the stilled crowd must have taken as the breaking of Smyke's neck. There were a few more moments of silence as, with awful concentration, they watched the last flinches of life pass across the swollen face of the limp and dangling form, whose bulging eyes and loose tongue now made almost unrecognisable. There was no celebration at the end; only a few mutters of righteous approval now came from the crowd. Some of them would remain to watch the lifeless body eventually cut down, to be tarred and caged in an iron basket and left to rot - and swung from a gibbet on the pier so that others of a criminal bent would be reminded of the penalty for crime. But most would soon drift away well satisfied with the morning's entertainment.

And neither would the Customs post-chaise linger. Jack had watched curiously unmoved as Smyke's body fell, yet had turned his head away in sudden distaste at the dying man's grotesque contortion at the end of the rope. White's gaze dwelled a little longer on the despised form of his former chief, but only so long as to be sure that he was dead, before shouting a curt instruction to the waiting driver to move on.

And so it was that Jack's long quest was brought to its conclusion. Smyke was gone, never to ply his corrupt trade again, his crimes at last punished. But as the post-chaise rattled down the ice-hardened track towards the town, Jack found himself sinking into an introspective mood, experiencing an unexpected and profound sense of deflation. There was no heady sense of self-congratulation at his victory, no triumphant euphoria; it was more a feeling of exhaustion and sorrow that filled him now - a deep and reflective grief that so much harm and loss had been caused, and that so much good had been extinguished through this one man's evil. In Jack's philosophy, he had begun to harbour the notion that such evil in man was the devil incarnate. But it had taken so much effort on his part, at so much risk, to root out this single outcrop of corruption that he had since begun to wonder what hope there could ever be for honest men's good nature ultimately to triumph.

Jack had noticed the tall-masted trader in Weymouth harbour earlier as he had joined Captain White at the Customs office before their short journey to the Nothe. The vessel was still there when they returned, the adjacent quayside piled with new provisions ready to be craned into her open holds. Jack had given the ship no more than casual inspection as the pair had alighted from the carriage, and he had not realised her identity until White pointed it out.

'Pettigrew will already have been taken aboard by now,' he said, flicking a desultory glance in the ship's direction.

It was not until then that Jack saw the ship's name stencilled in faded and peeling letters upon her stern.

'The *Rotterdam!*' he spat in a tone that mixed surprise with disgust. 'Andrew, that is the very ship on which I was transported seven years ago!' But the robustness in his voice thinned. 'And the ship on which Elizabeth died a pitiful wasting death - and her body cast into the sea with no more ceremony than galley filth,' he added bitterly, swinging a reproachful glare across the ship's cluttered decks.

'I know your story, Jack,' said White sagely, as he took hold of Jack's arm in a consoling gesture. 'And I remember the occasion of your departure well. Do you not recollect how you caught my eye from that very deck as I stood watching from Smyke's office window there?' he prompted, pointing at the bay window on the first floor of the Customs' house nearby. 'What was it that you shouted then with such anger?'

Jack frowned in thought, and then nodded in recollection of the incident.

'I will never forget it, Andrew! You may also remember that Smyke had stood at the window just prior to your appearance there?' he said plainly. 'It was to him that I was shouting - swearing that I would return to see him get his just desserts. And as far as I was concerned at that time, all of you were just as corrupt as he!'

'Then you have been true to your word, Jack,' White replied, simply. 'And now I hope that you will realize that some of us can be trusted. And a just and pleasing symmetry, I think, that Pettigrew will now go through the same horrors of that you experienced - the man was a disgrace to public office and his privileged class! And although Smyke and his sort were the rotten apples in the barrel, it takes greedy manipulative people of influence like Pettigrew to nurture and exploit the corruption; without him the rot might not have gone so deep and the Service not so thoroughly dishonoured. To my mind, Pettigrew's body should be rotting in a cage alongside Smyke's on the quay!'

Jack returned his gaze to the *Rotterdam's* quarterdeck from where he was surprised to find himself observed by the ship's captain, who seemed to be inspecting him curiously. At first, Jack was taken aback by the apparent scrutiny. He held the captain's eyes for a moment, and as he did so, he recognised the man's doleful features. It was the face that had looked down on him so dispassionately at the height of the mid-Atlantic storm when in vain Jack had pleaded for help for his dying Elizabeth. The two men's gazes locked fleetingly in a sort of mutual appraisal; but it was the captain who first broke eye contact and turned away. Jack was sure that he had been recognised and he felt an odd sympathy for the man. While he himself had been blessed with all kinds of new opportunities since the near ruin caused by his banishment, this poor mariner seemed destined to plough his dirty furrow to and fro across the Atlantic forever in this old and filthy tub. Jack recalled his desperation as he had lain on that wind-lashed deck so helplessly on that stormy night. His eyes had searched for a sign of compassion from the ship's master, a man who must surely have had it within his power to help those suffering below, but who had failed to respond to his silent plea. Who now was the master of destiny, Jack wondered, and who now destiny's slave?

'Your passage back to Maryland?' prompted White, seeing Jack's preoccupation with the vessel and misinterpreting his mood. 'She leaves in the morning on the early tide. There won't be another from Weymouth for at least a month.'

Jack shook his head and grimaced. 'I'd rather swim than set a foot upon her!' he answered gruffly.

The banker's draft from Captain Auld arrived by courier a few days later and was delivered to his mother Eleanor's Wakeham cottage where Jack continued to reside. He took it from his mother's hand and opened it impatiently. It was an important-looking document, written on velum in Gothic script with a fine and steady hand, and embossed with the bank's insignia in the top right-hand corner. The amount to be credited, as Captain Auld's accompanying note confirmed, was indeed one-thousand guineas sterling just as had been expected. Jack had already sought advice on how the money might be conveyed to Maryland but had found no one in provincial Weymouth or Melcombe who was entirely sure as to whether it would be possible to encash such a draft on colonial territory. Because of this uncertainty, and not willing to waste further time on enquiry in his haste to be on his way, he decided that it would be prudent to convert the draft into negotiable currency in the form of large denomination indented letters of credit. In this form, he could use the paper currency as sterling in exchange for goods and services as and when he wished to trade. This seemed to make good sense at that time, for the value of his money would thus be preserved at the sterling rate and not be affected by any colonial inflation that may occur; but it was a decision he would live to regret.

Chapter Two
Passage to Cowes

Jack leant on the stern rail of the Isle of Wight packet boat and watched the grey and hazy form of Portland diminish in its wake. There was a cold wind from the north on this gloomy February day, and it brought with it the further threat of sleet that had already transformed the grassy cliff tops towering close to larboard into a bleak winter scene as quickly as he had watched them pass. Jack raised the high collar of his thick mariners' coat and pulled his cap firmly over his ears to protect him from the icy chill. He was determined to see out the last glimpses of his island as it dissolved into the precipitation behind him. It now looked so ethereal and remote that it was hard to believe that most of those from whom he had just taken leave in Weymouth: his mother, his brother Luke, and Rose's parents amongst them, would already have returned there by now. It would be immodest for him to deny that their lives would have been changed for the better by what he had done for them, and he felt a sense of pride at his accomplishments as he gazed at the fading outline. But he would also readily admit that he had merely been an instrument in the transformation, a catalyst, and not the all-conquering hero portrayed so embarrassingly in news reports of the trial. The certain and sobering knowledge that all his little victories had been brought about only with considerable help and luck had kept the swelling bubble of his pride in check. He pictured Luke, freed at last from the anxiety of mounting debt at the quarry and with a new start in front of him; he saw his mother, once more her former peppery self, returning to a home no longer at risk of being repossessed; he pictured his new parents-in-law, the Dales, now reconciled to Elizabeth's death, content with Rose's new found happiness, and overjoyed at the prospect of a grandchild on the way. And he imagined them all leaving the quay, silence falling between them as they turned away, feeling the same emptiness at his going that he himself now felt, returning home with their hearts as heavy as his. 'When shall we see you again?' his mother had called from the quay as the mooring warps had been cast off, as if she had only then plucked up courage to ask - her eyes had been reproachful, as if she feared to know. Caught off guard, his mind had been thrown into confusion - perhaps because he had found it easier not to face up to the question that had been on everyone's mind except his. 'Soon!' he had stuttered as the water opened between them; but he had felt a terrible pang of conscience at his dishonesty, for he really did not know. The heartache of his parting had locked their fond images in his mind in their last remembered poses, waving him off as he slipped away – just as he had waved back – bravely, sadly – until, at last, they had become invisible to his view. Now these images had been committed to his memory and would call to him often in his dreams.

It was with a kind of mourning that he watched the last faint smudge of his island melt into the enshrouding mist, and with its disappearance came a sudden shiver as if a cold hand had taken hold of his heart. He suddenly could not bear to think that he would never see his island again. That his mother, his brother, his family and friends - all those whom he held dear – would be lost to him forever? His island! His rugged, scarred, beautiful island – with all the associations and memories that it held of his childhood and his coming of age – all gone, as if swallowed up by the sea? Kept only as a fading memory, never again to be seen by his eyes or tasted with his lips; its beloved stone never again shaped with his hands? It was only now that he recognised how cruelly his life had been torn apart - severed utterly, the two parts irreconcilable, separated by an ocean of such vast and intimidating proportions that they might have been on different planets. He had made a new life with Rose in Maryland, in the homestead that they had built there together, having carved out a place for themselves with their own labour within the community of New Hope. How could he contemplate abandoning it now? He had sunk too much of himself into building up that new future, and forced by his years of penal servitude to let go of his past. And yet? And yet now that past had reasserted itself with a stark and vivid reality that sent a stab of pain across his chest at the thought of losing it again - as if his heart had been cut in two - so that he knew keenly the magnitude of the choice that he must eventually make. It was thus with a kind of frantic longing that he searched the mist - like a falling man grabbing for the disappearing end of a rope, he was suddenly desperate for one last glimpse of those high cliffs and craggy playgrounds of his lost boyhood home. But, for all his searching, he saw no trace, nor even the slightest shadow that might have been his island. It was as if a curtain had descended to signal the end of another episode in his life, and it had an air of finality about it that troubled him deeply. He shivered as an icy gust swept over the deck and he pulled his coat around him tightly; and with one last and mournful glance astern, he turned from the rail and quickly went below.

On a strengthening beam-wind the little packet boat scurried across Bournemouth Bay on billowing sails with an exhilarating turn of speed that sent a salty spume whipping across her decks to drench her. Through expert timing by her skipper, the swiftness of the passage was further aided by the rip of the spring tide, which hurtled at its peak through the narrow channel past Hurst Castle, and propelled the vessel up the Solent like a slingshot. Even so, it took her almost twelve hours to reach Cowes, and thus darkness was already upon her as she nosed into the harbour and came alongside her permanent berth. The passage had been quick, but Jack arrived numb and chilled to his bones from the boisterous ride and the cold damp air, which had penetrated the packet's ageing superstructure. As soon as the gangway was out, therefore, Jack was off along the waterfront as fast as his stiff legs would propel him in search of good food and a warm bed. Even at the late hour, however, there was much activity ashore. Several large vessels were being unloaded by gangs of stevedores with a such frenzied industry in the dim lantern light, that passers-by would need their wits about them to avoid being mown down. Cowes was a designated port of entry where incoming vessels would have their cargoes assessed for customs duty, and it was thus a necessary first port of call for ocean traders delivering goods to other destinations on the south coast. Larger vessels would also offload cargoes here to be transported by coasters to the multitude of small harbours nearby; and thus, with morning tides to catch, stevedoring often continued through the night. Jack dodged his way through the litter of stacked cargo and the shouting melee of labouring men and made for the streets that offered some prospect of quiet accommodation. He was steered by his instincts and an aversion to noisy drinking dens and drunken ribaldry against which his introspective mood rebelled, and found himself in the south side of the town. Here the back streets were somewhat seedy and not a little threatening in the darkness, and after fruitless knocks on doors and several un-navigable referrals, he began to regret being so choosy. It seemed that the town was rather full.

It was by luck, therefore, that he spotted a handwritten note placed in the window of a tall private house on the outskirts that offered the promise of a room within. If his search had loosened his joints it had not much warmed him. Damp, tired, and still somewhat morose, he was in no mood for engagement with the landlady who greeted him at the door as if he were a long lost son. He was ushered in with suspicious haste, and led at a pace up four flights of stairs to a dusty garret, which such a climb was too much of an investment in his current state to reject. Thus agreeing the lady's somewhat excessive price simply to have done with it, he ordered the stove lit, a ewer of hot water to be delivered for his ablutions, and a meal to be served in his room. But although the soon-flickering fire lit up the draughty room with its flames, it failed to warm it by as much as one degree; and the water and the meal arrived not much warmer after the long ascent from the kitchen below. If Jack had sought some revival of his spirits by these little comforts, he was mightily disappointed. And thus, thrown into a gloomier mood yet, he crawled despondently into bed and fell into a fitful sleep.

When he awoke, he found to his surprise on pulling back the ragged curtains of his gabled window that, for all its cobwebbed recesses, his room enjoyed a fine view down the Medina to the harbour. The waterway seemed packed so tightly with sailing vessels of every kind that it seemed impossible that there would be room for more, yet several large ships could be seen waiting at anchor in the roads outside. In the crisp clear morning that followed the passing of the previous day's grisly weather front, the scene was a glistening cat's cradle of masts, spars, and rigging, which made it difficult to distinguish those of one ship from those of another. The Medina divided the two parts of the town into East and West, and there was such a busy thoroughfare of boats and lighters criss-crossing in between, that it seemed unlikely that any vessel could navigate a way through. But in seeing so many ocean-going vessels in harbour, Jack was at least sure that somewhere amongst the tangle, he would find an early transport to America.

Eager to be about his search for a suitable vessel, Jack packed his things and quit the house without delay, pausing only to cast a withering glance at the landlady who had at breakfast presented her bill with such a flourish that he half expected to hear her chuckle as he paid it. But his mood had unaccountably lifted overnight, and the bruising caused by this mean transaction could not dent it on this bright new morning. He thus made his way back towards the waterfront expectantly and in high spirits with the intention of finding the Customs House, whose officers, he thought, might assist him in finding a suitable berth. But he was saved from this diversion, for as he ploughed through the knot of people in the bustle of the narrow cobbled streets, he heard a voice behind him cry out.

'Jack! Good heavens! Is that you?'

It was the excited voice of non other than Philip Goddard, the former first officer of the *Rebecca* on which Jack had made his eventful crossing from America. Jack spun around upon his heels to see his friend, dressed in the uniform of a merchant captain, shouldering his way through the crowd towards him.

'Philip!' Jack beamed in delight to see a familiar face amongst the sea of plain-faced strangers. 'I never expected to see you still here,' Jack called as the other neared. 'I thought you would be long on your way back to the Chesapeake by now!'

The two men greeted each other with vigorous and prolonged hand shaking.

'But what's this?' Jack said taking a step back to appraise his friend's bright new uniform. 'A captain now!'

'Why, yes actually!' his friend replied in a show of feigned ostentation, before grinning broadly with manifest pride. 'They've given me the *Miranda*, *Rebecca's* sister ship, I sail for Annapolis within the week with a company of British soldiers en route to Philadelphia. If you are seeking a berth, Jack, I would be delighted to have you aboard as my guest. A little civilian conversation might prove a pleasant antidote to all that boorish military talk!'

While congratulating his friend on his promotion and accepting the offer of a passage, Jack could not help but reflect upon the rather brusque first greeting he had received from the young officer on the *Rebecca* in Charlestown. It had been their guilty secrets that had made them wary of each other at the beginning. But it had been those very impediments that had also made them such useful allies, since both had something to gain from the other. And the trials that they had subsequently faced together, first in battle against *L'hermine* and then in their near encounter with the Portland cliffs when steering the damaged vessel home, had bound them closer. Jack wondered at the transformation of their relationship as he again shook Goddard's hand, delighted at his elevation.

'But now tell me your news,' both said simultaneously, before bursting into laughter at the coincidence of their overlapping words.

'I assume that you have fulfilled your mission, otherwise you would not be here so openly?' continued Goddard, still chuckling.

'And I assume that you have resolved your little difficulty with Mr Judd, otherwise I would not find you in such good spirits?' laughed Jack in response.

'Safely behind bars!' Goddard affirmed with a look of satisfaction. But deciding that the busy street was not the place for them to speak further on either matter, they agreed forthwith to return to the *Miranda* to take refreshment together in the captain's cabin.

Goddard led Jack through a labyrinth of gloomy alleyways towards the waterfront at a brisk pace, and they came into view of the *Miranda* quite suddenly as the pair broke out into the bright open spaces of the quayside. And there she sat, resplendent in the morning sunshine in all her faded majesty. Like her sister ship, *Rebecca*, the *Miranda* was a redundant sixth-rate frigate converted to merchant use on her retirement from His Britannic Majesty's Navy, and she was identical in the details of her construction and fitting-out - right down to the eight nine-pound cannon in her prow retained to ward off privateers. Despite her age, she was still a handsome vessel of regal appearance and distinguished pedigree, and her three tall masts and high decks looked down upon those of other merchantmen nearby with haughty disdain. But it was the buzz of activity about her that impressed Jack at once. Her beamy hull sat proudly against the quay, her decks a clutter of attendant crewmen bent to preparation and repair. Her open holds gaped like hungry mouths as dockside derricks swung to and fro, craning in their heavy loads like automatons. A flash of bright red drew Jack's eye, and when he looked closer, he saw some soldiers standing about the deck in idle groups, finding refuge in quiet corners, their scarlet tunics and military haircuts seeming completely out of place amongst the rough hurly-burly of the stevedores. And high up in the black-tarred web of stays and shrouds, a dozen topmen, set to check the tackle and the rigging, scampered here and there about her yards with manifest indifference to gravity. Such scenes as this fascinated and excited Jack, and his heart took a little leap as if he were a young boy on an outing. And as he came closer he felt a tingle of pleasant anticipation arising within him at the prospect of the voyage home. It was this mood that now overtook him, sweeping all other feelings aside; and so for the present the sorrows and confusions that had dogged him throughout the previous day were quite forgotten.

Goddard's cabin, like his former captain's on the *Rebecca*, enjoyed a panoramic view aft through glazing which spanned the full beam of her high stern. On entering it, Jack now knew to duck his head to avoid the low beams that lay in wait. He seated himself at the dining table while Goddard went off in search of someone to muster some tea, and while awaiting his friend's return, Jack scanned the cabin in happy familiarity. It was laid out in just the same way as Auld's with matching furniture that must have come as Navy issue from the quartermaster's stores. He vividly remembered his last visit to Auld's cabin on the *Rebecca;* and tearing it apart in brutal haste to lay a battery of four aft-facing canon, whose barrage through the glazing would thwart *L'hermine's* attack. It had been a race against time as the Frenchman had closed to board, but the ship's carpenter and a desperate crew had managed it - witness the predator's devastating laceration by the cannonade at almost point blank range.

'A little more comfortable and not as draughty as Captain Auld's stateroom the way we left it!' Jack quipped as Goddard returned with a middle-aged crewman in his wake, carrying a tray on which a tea set of fine porcelain tinkled as he limped. Jack mused idly that the crewman must be a cook by the look of his greasy apron and his pale complexion; his infirmity would probably suit him for little else. Goddard waited for the man to set the tray upon the table and then dismissed him pleasantly.

'Our chef de cuisine?' Jack's tongue was held firmly in his cheek.

Goddard laughed as he nodded his reply: 'And I'm told, a passable surgeon too! Yes, we did leave the *Rebecca* in quite a state didn't we? She is still in dock being repaired, you know, and won't be re-commissioned for another month. Then she's due to follow us out to Annapolis to have a few weeks' finishing-off work completed in their yards – it is apparently cheaper there. And after that, I expect she'll return here with another shipment of tobacco – this time without our Mr Judd aboard to interfere with it!' he added with some evident chagrin. 'I am afraid that none of her crew have joined me aboard the *Miranda* – except one that is. I've made young Matthew my cabin boy!'

'He is a good worker, you'll be well served,' said Jack, remembering the times he and the fourteen-year-old ship's boy had been teamed up to assist in the repair work after the storm, and then later in patching up *L'hermine* for her voyage home.

Goddard displayed his teapot as if it were some prize exhibit at an auction. 'One of the privileges of captaincy!' he said ironically, then poured the golden liquid into the cups with such precision that he might have been measuring out gold nuggets. 'Ah!' he uttered suddenly as he poured, as if some memory had muscled its way into his preoccupation. 'I have something to return to you.' His measuring completed, he put down the teapot and went to his desk, returning immediately with an envelope in his hand. 'The letter you gave me to be delivered to your wife in the expectation that I would arrive in Charlestown before you...' he smiled apologetically as he handed it over, '...clearly, you will beat me to it now! As you will appreciate, events have rather got in the way, and I did not find anyone else to whom I would entrust it.'

'Oh, yes of course, I had quite forgotten,' said Jack, as a little wrinkle of disappointment became evident on his face. 'A pity; I had hoped that it would inform Rose of my safe arrival. Oh well,' he sighed resignedly, pocketing the envelope, 'I will have better news to tell her now!'

The cup clinked on its saucer as Goddard passed it into Jack's receiving hand. 'Well, you start with your story, then I'll tell you mine,' he said, seating himself comfortably as if in anticipation of some great entertainment.

'Hmmm!' uttered Jack taking a thoughtful sip as he wondered where to begin. 'I suppose I had better start from where you last saw me — when you had me sailed ashore in Church Ope Cove.'

Jack then launched into a summary of the events that had occurred since the pair had parted company on the morning of Jack's arrival in Portland aboard L'hermine. He left out nothing important, and added the news of his subsequent endowment from Captain Auld as a postscript, an item that raised his friend's eyebrows in surprise. When he had finished his tale, he sat back in his chair looking more than a little pleased with himself, while Goddard gave him an appraising look that combined astonishment with admiration.

'You *have* been busy!' Goddard exclaimed. 'Exonerated and now rich! Could you ever have predicted such a successful outcome when you first set foot on the *Rebecca* back in Charlestown last November?'

'And you so frosty when I first met you? Then nearly crushed to death in the hold with Mr Harding as we made our first inspection?' Jack chuckled, 'which, by the way, I firmly suspected as being by Judd's deliberate hand. No, Philip, I do admit to feeling somewhat surprised that things have turned out as well as they have, for I just trusted to divine intervention and luck, and took things one step at a time! Anyway,' he said impatiently, 'that's enough of me! Tell me about Judd. If he is behind bars, then he must have fallen into the trap we set for him - perhaps Captain Auld's swift departure to join you on L'hermine was enough to make him go through with it.'

'Indeed, Jack,' said Goddard, sitting forward in his chair and clearly relishing the opportunity to tell his tale. 'He was given enough of a free rein to hang himself with it! When the Captain and I returned from Spithead, Judd had already been apprehended. Your letter had done the job intended and the agent was thus well prepared – he is an astute man by all accounts, and probably not unused to dealing with matters of this sort. Evidently, he managed to avoid giving his observation away while he watched Judd prepare the hogsheads for sale. The normal practice is apparently for the loads to be stacked according to the plantation of origin so that buyers have the opportunity to assess quality before making their bids – the prices fetched could, of course, vary greatly depending on this. Like the others, Judd's re-branded hogsheads were stacked in batches as if from genuine plantations – only he arranged for these to be placed somewhat apart from the rest so he could do his dealing unobserved – or so he thought!' Goddard let out a little chuckle at the rejoinder. 'Do you remember that we discovered that he had falsified the manifest? Well, the missing hogsheads would never have been noticed - nor Judd's later private auction - but for your tip-off. Our boatswain was nothing if not devious, Jack, as we both well know; he waited until the main selling activity had been completed and then, quietly after nightfall, sold his little cache off separately, under the table, so to speak - to buyers he had apparently dealt with before and who were undoubtedly in on the game.'

'Just as we thought,' Jack interjected.

'Indeed. But this was what the agent was waiting for, and he moved in at that precise moment with his constables and apprehended Judd and several of the buyers too.' Goddard took a deep breath and gave out another little chuckle; but it was relief rather than amusement that was more evident in his expression. 'Anyway, the long and the short of it, Jack, is that our boatswain now sits behind bars in the cells at Newport awaiting trial! He denies everything, of course!'

'Slippery customer,' said Jack, thoughtfully. 'Let's hope the jury is not fooled and that the judge sends him away for a long stretch!' He paused as if struck by some new notion, and a frown of consternation flashed briefly across his brow. 'He'll be transported if he's found guilty, you know!' he said, but added with a wry smile: 'We get all the wrong sorts in America!'

Goddard laughed at Jack's ironic reference to his own transportation seven years before. 'They'll find him guilty, Jack; the agent's evidence is cast iron,' he asserted in a reassuring tone. 'But even assuming Judd escapes the gallows, he'll stew in gaol for a long while yet. With all my soldiers aboard, there'll be no room for any transports on my ship! And America is a big place; I doubt that either of us will ever encounter him again,' he laughed again. 'Anyway, Jack, it seems as if our plan to keep me out of it has succeeded: Judd cannot have guessed that I played any part in his demise so he will have no grounds to bear a grudge against me as I feared.' He sighed contentedly. 'I am so relieved that that unfortunate business now seems to be behind me; I have certainly learned a great lesson from it.'

Jack nodded sagely, although he did not share his friend's confidence that a man as devious as Judd would be as rational and as fair as his friend supposed. Nor was Jack quite so sanguine that they had seen the last of him. Time would prove him right to harbour such dark misgivings, but he would soon leave these worrisome thoughts behind.

Having accepted Goddard's offer of a free passage with alacrity, he was allocated the last available bunk in the officer's accommodation beneath the quarterdeck. It would be a crowded ship with all the soldiers aboard, and Jack was not at all perturbed to find himself sharing his cabin with the British army major in charge. Indeed he took a liking to the personable young Major Green immediately on being introduced, anticipating a companionable diversion from the expected tedium of the voyage.

Before Judd was moved upriver to the prison at Newport, the island's administrative centre where his trial was scheduled to take place in due course, he had spent some days held in the lock-up in Cowes. Here, as was common for those who could afford it, he was able to procure some additional victuals at his own expense. In the delivery of these comforts, made by a former inmate who brought them daily to him for a price, he was able to pass messages to the outside world. This was how he conveyed to his waterfront friends that help in effecting his escape might earn some annulment of the gambling debts owed. It might be added here that Judd had made it a principle in his gambling (for which he seemed to have developed a considerable aptitude) to build up such favours, for his success in fencing contraband goods depended on a cooperative network of indebted helpers. It was thus, after some weeks of discomfort in Newport Prison, crammed into a damp subterranean cell with scores of penniless petty thieves and ragamuffins from the gutters, that Judd managed his escape.

It had taken a relatively small sum of money and a bit of less-than-gentle coercion from Judd's friends to convince the senior warder that the new prisoner might be allowed to join some other inmates each day in the exercise yard. One of the high walls of this enclosure formed part of the perimeter of the prison and thus had the benefit of being adjacent to an outside service track that served a rear entrance to the kitchen. With the senior warder's collusion, the supervising guard was called away from the yard for just long enough for Judd to make his escape using a rope thrown over the wall from the other side. When the slow-witted officer returned to the yard some moments later, he did not notice that one of the prisoners had gone missing and, Judd's absence camouflaged by the passable mimicry of some old lag in the subsequent role call, his escape went unnoticed for the rest of the day. It was not until the following afternoon when Judd was absent in the line-up to join the exercise party, that something was seen to be amiss. At first, however, thinking Judd might have chosen not to exercise on that occasion, the guard was slow to make his report. And later, when the report was made, the head warder, still mindful of the threats made upon him, sought to delay things further by ordering a full search of the prison site. The upshot of all this delay was that Judd had two full days to get clear before the alarm was raised and before anyone outside the prison got wind of his escape. And it was during these two crucial days that the *Miranda*, Philip Goddard's proud new command, signed on the last of her new crew and set sail for Annapolis.

Anxious to escape the island before the inevitable hue and cry was raised to hunt him down, Judd was lucky to find a ship taking on hands at just the time he needed it. And it was more fortuitous yet that the ship would set sail even before the news of his escape was out. The disguises that he had hastily contrived for the purpose – the shaving of his head to stubbly baldness and the donning of an eye-patch – were merely the finishing touches; added to the camouflaging growth of facial hair, already quite impressive after his weeks of imprisonment, the alteration of his appearance proved remarkably effective. Indeed, he saw no hint of recognition in those familiar eyes that scanned him as he passed along his way towards the quay. And so he became quite confident, even if there were crew aboard the *Miranda* who had sailed with him before, that he would not be identified. And losing himself amongst the large number of men required to sail a former sixth-rate frigate, he would also avoid detection by the captain, his cabin boy, and Jack, who would anyway have recognised him only after prolonged scrutiny. In fact, it was not until the ship was ghosting down the Solent with all her sails ablaze in the fiercely yellow light of the dawn's new sun that Judd even noticed their familiar faces on the quarterdeck. Although he was at first somewhat alarmed by the presence of these three at such close quarters, he quickly realised that he was invisible to their casual glances. And thus, amused by his relative invulnerability, he resolved to make the most of it.

Chapter Three

Jack's reunion with Matthew, the tousle-haired ship's boy from the *Rebecca* whom he had befriended on his eventful earlier voyage, was a brief but happy one. The boy's eyes opened wide in surprise on entering the captain's cabin to find Jack sitting with the captain at his breakfast table, and he was evidently unable to stop himself blurting out:

'Why Mr Easton, sir!'

The captain and Jack had conspired to surprise the boy with the unheralded encounter and now they burst into laughter to see Matthew's face lit up in delight. But the ruse nearly backfired. So surprised was the boy to see Jack again, that he barely avoided distributing the entire contents of his tray all over the cabin floor. Indeed, had it not been for Jack's quick hands wresting the tray from its precipitous incline as the boy came closer to the table still agog, the captain and his guest might have suffered the discomfort of steaming porridge in their laps.

'I am very pleased to see you again so soon, young man,' Jack said, relieving the boy of his burden and placing it safely on the table, 'and glad to see you promoted from general dogsbody to captain's aide – and wearing shoes too!'

Matthew grinned from ear to ear but then seemed suddenly to become a little coy.

'My offer still stands, you know,' continued Jack, in a kindly manner. 'When you get tired of the sea, there is work and a home for you on my farm. I shall make my way there once we have reached Annapolis, and you may accompany me if you wish. If the captain can spare you, that is!'

'Yes, sir, I had not forgotten. Indeed, I have been considering it,' the young orphan replied, suddenly turning awkward at the captain's quick glance.

'What's this, Jack!' said Goddard in mock affront. 'Poaching my crew already!' But he gave the boy a reassuring look. 'No doubt we shall speak of this later, Matthew,' he said. 'But now, be off to the quarterdeck if you please and give my compliments to the first officer. Remind him please that I await his report as soon as he has the ship ready to slip; I am anxious to be off at first light.'

The Miranda slipped past the high chalk cliffs of the Needles' promontory and set course out into the English Channel, heading for the open sea. From a cloudless sky, the midday sun threw long winter shadows behind these last calciferous outcrops of the Isle of Wight, and lit up their tall south faces in dazzling reflected light; they stood like white knights as guardians to the Solent. And it made a stunning spectacle to watch these mammoths receded in the ship's wake, their brilliance contrasting with the grassy cliff tops and the mixed blues of sea and sky. The wind, set fair in the larboard quarter, gave the ship a good turn of speed, and with the full ebb behind her it was not long before those white precipices lay so low on the horizon that they might have been breakers on a distant beach. At this swift romp, the quartering breeze was reduced to a relative breath across her decks, so that even the February sun warmed those who turned their faces to it. A hundred youthful soldiers stood about thus in the ship's waist, enjoying their ease with nothing else to do; while a few still gazed forlornly at a beloved homeland vanishing rapidly astern. Mustered in pristine scarlet uniforms that were emblazoned by the sparkle of sunlight off the sea, the cohort patiently awaited the arrival of their leaders from below.

With Captain Goddard and his officers engaged in piloting the ship's departure or practising their quadrant technique on the noon sun, the messing area below the quarterdeck had been abandoned to the army. Seven redcoat officers now occupied this dingy space sitting at the central table, their earnest faces wan in the oblique reflected light entering from an open hatch. At the head of the table, and clearly identified as the most senior of all those assembled, sat Major William Green, officer-in-command of the embarked unit of the South Coast Fusiliers, a light infantry regiment assembled from volunteers from several southern counties. A trim, dark-haired officer in his middle-thirties, the major was distinguished by the quick humour of his eyes, the neatness of his moustache, and the strip of colourful campaign ribbons upon his chest. Jack sat on his bunk and observed the gathering discretely through the open door of his cabin. To be in military company was a new experience for Jack, and he was both interested and intrigued to listen in for he thought he might gain some new insights, especially into the character of his new cabin companion. And it was at once reassuring to see that the major was a popular leader, evidently well respected by his subalterns. The substance of the briefing concerned the duty roster and the shipboard training routines – physical exercise, firing practice, drill and so on – that would be adopted during the long voyage. Major Green had written down his list of items on a scrap of paper and was using this as a speaking cue, while his juniors listened attentively and made notes. As the briefing continued there was occasional discussion of detail and also a good deal of good-humoured banter that lightened the otherwise sober, business-like tone, but it proceeded in a manner that Jack judged to be both efficient and motivating. At its conclusion, the major dispatched his young subalterns to the main deck with directions to rally and instruct their platoons, and once they had departed he caught Jack's eye and beckoned him to join him at the table.

'One learns early on in one's military career, Jack,' said the major with a wry smile, 'that the two surest ways to bring about rebellion in a modern army are poor victuals and idleness! My officers and I will ensure that the men will retire gratefully to their hammocks each night, completely exhausted – so let us hope that the cook can send them there replete!'

'Don't count on it, Major!' replied Jack, with a puff of laughter. 'This is my third crossing, and I'll take a bet that within the week, half your men will be hurling the produce of his galley over the lee-rail! That is if they are instructed properly on the relative wind and don't want it thrown back in their faces!' he laughed again. 'Is this your first crossing, then?'

'Across an ocean, yes' conceded the major. 'But a few of us crossed the English Channel once or twice in the forties when we fought the French in Flanders, and so we should know what we're in for, don't you think?'

Jack felt a delicious sense of superiority steal over him as he contemplated what terrors might lie in store for these novices to the open ocean. He wondered how quickly the major's good discipline and order would last once a proper swell got up. 'Sounds like you are well prepared then,' he said with light irony, while swallowing his smile.

'So what happens when you get to Annapolis,' Jack asked, changing the subject.

'Oh, there's quite a push on now that Pitt has taken over,' Green said breezily. 'Don't know all the details yet, but our regiment has orders to meet up with General Forbes' army somewhere in Pennsylvania moving on Fort Duquesne, and there are a great many other units being deployed further north.' His tone became conspiratorial. 'Not sure I should tell you this, so keep it under your hat won't you, but the French and their

Indian allies are in for a major assault on several fronts. They've had it all their way for far too long.'

Jack recalled the disquieting conversation he had overheard in Charlestown on his way through. After his years of isolation at New Hope, those few words around the table in the hotel saloon had been his first awakening to the hostility faced along the colonies' western borders. 'They continue to pose a threat then?' he ventured, once again reminded of his perhaps too-lightly undertaken promise to join Sir Michael's militia should the threat to the colony ever warrant it.

'It is an out and out fight for territory, Jack,' the major answered simply. 'I have studied the situation since we received our orders. The cause of the conflict seems to me ultimately to be the relentless expansion of our colonial populations westwards. With each few miles that the settlers push further west, some new Indian village finds its people or its livelihood threatened, so one cannot blame them if they sometimes react violently. Earlier generations of Indians might well have been more acquiescent - mainly due to their desire to trade, I suspect - but now it seems as if they have begun to dig their heels in. Perhaps they realize that they have been taken advantage of – which they have of course! Their population has also been decimated by diseases brought in by the first settlers against which they had no immunity – so they may see it now as a fight for survival; you know, "so far and no further" so to speak. As for the French: they see our colonists' expansion as some grand British strategy to take over the north and west - and they naturally resent it. So they share a common interest with the Indians in pushing back the British settlement line - or at least halting its westward progression. And they use their trading links to build military alliances - well armed with French weapons of course.' Green paused for breath, but then continued as if something had just occurred to him: 'Did you hear of the attacks in Pennsylvania and New York?'

Jack nodded uncertainly. 'I did hear of it on my way through Charlestown, but I am afraid that I have been rather out of touch.'

'Well those are examples of their power to hurt us,' the major continued, 'and the London press regularly contains reports of western settlements razed to the ground with hundreds of settlers murdered – scalped even! Yet, as more new settlers arrive, the quest for land drives them ever westward - apparently regardless of the fact that they are stirring up a hornet's nest of resentment and retaliation. And then there was the disaster at Fort Duquesne in fifty-five, the loss of Fort Oswego in fifty-six,' he counted these off on his fingers, 'and of course the infamous attack on Fort William Henry last year where hundreds were massacred! It's war, Jack – just as much in North America as here in Europe!'

Jack's heart sank. 'I fear then that many of us civilians might find ourselves carrying arms before long,' he offered, gloomily. 'How strong are they? Should we fear being attacked in the east, do you think?'

'The Indians will certainly defend themselves around their territorial lines, Jack, but they also like to trade. I think that at the moment they're more interested in maintaining a balance between the French and the British colonists rather than seeing either side eliminated – it's gone too far for that, and they know it. It's a sort of canny pragmatism, really. They try to exploit the differences between the two groups to obtain better prices for their furs; and when they ally themselves to one side or the other it is because they see it as being in their interests at that particular time - perhaps a bit fickle, but it's the only card they have in their hand. It's my opinion that in playing that game they have become rather too dependent on European goods and weapons for their own good. Remember, it's not a homogeneous people we're talking about here; the Indian population is made up of many different nations who seem to fight each other as much as they fight the settlers. So once one tribe has guns, the others will want them too! And I suppose, in a way, that that is fortunate for us, for it would be an entirely different matter if they were united. Their division is definitely their weakness!' Green took a small flask from his tunic pocket, unscrewed its lid, and took a short satisfying swig.

'French Brandy!' He stated with ironic relish, wiping his lips delicately with an erect index finger. 'Want a slug?' Jack shook his head; he was entirely absorbed in the unsolicited lecture.

'The French military are another matter,' the major continued; he was unstoppable now, and clearly enjoying Jack's studious attention. 'But while they are certainly a determined and capable enemy, they do not maintain a strong enough force in America and they are thus too weak by themselves. You know, Jack, we already have one-and-a-half million colonists in British North America to only seventy thousand New French - and those are spread thinly all the way between Canada and Louisiana.'

Green sketched a rough map of the Atlantic seaboard and its hinterland with his fingertip in the thin layer of salt deposits that covered the table.

'Having said that, their regular forces are concentrated where we meet them head to head,' he said, indicating the sites, 'here, along a line from Virginia through Pennsylvania to the Hudson where they defend their territories in the Ohio valley; and here, south of the Great Lakes to the St Lawrence. But even though there have been very few British regulars on the continent to date, the French have still needed their Indian friends to make a reckonable army against our side's local defence militias. Without the Indians, I think that the French would already have been overrun by the sheer force of numbers!'

'So that is their weakness then?' Jack concluded simply. 'If we won the Indians over, the French would have no option but to retreat, surely?'

'Yes, but we have a lot more work to do to swing those allegiances in our favour, Jack. Some of the Indian nations already ally themselves to the British side, often as much for protection against other tribes as for trade, but the French seem more successful at winning Indian friends than do our own colonists. Maybe it is because the French are a lot less numerous - thus less of a threat and more dependent upon the Indians' good will – and perhaps therefore they have to be more generous to them than we are. I don't think that either the French or the Indians have any intentions to drive our colonists back to the sea, but they can certainly make colonial life difficult in the borderlands as well as prevent any further westward migration.'

'So, is this why you are being sent over?' Jack put in. '- to protect the colonialists and open up the way further west?'

'Along with twenty thousand or so other British Regulars and as many colonial volunteers who, because of Pitt, are now at last on British pay!' the major asserted. 'After a long time leaving the colonists more or less to look after themselves, the government seems to have put America at the top of their agenda. It's Pitt who has swung it, Jack; he has been arguing for a long time that America must be given a higher priority, and now he has got his way! I'm sure he wants to see the French entirely defeated in North America. And may be that's the way it has to be. But if we are to win, we will need as much guile as brute force while the Indians hold the balance of power. And our Navy will have to sever French supply lines down the St Lawrence too; for without weapons and wampum to buy Indian friendships, the French will soon be fighting unsupported - and that is a war they cannot win.'

It was in the few moments of thoughtful introspection following this conversation that sounds of orders being shouted on deck were heard, and Major Green seemed suddenly reminded of a duty to observe the progress of his soldiers' drill. Apologising, he began to rise from the table, but just then purposeful footsteps were heard descending the quarterdeck companionway and an instant later, Captain Goddard burst in.

'Major, I think that you should go on deck to see the spectacle!' he laughed. 'My sailors have never seen anything quite like it! Your redcoats have them doubled over with laughter as they march up and down the deck so awkwardly! The wind's got up, and without their sea legs, they're stumbling about like drunkards!'

Major Green grimaced wryly, excused himself politely, and departed at a swift pace.

'This is just the beginning, Jack;' Goddard said with a mischievous glint in his eye, 'the glass is falling fast. We're in for a blow by my reckoning - the wind's backing too! I'll get these lubbers below soon, we'll need to clear the decks and lash everything down before the day is out!'

The captain's weather eye proved uncannily accurate on this occasion. In the week of heavy weather that followed the ship's departure from the Solent, not much army drilling was seen either above or below decks, with most of the redcoats finding refuge in their hammocks for almost the entire duration of the blow. The ship heaved, plummeted, pitched and rolled continuously in a quartering sea that was whipped into a turmoil by an icy continental wind. The gyratory romp was both violent and nauseous, and to constitutions unused to such dizzying accelerations, it was unrelenting torture. If the motion were not enough to make these lubbers succumb, then the noxious stench of churned-up bilge water, mixed in evil alchemy with the reek of vomit in the close salt-laden air below decks, was sent to test even the most resistant of stomachs. Meanwhile, the *Miranda* ploughed on uncomplaining. She was in her element and she took the tossing in her stride. Only those frail beings below, swinging in uncomfortable unison to the rhythm of the sea, came close to any physical limits; and many even wished that they were dead. Even though in comparison with Jack's earlier crossings the pummelling was not extreme, at least half of the embarked soldiers had fallen into a state of total incapacitation as quickly as the sea had come up. And just as Jack had guessed, the orderly progress of Green's training schedule had rapidly disintegrated.

During such prolonged hammering by the elements, a sort of grim lethargy can sometimes settle upon a ship, which affects even the officers and crew - a collective siege mentality where speech is clipped and testy, and only chores that are absolutely necessary get done – and in poor humour too. This was how the *Miranda* felt for that first week. At first, the major had tried to chivvy his stricken comrades out of their lassitude in a brave show of pluck, but he had almost as quickly succumbed himself to the *mal de mer*, thereafter taking to his hanging cot - where he could sometimes be heard groaning. There was a small cohort of the major's men, however, who had the constitutions necessary to continue almost normally, and when these strong few were not looking after their stricken comrades, they continued their instruction - under the tutelage of the one or two subalterns who were still able.

Jack had sometimes listened in to the soldiers' tuition for want of something to do. But in the uncomfortable tedium of the constant motion, much of his time was spent indolently, passing many of his waking hours recumbent in his cot, swinging in soporific harmony with that of his nauseous companion. Or, during the occasional interlude when the weather became less inclement, he might stand around the quarterdeck or lean on the rail and gaze vacantly at the sea. Or he might simply sit at the mess table passing the time of day with any crew who had idle time to chat. And with the captain preoccupied for much of the time with the sailing of his ship, there was not much opportunity either for conversation with his friend or even with young Matthew who had been given other duties to perform in the galley.

In short, it was a time of unremitting boredom for a man who was not at all used to inactivity. But by the ninth day at sea, the strong north-easterly wind that had already swept the *Miranda* over fourteen hundred miles along her route began to abate and also to veer. Then, at last, in a position plotted on the chart as some fifty miles west of the Canaries, she was swung around onto a more westerly course to follow the equatorial current towards the New World. And with this change, the whole ship's complement breathed a collective sigh of relief.

Judd had taken some pleasure from the discomfort and disarray of the army cohort. He had watched them with smug amusement as he had gone about the allocated duties of his ordinary seaman's watch. And when not on duty, he had moved about the ship with an easy familiarity, taking advantage of any opportunity to get close to Jack and Captain

Goddard who soon became objects of a developing obsession. In nourishing this curiosity, he would even contrive duties of one kind or another to justify his presence in parts of the ship normally their domain. As his confidence in his disguise had grown, he had become so bold that he had courted close encounters with them on several occasions, brushing past unrecognised in the dingy corridors below-deck, sometimes even with an audacious touch of his forehead in salute. It had become a bit of a game with him to test how close he could come, and it gave him a strange feeling of empowerment to feel invisible to their glances. But with these encounters, he had also begun to feel some resentment at his state of relative discomfort. While they apparently lorded it, he had become a fugitive who had lost rank, power, and all the coveted gains of his thievery; moreover, he could not entirely dislodge the suspicion growing in his mind that one or both of the men he now observed so closely had had a hand in his demise – even if as yet he had not worked out quite how. And as he watched and overheard the pair further, this suspicion, fed by jealous fancy more than hard evidence, had turned into a conviction, such that he had begun to blame them entirely for his misfortune.

In the more comfortable conditions that accompanied the change of wind, order and purpose quickly returned to the company of Fusiliers; and with the major back in his saddle, so to speak, the platoons were soon seen exercising on the main deck once again. And Captain Goddard too, no longer preoccupied minute-by-minute with the demands of heavy weather sailing, now had time for other diversions. Thus, as dusk fell one afternoon towards the end of the second week of the voyage, the captain sought out Jack, whom he found sitting at the messing table, bent over a chart and apparently in some consternation. Earlier, Goddard had been amused to learn that his friend had joined the first-officer's navigation classes for the *Miranda's* cadets, and that he had engaged himself in following the ship's progress with his own plot. But when the captain came upon Jack that afternoon working so conscientiously at his chart work, he was impressed. Not for the first time had Jack shown himself acquisitive of the skills of big ship sailing: the captain well recalled Jack's voluntary deck apprenticeship on the *Rebecca's* homebound voyage when he had tutored Jack himself. Indeed, his friend's newfound skills had come in mighty handy when they had sailed *L'hermine* home together as skipper and mate! But on seeing Jack bent over his chart looking so baffled with his workings, Goddard almost laughed out loud.

'So where are we, Jack!' he said lightly, stifling his amusement.

Jack looked up, surprised by his friend's approach and smiled a wry and exasperated greeting:

'Well, by my midday sun shot, somewhere in the Amazonian rain forest!' he said, throwing his pen down in disgust. 'I'll never get the hang of these corrections!'

'It'll come, Jack. Keep working at it,' the captain reassured. 'By my plot, we are making somewhat better progress - and safely still at sea rather than up the Amazon - as far as I can tell!' he said, sliding himself along the bench to join Jack at his chart. Goddard studied Jack's workings for a moment, his forehead creasing in concentration. 'There,' he said at last, running a finger along a line of Jack's scribbled calculations. 'This date correction should be a negative integer. It is a common error. Work it out again, Jack; you won't find yourself far wrong next time if you pay more attention to the signs.'

The captain watched in silence while Jack re-worked his figures then transferred his calculated latitude to the chart, making a faint mark where this intercepted his estimated track and distance line. From the doubtful twist of his lips, it was clear that this construction was not accomplished with total confidence, but he placed his finger on the mark nevertheless:

'Here?' he said uncertainly.

'Hmmm.' The captain bent forward and scrutinised the chart closely. 'Not bad,' he said in a tone of mock admiration. 'After four hours of calculations, only about fifty miles out - getting a bit better I'd say. At least you now have us in the Northern hemisphere!'

The two men laughed as Jack once more threw down his pen in exaggerated frustration.

'The first officer still instructs you on the quadrant, I suppose,' the captain continued, still chuckling. 'The wind or the ship's motion affects the plumb bob too easily and it is difficult to get consistent readings of sun altitude when you bracket the local apparent noon,' he said, exuding the knowing confidence of a teacher encouraging a struggling student. 'The averaging will almost always introduce errors even to your best shots. But do not worry; when you have mastered the technique, I will entrust you with my new octant and you can try some Polaris shots with it – I think that you will find that a little more consistent!'

Jack looked perplexed. 'I begin to wonder how you can ever be certain where to steer, Philip!' he said, shaking his head incredulously. 'Latitude is one thing, but tracking longitude by dead reckoning - with all the course alterations and leeway, *and* the unknown strength of currents! – its estimation is a black art in my book!'

Goddard nodded his agreement with an indulgent smile. 'There is a method to obtain longitude by lunar observation but it is too complicated and long-winded for my limited intellect,' he smirked in mock self-deprecation. 'But, if you want to feel really rich, Jack, here's a challenge for you: invent me a timepiece that will give me the precise Greenwich time throughout our voyage – a clock that could withstand the rigours of being tossed about at sea. With such an instrument together with my octant, I could know my precise location anywhere on the globe without *any* dead reckoning at all – no knotted lines, no sandglass, nor even any need to log each change of course! The Government have offered a prize of twenty thousand pounds to the first to do so!'

'Now that *would* make me rich! But stone and wood are my materials, Philip, and I doubt that those materials would make a very accurate chronometer!' Jack laughed.

Judd had noticed the captain go below, and seeing Jack also absent from the deck, he decided on impulse to follow, having a notion that he might enjoy listening in to the conversation that may be taking place between them. Slipping down the forecastle companionway, he made his way along the full length of the ship using the interconnecting corridors and gangways that weaved through the orlop and the cargo bays. Underway, these dark spaces were not often trodden, and his familiarity with the ship's construction gave him an easy ability to find his way about without fear of being seen. Arriving at the base of the companionway at the rear of the ship leading from the orlop to the officers' messing deck above, he was soon aware of the sound of men's voices. At first the sound was no more than an indistinct murmur hidden in the noise of the sea sluicing against the hull, but as he brought his ears closer to the opening he recognised the voices. He climbed the first few steps, tentatively, on the balls of his feet, ready to make a quick escape back into the darkness should his presence be detected. He ascended in one slow smooth and silent movement, like a snake attracted by a scent, keeping his head below the level of the deck, yet bringing his ears as close as he dared to the open hatchway. He knew that the steps were rarely used and thus he felt secure as he seated himself on a tread to wait for his ears to adjust. The captain's voice was the next he heard.

'Well,' Goddard said, examining the chart and putting his finger down on it with some deliberation, 'we are *actually* about here. And if this favourable wind continues for a bit, the crossing should be fast. I even hope to break the company record!' he grinned, with a hint of triumph lighting up his eyes. 'And on my first voyage as captain, too!'

'Then we must be at least a third of the way there already, Philip?' Jack asserted, clearly impressed with the progress. 'I must say that I am becoming more excited by the day with the prospect of our arrival. It will be so good to be home again.'

'And you must be pleased to be returning with all that prize money at your disposal, Jack. That was an unexpected bonus for us all, by the way – and I must thank you for it. It was your idea that saved us from *L'hermine's* attack, Jack. If it hadn't been for that, we might be languishing in some French dungeon even now. You must have some ideas about how you will use your new wealth?'

'First, to get it home safely, I think, Philip! It is a large sum - a thousand guineas - as you may already know from Captain Auld. I keep it strapped around me in a body belt for security, and do not intend to let it out of my sight for one moment!'

'Hmmm! I have already put my share under lock and key,' said Goddard with some concern. 'And would advise you to do the same. I am surprised that you are carrying it with you - a little risky, Jack, don't you think? Could you not have more safely brought a bankers draft?'

'Perhaps I did not persevere with my enquiries sufficiently, Philip, but I could find no one to advise me better. And I suppose I felt more confident in having it in the form of negotiable notes rather than entrusting its encashment to some colonial bank of unknown credentials. At least its value will be maintained in sterling and I can exchange it at the best colonial rate as and when I need to. But better not to speak of it openly again, Philip, as I would not want the information to be picked up by the wrong ears.'

But it was already too late for such caution. And for Judd, listening at the nearby opening like some mongrel awaiting scraps from the table, this was a tasty morsel that had been so carelessly thrown down. His ears pricked up at Jack's confession; it was indeed an intriguing item that had fallen into his lap, and it gave more focus to his interest in Jack Easton. While brooding on his capture in his prison cell, he was already beginning to connect Easton and Goddard with his downfall, and these suspicions, as we already know, had since become firm convictions in his twisted mind. But now avarice had been added to his pique, and this mixture began to ferment a vitriolic potion in Judd's gut that now made him hungry for recompense as well as for revenge.

It was to be four weeks before a call of 'land-ahoy' would be shouted from the masthead lookout, during which time the *Miranda* trailed her steady wake upon a kindly sea in unusually favourable winds. Captain Goddard was in his element, measuring off the miles on his chart with the greatest satisfaction as his new command ploughed on at a record-breaking pace. After turning westwards abreast of the Canary Islands, her route took her straight down the latitude before eventually turning northwards for the Chesapeake. It was four weeks of plain sailing, during which the daily cycle of the ship's routines seemed to blur into a dull continuum, with no notable events to provide the punctuation. Hours melted away and days became weeks, the passing of which many aboard began to lose count. Only the ringing of the ship's bell at the changing of each watch, which for the *Miranda's* military cohort seemed a complicated ritual, gave any regularity to the passage of time. And for them, each day was identical to the one before, with endless repetitions of drills and exercises that had them, in the forenoons, firing at empty boxes cast into the ship's wake and, in the afternoons, panting in their shirtsleeves round and round the main deck and up and down the foredeck companionways until they dropped.

The ship's off-duty hands, tiring of the daily spectacle created by this military tattoo, soon returned to their usual recreational occupations. When they were not filling their faces or unconscious in their hammocks, which for most did not leave much time over, they might linger in the ratings' mess, swapping seamen's tales or sneaking off to some quiet corner to gamble away their pay. And while there may have been no calls of 'all-hands', nor much sail trimming required in the steady run of fair weather, they found their duty hours occupied with scrubbing deck planks, repairing canvases, and polishing the ship's brass.

Judd meanwhile melted into this routine and made himself inconspicuous. Since learning of Jack's money, carried so conveniently about his person, Judd had decided not to push his luck with further observations for the present. Instead, he now began to turn his thoughts to how he might relieve Jack of his pecuniary burden. Jack meanwhile had become so engaged with his navigation exercises that he, like his fellow passengers, might also have lost track of time altogether, but for his frequent referral to the declination tables in calculating his daily latitudes. The evenings too became rituals of their own: a time anticipated with some pleasure, when Jack, Major Green, and the subalterns would share their dining table with those of the ship's officers who were not required to be on watch. The captain might even join them for a time, and on these occasions, young Matthew would be there too, in attendance, hovering in the background where Jack and he might exchange a glance or a few words. And after the meal, the ship's officers and passengers would entertain each other with lively banter and storytelling that sometimes, especially when accompanied by saved-up liquor allocations, would develop into loud and jolly affairs that lasted well into the early hours. It was on such occasions that Major Green, unused to the strength of ship's rum, might strike up a tune on his fiddle and burst into song. And with his fine voice he might regale the convivial assembly with his ribald adaptations of some well-known English folk songs - aided in the choruses by some not-too-subtle harmonies from the military refrain.

The days and the nights of the Atlantic crossing slid past in this unthinking and unchallenging regime, and may well have continued thus until arriving at their destination for the weather was to remain unusually clement. But shortly after entering the Chesapeake, the comfortable routine would change in a rather dramatic way.

Chapter Four

It was at first light on the misty morning of Wednesday in the second week in March 1758, that the entrance to the Chesapeake was sighted. Having sailed along the latitude charted for the fifteen-mile-wide opening into the enclosed seaway, its northern headland appeared suddenly out of the mist, lying low and dark on a grey horizon. Captain Goddard accepted the congratulations of the first officer for his excellent landfall with quiet modesty, knowing that it was as much luck as skill with his octant that had brought him so accurately upon his objective. To Jack, who had come up on deck as soon as he had heard the bellowed call from the masthead, it was nothing short of miraculous to find the ship so well lined up, having seen no land since they had left the English Channel. His heart leapt knowing that it could not now be much more than a hundred miles, perhaps a day or two's sailing at most, that separated him from his farmstead at New Hope. And he resolved at once that he would ask the captain to have him ferried to the southern Maryland shore as they passed by - from where it would be but half a day's walk home. The vessel's track was bound to take her close, he thought, and it would save him a tedious three-day trek back from Annapolis. Moreover, it cannot be said that Jack relished the idea of being in the colonial capital; it held such unhappy memories that he had no desire whatever to see it again - to have been paraded there as a convict had been quite enough. He stood at the stern rail dismissing those unhappy thoughts from his mind; and with smells of land borne upon the breeze, and the squeals of gulls once more in his ears, he lost himself in the happier contemplation of his homecoming. He must have mused like this for some minutes before he became aware of another presence at the rail, standing quietly by Jack's side as if sharing his meditation. A glance sideways revealed that it was Matthew; but rather than acknowledge him with a greeting, Jack decided to let the boy take his own time to speak, and returned instead to his study of the sea.

After a long and pensive silence, Matthew cleared his throat. 'Er, Mr Easton, sir,' the boy ventured, 'I wondered if I might have a word?'

'Ah, Matthew, you crept up on me!' Jack feigned some mild surprise to see the boy. 'Well, what is it young man? Speak up.'

'I have been thinking about your offer, sir, and would like to accept it. I am rather tired of the sea and think I might quite like some time ashore for a change.'

'Why, I'm glad to hear it!' Jack spoke kindly. 'As I said, you'll find a warm welcome at New Hope Farm. But it'll be no holiday; I'll put you to work, and you'll earn your keep; make no bones about it!' He grinned. 'Now, are you quite sure? Working a farm and a busy workshop requires long hours, you know. And there will be chores around the house too.'

'But at least I shall have my own bed rather than borrowing someone else's hammock or sleeping on bare deck boards with no more than a blanket around me! And since cook seems to have run out of variations on his salt beef and oatmeal gruel,' he smirked, 'I'd rather like to give home cooking a try!'

And so it was agreed.

The entrance to the Chesapeake chosen by Captain Goddard as the most suitable given the ship's excellent landfall, was by way of the northern navigation channel, which cut quite close to the shorelines of Cape Charles and the nearby small island. These two low-lying but distinct features marked the end of a long and ragged peninsular that reached right up into Pennsylvania and formed the Bay's enclosing arm, protecting it from the open Atlantic. The navigation chart showed numerous dangerous shoals around the Cape that would trap an unwary mariner and, in the absence of any marker buoys, some tricky piloting would be required to stay in the deep-water channel and hence avoid grounding. The captain and the first officer had gone into a sort of private conference at the ship's approach, standing at the binnacle with the chart spread out before them on the wheel housing. Fearful of breaking their obvious concentration, Jack had remained at a distance while watching the two at work. It seemed a well-rehearsed procedure: the first officer called his bearings on several notable landmarks as the ship sailed by, and Goddard plotted these on the chart, triangulating the ship's position every few minutes. It seemed, by his frequent glances at the shore, that the captain continuously crosschecked his calculations with visual estimations of the ship's distance off. Sometimes there was a little nod of approval or a grunt of satisfaction, but often he called the helmsman to alter course, perhaps by five or ten degrees to one direction or the other – a glance astern would have revealed a crooked wake! Meanwhile, the aspect of the island and the Cape changed slowly as

Miranda progressed along her cautious track, the gap between the two opening as her heading turned more northerly. The two officers worked like this for the best part of an hour, but eventually the conference at the binnacle ended with the captain once more taking up his habitual supervisory position at the rail. 'Carry on, number one.' Jack heard him say. And it was at once obvious that the hazards lurking unseen beneath the opaque water had been successfully left behind.

It was one of those dull March days with a leaden overcast that foreboded gloomy twilight throughout the day. The muddy silt-laden water of the Chesapeake, served to depress the light yet further so that spirits aboard were curiously subdued at what should have been a time of great elation at the end of a long voyage. The wind fell off too, and against the slow drift of an outgoing tide, the ship's speed along track reduced perhaps to three or four knots; it was a snail's pace compared with her earlier romp across the open waters of the ocean. And in the fickle wind, the great canvasses flapped about like linen on a back-yard washing line: sometimes billowing boisterously – the yards yanking violently against the braces and the blocks - when the ship might surge briefly ahead; but just as often the sails would fall into an indolent sulk, when the ship might come almost to a complete stop. And without the steadying thrust of the wind against her sails, *Miranda* had a tendency to roll wildly in the gentle swell – a nauseous alternation that soon sent one soldier after another dashing to the bulwarks to communicate with the sea! It was intensely frustrating too for all aboard to be so close to the destination, yet be making such painfully intermittent advancement towards it. If longing could have been exchanged for wind, *Miranda's* wake would have boiled into a froth behind her; but as it was, even with the tide eventually turning in the ship's favour, she had progressed only forty miles up the seaway by the end of the afternoon.

Miranda's track from the Cape to Annapolis, a distance measuring some one hundred and forty miles, bore north-by-northwest almost in a direct line. For these first frustrating forty miles, the ship's course had run parallel to the inside shoreline of the peninsular, a seemingly endless procession of low-lying dunes riven with muddy creeks. It had been tedious in the extreme to have nothing except such monotonous terrain by which to mark the ship's progress. Some variation, a few landmarks of interest, might have helped to pass the time, but there was so little to distinguish one stretch from another that it sometimes seemed as if the same view had been visible for hours on end. For Jack, time had dragged awfully in his impatience to be home, and he had spent his day languidly alternating between his bunk and the mess table, or else he had paced the decks like a caged beast hoping vainly for something to engage him. Quickly tiring of the eastern shoreline, he had taken up an eyeglass and searched the western horizon for sight of land several times, hoping to be the first to catch sight of some familiar landmark. But he was wasting his time; the seaway at this point was over fifteen miles wide and the western shoreline would be too far away to be seen even from the lookout platform on a clear day.

Eventually, with the approach of nightfall, Captain Goddard announced his intention to anchor overnight. In the relative confines of the Chesapeake, with its treacherous shoals and absence of navigation lights, it would be an irksome labour and an unnecessary risk to attempt to sail up-channel on dead-reckoning alone, especially on such an unreliable wind. And the crew could not have agreed more readily with his decision, for the majority gleefully anticipated their first night of undisturbed slumber after all the previous weeks of continuous watch rotation while underway.

With the ship swinging to her bow anchor, all soon fell quiet on deck, with everyone except a skeleton anchor watch retreating to his quarters to escape the chill of the damp night air. Under the continuing dense cloud, it was a moonless, starless night, and the *Miranda* thus lay enveloped by an inky blackness that, but for the few dim pools of lantern light from open hatchways, seemed to have swallowed every aspect of the ship. It was so dark, that staring to seaward a man might have thought himself blind. But halfway through the evening, a lookout broke the silence with an unexpected call – a sighting of a single light that had become visible further up the coast, closer to the shore. The captain and the first officer, sitting at the mess table below in the usual company, came up to the quarterdeck immediately to investigate. It was too dark for their telescopes to be of much use in determining the nature of the light's source, but after some moments of observation, it was concluded that the light, by its unchanging bearing, must be from a stationary vessel.

'A riding light, perhaps?' offered the first officer, glancing up to the masthead to check that their own light still burned. 'Too misty for us to see her earlier, I expect.'

'Very likely,' replied the captain, 'but too close inshore for a large vessel surely, unless she is aground?' A short thoughtful pause ensued. 'Ah well, take a bearing and note it in the log, number one, and have the watch officer keep an eye on it overnight, would you? Wake me if there is any change,' he said, making to depart. 'And have the ship prepared to set sail at first light; I am determined that we shall reach Annapolis before nightfall tomorrow night.'

It was still dark when Captain Goddard returned to the quarterdeck eight hours later fresh from his morning ablutions, but a loom of pale grey light in the eastern sky heralded the arrival of dawn. The first officer had beaten him to the deck, and was standing at the binnacle with his hands behind his back in a proprietary manner while men moved about the decks with an early morning vacancy, suggesting that they too had only just been roused. Goddard joined him, acknowledging the morning with a sort of growl, and both men stood in silent communion for a while as the sailing preparations picked up some pace.

'The light seems to have disappeared,' the captain said at last. 'What was its bearing?'

'Zero six five, sir,' said the first officer, glancing at the compass card and flicking his eyes in that direction. 'The watch officer reported losing sight of it in the early hours, sir. Gone out - or moved on, perhaps?' he suggested.

'Most probably,' the captain replied distractedly, still squinting into the gloom. But the dawn was breaking fast now, and after a few minutes he put his glass to his eye and swung it steadily to and fro around the given bearing.

'There she is,' he exclaimed, fixing his gaze. His companion took out his instrument and levelled it in the same direction, soon fixing on the object of the captain's inspection. A ship, similar in size and configuration to the *Miranda*, sat stationary in flat calm water closer to the eastern shore. She lay some two miles further up the coast from the *Miranda's* anchorage, pale and lifeless against the grey and misty background, her three masts bare of any sails. Behind her, perhaps a mile or so further inshore, the low sandy dunes of the peninsular were just visible, looking lifeless and desolate in the dawning light. To see a vessel lying so forlornly and apparently abandoned was a dismal scene on such a gloomy morning.

'A large sailing vessel, sir, aground by the look of her,' muttered the first officer, his telescope still raised. 'Can't see any life aboard.'

Both scrutinised the grounded ship for some minutes as the daylight strengthened further.

'Ah!' uttered the first officer in some surprise. 'I see some activity on deck, sir.'

'Ah, yes,' said Goddard, his eye still pressed to his eyepiece. 'And needing help too by the look of it - she's signalling smoke. I think we had better investigate, don't you?'

It took the best part of half an hour to raise the anchor, set sufficient sail, and start a cautious approach towards the stricken vessel. By this time Jack and Major Green had joined the officers on the quarterdeck and both had taken an immediate interest in the unfolding drama. The *Miranda* was now sailing into water that was shoaling quickly and unpredictably, where the depths marked on the chart were few and far between. Captain Goddard had assumed direct command for this risky operation, ordering continuous soundings to be taken as the ship closed in. The leadsman's calls thus now signalled the passing of the anxious minutes, his voice resounding across decks on which an apprehensive hush had fallen, where keen interest in his vital information was evident in the faces of the crew. The last thing anyone wanted was to join the grounded vessel on the mud; it was always such an inconvenience to get off again, not to mention the wasted time - and the danger of being left high and dry if an on-shore wind got up.

'By the mark, ten fathoms!' came a shout from the larboard leadsman.

'At least we're on a rising tide,' Goddard muttered to the first officer under his breath.

'Nine fathoms!' Another call came quickly after the last.

'We should not get too close, sir,' cautioned the first officer, needlessly.

'I'll come no further in than six fathoms! We'll need some water under us to manoeuvre off in due course.' The captain's voice was tense; there were sand bars and shifting mud banks all the way up the eastern shoreline and the charted depths were unreliable. 'Shorten sail to slow the approach, number one, and have the anchor trailed at seven fathoms from the capstan,' he ordered. 'That should be enough to check her at six at this speed.'

'Aye, sir,' replied the first officer, who with his next breath yelled the order to the boatswain who had already mustered his anchor crew in position on the foredeck.

'Eight fathoms and a half fathom!' The call from the foredeck was audibly higher in pitch.

'Shoaling more quickly now, sir,' offered the first officer unnecessarily, shifting his weight in apparent unease as he spoke.

The *Miranda* was now only a few hundred yards away from the grounded vessel and still making way very slowly towards her as sail was progressively taken in.

Then a lookout stationed in the bow shouted: 'She's the *Rotterdam*, sir!'

Jack heard the name '*Rotterdam*' and looked up sharply with a frown. 'Of course!' he thought, at once realising why the vessel had looked so familiar. He glanced across at the captain who at that same moment glanced back at Jack, and their eyes locked briefly in a silent yet meaningful exchange. Goddard knew what the *Rotterdam* meant to Jack - he had been told the story of Pettigrew's capture, and knew that the disgraced ship owner would be aboard as a convict transport.

'You know the vessel, Jack?' queried Major Green, astutely catching Jack's glance.

'Oh yes,' Jack replied ruefully, keeping his voice low so as not to be a distraction on the quarterdeck. 'I made my first crossing on her – as a convict!' But any response that the major might have made was not given the opportunity to form on his lips before a cry rang out from the starboard rail:

'She's signalling, sir: "You are running into danger",' called the first officer from underneath his telescope, instantly capturing the two observers' attention.

'Does he think that I don't know that!' barked the captain, irritably. 'Signal: "We are rendering assistance" and raise the anchor ball to let him know our intentions.'

It was at this point that the trailing anchor bit into the mud, for the *Miranda* suddenly slowed as, in quick succession, her bow was pulled sharply askew by the tensioning cable and the sails began to flap.

'Six fathoms, sir!' came a final call from the leadsman.

'Very well, number one. Secure the sails, and tell the watch to monitor for anchor drag! Call me if the soundings reduce,' the captain ordered. 'And have a boat sent across to the *Rotterdam*, will you. No doubt her captain will wish to come aboard.'

Under the various Navigation Acts pertaining at the time, only British or colonial-laid ships were allowed to carry goods to or from the British American colonies – this being legislation designed to maximise advantage to the empire by excluding rival nations from profiting from colonial trade. While the *Rotterdam* may have been built originally in a Dutch shipyard, she had since been so substantially remodelled in New England, that she now qualified as Empire made - at least the Board of Trade had certified her as such twenty years before. Certainly, she now sailed under a British flag, and her port of registration was Boston, as indicated by the peeling lettering painted on her stern. That she still carried the name *Rotterdam* was because her nostalgic owners were descendants of Dutch immigrants to the former New Netherlands, now the English colony of New York. She lay fast aground. Her normal loaded waterline, clearly marked by the rim of dark weed that ringed her hull, was exposed a good six inches above the muddy water of the Chesapeake. She was an ageing workhorse well overdue for the knacker's yard: her canvasses were grubby and frayed, her rigging sagged, and her planks were grey and stained through long years of undistinguished service. It was not only Jack who felt gloomy at the sight of her.

The *Miranda's* boat returned with the *Rotterdam's* captain and purser aboard, having navigated the three hundred yards of calm water that separated the two ships. The two officers climbed aboard and were brought up to the quarterdeck where they were greeted cordially by Captain Goddard and his first officer. Jack hung back, not wishing to engage with the very men he held responsible for the tragedy of Elizabeth's death during his transportation. The memory of the squalid conditions of that terrible voyage and of these officers' callous indifference to the suffering on the convict deck, made the thought of polite conversation with them quite repugnant.

The *Rotterdam's* captain spoke without embarrassment as he explained his predicament. It appeared that he had navigated his ship into the Chesapeake in poor visibility and had been forced off course by unfavourable winds, eventually running on to an uncharted mud bank (at least this was his version of events). Unfortunately, the grounding had occurred close to high water a few days after the last spring tide. Unluckily for him, this inopportune timing meant that subsequent high-water levels would reduce for a period before increasing again according to the lunar cycle, and it was therefore not expected that his stranded ship would re-float for about a week.

'I was already running short of food and drink when I entered the Bay,' he said laconically. 'Indeed, I had already started to ration supplies to my transports some days before. Now this delay is creating further inconveniences for me, not to speak of the cost. Those who don't succumb through lack of nourishment will not fetch the best price if they look weak and feeble from under-feeding!'

'I see you are troubled by their distress,' replied Goddard with unveiled sarcasm. 'But how can I help you? With this company of ravenous infantrymen aboard,' he said, waving his hand airily at the red-coated soldiers once more exercising on the main deck, 'we do not have much to spare and would certainly not have enough to supply you for a week. How many souls are you transporting?'

'We have about a hundred indentured servants at the last count, sir, and a dozen convicts,' the purser chipped in, casting an indifferent glance back towards his stranded ship, and speaking in a strong Irish brogue. 'But we do not expect you to give up your supplies to feed them, sir. Oh no, indeed, sir! Better, I think, if you were able to take them aboard and sail them to Annapolis for us – a day or two's sailing at the most is my guess. I, as purser, would accompany you, of course, and bring some of my officers to administer their disembarkation – and a few guards to keep an eye on the convicts.'

The *Rotterdam's* captain nodded agreement. 'And I would hope to get off the mud a little earlier without their weight aboard,' he added, 'and thus should not be more than a few days behind you.'

Goddard seemed to ponder this for a moment. 'There would be a need for discussion between our owners in respect of any payment due, you understand?' he said, looking doubtful. 'And I am afraid that I would have no room to accommodate your people below – we would have to erect some form of shelter for them on the main deck – an inconvenience for my army passengers who would thus be denied the use of the space,' he added, clearly laying down a marker to justify a later claim for recompense. Jack was surprised that his friend could have turned so mercenary, but then his masters would certainly be more interested in commerce than compassion, and the captain would need to answer for his actions. Thus with a shake of hands between the two men, it was agreed; the *Rotterdam's* unhappy cohort of indentured servants and convict transports would at once be conveyed to the *Miranda's* decks for delivery to Annapolis as quickly as the winds permitted.

It took some hours for the transfer to take place, with boats from both ships ploughing repeatedly across the separating gap, each boat rowed by four sturdy crewmen and loaded with half a dozen pale-faced refugees hooded with blankets against the cold. By midday the *Miranda's* main deck was already heaving with scores of scruffy-looking people:

men, women, and children, standing about in pathetic little groups, many of them still nursing the mug of broth that had been ladled from a steaming cauldron as they had arrived. Jack had remained on the quarterdeck in the company of Goddard, observing the transfer, while Major Green had gone below soon after the first boat had arrived to supervise his company, who were now confined to the gun deck.

Jack eyed the continuing transfer pensively, watching for Pettigrew to arrive. The last time he had seen the villain, it was the day of his own triumphant acquittal in Dorchester when Pettigrew was led sullenly from the dock. Jack was morbidly eager to see what ruinous effect the intervening months had wrought upon this once aristocratic figure, rather imagining that he would see a humbled and broken man brought low by disgrace and the discomforts of captivity. Scanning the faces of the growing number of miserable and downcast refugees as they arrived on deck in such manifest exhaustion and confusion, he searched in vain for Pettigrew's despised features. But as the number swelled, still without recognising the face he sought, Jack began to wonder if Pettigrew had been aboard the *Rotterdam* after all. Perhaps, he wondered, like many on Jack's own voyage of transportation, Pettigrew had not survived the rigours of the crossing? This was not a thought that passed through Jack's mind with any trace of compassion or regret; indeed he was rather warmed by the possibility. And as more unfamiliar arrivals stepped onto the deck, his hopes in this respect were raised yet further. Pettigrew dead? Jack savoured the thought. But as he scanned the ragged assembly milling about on the main deck, it dawned upon him that the transfer of the prisoners must have been left until last since there were no guards yet in evidence. Swinging his gaze quickly towards the *Rotterdam,* he now spotted a cluster of three boats forming into a convoy, flanked by two other boats from which men could be seen watching with muskets in their arms; and Jack's heart at once sank in disappointment.

Pettigrew was amongst the last of the convicts to step onto the *Miranda's* deck. There were about twenty felons in all, all men, all wearing ill-fitting uniforms of creased and dirty calico, and all tied at the wrists. Once assembled on deck, they were herded by their guards into a roped off area under the forecastle rail and ordered to sit cross-legged in lines. Contrary to Jack's expectations, the former justice of the peace did not slump like many of his compatriots, but instead sat upright, holding his head up in an attentive attitude, his eyes alertly scanning the mass of humanity milling around him. He was not the emaciated and humbled figure that Jack had expected, but seemed to have fared rather well on the voyage. Certainly, he looked dishevelled and unshaven, but he was clearly in tolerable health, unlike most of the others shouldering for space on the cramped deck - who looked scrawny by comparison. Jack wondered whether Pettigrew had been able to use any residue of his former wealth to buy favours from his guards. The man had some cunning about him, and Jack would not have been surprised to learn that he had managed to evade some of the confiscations ordered by the court. And perhaps, through Pettigrew's corrupt network, someone had been inveigled to smuggle something into the gaol before his transportation? Jack was both intrigued and perturbed by the man's confident demeanour and could not prevent himself from returning frequent glances to the sitting figure.

The deck was soon alive with activity as crewmen swarmed the rigging and climbed into the yards, and this drew the interest and attention of most of those on deck. It was during this commotion that Jack's eyes were drawn to the convicts sitting around Pettigrew who, by their furtive mutterings and sly glances, were clearly communicating with each other. They were burly men, with mean and ignorant faces, the sort a decent man would fear to encounter in back streets and dark alleyways. There was something secretive about their behaviour that made Jack curious; and then he saw them begin to glance about quickly as if making some calculation. Too late, he realised what they were up to. Before Jack could utter an alarm they had somehow freed themselves, and they and Pettigrew were on their feet and moving the short distance to a nearby group of guards whose attention had been distracted by the activity aloft. The guards were taken totally by surprise and were stripped of their pistols and bludgeoned to the deck almost before they knew what had hit them. It all happened so quickly that no one outside the roped off area seemed to have noticed - until a single shot rang out, and a guard further from the group dropped where he had stood, the only one to have reacted to the assault. The clatter of his falling pistol resounded as a stunned silence descended upon the crowd; and all eyes turned in fright to see the five men backed up against the starboard rail, their pistols menacingly raised. A few gasps of horror were heard amongst the crowd and a young child's scream suddenly rang out. At the same instant, activity in the yards ceased abruptly as if by some signal; and now the topmen craned from their lofty perches to see what was going on below. Amongst the yardsmen, Judd looked down with special interest at the turn of events, perhaps wondering if an opportunity might present itself, while others around him seemed frozen to the spot. Then blind panic broke out on deck as the refugees shrank back in terror from the gunmen, their wild movement accompanied by shrieks and shouts of alarm. At this, the remaining convicts became restless; some started to get up, apparently intending to join their five fellows at the rail, but they were gestured back with an ominous wave of a pistol. Then another shot rang out, this time into the air, and a sudden silence fell upon the crowd as one of the gunmen yelled out to the guards still standing:

'Place your weapons on the deck and step back!'

The guards, struck into inaction at the sight of their fallen comrades, immediately took notice of the pistol barrels levelled at their heads, and obeyed without prevarication, falling back meekly into the crowd as instructed. Pettigrew now stood at the centre of his group with two men on each side. And with a flick of his head he dispatched one of these to collect the discarded weapons from the deck; the man returned quickly, distributing the pistols amongst the convict cohort. Now, with a weapon in each hand, the group became suddenly formidable.

On hearing the first shot, Captain Goddard had taken the few quick steps required to reach the quarterdeck rail, and had watched almost incredulously as the drama on the main deck unfolded below him at such lightning speed. Powerless to intervene, he now he found himself looking down the barrel of one of Pettigrew's pistols.

'Captain,' Pettigrew uttered languidly, 'you will ask your men to rig a boat for sail and put it over the larboard side, if you would be so kind. Otherwise I fear that there will be further loss of life. My friends here, as you see, are not slow to take offence.'

Goddard managed to look equally calm, but Jack guessed that he must have been assessing his options. From where Jack stood, the situation looked bleak: most of the crew were in the yards; Major Green and his troops were below decks with no unobserved ascent available; and the deck was cluttered with over a hundred refugees whose presence would impede any concerted retaliation. Moreover, a large amount of firepower was now aimed indiscriminately at the crowd and to attempt to turn the tables would inevitably result in innocent casualties. Pettigrew and his henchmen had planned their timing well, Jack realised; and he wondered if his friend, Goddard, had come to the same conclusions. Seeing the captain's shoulders drop in apparent resignation, he rather thought he had.

The captain cast his gaze about for the boatswain and spied him in the forecastle where he found the man's eyes already awaiting his signal to proceed. Goddard gave it with a flick of his chin; and with alacrity, the boatswain acknowledged, but his tone was sullen as he called a group of nearby deckhands to muster. Meanwhile, the refugees looked on silently as if stunned, their faces frozen into masks of ghoulish curiosity. Once assembled, the boatswain's group descended to the main deck with these same eyes fixed upon them as if they were condemned men heading for the gallows, a path opening before them as the crowd fell back – almost as if in reverence at their approach. Looking down from the quarterdeck, Jack was reminded of a painting he had once seen of Moses crossing the Red Sea. The seamen ploughed a path thus to reach the larboard rail, where they began at once to hook up the davit tackle to one of the ship's boats.

'You'll not get away with this,' said Goddard, grim jawed and tight lipped, but he had patently been out-manoeuvred and knew it.

'We shall see,' replied Pettigrew, coldly, 'but in case you are harbouring any ambitions to have your men fire upon us as we depart, I suggest that you think again.' At this, he flicked a glance at two of his companions who, clearly knowing what to do, started roughly into the crowd, pushing and shoving in a most brutal and intimidating manner. The crowd shrank back as these ruffians came amongst them, the nearest refugees cowering in palpable dread as the intentions of the pair became evident. The commotion was accompanied with cries of fright and alarm, and several children struck up a chorus of wailing that rang such a forlorn note that some women began to weep. Then out of this low moaning, a piercing shriek arose that assaulted Jack's ears like the stabbing of a knife. His attention was drawn thereby to a woman in the centre of the milling crowd who began to shriek and protest as if she were in some terrible pain – so much, apparently, that those nearest in the crowd closed around her to comfort and restrain her as gently as her fierce struggling permitted. At first Jack did not understand the cause of her distress, but then he spotted Pettigrew's brutes singling out two males nearby and grabbing them, an adult and a young boy. From the woman's hysterical pleading, it was immediately clear that the two males were her husband and her son and that both were doomed to become hostages. Their feeble struggling was futile against the strong arms of their captors who then manhandled these lost souls to the front where, with pistols to their necks, they were both bound with their hands tied behind their backs.

Jack was sickened at the sight. A distracted father and his terrified son, both cowed into submission and visibly in real fear of their lives; there was no doubt in Jack's mind that the pair had been selected as having both reason and imperative to behave. He watched in horror and with mounting fury as Pettigrew's thugs dragged the captives through the crowd towards the larboard rail. They reached it as the boatswain and his crew were just beginning to lower the boat to the water and soon only the mast remained visible as it descended below the bulwarks. While they waited for the craft to complete its downward journey, the convict group formed into a defensive line at the rail with the hostages pinned in behind them. Jack could see the father's face peering through a gap; the man was clearly doing his best to maintain control but his eyes were filled with dread and his lips trembled visibly. The boy meanwhile struggled resentfully against his restraint and cried out for his mother in a pathetic and hopeless tone that tore at Jack's heart. But his appeal died when one of the thugs swung back and struck the boy's cheek with the back of his hand, leaving only a mournful sob to heighten the tension in the air.

Hoping for a possible opportunity in this hiatus, Jack scanned the deck, desperate to find some means of foiling the escape. He spotted a number of hands watching from the foredeck - young Matthew stood amongst them – they looked angry and restless, but they were boxed in by the crowd. Jack wondered whether he could rally them in some way, but realised at once that it was a useless prospect - they were unarmed and had no easy line of approach. His gaze swept further. Then something bright red summoned his eye; it was Major Green in his scarlet tunic crouching in a hatchway in the centre of the main deck, hidden from the fugitive's view by the surrounding crowd. Jack caught Green's upturned gaze. The major thrust out his jaw and raised his pistol to show Jack that he was armed, but he shook his head slowly in a gesture that suggested no hope. It seemed that he had come to the same conclusion as Jack – that the possible consequences of retaliation against such firepower were frightening with so many innocent people as potential targets. Jack continued his scan. He was becoming desperate now. There seemed no way to intervene. Everyone appeared helplessly rooted to the spot; neither the topmen in the yards nor the crew scattered around the decks were free to act without attracting the immediate retaliation of the gunmen. And the centre deck was so clogged up with refugees that it would be impossible to move with the speed needed to overcome them. The whole ship seemed powerless and impotent. And over that stilled and horrified assembly, the distraught woman's continuous low moaning struck a bleak and doleful chord.

Eventually the hostages were ushered roughly over the bulwark to climb down into the waiting boat, and with their disappearance Jack realised that he was losing his chance to act. It was at this point that his frustration simply overwhelmed him. With no thought in his mind other than to interrupt the seemingly inevitable course of events, and thus perhaps gain some time, he could not prevent himself from blurting out: 'Pettigrew!' And with this, he strode to the quarterdeck rail and glared down at the five fugitives who were by now preparing to descend. At Jack's angry shout, Pettigrew had halted his manoeuvre and now looked back, apparently at once amused to see a single defiant and unarmed protester facing him. At first he sneered derisively; but then, in a slow and dawning transformation, his expression altered first to one of recognition and then to one of pure and unadulterated malice.

'Ah, Mr Easton, what a happy coincidence!' he said smoothly, as he calmly transferred the aim of his pistol directly into Jack's accusing eyes. 'And an unexpected opportunity to get even with the man who has caused me *so* much inconvenience,' he continued in a drawl.

Pettigrew's four companions' progress over the rail had also been arrested by Jack's shout, and they now resumed the threatening swinging of their weapons, while casting about pugnaciously as if to say 'try it if you dare!' One flicked a glance at the two hostages already half way down the ladder into the waiting boat, and waved his pistol irritably, gesturing them to continue their descent. The others swung their aims about the ship, lining up their sights here and there in rapid movements, watching for any sign of resistance.

Jack became enraged. 'You harm that man and boy, Pettigrew,' he spat vehemently, 'and I will hunt you down and finish you off with my own bare hands! You don't deserve to live anyway,' he added contemptuously 'You should have been strung up with your friend Smyke and left to rot on The Nothe!'

It was a defiant outburst but his threat sounded empty and impotent in his ears. He tried to put some menace into his voice:

'You can run, but you'll not escape! The passing of strangers is always noted; wherever you go, you will leave a trail which I can and will follow, believe me!' It was the best he could do, but he knew as he spoke that his words were futile.

'Brave talk indeed,' Pettigrew replied with a smirk. 'But what makes you think that you'll have the chance,' he said, cocking his pistol with a loud click that made the atmosphere suddenly electric.

Someone in the watching crowd gasped. A woman buried her head in her hands and started to sob. Jack held Pettigrew's calmly appraising gaze as the seconds ticked past, steeling himself for the moment of searing pain that he imagined would mark the end of his life. He had made himself a target and now there was no escape. He must bluff it out - to turn and run would demand more than his pride could bear even though death might be the cost; moreover, a hasty move on his part might precipitate a dangerous over-reaction from the other escapees.

But Pettigrew did not fire. And as Jack searched the eyes behind the ominous black hole of the barrel that aimed with such unwavering accuracy at his head, he began to wonder if Pettigrew might be balking at the act.

'The man has never had to pull the trigger himself,' he thought, 'he's always had others do it for him. Perhaps he hasn't got the guts?' This was a moment of hope.

But Pettigrew's henchmen were not so squeamish.

'If you don't shoot him, Pettigrew, then I bloody will!' swore one of them impatiently, swinging his weapon at Jack and cocking it. But at that moment, several more arming clicks were heard from the companionway as Major Green and two of his subalterns raced out from the cover of the hatch, their weapons already aimed at Pettigrew and his companions.

'You shoot, and the next is for you!' Green shouted breathlessly. 'One of us will get you in any event!'

The major's little posse was hopelessly outgunned but Pettigrew would certainly fall in any exchange. Green must have been counting on a standoff for he would most surely have realised the danger of a shoot-out to the crowd of people surrounding him.

Pettigrew gave Green a withering look. '*You* shoot, major,' he said languidly, 'and several of these good people will die with you!' He smiled condescendingly. But one of his knuckle-headed companions was a hot head not given to subtle reasoning; nor was he apparently blessed with patience. The thug swung his weapon and pulled his trigger. Within a quarter of a second, his flintlock lever arched, followed by a puff of smoke as the ignition powder flared. But an instant later, the first subaltern pulled his trigger too. And the two men were still standing face to face as the two projectiles exploded from the barrels of their weapons almost simultaneously and sped at sonic speed towards their targets. The speeding lead balls must have crossed paths midway, for both men appeared to be hit at the same time - and they both fell where they stood. As the echoes of the shots subsided, other red-coated infantrymen now rushed up the companionway, their muskets at the ready. They were on deck even as the smoke from the first two shots still hung in the air. But by then, panic and mayhem had erupted amongst the crowd of refugees who now tripped, stumbled, and fell over each other as they ran in all directions, trying to escape the shoot-out that they must have feared was about to start. One of the topmen, distracted by the chaos, lost his footing on the foot ropes and fell screaming from the yards, his limbs flailing wildly as he fell - until impact with the deck silenced him abruptly, splitting his skull with a sickening thud. In the horrified confusion that reigned for some seconds thereafter, Pettigrew and his three remaining companions slipped over the rail and dropped into the waiting boat. And by the time Major Green and his soldiers had fought their way through the melee and brought their muskets to bear, the boat had already been pushed off, its sail raised, and the two hostages bundled onto the stern seat as a shield.

'Hold your fire!' commanded Major Green to his men lining up their sights at the fast retreating vessel. 'You'll hit the hostages; we'll have to let them go,' he said resignedly. 'And may God preserve them both,' he muttered under his breath.

Throughout all this, Jack had watched helplessly from the quarterdeck, perplexed and shocked at the calamitous train of events that his intervention appeared to have unleashed. Should he have stood by and done nothing, he wondered. Would it have been wiser for him to hold his tongue? The upshot of his action had seen two men shot and another killed by falling from the yards! Hardly the outcome that he had hoped for! And the two hostages were now perhaps even more at risk than before with angry and perhaps vengeful fugitives their captors. As for Pettigrew, the man who Jack had already brought once to justice at the Dorchester trial, he was now free again, and Jack felt sick in the pit of his stomach to watch him slipping away into the mist. His thuggish companions had clearly been bent, like Smyke and the members of the Chesil gang before, to do his bidding, and Jack prayed that Pettigrew's hold over his fellow fugitives would last long enough to keep the hostages from harm.

Following the fugitives' departure, a sort of brittle order returned quickly to the deck, and the casualties immediately became the centre of attention. To the aid of the survivors of the shoot-out, came the *Rotterdam's* Irish purser and a guard to attend to the convict's injury, while Major Green and a subaltern at once rushed to their fallen comrade's side. Both casualties were conscious but subdued and preoccupied with their wounds, both remarkably to the shoulder, which at the time seemed to need little more than a tight bandage to stop the flow of blood. Around both men, in separate clusters, groups of onlookers from the crowd of refugees soon formed. But elsewhere on deck, there was less interest in the two casualties who had not been so lucky. While sombre crewmen attended the top-man who had fallen to his death from the yards, few could bear to watch his broken body straightened. And fewer still watched his corpse laid out and sown into the canvas square that would become his funeral garb. The brave guard, the only one to have attempted resistance and the first of Pettigrew's victims that day, would be similarly attended to in due course. If the ship had been afloat upon the open sea, both bodies would have been committed to the deep before the day was out, but so close to port and in enclosed waters, the corpses would be hurried to Annapolis for burial ashore. And throughout all this, standing at the larboard rail with only a single companion to comfort her, the abandoned woman had wept as she had watched her loved ones sailed away across the Chesapeake, eventually disappearing into the enshrouding mist.

Meanwhile Captain Goddard, the first officer, and the boatswain met on the quarterdeck in a hastily convened meeting in which it was determined to get *Miranda* underway immediately. But it would not be in pursuit of Pettigrew and the hostages – with his boat already out of sight, that cause was quickly dismissed as already lost. With casualties and corpses aboard and several hundred other souls to care for, the better option was to proceed immediately to Annapolis where the escape could be reported. Moreover, it was resolved that they would sail with every inch of canvas spread, for there was now no time to lose.

Hovering within earshot of the captain's short meeting, Jack understood at once that urgency was now the imperative, and that therefore he could not ask even for the short diversion to put him ashore early. But in reconciling himself to this disappointment, he could not possibly have anticipated the tragic consequences of this loss of opportunity. For had he and his young companion been landed nearer home as he had hoped, not only would a tedious journey have been avoided, but Judd would also have been denied the chance to follow them. On such capricious chances are the twists and turns of fate decided. But Jack was still entirely unaware of any danger and unsuspecting that, even at that very moment, he was being watched.

Chapter Five

It was not until dusk the day after her swift departure from the grounded *Rotterdam* that the *Miranda* was brought alongside the quay in Annapolis. And almost as soon as her mooring warps had been secured, the two casualties were being carried ashore to seek medical attention in the town. Both had suffered relatively superficial wounds to the shoulder that had at first not appeared to pose a threat to life. The ship's surgeon, otherwise the principal cook, whose skill with a knife was held in high regard, had removed the shot and dressed the wounds using rum as an antiseptic. But both victims had since fallen into a fever, and this had become a matter of anxiety by the time the ship had arrived in port. Major Green and his company were naturally concerned for their comrade, but there was a degree of concern for the convict too, since it was hoped to extract information from him as to the intentions of his fellow escapees. In the lull that followed the flurry of activity surrounding the casualties' hurried transportation by stretcher, the bodies of the dead were quietly slipped ashore and placed in coffins on a waiting undertaker's cart. Meanwhile, night approached. But before it was completely dark, the purser and his guards had taken charge of the refugees, disembarking them quickly to the quay where they were now assembling in rough order. From here they would be taken off to spend the night in a nearby warehouse that, bare and unheated as it might be, would nevertheless offer more comfort than an over-crowded open deck. Tomorrow, the auction of their indentures would begin.

In the fading light, Jack watched the downcast figures formed up and moved along the quay in a closely guarded line. And as he watched them led off, he reflected upon the run of mixed fortune that had befallen him since he had been in just their situation seven years before. It had not seemed so at the time, but in retrospect it was now clear that he had been exceedingly lucky that, on that very quay, it had been Sir Michael de Burgh who had bought his indentures. He thought it unlikely that others of his cohort would have been as lucky. Jack guessed that some of those who had shared his deck space on the *Rotterdam* in 1751 would already have perished from the hardships of their virtual slavery. And many of those who had endured them would even so never attain the freedoms that they had hoped to find. Jack wondered how many would find what they sought. It was said that these days, most new immigrants – reportedly as likely now to be Scottish, Scots-Irish, or German as English - would stand little chance of acquiring the freehold of any land at all. Indeed, it was said to be rare these days to obtain a headright at the completion of indentures. Thus, forced to migrate ever further westwards in a quest for living space, a newly freed man might find himself encroaching upon disputed land. And as Major Green had so graphically related, a settler could then face Indian resentment, or worse – angry resistance or brutal retaliation. Not everyone would want to take these risks, of course, and others would not want to burden themselves with mortgages that might become difficult to repay - especially from uncertain income. It was quite likely, therefore, that many of those who he could now see entering the warehouse door would become tenant farmers or itinerant jobbers – or else join the growing legion of the city poor. Jack sank into a melancholy mood as he mused upon their destinies, reflecting that it had been the blessing of his carving skills that had won him back the early prize of freedom. It had been this gift that had saved him, and he quietly thanked the Lord for the capabilities and good fortune with which he had been endowed.

That evening, Jack dined with Captain Goddard and Major Green in the captain's cabin, attended at their table by Matthew in his capacity of cabin boy. The company of soldiers had also stayed aboard since accommodation was yet to be found for them ashore. It had also been considered prudent to confine them to the gun deck to minimise the risk of friction with the people of the town who would undoubtedly be nervous of their presence. The muted cadences of their ribaldry, rendered mellifluous by the thickness of the intervening bulkheads, formed a musical background to the conversation at the table, which soon turned to the subject of Pettigrew's escape.

'Where in heaven's name would they have made for?' the major asked.

Goddard frowned. 'Well, what puzzles me is that they headed off northwest,' he said. 'Pettigrew was quite specific with his demands; he instructed me to have the boat lowered on the larboard side – almost as if he already knew which way they would go. I suppose that it is possible that someone aboard the *Rotterdam* could have told them of their location,' he mused, ' - after all they had been stuck on that sand bank for several days!'

'Pettigrew has a way of using others to his advantage,' Jack chipped in. 'I would not be at all surprised if he had somehow managed to make it worth someone's while to help him. And do not forget, Philip, that in his former life before his disgrace and transportation, he was a ship owner, and he is therefore likely to have at least some understanding of navigation. Who knows, he may even have been to the Chesapeake before aboard one of his own vessels and thus know the lay of the land in these parts.'

'But why set off across the Bay - *away* from the shore,' asked the major, with some incredulity, 'when they had land in sight to the East?'

'I wouldn't have gone eastwards either, major,' answered the captain, sagely shaking his head, 'that peninsular is inhospitable and very remote. They will certainly have better chances both of survival and escape on the western shoreline, even though they would have faced a long sail in an open boat. It would have been about thirty miles to the Potomac in the direction that they set off – a good six or seven hours sailing, and they would have been lucky to reach it before darkness fell. I would guess that they camped overnight on a convenient shore before proceeding up river the following morning. They could have either Maryland or Virginia in their minds as an objective. Perhaps we will learn that from our wounded convict?'

'And then what?' the major asked rhetorically, 'Knock on the door of some isolated farmstead, I suppose!'

'Most likely,' agreed the captain. 'They'll be away by now with a change of clothing and food in their bellies, no doubt.'

'Having ditched the hostages unharmed, we hope.' added Jack, doubtfully.

At that moment a loud burst of military revelry suddenly ruptured the tranquillity of the cabin like an explosion and it drowned out the response. Startled by the deafening intrusion, all heads turned to see a grinning Matthew standing in the open doorway carrying a tray. Caught in the glare of the captain's sharp glance, the youngster's smile wilted as he kicked the door closed behind him. The door slammed shut, all but killing the din, and the youngster made his way forward in the relative silence that ensued. The brimming pewter tankards crammed together upon his tray could now be heard clunking with each careful step.

'The sergeant thought you gentlemen might like a sup of Annapolis ale, sir,' said Matthew, his grin returning, unabashed. 'A barrel was sent back by the purser, sir, in thanks for your hospitality.'

Goddard laughed. 'And this is all we'll see of it, I suppose!'

The following morning, Captain Goddard and Jack made their way to the sheriff's office in the centre of the town to report Pettigrew's escape. They carried with them written details of the fugitives and hostages provided by the purser. In the absence of the sheriff, Jack and Captain Goddard were at first attended to by a clerk, who was already engaged in noting down details of the escape when the senior law enforcer arrived. The clerk, a timid little man, immediately deferred to his bluff and portly superior who at once assumed command, relieving the clerk peremptorily of his seat in the process. After some discussion of the location and nature of the escape, the sheriff sucked his teeth in an expression of some doubt.

'I'll get the word out,' he said, shaking his head doubtfully after reading the purser's notes, 'but I doubt that they'll be apprehended on the basis of these descriptions!' He waved the paper airily. 'There must be scores of posters scattered around the colony with descriptions of runaways that read identically to these! A likeness would do a better job!'

It had not occurred to Jack before, but the mention of a likeness posed an interesting challenge. Pettigrew's face was etched vividly in his memory having studied it long and hard during the day of the trial in Dorchester and now more recently behind the barrel of a pistol. He found himself suddenly quite taken by the idea of experimenting with his artistic skills.

'I'll have a go at producing a sketch of Pettigrew,' said Jack, bravely. 'The others, I'm not so sure about. But is there a printing facility in Annapolis that could print it?' He queried this with some apparent scepticism.

'We're not *that* far behind England, you know! The *Maryland Gazette* is printed here - by one of our aldermen: Jonas Green. He took over the press works founded by William Parks himself - you must have heard of him, surely?' the sheriff answered proudly, flicking a triumphant glance at the clerk still hovering nearby. 'You draw a picture, Mr Easton,' he challenged, 'and one of the firm's engravers could cut a printing block from it within a day or two! The Gazette's a weekly, so you bring a sketch to me by tomorrow night, and it'll be all over the colony by the end of next week, and throughout Virginia the week after – Jonas still has links with the old Parks' press in Williamsburg.'

Jack spent much of the rest of the day sitting wrapped up in his overcoat on the *Miranda's* empty quarterdeck having decided that this was where he would obtain the best light for his sketching. But it took some time before he actually put pen to paper, so to speak. The thought of Pettigrew roaming free had placed the man's recapture uppermost in Jack's mind, and he had resigned himself to contributing this one day to help secure it, despite his impatience to be on his way home. This was no mere citizenly duty either, for the manner of Pettigrew's escape and the callous treatment of the boy and his father had enraged Jack almost beyond endurance. Jack now sat with a board upon his knees, ready to commence. The deck was relatively quiet. The fusiliers had been stood down and most had now retired below, and Major Green and Captain Goddard had been called ashore to receive new orders from their agents. Jack had thus found some peace at last and had no reason any longer to delay. But he found himself distracted.

After a grey start to the day, the sheet of low overcast dispersed to reveal a bright blue sky and, although the air remained cold, Jack soon felt the pleasing warmth of sunshine upon his face. For a time he basked in it, wondering how he might begin to draw a likeness. But then his attention was diverted by the activity at the nearby warehouse, into which the previous evening he had seen the *Rotterdam's* refugees led. It was immediately clear what was going on inside by the numerous wagons and traps drawn up outside the wide-open double doors. It was an ugly and dilapidated edifice, set apart from other commercial buildings on the quay, and Jack guessed that it had seen long service as a market for bondage. From its hidden depths, sounds of human misery resonated from time to time, as if drawn out by some unseen torture within. Jack guessed that some of those inside would just be learning of their separation from those they loved; indentures were sold at the best price - sometimes with indifference to relationships or family ties. It was an idle notion, but to Jack the yawning doorway of the warehouse was an mouth opened wide in pain. And while to other ears at this distance the cries would have sounded faint, to Jack's tuned hearing they struck a depressing chord. He watched dolefully as groups of dazzled individuals were brought into the sunlight and hustled onto wagons and carted off. Jack recognised some faces as they rattled their way along the quay, and his heart went out to them, his pulse thumping to the same dread beat that he had felt when he had trodden the same dread path. But at least, unlike him, most of these people had chosen of their own free will to come to the New World, and for all the uncertainties and hardships that they now faced, most would still be better off in America than those they had left behind.

Trying to shake off his melancholy mood, Jack gazed about him listlessly, impatient to get his drawing done yet seemingly unable to make his first mark. He studied his blank canvas again. But no sooner had he started to picture the image that he would try to draw he found his thoughts drifting. This time it was visions of his imminent return home that took him. He was so near to Rose – perhaps now only a few days away – that he could almost feel her presence. It was *her* face that he saw before him, not Pettigrew's! He let his mind be taken by thoughts of a reunion - their first gentle embrace, a tender kiss - the warmth of her body lying next to his. With only a month to go before the expected birth of their child, he imagined her belly well rounded, and he was suddenly rather proud to think that he would fulfil his promise to be with her at this important time. He thought of life once more returning to normal at the farmstead now that his mission had been accomplished: once more working alongside his faithful friend, Ned Holder, a giant of a man with a heart as big as his hands; and wise old Sebi, the former black slave who had become a cherished elder in Jack's adopted family. He imagined the two of them working in the kitchen garden - seeing him arrive at the gate, dropping their tools and rushing to greet him. He pictured them with Rose in the kitchen, sitting at the table before a roaring fire at the end of a good day's work, discussing the day over a jug of Sebi's cider - just like they used to before he went away. And he let out a nostalgic sigh.

But the blank canvas still taunted him, and he shook his head in an attempt to free himself from these distracting thoughts. His mind cleared, and he became aware, as if he had not been aware before, of the clatter and clamour of the busy waterfront around him. He noticed the crates of metal tools and agricultural implements, and boxes of fine furniture and cloth that had been unloaded onto the quay. And nearby, labelled according to ship and destination, there was tobacco and wheat – for export to England and her Caribbean possessions – and not a single foreign flag in sight in all the port. Behind the commercial properties lining the waterfront, the buildings of a prospering capital rose up proudly, their facades bright and colourful under a misty mantle of blue-grey wood-smoke from a hundred smoking chimneys. It was only when he caught sight of the large clock above the harbour master's office that he realised how time was slipping away. It was already eleven o'clock!

With a grunt of self-admonishment for his tardiness, he pulled himself up and forced himself at last to make a start.

Jack had earlier found some shards of charcoal in the ashes of the galley stove and now he took up a suitable piece, flourished it before him as if displaying some coveted prize, and set himself immediately to work! At first, he experimented on scraps of old sail canvas with simple lines and shapes, but he quickly progressed to representing depth and form by varying the density of the charcoal laid down. It was a messy business and the results were not initially encouraging, but after a short time he felt confident enough to try a number of rough sketches. With these, he learned quickly that the best technique was not unlike that used when creating his designs for carving stone. Indeed, the medium had a similar feel to his touch and his fingers were soon quite blackened by his tactile technique. In some ways, he thought, working charcoal was quite like sculpture - and the effect produced, almost as three-dimensional. Having put his distractions aside, he now moved on rapidly, and he was soon satisfied that he could produce the semblance of a well-proportioned human face. 'Now,' he thought at last, exercising his fingers with an eager relish, 'let's see if I can capture the dimensions of Pettigrew's evil features!'

As Jack worked, Matthew brought him refreshment from time to time, but the artist was too engrossed to utter much more than a simple grunt of acknowledgement or at best a distracted 'thank you', and it was clear that any conversation that the boy might have had in mind was going nowhere. Goddard returned eventually from his trip ashore, muttering his impatience to disembark the soldiers so that he could load up his new cargo and be off again to sea. But seeing Jack sitting on the quarterdeck he approached his friend, and craned inquisitively over Jack's shoulder. He even offered a comment on Jack's work, but he may as well have been speaking to himself, for he received little response. Crewmen had also appeared on the quarterdeck from time to time, perhaps attending to some aspect of the rigging or the sail machinery. Jack was conscious of their presence but took no particular note of their identity, and he certainly did not register the bearded seaman with an eye-patch who watched him at his work with more than idle curiosity.

Creating Pettigrew's likeness was more difficult than Jack had thought, and it took some hours surrounded by an ever-deepening pile of discarded sheets of canvas before he sat back, satisfied that he had achieved it. He surveyed the sketch critically: the fair hair swept back over a high forehead, the prominent cheekbones, the long chin depicted shaved of the untidy growth acquired during the voyage, the aquiline nose that gave the man that very English upper-class look. All these features were well enough drawn, he thought. So too, the full lips set in an affronted sneer, and the eyes: condescending, as if viewing something of mild distaste.

Feigning some modest doubt, he later offered the sheet up for Goddard and Matthew to inspect. At first, Jack's face was an inscrutable mask as he waited for their comments. But by their admiring nods, it was at once clear that his friends approved.

'Hmmm,' uttered Goddard, 'that's the man all right! I'd say you've captured him, Jack.'

'Let's hope I have, Philip!' replied Jack, chuckling at the ambiguity. 'What do you think of it Matthew?'

'Not sure, sir,' the boy replied honestly, after a little pause for thought. 'I did not have much opportunity to study him from where I stood. But I think that it is very well drawn. You are quite an artist, sir,' he said, looking more than a little impressed.

'Well, let us see what the sheriff and his printing friend can make of it;' Jack said. 'And while I am gone, Matthew - if you've not had second thoughts – you can get yourself ready for an early departure tomorrow morning! While I'm in town, I'm going to see what possibilities exist for transportation. I'm rather anxious to catch up on lost time!'

As Jack descended the *Miranda's* gangway, heading in some haste for the sheriff's office with his canvas clutched underneath his arm, he nearly collided with Major Green who was returning with similar urgency from his meeting ashore.

'Jack!' Green shouted breathlessly, stepping out of the way just in time. 'Where are you off to in such a hurry?'

Jack explained the reason for his journey, unrolling the canvas proudly to display his work.

Green glanced at it briefly and nodded an ambiguous approval, 'Hmmm! Not bad!' he said, but he was clearly impatient to be on his way. 'I've got my marching orders; I need to get preparations underway for departure first thing tomorrow, so excuse me if I hurry on.' With this, he eased past his friend and continued up the gangway two treads at a time, calling over his shoulder as he went: 'I'll tell you all about it later.'

With the sketch delivered to the printer, and arrangements for the following day made, Jack returned to the ship some hours later in a positive frame of mind. And soon after, the three men met again in the captain's cabin for a final evening meal. Like the night before, the conversation had to compete with the muffled accompaniment of the raucous harmonies from the gun deck. No doubt, the men's musical renditions were given added stridence by the imminence of release from their unnatural confinement. And Major Green was in equally garrulous mood at the captain's table, with a glass in his hand. He should probably have been more guarded in revealing the nature of his orders, but the young officer's pride had clearly been fanned by the great duty thrust upon him, and he was easily drawn out. The solemnity with which he swore Jack and Goddard to secrecy seemed to swell him yet further, but he had a modesty about him that made his mildly inebriated manner more amusing than ostentatious to his friends.

His unit had evidently been ordered northwards. They would move initially by water up the Susquehanna River, to meet up en route with other units of General Forbes' army who were already on the move. This massive force would be making their way through Pennsylvania and across the four ridges of the Allegheny Mountain range into the Ohio valley. It had been at the fork of the Ohio with the Monongahela River at Fort Duquesne that General Braddock's army had been decimated by the French and Indian coalition two years before. It seemed that the British would not make the same mistakes again. This time there would be a concerted effort of British and colonial troops on several fronts to defeat the enemy and drive them northwards into Canada. It appeared that a new road was being cut through the colony to facilitate logistic support, and so Green anticipated that his unit would intercept this route and quickly catch up the other units of his regiment as they advanced. As Jack listened, he could not help feeling the same unease he had felt before at such talk of war. During all the years he had spent working at New Hope, isolated and insulated from news of the outside world, he had been unaware that the British colonies had faced any threat at all. Now it was becoming clear that there was to be a pitched battle to protect colonial territory or to win yet more, and with his commitment to Sir Michael brought again into mind, Jack had the horrible feeling that he would soon find himself embroiled in it.

'But let us not depress ourselves further on this,' interjected Goddard, as talk began a slide into gloomy conjecture. 'A toast to the major and his men!' he said brightly, catching Jack's eye and lifting his glass. 'For all our sakes, may God protect you, William - and guide you to the successful accomplishment of your mission!'

Jack followed Goddard's lead, lifting his glass too and echoing his friend's sentiment with heartfelt sincerity - for he saw his own security depending upon it. And in the pause for Green's overly grave acknowledgement that followed, the captain took the opportunity to move the discourse away from weighty matters of state and onto the happier subject of his sailing instructions.

The *Miranda* had been ordered to proceed from Annapolis forthwith to the West Indies with a cargo of wheat and timber, returning immediately to New England with sugar, calling in at Wilmington, Carolina, to pick up a small consignment of indigo en route. From Boston, Goddard would then return to the Potomac in early summer for minor work to be carried out before eventually returning to England with a full hold of Virginia and Maryland tobacco. Goddard peppered the details of his itinerary with such colourful anecdotes and descriptions of far-away destinations that exotic and adventurous images were conjured in Jack's mind. He listened, enraptured, and could not help but envy the apparent simplicity of a mariner's life: a life dictated purely by wind and current; directed as to where to go and what to carry by some external authority, within a disciplined and ordered framework with all needs met. Jack envied a life so straightforward. It seemed a sort of primeval existence where a man could pit himself and his ship against natural forces, where practical accomplishments would determine the outcome, and where the challenges would be calculable and without guile. Contrast that, he mused, to the life that most men faced: scraping a capricious living from the soil in a perpetual round of repeating tedium that could dull a man's brain; or, with his own recent experience in mind, to covetousness and corruption conspiring with such devious malice. But, he asked himself, would he want such a free-floating existence: a life apart, a life where he would be always be transient even in his own home? Thinking now of his homestead, of Rose, of his new family, and of the community in which he was making his mark, he rather thought not; but it was an alluring notion to play with in his fantasies.

The evening's conversation continued thus over several glasses of Madeira wine while the captain puffed his pipe contentedly, filling the cabin with the aromatic vapours of his Virginia tobacco. But eventually the evening was brought to a reluctant close with Goddard's stifled yawn - taken by both his visitors as the signal that it was time to retire.

'But one final matter before you go, Jack;' the captain said dramatically, putting down his pipe and reaching behind him to open a draw. 'I have a parting gift for you: a belated token of my gratitude for your assistance in sorting out my unfortunate difficulties with Mr Judd on the *Rebecca*,' he said, presenting Jack with a polished rosewood box embellished by shiny brass hinges and clasp. 'It was a happy resolution for which I shall be eternally in your debt,' he continued, smiling at Jack's surprise. Jack took the box, adopting an expression in which embarrassment and delight were mixed in equal measure as he lifted its lid. Inside the box, lying snugly on a bed of faded crimson satin was the brass quadrant with which he had become so familiar during his long voyage. It had been polished to a gleaming lustre.

'You will be acquainted with my old instrument I believe,' continued Goddard, shrugging off the handsome gift as a mere trifle. 'It has been superseded by my new octant now, and so I have no further use for it; and since you have proved yourself so adept at navigation (said with tongue only slightly in cheek) you may find the device useful on your travels. I can't give you my almanac, I'm afraid, so you'll have to interpolate the sun's elevation by counting days either side of the equinox – remember...' And here Jack leapt in, anticipating his friend's instruction by echoing: '...twenty-three point four five degrees – and don't forget the sign!' Both laughed out loud. 'But use Polaris and you'll not have to struggle with the arithmetic!' Goddard smirked, 'and with no swell ashore to disturb your measurements, Jack, you'll no longer have any excuse for your errors!' The three men chuckled. For Jack and his sea-faring friend, the matter of Mr Judd's blackmail seemed now to be relegated to the distant past. It was indeed an episode best laid to rest, but as we already know, the affair was far from closed.

Chapter Six

From his secret listening position at the foot of the orlop companionway, Judd had waited patiently on that final evening, hoping to discover Jack's plans. Against the muffled but unrelenting ribaldry on the gun deck, it had been impossible to hear a word of the conversation in the captain's cabin, and lulled by the sheer tedium of his waiting, Judd had eventually dozed off. It was the sound of voices and the closing of a door that woke him, almost as if his subconscious mind had awaited it, and he was immediately alert even as he raised his head. The musical background had by now reduced markedly in its amplitude, the ranks of the regiment having thinned through attrition as the hours had passed; and thus Judd could hear that it was Jack and the major who now talked on the mess deck above his perch. At first, he could not make out the words spoken, but from the mellow tone of their speaking it was clear that both had enjoyed a glass or two of wine over their meal. It appeared also that the two men had seated themselves at the mess table to linger over a concluding chat before retiring to their cabin. Treading with utmost care, Judd raised himself silently up the companionway to bring his ears closer to the opening where he settled himself again, being very careful to remain out of sight. Meanwhile, the conversation continued uninterrupted:

'We'll be on our way first thing tomorrow morning,' he heard Jack say; 'leaving the ship probably at much the same time as you.' There was some amusement in his voice as he continued: 'I've bought myself a horse, William, big and sturdy enough for Matthew and me to ride in tandem. Can you imagine the sight of the two of us on horseback!'

'And you are able to ride too?' came the major's reply, affecting admiration. 'Such a catalogue of skills, Jack!' he laughed ironically. 'What will you turn your hand to next?'

'Hah! Well, at least I should be able to sit astride the old warhorse that I have managed to procure!' Jack joined the laughter. 'I doubt that the old nag is capable of more than a steady plod anyway; but he'll save our legs and extend our daily range a bit, I hope.'

'A pity you're heading south for Charlestown, Jack. It would have been a pleasure to have had your company on our route northwards.'

The conversation between the two men continued in the same vein a while longer yet, but Judd was satisfied that he had heard all that he needed to know; and thus he crept away, returning to his hammock in the forecastle. But he would not be there for long.

In the early hours of the following morning, Judd slipped quietly ashore before anyone was awake. He wore a seaman's coat over breeches and calf-length boots, and to cover his head, he wore his tricorn hat pulled well down. His eye-patch, now as likely to be more an identifying encumbrance than a disguise, had already been discarded. Amongst the articles that he had about him, a pistol with some shot and powder and a knife were the most notable, but he had also brought some food, a few items of spare clothing and a small amount of coinage acquired through an aptitude for winning at cards. The most bulky of these items, he carried in a knapsack made of old sailcloth slung over his shoulder. That the currency in his pockets would not provide subsistence for more than a few weeks did not overly concern him since he confidently expected to come into a small fortune once he could get Jack on his own.

There were only a few early workers about as Judd strode out along the lantern-lit quay and disappeared into a dark alleyway that led into the town. His intention was to get ahead of Jack on the road to Charlestown so that he would have an opportunity to surprise him in a secluded spot where his ambush would be unobserved. By sunrise, the town was well behind him, and he soon identified a suitable place to lie in wait - in a gully beside a bend in the road, covered by scrub and trees, with a view commanding the approaches. Satisfied that he would not be seen, he thus wrapped his coat around him and settled himself down.

Jack and Matthew meanwhile had already saddled up and departed the livery stable sitting astride the old warrior that Jack had procured the previous day. If Jack had been apprehensive of falling off the beast, he need not have been concerned, for this retired military quadruped would never startle its rider with his alacrity. The threesome now proceeded through the town at a stately pace, drawing the attention of passers by who seemed amused at the sight. The old war horse was a large and hefty beast: a dappled grey with shocking white mane and tail - he might very well have pulled a wagon by the thickness of his fetlocks and certainly would never have led a battle charge. Atop the lumbering animal plodding mindlessly through the narrow streets at the only gait he knew, perched Jack and Matthew in tandem trying to look at ease, the former, six feet tall, the latter, five, conjuring into the imagination a quixotic scene in a medieval tale of derring-do. As they neared the town's outskirts, the road widened and other travellers converged upon them heading the same way. It appeared that the road was a major thoroughfare linking the Port of Charlestown on the Potomac with its capital on the Chesapeake, the distance between the two settlements, some forty-five miles.

When travelling in open country, it was generally considered wise not to travel alone and there was therefore a natural propensity for individual travellers to join up with others. Jack thus found himself assimilated into a band of itinerant tradesmen travelling the route in search of work. They were a motley bunch of yokels and artisans but were immediately friendly and engaging, incorporating the pair on horseback as if fellow members of some guild. When Jack revealed that he was a stonemason by trade, he was adopted as a brother, and Matthew, a run-away orphaned ship's boy, as a long lost son. They passed Judd's hiding place in animated and jocular discussion completely oblivious of the skulking presence nearby, and continued thus not noticing the dark figure emerging from the bushes behind them and following at a distance. If Judd had harboured ideas of ambushing a lonely pair of travellers in an isolated spot, he must have been disappointed that the road was suddenly so cluttered with potential witnesses.

As dusk began to fall, the chattering group found themselves approaching the settlement of Brandywine, amongst whose few small buildings stood a wayside tavern and lodging house identified, perhaps rather grandiosely, as the Brandywine Hotel. The itinerants at once made for its door and entered, seeking accommodation and intent upon refreshment. Having stabled their mount, Jack and Matthew followed their good-natured friends and found themselves billeted in the same first-floor dormitory. The day had been long and wearisome, and, neither changing nor even washing off the grime, the whole party dropped their bags and descended upon the adjacent tavern en masse, ravenous for food and drink. The dingy saloon was already heaving with fellow travellers as they entered, and several faces turned to watch the newcomers fight their way through the smoke to an empty table opposite the bar at which a line of men stood drinking. Elsewhere, the noisy room was filled with tables whose occupants engaged in gaming of one kind or another.

The first priority at Jack's table was to satisfy an urgent desire to fill bellies, and this was done without much decorum or conversation. The evening thence proceeded pleasantly and without incident until Jack noticed a face within the crowd that was familiar. He peered through the smoke, trying to get a proper look at the man who sat side-on to Jack's perspective, playing cards at a distant table. He was well dressed and full of self-assurance, and his quick eyes were calculating as he held his cards close to his chest. Suddenly it dawned upon Jack who the man was. It was Hayward, the trickster who, with his band of muggers, had waylaid Jack and Ned in the alleyway in Charlestown on the way through - and relieved them of their purses. Jack well remembered the vicious fistfight in the darkness, the eventual capture of four of the ruffians aided by the timely arrival of the sheriff and his constables. But Hayward himself had escaped with Jack's money - and patently he was still at large. Moreover, judging by his brazenness in such a public place, he had probably never been identified as the perpetrator. Reflecting on the unpleasant incident, however, Jack was now ambivalent. He had come to see Hayward's robbery as strangely fortuitous for it had put him in contact with Harding, the Charlestown agent, who had in turn got him aboard the *Rebecca* and thus to England. It was Hayward, therefore, who indirectly had facilitated Jack's escape, since Harding's subsequent adoption of Jack's cause had made it possible for him to travel without papers – papers that as a convict exile he would not have been able to obtain. Jack examined Hayward coolly with these thoughts running through his head, undecided whether to act or to leave the man be and thus avoid a risky confrontation. But as he considered his options, he saw Hayward stand up, throw down his cards in a careless manner, and move towards the doorway, through which he passed nonchalantly putting on his hat. Now, if Jack had one fault it was his impetuousness, and this is why he found himself suddenly on his feet, seized with the notion that, at the very least, he should try to establish where the man was going. This may have been irrational, but then such rash actions often follow when impulse is the driver and not logic; and once outside in the darkness, he began to realise this and that pursuit was not after all worth the risk. Clearly he had begun to learn some caution from his last encounter with Hayward in the Charlestown alleyway - but unfortunately it was already too late. As he turned back, he was startled by a voice spoken from the shadows. It was, of course, Hayward's refined accent that cut the air, and so suddenly that Jack's heart missed a beat:

'Ah, Mr Stone, I rather hoped that you might follow me,' he said calmly, stepping from the shadows into the dim light of the front door lantern. 'I enjoyed reading of your exploits in the *Charlestown Reader* last November. And two of my men are still inside because of you; quite a brave one are you not? Alone too, I see - and not escorted by your big friend this time? How very unfortunate.'

Hayward's voice was irritatingly complacent, and Jack curled his hands into fists as he prepared himself for a fight. He cursed himself for leaving his pistols in his bag - they would be no use there, he thought wryly.

'Don't take another step,' he called defiantly, 'unless you want another thrashing!'

But as he puffed himself up and took a bold step forward trying to intimidate his attacker, he saw immediately that his posturing would fail. Hayward raised his arm unhurriedly. The pistol in his hand became visible as the light found it and glinted off its barrel. Its flintlock clicked as Hayward pulled back the firing arm.

'It is you who had better not take another step, Stone!' he said sharply. Hayward still used the name Jack had given himself in Charlestown, the name he had used to conceal his identity as a convict, but he did not bother to correct it. He raised his hands in a submissive gesture. But as he did so, he felt the canvas money belt under his shirt settle around his waist and was suddenly reminded that he carried his fortune about him. The realisation of how reckless he had been to put himself in such danger hit him in a rush and he felt beads of sweat tickle his brow almost instantaneously. He stepped back instinctively, wondering for a moment if there was any escape.

'Stay where you are!' Hayward said menacingly, and began to close the distance between them, his pistol steady in his hand.

Jack knew that he was in a most precarious position; although Hayward could not yet know that Jack carried such a prize about him, if he were physically searched, his bulky money belt would not be missed. Jack groaned under his breath in sudden fear of what appeared inevitable. And if he were to lose his money, then all his grand plans for home and farmstead would be thwarted, and his path to land ownership and true freedom made more arduous and greatly lengthened. He mouthed a bitter oath as despair rose up and engulfed him. There seemed no escape. If he ran, he risked being shot in the back; and his money was certainly not worth that – especially not with Rose and their new baby dependent upon him. Hayward came closer yet, his pistol hand unwavering, his eyes calculating and acquisitive. Jack tensed. Perhaps he could surprise the man yet, he wondered – first lull him into believing that he would acquiesce, then spring upon him, and wrestle the pistol from his hand?

It was probably fortunate that Jack restrained himself, for at that very moment a curiously anxious expression came over Hayward's face, and it took a second or two for Jack to interpret it; it was a mixture of astonishment and pain. At the same time, Hayward's menacing advance had halted abruptly, like a dog at the end of his chain - and now his head jerked backwards and his spine arched as his face broke into a grimace of sheer agony. It was only then that Jack realised that his attacker had been grabbed from the rear and was now being held in an arm lock with a knife to his throat. Then, from behind Hayward's contorted features, another face appeared, half hidden in shadow – a bearded man in a tricorn hat.

'Thank God!' Jack let out in relief, and strode forward to assist his rescuer.

'Take his pistol,' the bearded man growled through clenched teeth, 'then step back! He's still dangerous!'

Jack did as he was told and stood waiting in the dim light while Hayward was taken roughly by the scruff of his neck and pushed stumbling into the darkness.

'You've let him go!' shouted Jack incredulously, and started into the gloom in pursuit. It was another instinctive reaction, but this time he only got a few steps before he stopped and turned back. His rescuer now stood waiting for him, silhouetted by the light of the lantern; his face was a dark shadow.

'Why on earth did you let him go?' Jack quizzed crossly as he made towards the mysterious figure, his own features illuminated by the lantern thus putting him at a disadvantage. But his shadowy rescuer did not answer; he merely stood there motionless as Jack come closer.

'Better give me the weapon,' said the rescuer calmly, holding out his hand.

Without thinking, Jack handed the pistol over, letting out a heavy sigh of relief. 'Anyway, I can't thank you enough!' he said, breaking into a grin and offering his hand in gratitude. But his gesture was not reciprocated, and Jack now began to think that there was something odd about the man's attitude: there was a hesitancy about him, as if he were intending to do or say something but had not yet decided what. But since his features remained invisible in the darkness, it was impossible to gauge the man's character or intent. The strange hesitancy continued and Jack felt a new sense of uneasiness creep over him. 'Well, thank you all the same,' he said, beginning to feel nervous of the weapon still hanging in his rescuer's hand. 'Perhaps we should be getting in,' he suggested nervously, his voice sounding a little lame in his ears. He made to turn back to the door. 'I owe you a drink at the very least,' he proffered.

But at that moment the tavern's door was flung open and several men tumbled out, shouting and laughing in an explosion of sound and light that shattered the night's still air. Startled almost out of his wits, Jack saw the men now dropping their trouser flaps and urinating into the street. They stood in a line, their backs lit up in the light from the open door, their shadows stretching out into the distant darkness. They were the members of his happy band of itinerants made merrier by drink. And Matthew was stood at the end of the line following the men's rude example, laughing his head off as he watched his stream arc into the night sky. It then seemed to become a competition between the men to see how high a trajectory could be achieved. Someone broke wind with such terrible force that it ripped the air like the tearing of blown-out canvas in a storm, and it was followed by the inebriated sniggering of its proud progenitor. Jack could not help joining in the ensuing laughter, and he felt a rush of comfort once again to be in a friendly presence. Still laughing, he turned back, thinking to draw his mysterious rescuer into the laughter and thus break the uneasiness that seemed to have had formed between them. But the man had vanished into the night.

Jack shouted into the gloom after him. But there came no answer.

Jack slept fitfully that night, his slumber disturbed by recurring imaginings of Hayward on the prowl outside. From now on he would carry his pistols loaded and ready to hand, in case he encountered him again. The sudden disappearance of his rescuing Samaritan also troubled him. Why should the man have acted so strangely, he wondered; and where had he come from to be so readily on hand in the darkness - just when he was needed? Perhaps he might have been a deputy on night watch - or else a local thief, jealous of someone poaching on his patch? It would remain a mystery, but whoever his saviour had been and whatever his motive, Jack concluded that he should be exceedingly grateful. Perhaps he had a guardian angel after all, he wondered dozily as he finally dropped off to sleep.

It seemed only an instant later that he was awoken by rustling noises in the dormitory, and for a moment Jack thought there must be something wrong. Instantly alert, his heart pounding like a drum, he shot upright in his bunk only to see his compatriots awkwardly pulling on their clothes in the tight confines of the room. In the unearthly light of a single flickering candle, their shadows on the wall seemed to be performing some macabre ritual as the men huffed and puffed in their contortions. Through the open window, the sky seemed pitch black, yet strident birdsong already heralded the approach of dawn. And then another strident sound was heard: it was his flatulent fellow traveller again making his presence felt! Amidst the several strangled groans that soon followed, the man sniggered in a falsetto voice: 'Your early morning call, Jack!' In the semi-darkness, it was impossible to see Jack's expression, but he was out of his bed in seconds, and fighting for fresh air at the window with the others as if the hotel were ablaze. Meanwhile Matthew, oblivious of the commotion, slumbered on in the upper bunk. One of the group, the first to brave a return from the window and seeing the boy still lying there, laughed disbelievingly: 'I think your young companion must have died, Jack! No one could have survived that one!'

Forty minutes later, with the crimson-streaked light of the dawn sky serving as a backdrop, the group was on its way with Jack and Matthew once more seated on their dappled grey and plodding at its centre. If the mood amongst the travellers seemed more subdued than the day before, it was the early hour and the lingering after-effects of the previous evening's excesses rather than Jack's lingering disquiet that caused it. Nevertheless, his encounter with Hayward had made him more wary, and he found himself anxiously looking behind from time to time to reassure himself that he was not followed. But after a morning of rearward glances, throughout which the road behind was always clear, Jack soon started to relax again. It was, however, not Hayward that need have worried him. That suave trickster would not dare to show his face in Charlestown with Jack once more on the scene - he would lie low for a while for fear of being identified by the only man who could do so. It was the bearded man in the tricorn hat that continued to be Jack's greatest threat. And having intervened the night before to save his goose with the golden egg, Judd was already well ahead on the road to Charlestown, where he would wait for Jack again, hoping for another opportunity to make his move.

Chapter Seven

It felt very much like a home-coming as Jack led his weary band of itinerants through the familiar streets of Charlestown towards the Centennial Hotel; and he left them there with Matthew to check in while he sought out a stable for his mount. The creature's livery efficiently arranged, Jack at once set off in the direction of Harding's office in the hope that he would find the agent there. There would be much to report.

An amber sun sank quickly on the horizon in the last moments before sunset as Jack navigated his way around the boardwalks avoiding the muddy streets. The town square was already in deep shadow, but a single shaft of sunlight had found a momentary alignment along a thoroughfare and it now blazed a path across the square, cutting it in two. Directly at the focus of its dying beam, the church first turned gold, then pink, then purple as the light faded on its white clapboard facade; the colourful illumination was as much a call for prayer as the little bell which now rang urgently from its steeple. Amongst the people now hurrying to its chimes, Jack recognised a few faces, acknowledging their glances as he passed – some had evidently not forgotten his brief moment of acclaim five months before. Finally, he reached the quay. It was strange again to gaze down the empty river to the bend where he had last seen Ned sailing his little boat back to New Hope on the afternoon of Jack's embarkation. He recalled how alone he felt on seeing his friend depart, daunted to be facing his self-imposed crusade without his staunch support. He could see Neal's Landing in the distance too, the port of entry from where he had set sail. It was deserted now, and would not see a tobacco ship until later in the year when the crop would be cured and ready for shipping. Goddard had said that the *Miranda* would be berthing there in a month or two for her refit, and Jack resolved there and then to sail up from New Hope to meet him. He continued along the waterfront until the shipping office stood before him. It was a single story extension added to the northern end of the courthouse; and running along its far side was the alleyway in which he had famously fought off Hayward and his thugs. He glanced into its dark recesses as he approached, remembering the fight; and it occurred to him that, but for the intervention of his mysterious rescuer the night before in Brandywine, Hayward might have had him and his money again. Jack felt himself shudder as he contemplated that near catastrophe.

Harding was sitting at his desk scribbling with his quill on the page of a large ledger as Jack entered his open doorway, and it was not until Jack spoke that the tobacco agent looked up.

'Mission accomplished, Mr Harding, sir,' Jack said simply, smiling a greeting.

'Jack, good Lord!' Thomas Harding exclaimed, jumping to his feet in surprise, his round flushed face beaming under his short silver hair. 'How nice to see you back.' Harding reached both hands across his cluttered deck to grasp Jack's in welcome, shaking it warmly. 'Now, take a seat and tell me all about it!' he said, immediately getting down to business.

Harding had suspected that some of his tobacco was being misappropriated during shipment and had taken on Jack as his agent to supervise the *Rebecca's* last consignment. Indeed, it had been this employment that had secured Jack's passage, for, as has already been said, he would not have been able to leave the colony otherwise. Jack decided, therefore, to confine his report to the points of Harding's likely interest, explaining at once how Judd had gone about his thieving. Jack kept it short and to the point adding only enough supplementary information to bring the agent up to date. The rest would have to wait until later. Besides, he was tired and hungry.

'This boatswain, Judd: I'm trying to put a face to him,' said Harding, gazing into the air thoughtfully. 'Ah yes. I remember him; I dealt with him from time to time - a rather shifty sort if I recall.' He paused, evidently thinking further on the matter, before seeming to dismiss it from his mind. 'Well, Jack, in any event, you have done me a great service. Without your intervention, who knows how long his mischief would have gone on.'

In his telling of the story, Jack had carefully avoided any mention of Judd's blackmailing of Goddard and his predecessor to become reluctant accomplices in the scheme. And Harding seemed so delighted to have his suspicions proved that he did not enquire further of the details.

'It seems that I was right to put my faith in you.' Harding got up from his desk and moved over to a drop-leaf cabinet in the corner of the room. 'A drink to celebrate your safe return, I think, don't you?' He poured himself a glass of red wine, flicking a glance over his shoulder with his eyebrows raised in enquiry.

'Why not,' Jack replied, 'but a small one if you please, sir, I must be away to the hotel where young Matthew awaits me. And both of us need a bath before we get ourselves something to eat. We have been on the road all day!'

'Young Matthew?' responded Harding, 'the *Rebecca's* boy?'

'And late of the *Miranda*, promoted to Captain Goddard's steward too!' Jack replied with the air of one especially impressed, and he then related his offer to give the orphan a decent home ashore on his farmstead at New Hope.

'Then here's to you both,' Harding replied lifting his glass. 'And to your new life as a freeman in our colony! I am so glad to hear that things have worked out as you hoped, Jack. You should know that Sir Michael and I both thought you reckless in the extreme to be taking the chance of returning to England with a price upon your head. Now, we shall have to eat our words, won't we? By the way, I am meeting him at Chaptico tomorrow night for our monthly get-together to discuss the shipment of his crop; I plan to set off tomorrow morning early,' he explained. 'We could travel together perhaps?' he asked brightly. And with this, he downed the last dregs of his wine in the manner of one making up his mind. 'And you shall both stay the night at my home this evening and we shall dine together,' he said emphatically. 'Hmmm - once you have bathed and changed out of those clothes that is!' he added with a mischievous wrinkle of his nose. 'I'll walk with you to collect Matthew from the hotel!' he said, while reaching for his coat.

And so the following day, like the one before, Jack and Matthew were awoken early. But this time they dressed not in the rudimentary confines of a dormitory, crowded with rude and boisterous itinerants, but in the domestic comfort of a family home. Mr and Mrs Harding had fed them well the previous evening and Jack had retired far too late to bed having entertained the agent and his wife with his adventurous tales. His head throbbed with each delicate step as he descended the stairs for breakfast, while Matthew, wisely not so late to bed the night before, raced ahead following the smell of bacon. The house was well proportioned and of brick and timber construction, and it was situated on the shallow ridge that rose to the east of the town. The view from the breakfast table thus encompassed the wide sweep of the Port Tobacco River valley stretching to the south with glimpses of the Potomac beyond. Despite his throbbing head, Jack could not stop himself comparing the relative luxury of the Hardings' home with the basic rusticity of his own, and he decided there and then that he would spend some of his new wealth on improving the farmstead at New Hope. In the flights of fancy that then overtook him, he voiced some of his thoughts to Harding across the table, mentioning in passing that he carried the prize money with him in a money belt.

'Jack, my friend,' said Harding, looking shocked, 'you did not tell me that you were carrying so much on your person? I should advise you straight away to make use of our depositary here in my strong room, where your money will be safe.'

Remembering his fright at Brandywine, Jack immediately saw the sense in this and agreed at once, grateful at last to have someone with commercial acumen to advise him.

'And when it is necessary for you to make use of it,' Harding continued earnestly, 'Charlestown is certainly the best place for you to obtain the highest rate of exchange. Sterling is always in demand here; it is much more reliable than some of the other specie that flow through traders' hands - and necessary for the purchase of English goods, of course. If you will trust me with it, I will secure it in my safe here in the house forthwith and will see to its deposit in the shipping office strong room as soon as I return from Chaptico.'

The matter was quickly settled, and Jack divested himself of the worrisome encumbrance with evident relief, retaining a sum of twenty pounds or so for his pocket. He was thus easier in his mind and more comfortable around the waist some half an hour later as the threesome set off from the house and descended into the town.

Judd had followed Jack and his conspicuous mount to the stable the previous afternoon and had then trailed him to the shipping office at a discrete distance; there were people about and so he could not be too blatant in his observation while it was still light. He had expected Jack eventually to walk back to the hotel alone, planning to intercept him in the alleyways along the route. He had thus concealed himself in a nearby doorway to wait patiently in the gathering darkness. When he saw Jack leave the building some time later accompanied by the agent Harding, he swore under his breath in exasperation. He did not want to be outnumbered or leave a witness to his act, especially someone like Harding who might well recognise him in a close encounter. His resolve had thus wilted as the pair had passed close by, shrinking back into the deep shadows of the doorway. While Jack remained accompanied, he had unwittingly given himself some protection from attack, and Judd was becoming increasingly frustrated by it. Now, short on sleep from an uncomfortable night in a Brandywine barn, he faced another night of discomfort, for despite his disguise he could not risk identification in a public hotel. Thus, knowing that Jack must eventually return to the stable to pick up his horse, he returned there to wait until morning when perhaps he might get another chance. But again his plan would be thwarted, for when Jack arrived to saddle up the grey, not only was the burly liveryman already mucking out the stalls with a worrisome pitchfork, but also Harding and Matthew accompanied him.

By the end of the day, the threesome - Harding on his sleek brown gelding, Jack and Matthew astride their old grey charger - had reached their destination: the small harbour town of Chaptico, distinguished by its handsome brick-built church built some twenty years before apparently to a Christopher Wren design. Chaptico lay at the head of a tributary of the Wicomico River, which flowed into the Potomac approximately half way between Charlestown and the southern extremities of St Mary's county. It was thus a convenient meeting place for Harding to meet the plantation owners of those southern parts who used him as their agent for the shipment and sales of their tobacco. His meetings with his southern clients generally took place in the Chaptico Hotel, the only establishment for miles around where a gentleman could find accommodation of reasonable comfort - and a saloon not overrun with ruffians off visiting vessels. It was thus here that Harding had planned to meet Sir Michael and several other important clients that evening, and after seeing to the stabling of their mounts, the three travellers went inside. Sir Michael was already sitting at his customary table adjacent to the window as the threesome entered and shook the dust from their coats. Sir Michael had apparently not noticed their arrival, for he stared through the window, with his mind apparently lost in thought. Forming a backdrop to his contemplative pose, the dramatic blood-red bloom of dusk set nearby warehouses ablaze in its fiery light, and drew the eye to a distant view of the flat and marshy landscape that was now darkening in the descending gloom. He wore a fawn coloured coat of fine cut with a high collar of darker material, pale riding trousers and calf-length black leather riding boots with tan tops. His hair, fair and swept back into a short ponytail tied with a black ribbon, was of that neat and shiny appearance that looked as if it had just been groomed. Clearly, he had been waiting for some little time for he appeared somewhat bored.

Harding led the way across the room towards his client, picking his way between the empty tables that lay in their path. Sir Michael turned at the sound of their approach, but to him at first only Harding would have been seen as leader of the line.

'Ah, Harding,' he said brightening, but in that sort of slightly condescending tone that men of breeding reserved for their servants, albeit a respected and senior one. 'Good that you have arrived early; I hope you...' But at that early point in his opening discourse, he saw Jack appear from behind Harding's back and his sentence proceeded no further, his mouth sticking for a moment in the shape of his last syllable. A look of astonishment at once animated his features. 'Why, Jack Easton!' he exclaimed, changing his manner instantly to one of hearty bonhomie, 'I was talking about you only this morning - just before I left New Hope!'

'Nothing defamatory I hope, sir!' retorted Jack, breaking into a wry smile. 'It is good to see you again.' Jack took Sir Michael's proffered hand, but it was done briefly and with some slight reticence in his manner. 'And good to be back again on home territory, sir. All is well at New Hope, I trust?' he enquired politely, clearly fishing for news from his farmstead in particular.

'All is very well indeed,' replied Sir Michael, emphatically. 'And at your farmstead too, as far as I can tell,' he added, sensing Jack's meaning. 'Rose came to the house again this morning, knowing of my intended meeting here, and reminded me to enquire of any news of vessels arriving from England,' he chuckled. 'She constantly badgers me in case I might have heard anything which might give a clue as to your return. She will be delighted to see you safe - and I will be delighted from now on not to be so pestered!'

'An did she look well, sir?'

'Rose by name and rosy by appearance I would say, Jack,' Sir Michael winked conspiratorially. 'She looks very well indeed, with a fine and full shape on her too! Oh, you knew of course?' he asked quickly, suddenly seeming unsure of himself.

'Indeed I did, sir. And have made all haste to be back in time for the birth!'

'Then Harding and I will conclude our business this very evening and you and I shall travel back together tomorrow; I have some important business to discuss with you, and your arrival is very timely.' Sir Michael threw a commanding glance at Harding as he spoke, leaving Jack wondering what business he could be referring to. But then Matthew, until now hidden behind his two companions' backs, chose this moment to shoulder his way gently between them. 'And who is this young scallywag?' Sir Michael retorted, bemused.

Sir Michael's business with Harding was kept short, and the four travellers retired briefly to their rooms before returning for supper later in the evening. By then the room had filled up with other travellers or seamen officers from the wharf, and the atmosphere in the room had taken on that gentle and smoky ambience characteristic of a respectable tavern. Seating themselves at the same table, Jack soon became the centre of attention with tales of his adventures, this time related for Sir Michael's sake. His two other listeners had, of course, already heard it all before, but seemed content nevertheless to be hearing it again; Matthew even interjected some missed out detail from time to time. Sir Michael listened intently as Jack's tale unfolded, sometimes falling grave, sometimes amused, and occasionally erupting into loud guffaws of uninhibited laughter, depending upon the episode related. Jack had them all eating out of his hand.

The meal and Jack's entertaining monologue came to an end more or less simultaneously as the landlord arrived at the table to clear away their plates. At this point Matthew rose politely to excuse himself to retire to his bed, and Harding chose the same moment to announce his removal to another table to join clients he had arranged to meet. The pair's departure seemed to spark an uneasy shift of mood at the table for the two remaining men, and for some seconds neither Sir Michael nor Jack offered anything to fill the awkward silence that ensued. Meanwhile, the burble of background chatter ebbed and flowed, creating a rescuing diversion that bridged the hiatus as the two men affected to find interest elsewhere in the now crowded room. Although Jack's gaze swung to and fro, it was unfocussed - more out of wanting to seem at ease than purposeful. He thus failed to notice the bearded man in a tricorn sitting at a table in the far corner of the room, who happened at that moment to be in conversation with the landlord. Had Jack paid attention to the pair, he might have found it curious that both threw occasional glances across the room towards the table at which he sat.

Meanwhile the awkward silence continued for a few seconds more, before Sir Michael spoke: 'You should have told me what you had in mind, Jack,' he said in a slightly disappointed tone, 'I may have been able to help you. Instead you simply disappeared, leaving me to draw my own conclusions. I might have set the law upon you had not Rose explained your sudden absence.'

Jack's expression revealed some slight embarrassment but it was stiffened with a streak of self-justification.

'Sir Michael,' he hesitated as if collecting his thoughts, 'as soon as Mr Harding relayed your message to me in Charlestown just before my departure, I realised that I should have advised you of my plans. But until then I could not be sure how you would react. You might very well have tried to stop me going; and if you had, I would never have been able to obtain justice. And, despite your earlier generosity in making the farmstead available to Rose and me, I would never have been truly free had I not cleared my name in the courts. Besides,' he added with some irony, in an attempt to break the serious mood, 'I had to contend with quite stiff resistance from Rose at that time, and that gave me more than enough to think about – I needed to go quickly or not at all!'

Sir Michael pursed his lips and nodded thoughtfully, eventually appearing to accept Jack's half-apology. 'Well, it is as well you have returned and I am glad to see you back.' he said in a conciliatory tone, which seemed to draw a line under the matter. But there were evidently other matters that still troubled him, and after a further uneasy hesitation, he continued diffidently:

'And so you are no longer a convicted felon, Jack, no longer exiled from England, and no longer poor!' Sir Michael summed up Jack's position quite succinctly. 'But I hope that you have not forgotten your undertaking to join my militia?' His words were lightly spoken but highly charged.

Until that moment, the thought that his windfall would alter anything with regard to his undertakings to Sir Michael had not entered Jack's mind. His early release from indentures had come at the cost of certain promises to his former master and he had accepted the conditions willingly. But prompted by Sir Michael's words, it now occurred to him that he might negotiate to buy the freehold of New Hope Farm and thus remove the encumbrance of the annual quota of stonework due in lieu of rent. This might well be possible, he now realised; but the tone of Sir Michael's rhetoric made it quite clear that Jack's other undertaking - to join the militia - would not be so easy to negotiate away.

In truth, Jack knew that given a threat to life and home, he would fight to the death in its defence. And so, if the circumstances ever demanded it, he would be amongst the first to volunteer for military service. But it was a shock nevertheless to be reminded of his duty so starkly, and his heart sank at the unexpected prospect of leaving Rose and his new baby so soon after his return.

'Then it has become necessary, Sir Michael?' he asked evenly.

'I am very much afraid that it has, Jack, and I shall want you at my side.'

'When?'

'Soon, Jack, very soon. General Forbes is already on his way to the Ohio valley and I mean to support him. Besides, several thousand American volunteers, including two Virginia regiments and the Pennsylvania Regiment, will be joining him and I do not want to be left out of the party! New land could well become our prize as well as putting a stop at last to French and Indian incursions!'

Sir Michael spoke with such unchallengeable conviction that it was difficult to disagree with him, but Jack thought that his former master's anxiety not to be 'left out of the party' was revealing. He now wondered if Sir Michael's intentions might be driven by some petty vanity or even avarice rather than a noble cause.

'And your men are already trained?' he queried, trying not to sound a negative note.

'In training, Jack, but soon ready,' came the landowner's confident reply. 'One hundred men from southern estates as well as farmsteads like yours.'

'And have you received orders?' Jack probed gently.

'Orders, Jack?' Sir Michael retorted. 'Heavens no! We'll grow old waiting for the Maryland Assembly to make up its mind! We need no orders! I know my duty though, and I intend for us to join up with Forbes' army and be put under his command. A hundred extra men will not be sneezed at!'

'And how will you find him, sir? Do you know his route?'

'A road is being cut through Pennsylvania as we speak, with fortified supply depots and encampments all the way along it,' Sir Michael retorted confidently. 'It should not be difficult to intercept. We shall sail up the Potomac to Georgetown then strike north overland from there until we do. From New Hope, ninety miles upriver, and then the same again on reasonable terrain to pick up Forbes' new road.' Sir Michael now began to sound slightly less convincing. 'The road runs due west from there about one-hundred-and-fifty miles straight across the Appalachians, so the going might get a bit hard,' he said a little uncertainly, 'but at least we'll have a route to follow and should obtain assistance from the depots.'

' A hundred men's rations to be carried over that distance?' Jack's voice was measured, but alarm bells had begun to ring in his mind. 'Muskets, shot, and powder too – that's quite a load, sir,' he cautioned. 'Perhaps not so bad by boat, but once we are on land, we'll need horses and wagons to transport it all. It'll be a tough journey, sir, – and worse still if we encounter hostile Indians on the way!' Still feeling far from being part of the venture, Jack had nevertheless used the first person plural deliberately to soften the edge of his critical enquiry; but he was beginning to gauge the scale of the undertaking, and it frightened him.

'With a fair wind, Jack, it should only take us about two to three days to sail up to Georgetown, then perhaps seven or eight days on foot northwards to General Forbes' road and the first of the depots.'

Sir Michael countered Jack's probing soothingly - apparently trying to make light of Jack's concerns - but his manner was now becoming a little tetchy.

'Anyway, once we are on the road, we'll be able to travel light and restock from the forts every few days or so. I don't think that we should find it *too* difficult,' he said blandly.

Jack was now not only uneasy at the scale of Sir Michael's grand strategy, but he was also beginning to harbour some serious doubts as to the man's competence to lead it, wondering if he had really thought it through. Sir Michael was, after all, a plantation owner, and despite his aristocratic lineage, he had no military background at all. Jack liked and respected his former owner, a man who had shown him kindness and generosity, but the very thought of following him into battle was suddenly quite terrifying. Major Green's astute summary of the current military situation came to mind, and he decided to risk one further question:

'Your officers, sir, will they have experience of Indian warfare? If not I fear...' but he got no further with his question, for Sir Michael interrupted at that point:

'You do not need to worry on that score, Jack,' he said dismissively. 'I have recruited a friend of mine, a fellow landowner with considerable militia experience, as my second-in-command. He will be our military adviser, Jack, and he brings several former militiamen with him who will act as platoon commanders and scouts. They are also supervising our training and attending to the details of our logistics.'

Jack sat back not knowing whether to be comforted by Sir Michael's confident response. Every answer seemed to prompt yet more questions in his mind but, much as his instincts cried out for him to press Sir Michael further, he could neither prolong nor sharpen his scrutiny without risking it being seen as a direct challenge to his authority. He thus decided to leave his enquiry at that – at least for the present. Nevertheless, when Jack eventually retired to his bed that night, he lay awake for some considerable time before drifting off to sleep.

Chapter Eight

At dawn, in a hayloft not more than fifty yards from the hotel room in which Jack had slept so poorly, Judd awoke after a third night sleeping rough. He rose quickly, clambered from his dusty nest in crumpled dishevelment, and crawled on hands and knees across the loft to the half-open shutters, where he resumed his watch. Outside in the street and on the nearby quay, the first few early risers were already about in the half-light. Directly opposite his observation post, the hotel stood almost in total darkness save for the dim light that burned in the window of the ground-floor saloon. 'Breakfast,' he thought longingly, but he knew that it was a hopeless wish; his meal the previous evening would have to see him through the day. He yawned unrestrainedly and rubbed the sleep from his eyes, then ran a hand over his shaven head and scratched the itching in his beard, removing some strands of hay that he found entangled within it. Yesterday's long walk from Charlestown had taken its toll; his legs ached as if they had been trampled, his thighs were chafed and sore, and his eyes stung sorely from the dust of the road. Keeping up with the threesome, riding at a walking pace but never pausing for a break throughout the day, had drained him. Wearily, he propped himself against the frame of the opening and settled down to wait, almost immediately finding himself fighting to stay awake. But a movement on the boardwalk of the hotel opposite soon drew his eye and he sat up to see Jack emerging from the tavern carrying his bags. When he saw Sir Michael and Matthew following him out, he swore under his breath; once again his patience was being sorely tried. He needed to get Jack on his own and it seemed that this day would repeat the inconsequential pattern of the days before. Despondently, he watched them saddle up, and for a few seconds he contemplated giving up his pursuit and making his way back to Annapolis to find a gambling table to top up his depleting resources. But just as quickly, he thought better of it. Bide your time my lad, he thought grimly, the prize is worth the waiting! This was the inner voice of wise counsel speaking again, for he had already resisted several earlier impulses simply to waylay Jack and his various companions on the road and be done with it once and for all. It was the possibility of messy complications that deterred him: For a start, although he might have surprise on his side, he would still be outnumbered and possibly outgunned. But it was the thought of being identified and then later hunted down that worried him more. Somehow, he hoped to steal Jack's money unseen and unknown, and vanish without trace to live as a free man rather than as a fugitive from the law. And since he could not guarantee to silence all witnesses, even if he had the stomach for it, he would have to be patient. Consequently, perhaps because he could think of no better idea, he resigned himself again to follow on as the group climbed into their saddles and set off. But this time he could follow at a greater distance and take his time. His casual enquiries of the landlord during the previous evening had revealed the identity of Jack's new companion, and it would not be difficult to find the well-known estate of which he was the owner. But had Judd also known that Jack now carried a sum of only twenty pounds upon his person, he might have been less persistent and given up his obsession there and then.

The terrain of St Mary's County, Maryland, undulates so gently that in places it appears almost entirely flat. And being quite densely wooded, it is difficult for a traveller to gain any distant perspective - unless he comes upon one of the many creeks or rivers that penetrate the narrowing peninsular, thus gaining a view across open water to distant banks – or else catches glimpses of the Chesapeake or the Potomac shining between the trees. Or perhaps he might cross one of the many plantations, which most commonly descend to the water's edge or to a broad navigable inlet around which, cut into the dense greenery of mixed woodland, broad fields of many lighter textures have been set. Here, he might obtain a view of some wealthy tobacco planter's house nestling into a pleasant dell, surrounded prettily by its outbuildings in a pleasing agricultural scene where colourful denizens labour amongst the rows of newly planted tobacco plants. Not until the traveller comes closer will he see no smiles upon their dark faces, or hear their slow lamenting voices, or notice the ostentatious batons swinging from their overseers' belts.

Movement through these tidewater regions is generally most easily accomplished by boat since most habitations lie adjacent to water; but a lattice-work of rough roads also criss-crosses the peninsular, linking place to place. It was along these by-ways that Sir Michael now led his little group towards New Hope in a roughly south easterly direction. Curiously, neither Sir Michael nor Jack returned to the matter of the previous evening's somewhat prickly discussion. Perhaps the subject was avoided because of Matthew's presence; but more likely, it was because both participants had sensed the fragility of Sir Michael's battle plan and thus neither had dared to reopen talk of it, lest it turn into an argument. Conversation along the way was therefore somewhat stilted, aided only by Sir Michael's tuition on geography in territory that was at first unfamiliar both to Jack and Matthew. But by early afternoon, having made a brief stop for refreshment at the Leonardtown ordinary that Jack knew well, they were already entering the northern boundary of the New Hope estate, distinguished at once by its almost manicured appearance. Having started cloudy, the day had brightened quickly and the sunshine now drew out the budding colours of springtime that gave a hint of new life to the winter landscape that lay before them. In the distance, the shingled roofs and the glistening steeple of the church at New Hope were conspicuous amongst the trees; and just beyond these beacons, the wide expanses of the Potomac stretched towards the haze layer that lay upon a blue horizon like a blanket. A fork in the road was soon reached where two tracks led off: the main track continued straight ahead towards New Hope itself, while the other, a narrower track, wound off to the left towards Jack's farmstead, still hidden in the woodland canopy. Jack pulled the grey to a halt to savour the moment of his arrival, allowing Sir Michael go ahead.

'Tomorrow, Jack! Come to see me tomorrow and we'll talk more of my plans,' Sir Michael called over his shoulder as his horse carried him onwards without a pause. Jack's acknowledgement was perfunctory, for, as he gazed upon the familiar panorama that lay before him, he was suddenly taken with the importance of this moment of return. It seemed somehow incredible that he was here at all after such a long and hazardous itinerary. But even as his mind sifted through the many images of his long and hazardous journey, the memories began to blur. They flashed across his inner eye and receded so quickly that it felt as if they were somehow being sorted and filed - posted to some distant archive where they might only have been dreams rather than real. It was the here-and-now at New Hope that rose up to assert itself where it had left off nearly six months before. And suddenly it was as though he had never been away. It had been an eventful, exhausting and, sometimes, dangerous venture, but now, at last, at *long, long* last, he had come home.

Rose was kneeling in the kitchen garden selecting a few leaves in her herb corner when she heard the soft clip-clop of hooves approaching. When she looked up, she saw a fair-haired boy astride a large grey horse walking as if mindlessly towards the gate. The boy was dressed in a sailing jacket and wore a sailing cap; his trousers, made from some light-coloured coarse material, were baggy and too short for his legs, and although he wore leather boots, there seemed to be no socks upon his feet. His bonny face beamed with a broad and cheeky smile as if he recognised her, and he had the sort of ruddy countenance that comes from exposure to the full force of the sea air. *A ship's boy*, she thought. The sight was so unexpected that at first she was bemused, and she returned the smile not knowing if she should know the boy or not. He was so dwarfed by the great creature upon which he sat that she wondered how he had ever climbed upon it, let alone have been given control of the reins. She raised herself ready as he drew nearer, carefully depositing the picked leaves into her basket and brushing her hands clean upon her apron. Her rising sparked a stirring in her womb, signalling a protest, and she placed her hands upon her belly to calm the infant within, smiling to herself in happy contemplation of imminent motherhood. It was not until then that she become aware that someone, clearly a man, must be walking behind the approaching steed, for she could see another pair of booted legs. She straightened her linen bonnet and tucked some loose strands of her long dark hair back behind her ears in preparation for a greeting. And then she cupped her hands under the pregnant bulge in her long full skirt and waited for the man to come into sight, her face by then a picture of mystified but pleasant anticipation. The horse stopped when it reached the gate almost as if it had a will of its own, but the man did not emerge from his concealment straight away. It seemed by the movement of his legs, however, that he must be attending to the bags attached to the other side of the saddle. 'A delivery of some sort?' she contemplated. And then she felt her heart race a little as a new thought entered her mind; 'perhaps it is a letter from Jack?' Her expression at once took on that look of someone filled with eagerness and hope, and she stuttered anxiously:

'Are you carrying a letter for me, young man?'

'I bid you good afternoon, Mrs Easton,' replied the boy politely, still smiling as if participating in some secret conspiracy. 'I have brought you something, but it is not a letter,' he said mysteriously. Rose sagged visibly and her face fell a little in disappointment. But then, seeing the boy still smiling enigmatically, she became at first puzzled and then elated as Jack stepped from behind the grey and stood out in full view for the first time, his face cast in an expression somewhere between hilarity and tears.

'Jack!' she screamed ecstatically, bringing her hands to her cheeks in a gesture of consummate elation, her eyes wide like saucers, her mouth agape. 'Jack, Oh Jack! It is you!' And with that she rushed through the gate and flung herself into his waiting arms with nothing more than a little shriek of glee. And the two clung to each other for several minutes, feeling the urgency of each other's fierce embrace, while each whispered most tender words of reunion into the other's ear. It was Matthew's consoling mutterings to the abandoned grey that eventually reminded the pair that they were not alone. Reluctantly, Jack and Rose loosened their embrace, drawing back from each other until they stood a foot apart still holding hands, their gazes meanwhile, lingering and fond. Jack was the first to break the tender mood: 'You've no idea how I've longed for this moment!' He threw back his head and laughed exultantly. 'And now I can't believe I'm back!' And with the grin still upon his face he examined his wife with affectionate and appraising eyes - then stroked her swollen belly in an unspoken acknowledgement of the imminence of the birth.

'A few weeks,' she said, smiling demurely. 'And you have kept your promise to be back in time.' Her smile, first sweet, became mischievous, and her voice took on a sharper edge. 'And perhaps our baby will have a father around to rear him after all,' she added in playful sarcasm. 'Although it will be a mixed blessing if it turns out to be as obstinate as you!' And they both burst into laughter and fell once more into each other's arms and kissed each other for several seconds more, while Matthew and the grey looked on - the one, patently baffled, the other, evidently bored.

It was in this pose that Ned and Sebi first saw the little congregation at the gate as they came out of the rear door of the cabin with expressions on their faces that suggested that they had been wondering why Rose was not at the hearth preparing their meal. Jack threw the men a grin, but for a moment they stood gazing back with some uncertainty. Jack waited amused for recognition to dawn. Ned's square frame and ponderous bulk stood in comical contrast to Sebi's lanky gauntness, and the old man's crinkly hair was whiter than he remembered it. By now, dusk was gathering, and in the diminishing light it took the pair some seconds to realize who it was that stood before them. But then both, simultaneously, let out the same delighted yell: 'Jack!' And both at once sprung forward, their faces split by broad grins of pleasure as they galloped at a pelt across the garden towards him, oblivious of Rose's careful planting. Judging the momentum of the oncoming pair to be unstoppable, Jack took a careful step to one side to protect Rose from the imminent collision. He was just in time, for a fraction of a second later, he found himself in an asphyxiating bear hug from Ned while at the same time Sebi seemed intent on strangling him. As soon as he was able to extricate himself from their tenacious grips, Jack returned the obvious fondness by wrapping his arms around his friends' shoulders.

'Well boys?' he said, grinning into their beaming faces. 'Time for a jug of cider to celebrate the return of the prodigal son, eh?' he said. 'And I have some excellent news for us all!' And with that, he pulled the two men in towards him roughly in a show of manly affection that nearly knocked their heads together.

'The good news can wait,' Ned chuckled, 'cider first!' Breaking free from Jack's grip, he quickly turned the tables and wrapped his thick arm around Jack's neck, knocking off his cap in the manoeuvre. Like a ruffian in a schoolyard, he messed up Jack's hair with his free hand, leaving him looking like someone dragged through a hedge backwards. Jack knew what was expected of him and he retaliated immediately. Twisting, he took hold of Ned's girth with both arms, and tried to wrestle himself free. Sebi sensibly leapt aside at this point, clearly unwilling to let his fragile frame become entangled in such boisterous behaviour, while Rose looked on, bemused. The two men finally pulled themselves apart, grunting and panting with exertion. By this time, Jack had had enough and raised his hands in surrender. If Ned might find it difficult to articulate his feelings, Jack thought, this rough and tumble was as clear a manifestation of his friendship as any. Jack let down his guard thinking himself safe; but without warning, Ned lunged again, precipitating a further bout of playful cut and thrust that developed quickly into another wrestling match – the pair laughing and sniggering throughout like children at a party. Meanwhile Matthew and the grey stood by dumbfounded by the spectacle of two grown adults behaving in such an imbecilic fashion - until finally the boy could not prevent himself from bursting into laughter. The sparring twosome, brought up by the sound of mirth, paused to look, their expressions turning from surprise to sheepishness to see the boy clearly so amused. It was now the turn of the adult assembly to stand and stare at the boy, still doubled over in spasms of hilarity. Becoming aware of the inspection, Matthew brought himself under control, his laughter withering in an instant into an embarrassed smirk. He cleared his throat nervously, pulled himself into a more sober pose, and ventured rather coyly: 'Er, I'm Matthew,' he said, thrusting out his hand.

The celebratory evening that followed was not spoiled by news of Jack's probable conscription into Sir Michael's militia, for he decided not yet to speak of it. And while the arrival of a military encampment on the estate in recent weeks certainly sparked some comment around the supper table, Jack had carefully avoided being drawn in. Moreover, if Rose had held any concern about Jack's possible involvement, she had not shown it.

To Jack, sitting once more at the table in the cluttered room that served as kitchen, scullery, dining room, and parlour, it felt as if he had travelled back in time. The same fire burned in the open inglenook with the same flames, and the oil lamps cast the same warm glow on the same odd collection of furniture that seemed hardly to have changed position since he had left. Around the table, the same faces, caught in the flickering light of the candles arrayed at its centre, were the same rosy images that he had carried with him on his journey: my dearest wife and my good friends, he thought with a sudden up-welling of fondness for them all. Jack's heart felt full as he watched them chattering in that spontaneous way that families do when completely at ease, their faces flushed on this occasion with the happiness of a reunion, their moods yet further elevated by Sebi's heady well-fermented brew. And behind them on the walls, their lively shadows danced the same dance to the candles' wavering flames as if the party from which he had excused himself six months before had resumed with the same gusto, hardly noticing that he had been away.

After the long winter months of Jack's absence, the group was once more complete - indeed it had now been enhanced by Matthew's arrival - and the five sat at the supper table over an evening meal that was drawn out by Jack's entertaining narratives (which in Matthew's estimation, were maturing royally with each telling). Discussion of Jack's new wealth, only latterly revealed so as not to divert the discourse too early from his tales, then soared to heights of unachievable extravagance before finding root in more realistic ground. And chief amongst the ideas mooted was the building of a new workshop for stone and woodwork to which Jack professed an eagerness to return, while Rose, of course, had other things on her mind of a more domestic nature - like the building of a nursery for the new baby. Sebi suggested a new trap for his trips to Leonardtown, while for Ned, a bigger boat with some weather protection for more comfortable fishing was required. Throughout all this banter Matthew had said very little, seeming sometimes even overawed. Instead, he listened avidly, his eyes flicking from face to face, the expressions on his own mirroring those of his animated companions just as if he were taking a full part.

Throughout the meal, Jack and Rose had sat side by side. And when Jack's right hand was not playing its essential supporting role in pictorial reinforcement of his words, it sought hers under the cover of the table or it rested on her thigh where her hand found it and held it tenderly. And their eyes would often meet in lingering glances that made their mutual affection plain for all to see. Moreover, although Jack clearly took great pleasure in regaling his wider audience with his tales, any tally of his glances would have shown that it was Rose who was the main focus of his attention, hers the approval that he sought, and her that he strove mainly to impress.

The evening thus ran its convivial course, and eventually it became clear that an appropriate time had arrived for Ned and Sebi to return to their own cabin nearby. It had been decided earlier that Matthew would sleep on the long settee in that multi-purpose room until more comfortable arrangements could be made for him. Before the pair departed, therefore, their help was enlisted to clear some space by shifting some items of furniture. It was during this kafuffle that a movement drew Matthew's eye to the little single-paned window adjacent to the outside door where, just for an instant, he thought he saw a human face illuminated in the light coming from inside the room. His eyes sought out Jack immediately, as if some inner alarm had triggered him to alert his friend, but seeing him busy bringing out a pile of blankets from the bedroom, he hesitated, suddenly unsure of what he had seen. He returned his glance to the window but the face was no longer there. The glazing now reflected only the movement inside the room, and thus he began to think that this must have been what he had seen before. He therefore held his tongue while the reorganisation of the furniture was completed and the settee was made up into a bed. And by the time the work was done, Matthew had convinced himself that his eyes must have been deceived. With Jack and Rose soon departing hand-in-hand into their bedroom, he undressed, snuffed out the lantern, and climbed into his bed, quite forgetting the incident for a time. But as he swept his gaze around his new surroundings in the rosy glow of the fire's dying embers, he found his eyes alighting more than once on the little window through which now only the bare branches of a nearby tree could be seen, silhouetted against a pale moonlit sky.

In the adjacent room, Jack found that the pleasure of sleeping with his wife again was diminished only by the frustration of not being able to consummate his almost irresistible urge to make love to her. It was a mutual if unspoken acceptance of her tender state that held them back – but only just! While every inch of his body yearned for her, and every movement of his tingling flesh against hers caused a throb of anticipation in his loins, he denied himself his own fulfilment with a will that tested his resolve. It was a supreme act of restraint on both sides. But instead, they held each other naked front-to-front in a long and tender embrace, each delighting in the intimacy and warmth of the other's body: his – lean, firm, and muscular; hers – soft, full, and velvety smooth. Their hands explored, stroked, and caressed within the radius of an arm's reach, their skins trembled in almost unendurable ecstasy to each electric touch. He felt her breasts firm against his chest; she felt his manhood swell against her belly - so hot against her skin that it was hardly possible to resist yielding to it; for she could feel the mounting urgency within her to receive him. And both might have thrown all caution to the wind and given in to passion had they not at that moment felt their unborn infant stir between them. It was almost certainly a tiny limb that moved across the inside of her womb in a wide arc – like the wave of an arm - as if in salutation; as if reminding the couple that they were no longer alone. The impression was so strong that both gave out a startled breath of mirth. It was the strangest of feelings. But the profundity of the creation inside her suddenly struck home, and the thought of it cooled their ardour instantly, their earthly urges ranked to puerile self-indulgence in the face of such a heavenly blessing. In the candlelight, their eyes met in fond acknowledgement, and they kissed and spoke of cherished dreams in that abbreviated way in which lovers communicate their deepest desires. And with these tender, hopeful, words, and still intimately entwined, they fell into a blissful and contented asleep.

Chapter Nine

The following day, just as the sun reached its zenith in a clear blue sky, Jack and Ned set off to visit Sir Michael at New Hope, leaving Sebi and Rose to introduce Matthew to his new home and duties. They walked the well-worn footpath that linked Jack's fifty-acre farmstead with its parent estate a mile or so distant. Ned had seized the opportunity to accompany his friend, mainly to satisfy his curiosity about activities at the encampment, but there was also a possibility that their stonework quota would be discussed, and thus Jack had not discouraged him. Their route first climbed the gentle gradient skirting the top field, an area of about two acres of sloping ground through which the fresh green shoots of winter-planted wheat now poked like a show of eager young hands.

'You got it sown, I see,' said Jack, sounding impressed. 'Looks like it's taken too. Well done!'

'Yeah. An' I've started plantin' out the tobacco on the lower field, Jack, now that there's no further risk of frost,' returned Ned, equally businesslike. 'We'll put young Matthew to helpin' us once he's got himself settled in.'

As they reached the top of the incline, the New Hope estate began to reveal itself in panoramic splendour over the rise, stretching out before them along the shores of the Potomac to the northwest. The first impression from this relatively low perspective was that the estate was almost entirely wooded, but closer inspection revealed the many fields and meadows carved out in a roughly radial pattern from the buildings at its centre. Sir Michael's house was not ostentatious either by size or design but, painted white like the nearby church, it stood out clearly amongst the cluster of tobacco drying sheds and the several rows of slave houses and other farm buildings that formed the built estate. The house was a timber-clad, single-story edifice with gables in its shingled roof and a long veranda that ran the length of the house; it sat overlooking a bend in a navigable tributary that flowed into the Potomac half a mile to the southwest. Behind the house, a tented encampment could be seen in the adjacent meadow.

'So that's Sir Michael's Southern Maryland militia?' Jack muttered, with more than a little derision in his voice 'let's hope that it is better organised than it looks. You'll remember, Ned, that I agreed to join it as a condition of accepting the land that we now farm!'

'Aye, Jack, I do,' replied Ned, nodding sagely, 'D'you think he'll hold you to it?'

'I rather think he will, Ned. He's as much as told me so; and I'm afraid that I'll be off again before a month or two have passed. He'll probably want to talk about it when we meet, so we'll find out soon enough.'

'I already got wind of where they're to, Jack,' said Ned dismally, '- the Ohio, - to help the British have another go at Duquesne; 'though whether they'll be a help or a hindrance, I'm not so sure, having watched them at their training!'

'Yes, Sir Michael told me it would be the Ohio - and my military friend aboard the *Miranda* filled in the background during the crossing. Sir Michael apparently intends to join up with British regulars and other militias as part of their bigger strike against the French across the whole of the northwest frontier. I suppose they are our enemy now that war has been declared in Europe, and our once indifferent government now see them as an irritant and an obstacle to be removed! And more than likely they'll have had the proprietors and governors bending their ears about all these Indian raids in Pennsylvania and New York – after all there'll be money at stake with all these new settlers so eager to buy, providing the land's made safe. Never mind the fact that it's the Iroquois' homelands!' said Jack, his irony going entirely unnoticed.

'Hmmm,' uttered Ned quickly. 'Land – now that's something I do understand, Jack, 'specially having been pushed off our common back in England!' He said this in a bitter tone and with the particular insight of one forced into the gutters by the enclosure of the common land on which his family had once made their living. 'This new land's given me somethin' I never could have got in England – my independence from people who couldn't give a damn about the likes of me! You can't blame them as wants it.'

Jack nodded thoughtfully, but did not have a chance to reply since Ned continued without a pause.

'And I'm going to come with you, Jack,' he said insistently 'If it comes to a scrap, I've as much to fight for as anyone. Anyway, you'll need me to look after you if our trip to Charlestown was anything to go by!' (This was a reference to the fight with Hayward and his gang, and he made the gibe with a mischievous smile.)

'No chance, Ned,' said Jack emphatically. 'Sir Michael has no contract with you! Besides, someone will have to run the farm!'

Hidden from the view of the cabin in a small copse some fifty or so yards distant, Judd had watched Jack and his companion stride off along the path. He waited for a while, wanting to be certain that they would not immediately return, and soon saw Matthew also leave the cabin accompanied by a lanky white-haired Black. A barn stood directly opposite the cabin creating a spacious bare earth courtyard between the two buildings, for which the spreading branches of an old willow formed an eminent centrepiece. Judd saw the pair make towards its trunk where a bench had been located, presumably to take advantage of summer shade. They settled themselves upon the bench and fell at once into conversation that seemed by its manner to be both instructive and entertaining. Indeed, their laughter was occasionally loud enough for Judd to catch the sound from where he lay. After some little time, however, the pair stood up and, still chatting amiably, they strolled into the barn, thus disappearing from Judd's sight. From his previous evening's observation through the window, Judd now knew that the woman left behind in the cabin would be alone. Thus, without hesitating for a moment longer, he decided to risk an approach.

Rose answered the knock at the door to find a shabbily dressed and bearded stranger waiting outside. She thought him a rough looking sort and was immediately put on her guard by his appearance, flicking her eyes across the courtyard nervously to ascertain Sebi's whereabouts. She saw the barn's open door and thought of calling out, but before she could do so, the stranger smiled disarmingly:

'Is it Mrs Easton to whom I have the pleasure of speaking?' Judd enquired, affecting a politeness to which he was unused, and thus neglecting to remove his tricorn, 'Only, Jack told me I should call upon you if I was passing – and well here I am. My name is Goddard, by the way,' he said, calculating she might have heard the name spoken by her husband and thus be lulled long enough for him to take advantage. He held out his hand and Rose could not stop herself from taking it. Her courtesy was instinctive and involuntary, but his firm grip surprised and frightened her and she recoiled a little as he stepped towards her.

'Jack and I sailed together on the crossing,' he continued in a curiously even tone. 'I am making for St Mary's on business, and wonder if I might ask you for some refreshment; I am fearful thirsty,' he said, taking another step.

Rose found herself retreating backwards into the room as he pressed forwards, her mind in a dither between hospitality and assertion. She yielded uncertainly. There was something in the man's voice that sounded false; yet she would not wish to be rude to a fellow of Jack's acquaintance. A little flustered now, she turned away and moved towards the dresser on which she stored the water jug. But when she turned back with it and a beaker in her hand, the visitor was squarely in the room and had closed the door behind him. She noted that the man appeared to be scanning the room as if searching for something, and his manner began to alarm her.

'Some water?' she asked, pouring the liquid into a mug with an unsteadiness that betrayed her mounting apprehension. 'My husband will return at any moment, but perhaps you would like to wait?' She said this nervously, waving her hand as if to indicate that he should take a seat at the table.

The stranger smiled curiously but declined; and then quite suddenly he seemed to grow impatient, his face losing the earlier gloss of civility, his lips forming into an ugly curl.

'Alright, where's the money?' he rasped, taking out his knife and brandishing it threateningly. 'I haven't got time to play about, so be sure I'll use this if it's necessary. Now, where is it?' he demanded roughly.

'Oh!' gasped Rose, dropping both items and bringing her hands to her lips in alarm, her face suddenly draining of colour. The jug and beaker clattered noisily as their contents sloshed onto the floor. Rose backed away. 'I...I don't know what you mean,' she cried.

Judd took a few steps towards her, his knife pointing at Rose's pregnant belly. 'You tell me where it is and you'll not get hurt;' he said with a sinister leer, 'if not you'll both get it!'

'No!' Rose screamed in horror, wrapping her arms around her belly as a shield, still backing away as panic began to take hold. He followed her step by step, his knife hand becoming more menacing as he advanced.

But Rose's retreat was brought up short when her foot made contact with the lip of the hearth. She almost lost her balance, her arms going out instinctively to arrest her incipient fall into the flames of the fire behind her, but she was steadied when her head made contact with the low beam spanning the opening. Her flailing hand stumbled upon the poker lying against the wall and she took it up and held it out before her as a weapon.

'Get back!' she cried, now almost hysterical, and brandished the poker in his face. But he grabbed it in a flash and wrenched it from her hand, laughing derisively; and he threw the implement spinning behind him, where it landed with a fearful crash upon the table still bedecked with the detritus of the early midday meal. The clatter seemed to make her attacker more vicious yet, and he closed the gap between them and grabbed her by the throat in one terrifying move. She felt his horny hand close around her windpipe with such force that she could hardly breathe.

'Help!' she tried to scream, but the sound was strangled in her throat.

'Tell me where the money is or you die, and I'll find it for myself!' he said, his voice edged with such venom that she felt her legs begin to buckle in shear fright. Her vision dimmed as she fought for breath. Frantically, she clawed at his hands, trying to break his grip, but all strength seemed to have gone from her. Her mind reeled. She seemed lost - but then in one desperate bid to save herself she flicked her bulging eyes as if to indicate the bedroom to her left. She saw him glance towards it and then look back at her with a glint of triumph in his evil eyes.

'That's more like it,' he sneered.

Rose felt his grip loosen as he pulled away but now, almost in a faint, she could not prevent herself from slumping to the ground. He left her there and strode towards the door quickly, evidently anxious to do his business and get away. She watched him go as relief welled up so palpably that it almost brought her to tears; but she forced herself to act, knowing that she had bought herself at best a minute with her simple ruse. She clambered to her feet and, staggering across the room like someone blind on drink, she reached the door and flung it open. But just as she was about to let out a scream for help, there, racing up the steps towards her, was Sebi into whose arms she fell.

'I heard the noise, Miz Rosy, an' I came ...' But his words died in his throat as Judd stepped through the open doorway holding a pistol in his outstretched hand.

'Inside, both of you,' he ordered, gesturing with his weapon as he glanced around the courtyard as if to check the coast was clear (Matthew hiding behind the willow not being seen). Rose sobbed desolately as Sebi took her weight and supported her through the door - with Judd on their heels, pushing them roughly at gunpoint and kicking the door shut behind him. Inside, Sebi held Rose to him in a protective embrace as she buried her face in his breast. He threw the intruder a defiant scowl, but things were moving faster than he could think.

'I'll ask you one more time,' Judd spat, grabbing at Rose's hair and yanking it back fiercely so that he could glare into her face.

Sebi exploded into a rage at this show of wanton violence. And with a defiant roar he shifted his weight and turned in one swift movement to pull Rose from her attacker's grip and make himself her human shield. Judd, evidently surprised by Sebi's strength, stepped back in some consternation. A flash of fearful anticipation crossed his features as Sebi puffed himself up angrily to his full height. For a moment, the tables had been turned. Sebi might have been old and gaunt but he was used to standing up to the bullying of white men, and fear of punishment had never quelled his boldness. But Judd still had his pistol and now he raised it again, and this time it was pointed directly into the old man's face.

'You only got one shot in that there pistol, mister,' Sebi drawled in his plantation English, 'so you gonna have to shoot me first!'

Judd smirked and cocked his weapon, and might have pulled the trigger had he not been distracted by the creak of the door opening behind him. Sebi had seen the latch lift silently behind Judd's back and so had prepared himself to leap, and with Judd's momentary backward glance, his chance came. He launched himself across the intervening gap just as Matthew's head appeared at the door's edge. Even in the instant of flight, he saw the boy's eyes open wide in fright before pulling the door rapidly shut before him as a shield. Matthew was just quick enough to avoid the collision - Sebi hit Judd square on, cannoning the two men heavily against the door where they fell in a heap at its foot.

Rose screamed as the deafening boom of Judd's pistol shot resounded in the close confines of the room, and she cowered instinctively. When she regained her senses and opened her eyes, she saw Sebi lying motionless across the stranger's body as smoke from the shot dispersed. The acrid smell of it caught in her nostrils. Then, with sudden urgency, the door latch lifted repeatedly. Matthew was trying to get in - but he would not now be able to open the door with the weight of the two men against it. Both men seemed either to be stunned or unconscious. Rose stepped forwards tentatively, not sure if Judd still posed a threat. She reached for Sebi's leg and shook it gently, hoping to get some reaction from her fallen friend. But he did not move. She tried again. But this time, instead of Sebi, it was the stranger who stirred; his tricorn had fallen from his head, and the rough patchy stubble of dark hair on his scalp and the wildness of his beard made him look grotesque. He opened his eyes and glared at her. Rose leapt back in fright, fearing for Sebi and herself at the same time. She turned away and scanned the room, frantic to find her poker or something else with which to defend herself. But her poker was nowhere to be seen and in desperation she ran to the hearth to find the kitchen knife. She had only just reached it when Judd grabbed her hair roughly from behind. He had thrown Sebi's old body off him like a straw and had crossed the floor like lightning; and in a fearful rage, he now yanked her backwards and spun her to the floor. But he had not noticed the knife clasped in her hand and he was slow to follow up his manoeuvre. Rose saw his hesitation and came to her knees quickly, her veins now surging with the adrenaline of survival and she leapt at him, cat-like, slashing out wildly with her knife even as she was cast bodily aside. Her quick movement had, however, caught him off guard and her knife had met its mark. His scream of pain split the air as he clutched his cheek and staggered back, and Rose looked up from the floor to see vermilion oozing through his fingers. Seizing the moment of his distraction, she leapt to her feet and scrambled for the door, reaching it just as Matthew pushed it open. In full flight, she grabbed him and bundled him outside and raced away in sheer terror, dragging him by the hand in a wild bid to escape. She heard the door slam behind her as she ran, and for a moment she thought her attacker must be in hot pursuit. Still dragging the boy with her, she forced herself ever onwards, fleeing like a child caught in a nightmare, terrified to look back in case clawing hands might even now be reaching out to grab her. Her heart was palpitating; her lungs were on fire; she gasped for precious air. It was all too much. Suddenly, the light began to dim and her legs began to fail. And without warning everything went dark as she felt the grit of the courtyard grind into her face.

It did not seem more than a moment later that Rose regained consciousness with the distant sound of Matthew's imploring calls in her ears. In a daze, she lifted herself to her knees. The salty taste of blood and dirt came into her mouth. She spat it out, examining the murky globules that splattered the ground in front of her. She ran her fingers over her badly swollen lips. A wave of nausea passed over her and she suddenly felt faint, but she forced herself to stagger to her feet, her instincts still driving her to the boy's continuing calls. He sounded desperate. But she was not prepared for what she saw when she eventually looked back towards the cabin.

Heavy grey smoke now billowed from the top of the open doorway while Matthew crept on hands and knees into the dark black void that was clear beneath it. Rose realised immediately that Sebi must still be inside and that the boy must be making an attempt to rescue him.

'Matthew!' she screamed. But it was too late. The boy had already disappeared inside and would be unable to hear her against the cracking and spluttering of the fire that was now clearly taking hold. 'Matthew!' she screamed again, and started forward at once, frantic to save him. But her legs felt like lead and the dull ache in the pit of her belly slowed her pace to a stagger. She was panting heavily when she reached the foot of the steps where she stopped abruptly, feeling the raw heat on her face radiating from the open doorway. The issuing smoke was now mixed with tongues of yellow flame that licked the lintel as it poured out in dark billowing clouds. The roar of the flames coming from inside was growing louder by the second, but as yet, the outside structure had not burnt through. She crouched down and peered inside, shielding her face from the heat with her hand. Beneath a dense black canopy of smoke, there seemed to be a thin layer of clear air just tall enough for a man to crawl, but the clouds of billowing filth above the gap threatened to close it at any moment. Inside, she could just make out Matthew's form in the dim grey and orange light - he was on his haunches, wrestling with Sebi's prostrate body - but he was clearly too weak to shift it. She screamed at him through cupped hands:

'Matthew! Come out! It's too late! You can't save him – save yourself! For pity's sake, come out!'

But either he did not hear her or he chose to struggle on regardless, for he continued to strain and yank at Sebi's legs, apparently heedless of the peril. Meanwhile the roaring of the flames grew louder and more intense. Desperate now, Rose, could see that the boy would perish in seconds if she did not act. Tearing off her full top skirt, she plunged it into the nearby water trough, and draped the soaking cloth about her head and shoulders like a cape. With this as her shield from the heat, she fell to the floor in her underskirts and crawled inside the fiery chasm on hands and knees.

It was not until the approach of twilight that Jack and Ned set off from the encampment along the path towards the farmstead, having spent the afternoon in the company of Sir Michael, and watching the militia in their training.

'So you're goin' to be his adjutant,' said Ned in a sarcastic tone. 'What's a adjutant, when he's about?'

'A general dogsbody, I should think,' replied Jack wryly. 'But at least I'll get paid for my service, and be able to keep an eye on Sir Michael and stop him from leading us into too much trouble!'

'Sounds a bit highfalutin to my mind, Jack; dogsbody is what dogsbody does - I don't hold with all this military strutting about. They'll be putting you in a officer's uniform next – and its officers with their shiny buttons as uses ordinary folk as cannon fodder for their own glory!'

'I certainly won't be seeking glory, Ned! I'll just be looking to get this over and done with as soon as possible and come back home.'

The pair walked on in silence for a while, electing to take the long path back by way of the bottom field in order to inspect the progress of Ned's tobacco planting. It was not until they passed through the adjacent trees that they first realised that something must be wrong, for there was a strange loom of amber lightness in the darkening sky ahead. Its source was still obscured by the intervening canopy of budding branches but, becoming apprehensive, both men instinctively quickened their pace. The same thought must have entered both minds simultaneously, but it was Jack who first uttered the word: 'Fire.' He said it in such a low tone that it might have been a statement rather than an expletive, but both men immediately broke into a run. Jack sprinted ahead, crashing through the undergrowth in a direct line for the glow, shouting louder this time: 'Fire! Ned, the farm's on fire!'

The distance that Jack ran must have amounted to several hundred yards, through rough and spindly woodland, darting from side to side to dodge the fallen branches and leaping over bramble in his headlong race. Panting heavily, he broke into the open at last and was stopped in his tracks by what he saw. Before him, his cabin was consumed by a conflagration that licked high into the night sky, a torrent of glowing embers sweeping upwards at such speed that it might have been an eruption from the very bowels of the earth. His pulse beat loudly in his ears as he vainly scanned the courtyard, at once frantic for some sign of Rose, and hoping against hope that she was safe. It had become quite dark now except for the bleak light of the flames; and wafts of smoke, whipped and billowed by the fire's own draught, maddeningly interfered with his view. Ned's heavy footsteps came crashing up behind him and the big man pulled himself to a halt right beside him like some carthorse pulled up sharply by his reins. Ned's breathing was just as laboured as his own as both men now stood transfixed by the desolate spectre that confronted them, their eyes inexorably drawn to the fire, unblinking and incredulous.

'Rose! Matthew! Sebi!' Jack shouted, spurring himself forward towards the courtyard and into the swirling smoke, with Ned following close behind. But in the gloom and made more difficult by the drifting smoke, their sweep revealed no sign of life.

'You go that way, Ned!' shouted Jack, pointing towards the barn. 'I'll look over here.'

The two men split up and vanished from each other's sight into the smoke as they widened their search. Minutes passed without further contact between the pair while echoes of their plaintive calls resounded in the darkness in tones that were at first urgent and hopeful but became, as time passed, raggedly desperate and forlorn. Jack had rushed from one corner of the domestic patch to the other to no avail and now he ground to a halt, suddenly exhausted, his head reeling and dizzy, his lungs stinging from breathing in the smoke; and he doubled over with his hands upon his knees in an attitude that signified defeat.

'Rose,' he panted, dismally. 'Rose,' he panted again more desolately as his breathing calmed. And he raised himself and gazed in abject misery at the dying flames; and seeing there the charred and smoking timbers sticking up like bones at morbid angles, he wondered if he looked upon a funeral pyre.

In Jack's melancholy, it took some moments for Ned's call to grow in Jack's distracted hearing from distant echo into comprehension, but eventually his friend's urgent words reached the depths of despair that had swallowed him up:

'Jack! Over here – in the barn!'

Jack burst into the barn like a sudden gust of wind to find a scene that changed his expression in an instant from one of fearful anticipation to one of outright relief; but then he realised that his relief was premature. In the dim light of an oil lamp, Rose lay in a semi-upright position propped up on a bed of straw: she panted in short breaths as if in pain and her arms were wrapped around her belly as if already cradling her unborn child. Her face was blackened with soot, streaked with sweat, and her eyes were clamped tightly shut in a fierce grimace that frightened Jack with its intensity. Sebi was laid out beside her on his back, deathly still, as if he had been placed in that position and had not stirred since. Some fabric had been wrapped around his head roughly – Jack recognised it at once as Matthew's shirt, and it was soaked with blood. Ned knelt between the two injured forms; evidently he had been doing what he could to make them comfortable, and he was now tending to Sebi's wound, using his neckerchief as a pad to stem the bleeding. Sebi's face seemed drained of lustre, his skin no longer its usual shiny ebony but pale and pasty with dust. Ned looked up from his ministrations to meet Jack's bewildered gaze.

'I think she's gone into labour, Jack!' he whispered urgently, casting a concerned glance in Rose's direction. 'I've sent Matthew to the house for help. The boy said somethin' about an intruder and that Sebi got himself shot putting up a fight. He's lost some blood, Jack, but it's a nick by the look of it, so I think he'll pull through.'

Jack sank onto his knees at Rose's side and smoothed away the loose hair from her forehead with the palm of his hand. He took out his handkerchief, licked it, and used the dampened cloth to wipe away some sooty smudges from her face, while uttering affectionate, encouraging words under his breath.

'Hold on, Rose,' he said softly, kissing her cheek. 'Help's on its way.' He saw a brave smile flutter across her taut lips as she opened her eyes, and heard her strangled breath as she attempted to speak. But she seemed too weak to form the words. She tried a few more times, moving her lips painfully; but then she seemed to give up, her face resuming the troubled mask that had characterised it before. Jack placed a hand upon hers and squeezed it. 'Don't try to talk; you'll need your strength; just rest now,' he said soothingly.

'What's this about an intruder, Ned? And with a pistol?' Jack searched his friend's face for an answer. 'What in heaven's name could he have been after?'

Ned shook his head, returning Jack's uncomprehending stare with one of his own. But then Rose groaned and clutched her belly, and Jack became immediately more concerned with her condition than pursuing his question further. The two men thus fell into a thoughtful silence, remaining attentively at their stations - until the sound of a chaise was heard arriving in the courtyard at a canter, and Lady de Burgh hurried through the door with Matthew and Sir Michael in her wake.

Chapter Ten

Caroline de Burgh, born into a plantation family in Anne Arundel county, Maryland, had known Michael de Burgh man and boy, the pair having practically grown up together as cousins. By bloodline, they were not related at all, but it may have felt as though they were cousins, since their parents were on such frequenting terms that, respectively as children, they had called them aunt and uncle. Their childhood relationship had weathered puberty and adolescence and had matured into something that might pass as love by the time they had reached their middle-twenties - even if neither one of them had spoken of it. It was almost a surprise, therefore, that they soon found themselves engaged to be married, the moment simply arriving like a long awaited carriage, when it somehow seemed necessary to climb aboard - especially since their parents had agreed the union in advance as being a most appropriate match. The betrothal had passed without any great dissension, or indeed involvement on their part; there had been no fluttering of hearts, no wistful glances, nor any of those furtive meetings in secret places that might have been the norm in unions of lesser rank. And so, following their wedding, both had taken a little time to adjust to the intimacies of conjugal living. Indeed, it was often wondered if they had ever taken to it at all, since their union had not, in the ten years of the their marriage to date, resulted in any issue. Moreover, because both of the enjoined families were of the class where it was not considered seemly to display affection in the sight of one's servants and slaves, most outsiders would regard the couple's relationship and personalities as somewhat stiff and formal.

It was a revelation to Jack and Ned, therefore, at the moment when Lady de Burgh hurried into the barn in a flurry of skirts, to see her in a very agitated state. Clearly, she had been shocked at the sight of the smouldering wreckage of Jack's cabin outside, but on seeing Rose and Sebi lying in the hay, her face became puckered with such vicarious discomfort that she herself might have been injured. She was a slender woman, who habitually set her fair hair at both sides of her head into ringlets to compensate for the narrowness of her face, sweeping the rest up into a bun that was usually held in place with pins under a patterned bonnet. But after the headlong canter in the cold night air, her careful contrivances had fallen around her windblown and reddened cheeks in some disarray.

'We must get them to the house, Michael!' she said in some fluster, immediately taking charge. 'Matthew, fetch me two blankets from the chaise quickly, we'll use them as stretchers to carry these poor people out,' she said, '...and lay out the other blankets as a bed on which to lie them,' she called, even as the youngster, responding with alacrity to her command, was already on his way.

There not being room aboard the chaise to accommodate everyone, it was decided that Sir Michael and his wife would drive the casualties to the house where servants had been put on alert to receive them. This left Jack, Ned, and Matthew to make their way there on foot. And by the time this threesome arrived at the front door, having made the distance at a steady jog in less than twenty minutes, Rose already lay in a bed prepared for her confinement, and the midwife, a black slave of considerable experience in the art, was already heating water in the scullery. The unconscious Sebi, meanwhile, his bloody wound already cleaned and re-dressed, had been moved to a bed in the servant's quarters nearby where he was being watched over by his son, called to attend with some urgency from his hut on the plantation. A shiny-black-skinned housemaid answering the door to Jack's frantic knocking had evidently received instructions to send Ned and Matthew to join the son at his father's side, and she did this commandingly, while permitting Jack to enter the house only after he had taken off his muddy boots.

It was the normal expectation in these times that the place of childbirth was exclusively a matriarchal domain, and so when Jack attempted to push through the hall and climb the stairs to go to his wife's side, the housemaid, a woman of intimidating proportions, barred his way.

'You are not to go up, Mr Jack, sir,' said the housemaid, puffing herself up ready for a fight, for she knew him only too well. 'The midwife don' wan' no man clutterin' up her room!'

As if to emphasise the point, a low wail, instantly recognisable as from Rose's throat, was heard coming from the bedroom above their heads, and it quite enflamed the rebellious thoughts that were brewing up in Jack's mind. He took the moment of the distraction to try to squeeze past the seemingly immovable object in his way, but was again prevented. The maid had anticipated his manoeuvre and had been quick to move her broad hips to block him. 'There now,' she said in a proprietary tone, 'sounds like the baby's on its way - you sit yoursel' down an' wait patiently like a gen'lman should!'

And with that, the maid turned and vanished up the stairs clutching her skirts, leaving Jack bewildered, a little frightened, and alone.

The entrance hall at New Hope house was a spacious room of rectangular proportions that smelled of beeswax and floral fragrances that had always reminded Jack of his mother's home in Portland. In the centre of the polished oak floor, an oval Queen Anne table stood decorated with spring flowers flanked by two silver candlesticks in which candles burned with dim and wavering flames. Against one wall, a long case clock ticked somnolently in stark contrast to Jack's heart, which raced palpably in his chest. After the exertions and shocks of the last hour, Jack felt drained and his head spun. Suddenly overwhelmed with gloomy misgivings, he sagged onto a nearby chair and buried his face in his hands. How quickly, he thought, had the triumph of his return been washed away by the torrent of misfortune that was now engulfing him? Where was his guardian angel now, he wondered, as he sank into a trough of bleak despair?

Rose's wailing had in the meanwhile subsided to sporadic moaning and now this stopped completely, leaving in its place a terrifying silence that was just as disquieting. Jack's stomach churned as disquiet turned into alarm. The silence continued and he found himself on the edge of his seat, straining his ears for the slightest indication from the room above that might reassure him that all was well. At last, the sound of a softly spoken voice was heard; it was only a murmur and the intervening floorboards muted it, but it was unmistakably that of Lady de Burgh. And then another female voice spoke softly in an encouraging manner. Jack breathed his relief and sat back in his chair again; it was the midwife's voice he had latterly heard and was thankful that his wife appeared to be in capable hands. It fell quiet for a time thereafter but then sounds of floorboards creaking with soft footfalls broke the silence again. The paces seemed to move first to one side of the bedroom and then to the other. The movement was unhurried, as if someone were collecting an item from a drawer, but then the steps quickened as another of Rose's muted cries penetrated the thick floor. Jack's heart skipped a beat at this; and in sudden empathy of Rose's evident pain, he shot from his chair and made towards the stairway, intent this time on forcing his way to her - but he was checked by his own conscience not to intrude. The women would know what to do, he reasoned, and his intrusion might make matters worse. Instead, cursing the silly protocol that enshrouded childbirth in female mysticism, he paced anxiously up and down the hall floor, his mind a muddle of images of Rose in distress. He desperately wanted to be with her - to comfort and console her - but some inner restraint had held him back. As he paced to and fro, his resentment at this feeling of exclusion rose to an anger that was just as powerful as his mounting premonition of doom, and the two emotions fought to cripple him into uncertainty. He wanted desperately to have some conclusion to the drama unfolding above his head, but he feared it too.

Time passed slowly - and Rose's cries, moans, and silences fell into a pattern that ascended and subsided in a rough rhythm, each cycle becoming more agonizing in Jack's ears than the last. But then the frequency of the cycle seemed to quicken and her cries increase in intensity so that Jack could hardly bear to listen; he wanted to cover his ears yet he could not bring himself to blank her out. He heard a voice call out: *'Quickly!'* And it was followed by the sound of feet shuffling as if some commotion were taking place around Rose's bed. The floorboards creaked wildly. Then another pair of feet resounded across the room towards the others with a hasty tread and the tone of the voices became suddenly more anxious. Alarmed, Jack stopped in his tracks and pricked up his ears, straining to understand the words spoken. But he could not. And then the commotion subsided and the voices died away to a low disconsolate murmur. Jack hardly dared to breathe lest its sound mask any signal from above; his heartbeat was beating so fast that it began to make him feel light-headed. Time seemed to slow as the near-silence endured, the light seeming also to dim in his unseeing eyes. Then the floorboards creaked again and, with a sharp intake of breath, he came back to his full senses. But the tone of the voices had changed in some indefinable way. Jack registered the change but did not analyse it further for, at that moment, a brief and tiny note, heard upon the air, arrested him. The sound was strangely frail, and so faint that it might have been nothing at all, but he distinctly heard it and took it immediately to be the shrill first call of a newborn child. His heart leapt into his throat. At once, all the fears and agonies that he had pent up inside him were released - as if a dam that had held back his feelings had suddenly split asunder. And he dropped to his knees and wept, burying his face in his hands, his body becoming wracked in the tearful convulsions of the overjoyed.

'Praise the Lord!' he sobbed, wiping his face with the back of his sleeves. 'Praise the Lord!' he cried again, raising his reddened, smiling face to the ceiling as if heaven were there; and he lifted his clasped hands upwards in a prayerful offering of thanksgiving.

For a time thereafter, activity in the room above seemed to grow calm, but the relative quiet and the apparent lack of movement soon began to worry him again as it persisted. It was somehow not as he expected it to be. But then at last, the sound of a door being opened and a creak of the floorboards at the head of the stairway told him that someone was about to descend. Jack raised himself expectantly to his feet, quickly wiping his eyes and smoothing his hair with tear-wetted hands, making himself presentable, he thought, to go to his wife's side. He saw the midwife's feet appear at the top of the winding stairway and could not help himself smiling in anticipation in that tight-lipped, bleary-eyed way that men do when they are struggling to control their emotions. As the woman descended further, he saw her skirts and then her waist revealed; and carried in her arms was a baby wrapped in swaddling clothes. He rushed forward to the foot of the stairs joyously to meet the pair, but as he did so the midwife's tearful face came into view. And her expression stopped him short. She did not need to utter a single word, for her face said it all.

'But I heard a baby's cry!' he protested at the shiny black face of the midwife who stared back at him in gentle denial. 'I heard my baby cry!' he insisted, shaking his head fiercely, his eyes wide and disbelieving, as if by will alone he could change the very state of things, and make a comforting lie of a harsh and evident truth.

The midwife bit her lip. 'A li'l boy, Mr Jack,' she said, sobbing. 'The li'l mite never even took a breath of this sweet air.' And with this she sobbed again and gave the lifeless bundle a gentle squeeze to her bosom, before handing it with some reluctance into Jack's receiving arms.

'But I heard…' started Jack again, still not willing to accept the facts before him, yet his voice faded into nothingness as he looked down at the pale and puckered features of his dead son's face.

Jack sank onto the chair, cradling his son in his arms as if rocking the little soul to sleep, and his eyes welled with tears so profuse that they ran down his nose and dripped onto the swaddling cloth in a steady stream. 'I heard you calling me, my little one;' he choked, his voice catching in the back of his throat, 'may God guide you on your way.' With these words of parting, Jack recalled the boy's movement in the womb the night before, which he and Rose had both felt as they had held each other in a loving embrace. That movement then had evoked the image of happy salutation - a wave heralding arrival. In Jack's present distress, his mind now conjured the gesture as the boy's sad farewell, as if the tiny infant had somehow known what lay in store. It was a bitter comfort.

The world closed in on Jack for a while so that, in his grief, he and his son were its only inhabitants. But eventually he became aware of the gentle pressure of a hand upon his shoulder.

'Miss Rose is ready now,' a voice whispered, 'she wants to see you.'

The boy's tiny coffin was buried a week later when Rose had at last recouped her strength sufficiently to undertake the gentle ascent to the burial site. On Jack's instructions, Ned had already dug a grave in the grassy knoll on which Elizabeth's memorial headstone had been placed so lovingly some years before. It was thus already a revered site, and a chestnut bench had been positioned there for remembrance in the shade of a few surrounding trees. It was a pleasant place in which to sit at the end of the day because it caught the last rays of the setting sun and enjoyed a view of the farmstead and the creek behind. Before he had left for England, Jack and Rose often went there on a summer evening after work was done; it was a private place, reserved for them alone, which Ned and Sebi tactfully avoided as if it were a shrine. The couple might sit there and talk fondly of their lost Elizabeth; or lose themselves in quiet introspective thoughts; or sometimes, at sunset, simply gaze fondly at the amber-tinted view, relishing the warmth of the sun upon their backs. And from now on, as grief ran its bitter and inexorable course, they would go there to commune with their lost son.

Jack led the procession up the slope carrying the little coffin upon his shoulder at a pace that seemed as slow as it was reluctant. His burden was so light that he hardly stooped, yet dread weighed upon him more with each step closer to the grave. It was the thought of leaving his little boy in the cold ground alone that checked his stride. He had made the casket from oak planks, cut and planed lovingly with his own hands, and he had carved upon its lid the figure of a winged cherub, smoothed and polished with beeswax to such a state of perfection that it seemed to radiate life in the dead light of the day. The carving of it had obsessed him throughout the preceding week. He had hardly broken for food or sleep, excluding all others from the task, and working in fretful solitude while Rose had recovered from her ordeal. It had been his deliverance from the depths of grief that had engulfed him; but it had not quelled the undirected fury that had screwed his tortured thoughts into knots as he had worked. He wanted to lash out and strike down the mysterious intruder who had brought this catastrophe upon them. But his wrath had no object upon which to focus; the perpetrator as yet had neither shape nor form in Jack's imagination, and this had both frustrated and enraged him. And it enraged him still.

Walking behind Jack in the sombre procession, flanked on one side by Sir Michael and on the other by Lady de Burgh, a stoic Rose walked stiffly, her face a pale mask of self-control. Ned followed at a respectful distance supporting Sebi on his strong right arm. The old man walked proudly now but could not hide his limp, and his head was bandaged with fresh white linen; it was the only cloth in the procession that reflected any light on this grey and windy April morning beneath the gloomy overcast that shrouded the cortege. Matthew came next. His head held low, the boy walked alone behind his new friends, while others from the estate, servants and slaves, followed in a loose and solemn gaggle.

Reaching the graveside, Jack gently placed the little coffin on two planks above the opening while the congregation shuffled closer in a mournful silence. Rose took Jack's arm as he stepped back, and the pair stood for a while gazing at the oaken box with heavy hearts, while the dismal day reflected the glum mood of all those who looked on. It made a bleak sight, against the threatening sky and leafless trees, to see the mourners standing so hushed and so still. Meanwhile the wind played in the bare branches to intone a desolate lament upon the air that mourned that there was no more joy left in all the world. At last, perhaps judging that the silence had lasted long enough, Sir Michael took it upon himself to step forward. But in their mutual grief, neither Jack nor Rose heard his comforting soliloquy; nor would they have been comforted by it if they had, for it would take time not words to heal their aching hearts.

Rose almost lost her composure as the little box was lowered into the ground and Jack had to put a bracing arm around her waist as her knees began to give. But she pulled herself up and took a deep breath and, sighing a last farewell, she threw a handful of Maryland soil onto the coffin. She turned away quickly and held Jack's sympathetic gaze for several seconds. Her lips parted. 'At least we have each other,' she said softly, 'and if God has thought it fit to take our baby from us, he has also thought it fit to spare me. And with His blessing, we'll soon give life again.'

The following morning dawned bright and fresh and, intent upon making a start on a new beginning, Jack and Rose got up early and drove to the farm in the two-wheeled trap made available for their use by Sir Michael. They arrived to see Matthew struggling across the courtyard, weighed down by a pail of water, towards Ned and Sebi's cabin. Evidently, his duties had already been drawn up to include the early morning trip to the stream. And no doubt he would already have the fire lit so that the others might have the luxury of warm water for their morning ablutions. Hearing the trap's wheels arriving, the boy stopped, put down his pail, and beamed a delighted greeting, which neither Jack nor Rose could help returning in like measure. These smiles were the first small steps back to normality for the pair, helped inadvertently by the guileless innocence of the youngster, for whom the previous day's funeral had signified the end of gloom as though that it were a process completed. Jack picked this up in the boy's face and thought: 'this is the way it must be,' for he knew that it would be easier for everyone if that sad chapter could now be closed.

'Matthew,' he called, bringing the trap to a stop, 'when you and those two idlers have had breakfast, would you all please join us in the courtyard for a meeting? There are some things to discuss. Rose and I will take a ride around our fields for a while and return in half an hour.'

And without allowing time for the boy to do much more than touch his head in acknowledgement, Jack flapped the reins and set the trap off at a trot. When they returned, they found Ned and Sebi sitting with the boy on the bench under the scorched branches of the old willow in the centre of the courtyard. The courtyard had once been a pleasant place to sit. But now it was empty and rather desolate, and dominated on one side by the wreckage of the fire. After several heavy bouts of rain during the past week, the ashes and debris from the conflagration had been reduced to a glistening black sludge, through which several charred stumps of timber still stuck up at odd angles like headstones in an ancient graveyard. And the air still bore that bitter, acrid smell of incineration.

Jack brought the trap to a stop and he and Rose stepped down to greet the two men warmly. Other than at the funeral, it was the first time that they had talked together since the fire, and although the mood was still somewhat uncertain, it was obvious to Ned and Sebi at once that the pair wanted, indeed, demanded no sympathy to be shown.

'Sir Michael has generously offered us accommodation at New Hope for the time being, and Rose will stay there with Lady de Burgh when I go north with the militia,' Jack said in a tone that permitted no argument.

Ned cleared his throat, threw a sideways glance at Sebi as if to say: 'Alright, I'll also act as if nothing untoward has happened,' and responded in an equally forthright tone: 'Well, thank goodness for that! Sebi and I were beginning to worry that we might have had to share a bed if you'd moved in with us! And Matthew would have been put out in the barn!' The relieved glances exchanged between the men showed amusement, but there was a glint of gratitude in Jack's eyes that told Ned that he had picked up the coded signals perfectly. 'No sense in broodin',' Ned thought, 'what good has that ever done!' He then gave out a little grunt as if something had triggered his memory. 'I've got somethin' for you, Jack.' Fumbling in his shoulder bag, he produced a blackened metal contraption of angular proportions whose intended purpose would have confounded anyone but a mariner. 'I was kicking around the ashes during the week, and I found this,' he said, holding out the article proudly.

'My quadrant!' said Jack, looking genuinely pleased to take the instrument in his hands again. 'I had quite forgotten it,' he said, examining it closely. 'A bit of cleaning up and a new plumb-bob and it'll be as right as rain.' But a frown then wrinkled his brow. 'My pistols: did you find them too, Ned? I kept them together in the same drawer - along with my twenty pound note - not that that would have survived the fire.'

'That's just it, Jack: no pistols and none of our coinage either. You remember, we used to keep our few sovereigns and other coins there in that same drawer, and I found no trace of them - that's what I went looking for in the first place - and yet your device lay there clear for all to see - and the frame of the drawer was still intact!'

'So that's what our intruder was after then:' suggested Jack simply, 'our money!'

'He was after more than that Jack,' said Rose, quietly. 'I've not wanted to talk of it before, but that is what has been troubling me. First, the man introduced himself as having travelled with you – he called himself by a name I'd heard you speak the night before – "Godwin" or something like it. He said he was on the way down to St Mary's and had stopped by for some refreshment – but it was a ruse to put me off guard. I couldn't prevent him pushing his way in. Then suddenly he pulled out a knife and threatened me with it, shouting 'where's the money', like he knew something. It's been playing on my mind these last few days,' she said, 'I think he was looking for your money belt, Jack. It's just as well you left it safe in Charlestown, for one way or the other, we'd have lost that too.'

'How would he know about that?' retorted Jack, dumfounded. He fell into a puzzled silence for some seconds. 'Goddard! Did he say his name was Goddard?' shot Jack suddenly.

Rose nodded. 'Yes, that was it. Your captain friend, wasn't it? But he was no captain, Jack! Scruffy seaman more like it – shaven head and beard – and a mean look upon his face.'

'If he used Goddard's name, he must have been aboard the *Miranda* – one of the crew maybe? I know I mentioned my prize money to Goddard – I believed in private at the time – but it may be that I was overheard.'

Matthew shuffled his feet and muttered something inaudible, drawing the quick glances of his new friends. ' I thought I saw a face at the window the night before the fire,' he said rather hesitantly, and then looked a little abashed at his friends' show of astonishment at the revelation. 'I wasn't sure what it was I saw,' he protested quickly, '- and you were busy making up my bed – I thought it could have been reflections in the glass from inside – that's why I didn't mention it. But it must have been the same man – bearded like you say Mrs Easton, but wearing a tricorn then so I couldn't see his head. I think it was the same man that I saw running away as the cabin caught fire - with Mister Sebi still inside. The man's left cheek was all bloody...'

Rose chipped in: '...from my kitchen knife, Jack; I slashed at him trying to escape! I wish I'd caught his throat instead!' she said vehemently.

Matthew picked up his thread: 'Anyway, he ran off - he'd lost his hat by then. I saw him glance in my direction as he came out of the doorway. He must have seen me watching because he brought a hand up to his face as if trying to hide it from me. And he ran off without looking back. I keep seeing his face in my dreams - and if I close my eyes, I can see him now,' he said, doing exactly that for a second or two. 'There was something about him that struck me as familiar even then. And I've thought about him a lot since. But for his beard and shaven head I would have said that he resembled Mr Judd; when he saw me, his eyes flashed for a second just like his used to on the *Rebecca* when he got angry. If I didn't know for certain that he was in gaol ...'

'Judd!' Jack retorted, breaking in. Suddenly everything dropped into place. The image flashed into his mind of his mysterious rescuer at the Brandywine inn when he was so nearly Hayward's victim for the second time. Jack's stomach churned as he began to comprehend the likely train of events. 'Judd must have escaped and got aboard the *Miranda* in Cowes!' he muttered almost to himself, his mind conjuring the many occasions during the voyage when he might have been watched or overheard. The idea of Judd lurking unseen somewhere nearby as he and Goddard or Green had swapped tales at the mess table frightened him. It was certainly possible that Judd had found out about Jack's prize money, but could he also have discovered that it was Jack and Goddard who had set him up for capture and imprisonment? If so, neither was now safe from Judd's vindictiveness, for the former boatswain had shown his spitefulness before. And the fire could hardly have been an accident, Jack thought. That must have been Judd's way of getting his own back! Jack felt himself shudder at the thought of being followed to his home by such a nasty character, and with such stealth that he had been completely unaware of it. 'And if he did not get what he was after this time,' he wondered in alarm, 'perhaps he will try again!'

'Jack, my dear, you've gone as white as a sheet!' said Rose, suddenly concerned.

'My God, Rose,' Jack gasped at last, his mouth remaining agape as realisation dawned. '*I* am responsible for all this; *I* brought all this upon us!' he cried, sweeping his unbelieving eyes from her to the charred remains of the cabin. 'I led him here!'

Chapter Eleven

'No Jack, I'm sorry; that must be my final word on this.' Sir Michael was becoming quite cross now. 'You must put your duty to the King and the protection of our colony before you go racing off on some reckless mission of personal revenge! You and I have a contract, I'm afraid, and I intend to hold you to it – as much because I need you with me as to protect you from yourself.'

Jack was crestfallen for he knew his farmstead was at stake if he disobeyed. Sir Michael had not yielded to Jack's earlier entreaty to buy out his contract, and thus, despite his new wealth, he was still bound legally by his undertakings. Yet he was still about to continue his remonstration when Sir Michael's manner softened.

'And besides, think of Rose,' he said. Sir Michael's manner had changed from stiff formality to fatherly at a single stroke. 'Until we depart, she needs you here, not gallivanting around the colony on some wild goose chase looking for this man, Judd!'

Jack knew at once that Sir Michael spoke some sense, even though he disliked being lectured to. Capitulation came with a heavy sigh.

'You may be right, sir,' he admitted somewhat grudgingly. 'Perhaps it's not the time right now. But when I have done my duty by you, my time will be my own again, and I will set myself to find him and bring him to justice. I don't want to live a life looking over my shoulder in case he tries some other mischief! And besides - a man like that cannot be allowed to roam free!' Jack spoke as if a bile were upon him for the loss that he and Rose had suffered, and the knot of anger in his gut tightened.

'You'll never find him Jack!' Sir Michael shook his head, exasperated. 'Why, he may find himself a ship and leave the colonies altogether. You'll be wasting your time!'

'I know the man, sir;' Jack retorted. 'He'll not to return to England for fear of recapture, and where else would he go to find refuge? To the Spanish or the French? I don't think so. He may be a thief but he's not a traitor. No, my guess is that he'll make for one of the ports to find a living, probably off gambling or thievery - somewhere where he might have friends on the waterfront to help him. His options are therefore likely to be severely limited, and that will make him easier to find.

Besides, I doubt that he knows that I'm on to him, so he may drop his guard.'

'Then that will be your business, Jack,' Sir Michael said irritably, his manner once more turning rather stiff, 'for I will not condone it, and I shall still expect you to honour your stone-working commitments to me until your term is over! If you default, you will forfeit the farmstead, plain and simple! Those were the terms of our agreement; and I will have my quota or you will be forced to find land anew – and you will quickly find that to acquire a plot in Maryland as good as the one you now occupy will be difficult if not impossible, even if you can afford it. I hope I make myself clear!'

Sir Michael realised that he must appear pompous and obstructive, but in truth he found himself mildly affronted by Jack's new assertiveness. He had felt the irritation even in Chaptico when his military plans had come under Jack's critical scrutiny. The mason's newfound confidence had rankled and unsettled him. Since Jack's return from his escapades abroad, his exoneration under the law and his windfall seemed to have given him aspirations inappropriate to his station. He was after all still merely an artisan, and that of only modest background too; and his new money could never be a substitute for breeding. Was it possible, Sir Michael wondered, that Jack had misconstrued his recent sympathy for friendship? Or did he now actually believe himself an equal? If so, it was a preposterous notion to be sure! And to make matters worse, he thought, Lady de Burgh had now taken it into her sentimental head to give the grieving couple accommodation at New Hope, and this had exposed him to an uncomfortable domestic familiarity with the pair. Sir Michael had been brought up to expect deference and servitude, and Jack's attitudes posed a challenge in just the same way that some of the common men of his new militia had been so insolent as to question some of his evident wisdoms. Lamentably, such impertinences were becoming commonplace, but they struck at the very foundations of authority. As lord of his domain, with almost literal power of life or death over those who served him, he had a duty to his class to preserve order. Without it there would be chaos, he thought, and he and his kind must therefore stand together to nip such insubordination in the bud lest it become subversive. 'The common people will be thinking of revolt next - of overturning the natural authority of those who rule!' he thought wryly. 'And then where would we be?'

Sir Michael's mind, working thus, resolved forthwith that he must try to keep himself aloof and not demean himself by being drawn into the petty debates of subordinates - that he must in future shield himself with trusted officers of his own standing. Jack might have gained his master's respect as a servant – for he was certainly a man of initiative and skill - but others might see the man's articulate and forthright manner towards Sir Michael as accepted, and so it could not be tolerated lest it be taken as a model.

'And I will expect you to start work first thing tomorrow,' he said, crossly. 'Your late start as my adjutant has already put several important matters well behind schedule, and I will need you to attend to these before you begin your military induction!' And with this he turned and walked away.

In the six or so weeks remaining before the militia's planned departure, Jack found himself torn in several directions at once by the multitude of tasks placed upon him. A backlog of logistical difficulties had built up and now waited to be sorted out the moment that he started. Moreover, his instructions from Sir Michael, usually conveyed in a deceptively offhand manner, were never quite as straightforward as they at first appeared. In particular, the collection and assembly of goods and victuals from nearby trading posts became a bit of a lucky dip after it became apparent that Sir Michael's orders had been so loosely written that they were often misinterpreted. For example, instead of the twenty, one-hundred pound sacks of wheat flour Jack had been led to expect, he was dismayed to find that two hundred had been provided; instead of twenty casks of gun powder, there were twenty barrels; instead of ten boxes each of two-hundred lead shot, he got two-hundred boxes! And these were just a few of the inaccuracies in a long list of items written in Sir Michael's ambiguous hand. When Jack once declared some surprise at the unexpectedly large pile of containers stacked high under cover behind the trader's emporium, the trader flew into a tirade:

'This is what Sir Michael ordered!' the man insisted, waving the order in Jack's face as if he had encountered difficulties of this kind before. And when Jack later showed Sir Michael the invoices, the colonel simply raised an eyebrow and gave out a sort of non-committal grunt that Jack would soon recognise as signalling the man's reluctance to be drawn into the details, especially when they became inconvenient. The net result of these misunderstandings was that instead of one day, the assembly task took five; moreover, Jack was left with the feeling that it was he and not the colonel who had been awarded the blame.

Jack's time was peppered with uncomfortable incidents such as this, and it made him yearn for the simple endeavours of farming and stonework that had formed the routines of his life before. His duties required him to travel here and there about the area, visiting nearby landowners who had offered support for Sir Michael's venture. As he travelled, Jack often caught glimpses of his farm from distant vantage points. But the wreckage of his cabin always drew his eye from wherever he gained a view of it; it stood out like a sore on the fair face of the land, and it was painful to be reminded of the catastrophe that the burnt-out pyre represented. These frequent sightings contributed to the general feeling of despondency that gnawed at his soul. From time to time and from afar, he also sighted Ned, Sebi, and Matthew working the fields and envied them their uncomplicated lives, while he himself seemed entirely consumed with the irritating little details of a mission with which he found it hard to empathise. He tried so hard to shed the gloom that dogged him, yet one thing after another conspired to drag him further down.

Foremost of these was the continuing frustration that, with many of the hands at New Hope put to supporting the militia's preparations, no one would be released to assist in the rebuilding of his cabin until after the troop had departed. This meant that the temporary and sometimes awkward accommodation arrangements for Jack and his wife at New Hope would drag on. It also meant that Jack would have no hand in the construction or supervision of the work, and this vexed him because Rose would now be left to attend to the many details herself. While he would not have had any qualms as to Rose's competence in this respect in normal circumstances, he had wanted, in deference to her tender state of recovery, to spare her that responsibility. Ned and Sebi could certainly contribute, but discussion with them had quickly revealed that neither was particularly gifted with architectural insight. In short, left to them, Jack felt that the result would undoubtedly be a bit of a botch-up, and if Rose wanted a comfortable home to her own specification, she would have to manage the project herself. Besides, Ned and Sebi would have enough to attend to with planting-out now becoming an urgent priority as the warmer weather approached.

The second discomfort was the inexplicable cooling of Sir Michael's attitude towards him, and this had led to a number of difficulties including the rather strained atmosphere at the residence where it had seemed so generous and understanding before. The day of Jack's frustrated demand for leave of absence to go off in pursuit of Judd was not out before the change in temperature had been felt. Where it had become routine for the de Burghs to have Jack and Rose dine with them convivially in the room in which Jack's carved stone grandly embellished the hearth, the homeless pair now found themselves dining alone in the kitchen, with little by way of explanation.

'I thought us on easy terms, but I must have offended him in some way,' wondered Jack aloud one evening over a lonely supper. 'Perhaps with the directness of my speech, I have questioned him too much - and thus dented his pride? I shall have to be more careful as I tread from now on.'

Rose had also been somewhat bewildered by the cooling of relationships and had enquired of Lady de Burgh privately as to what might be the cause. With some unease, the lady had surmised that her husband may be wanting to distance himself a little from Jack, since for him to become too intimate with any of his subordinates might compromise his authority in command. Nevertheless, by her manner and delicately chosen wording, Lady de Burgh could not help herself revealing a certain difference of opinion with her husband on this matter, and Rose thus drew some hope that their own relationship might resume once the men had finally departed.

'You must not be too hard on him, Jack,' Rose counselled, assisted by this insight. 'I think it likely that Sir Michael feels the glare of inspection upon him in his new position, and if he seems to have become aloof it is likely to be because he is not yet fully confident in it. Lady de Burgh and I have talked of this; and you need not feel concerned on my account for we have an understanding.' Thus do women often understand their men better than the men understand themselves.

The training area lay at a discrete distance from the residence on level ground that had been left fallow during the previous year and had thus become covered in grasses and rough vegetation. A bird's-eye view of the area, a rectangular field of some twenty acres, would reveal a multitude of churned-up tracks, the result of wagon wheels and marching feet, criss-crossing the terrain like the scars on a flogged man's back. In one corner of the field, four tents had been erected using canvas sheets and poles. These had been stayed firmly with hawsers against the likelihood of wind off the Potomac, which lay open and unshielded by trees along its western edge. It was to the largest of these tents, a veritable marquee, that Jack had been directed to affect his introduction to the men and fellow officers of the militia. He thus made his way towards it with some trepidation.

Emerging into the field through the belt of trees that screened it from the house, he was surprised to see so little activity for, from Sir Michael's description, he had expected training to be ongoing and intense. The reason for the apparent quiet became clear as soon as he pulled back the entrance flap of the tent, for he found what appeared to be the entire troop assembled within in the course of a briefing. The musty smell of damp canvas and trodden grass mingled in his nostrils with the odours of unwashed clothes and sweat. He had apparently entered at the rear of the tent for he was now faced with the broad backs of scores of common soldiers dressed in hunting jackets of various designs and indifferent state. There was a certain uniformity in their dress, but it was hardly military, and would undoubtedly fail the regimental inspection of Major Green whose smart British redcoats might mock the rag-tag for their unkempt appearance. In Jack's estimation, these men were subsistence farmers like himself, ex-indentured servants with a mere headright of land, or tenants struggling to pay their former masters' quitrents and thus still beholden. One or two of them turned to inspect the new arrival, casually catching Jack's eye without acknowledgement, but they snatched their glances as quickly back to the front.

It took a while for Jack to tune himself into what it was that was being said that kept the men so attentive; and raising himself upon tiptoe, he peered between the forest of heads before him that obscured his view. Elevated upon a platform at the far end of the tent stood a bearded man of medium height and build, dressed in a weather-faded hunting jacket with powder straps draped diagonally across his chest.

'...and that's the way it was!' Jack heard him say. 'So it's not the French you'll need to watch out for – they march like the British and you'll hear them coming from miles away - it's the Indians who are the real threat! And if you want to stay alive out there, you'll have to have eyes in the back of your head, for they'll creep up on a man and have his scalp while he's taking a piss against a tree – and the poor sod will still be shaking it off before he feels the draft around his ears!'

There was some uncertain laughter at this remark that quickly died away. 'So, when we're moving in frontier territory,' he continued as the silence resumed, 'we'll not march in neat lines like the British with our eyes to the front, we'll tread careful in a loose formation covering each other. And we'll have scouts out with muskets primed and fingers wrapped around the triggers. We might lose a scout or two if they get jumped, but the rest of us at least might be alerted!' Jack wanted to suggest that Indians intent on ambush might be subtle enough to let a scout pass by in order to surprise the rest coming on behind, but he reckoned the measure a sensible precaution nevertheless.

The bearded speaker continued in the same laconic vein for a few minutes more, before Sir Michael eventually took his place in the centre of the platform.

'So gentlemen,' he started breezily, 'our thanks to Major Lawrence for those valuable insights; he will advise me on operational strategies once we enter hostile territory. And Lieutenant Colonel Sanderson here...' He paused and waved a hand behind him at a man even taller than himself, who now came forward with an expression upon his face which Jack took as either complacence or disdain. He was dressed similarly to the major but his attire, like Sir Michael's, appeared newly cleaned and pressed.

'Colonel Sanderson,' Sir Michael continued, 'will be my second-in-command.' (At this, the half colonel eked out a thin-lipped smile and gave a little bow of his head.) 'Some of you men are tenants of his and so will already know him well.' Sir Michael went on with a description of Sanderson's credentials, to which Jack listened with interest, hoping to find some assurance that the leadership of the company knew its business. Sanderson, it appeared, like Sir Michael, was the owner of a large estate. He was also clearly a man of similar lineage, undoubtedly someone used to command, and likewise an inheritor of privilege and power from a family line of gentry. While it appeared that he had served before as a militia officer, Sir Michael did not say for how long or in what capacity, nor did he mention if the corps in which the gentleman had served had ever seen active service.

Jack therefore did not receive the boost to his confidence that he had hoped for, being left at best unsure; and he was also left feeling that Sir Michael had been somewhat disingenuous at Chaptico to claim that militarily he would be well advised. Moreover, as Sir Michael continued his oratory, Jack became aware of sideways glances between the men assembled at the rear of the crowd. He could have no way of knowing what hidden meaning their expressions symbolised, but it was clear that these men did not hold Sanderson in the highest regard. And he wondered if they, like he, were under an obligation to their landowner to participate in a distant venture that they did not fully understand. Trying to gauge the mood in the tent, he let his gaze wander, musing upon what other motives might have driven those who stood before him to be here. Undoubtedly, many would have answered the stirring call of duty in the name of defending homeland and a way of life - or at least would have bowed to the pressure of their patriotic peers to rally to the flag. Some, as previously revealed inadvertently by Sir Michael himself, might have other rewards in mind: the opportunities for bounties or grants of title. Perhaps the military pay might have attracted some? And certainly there would be a few adventurers and glory hunters too. But there would also be those who might be using the venture to find new land away from the suffocating hierarchies and restrictions that were becoming almost as feudal on the eastern seaboard as in the mother country. The motives of the British were also interesting. What drove the distant government suddenly to invest such huge resources in the battlefront when they had neglected it for so long? Were they coming as knights in shining armour, arriving like cavalry over the hill to the aid of besieged colonists under attack? Or was it the ultimate defeat of France, the perpetual enemy, that they had in mind - to take North America and its riches for themselves and build an empire to compete with Spanish possessions in the south? And if they succeeded ..?

'Is Jack Easton here?' It was Sir Michael's voice that cut through Jack's meandering speculation; and he found himself suddenly the object of several rearward glances from the floor. There was no hiding the wince that crinkled his features as he found himself in the glare of inspection; but clearing his throat and puffing himself up to look more confident than he felt, he shouted crisply:

'Aye, sir.' And he put up his hand.

'Then come forward, man!' Sir Michael commanded - to which Jack obediently responded, making his way through the assembly and up onto the stage, feeling at once excruciatingly ill at ease.

'And this is my adjutant, Lieutenant Jack Easton,' Sir Michael announced - to which Jack managed a perfunctory nod at the sea of expectant faces raised before him. Now he knew how the lieutenant colonel had felt earlier, and began to feel more charitable towards the man.

'Whilst you men have been in training these past few weeks, Lieutenant Easton has been busying himself behind the scenes with logistics and supplies - under my instructions,' Sir Michael started. 'And that will continue to be his main task on our way north. However, once we are on potentially hostile ground, he will take one of the reconnaissance platoons under Major Lawrence's command to scout ahead for trouble and keep the main party informed.'

This was the first Jack had known of his operational duties and he had difficulty in keeping his alarm to himself. While outwardly, he tried to act the part expected, he groaned quietly under his breath at the sudden acceleration of pace. It suddenly felt as if he were on skids, and no longer in control of his own destiny. There comes a point in the course of any venture beyond which it seems impossible to go against the flow whatever the misgivings. The fear of being branded feeble or thought irresolute inhibits dissent. Or else, unchecked rhetoric decides the way - when men are too shallow to think for themselves, too lame to argue, or too uncertain to stand up and shout *stop*! Jack wondered if any of these might apply to him but, in truth, he did not know enough to understand what troubled him. Moreover, Sir Michael's public announcement of his role in front of a southern Maryland community on which he would inevitably depend for his security and well being gave him a distinct feeling of ensnarement. And having only just shaken off the ostracising label of 'ex-con', he found himself averse to putting at risk the comfort of social acceptability again. If he had harboured any notion of escaping his undertaking, of slipping away to attend to the hurt and damage of recent events, then this was the moment when he gave it up. Everything on that score would now have to be put on hold. This was also the moment that Jack finally reconciled himself that the pursuit of Judd would have to wait.

'So these are your officers, men,' continued Sir Michael, stridently. 'You will have time enough to get to know them better once we are on the way, for we have some weeks of hard journeying before us. But for now, I declare that we are ready for our task, and thus we have earned ourselves a few days leave before departure. So men, return to your homes and loved-ones to make ready and take your leave! And make them know that we go to fight in their names and in the name of King George to remove the Gallic and Indian scourge from this precious land!' By now, Sir Michael had worked up his rhetoric to a rallying pitch, adopting that sort of bold and upbeat tone required of military commanders at the outset of a mission. 'Report back to your NCOs on

Monday by noon, kitted up and ready to go! And may God be on the side of the righteous!'

Jack wondered if the Lord would take sides in a squabble over the possession of mere land, especially if those territories already occupied by European colonists had been extracted from their original inhabitants by force or subterfuge. But, despite himself, he found it impossible not to respond in similar measure to the triumphant grins of many in the crowd who stood before him with such unquestioning belief in their eyes. Yet it was apparent that not all the men had been swept along by the conquering mood, for some, those at the back in particular, were already making their exit through the flap at the rear of the tent even before Sir Michael had finished.

Jack was unsure what was expected of him following the dismissal, and so he lingered on the platform feeling slightly ill at ease while the confusion of the men's departure reigned below. Behind him, Sir Michael and Lieutenant Colonel Sanderson had found something to discuss, and so for a time Jack was left standing alone with no one apparently taking any notice of him. Warming to the anonymity, he scanned the departing faces, hoping to find some familiar amongst them. It was like watching a pond drain as the men surged out of the several flaps that had been opened in the canvas walls like sluice gates. A few black faces punctuated the ebbing tide of white, and Jack recognised some of these as New Hope slaves, those that he had once worked alongside in the tobacco fields of his earlier penal servitude. And amongst the white faces, he spotted some of his former fellows, indentured servants still working their time. And there were a few of the overseers there too, men who had once ensured that he and his compatriots had toed the line – with their beating sticks and their power to make a life of poverty, poorer yet. He found a few eyes in those familiar faces turned towards him, and held their gazes for a moment here and there, acknowledging them with a nod of his head. But save for the uncertain cast of their glances, their faces conveyed no warmth, even though he would have counted some of them formerly as friends. It was as though that by being marked out by his arbitrary commission, a line had been drawn that now separated him. Jack had the uncomfortable feeling that somehow he was no longer one of them; that he had been taken out of one group but not placed within another, and thus he felt that he now stood in a void somewhere in-between.

In his isolation, a curious feeling of vulnerability arose within him that made it suddenly important to belong. Then, as the crowd thinned, he noticed that a knot of half a dozen men remained behind engaged in conversation that struck Jack immediately as convivial. These, Jack guessed, were the non-commissioned officers, the backbone of the corps, the men who would really be in charge. As Jack alighted from the platform, he noticed Major Lawrence move towards the group and join it with such an easy reception that it was clear that a fellowship had already been established. The major glanced about and caught Jack's eye, and beckoned him to join them with a flick of his head that was both friendly and commanding. It is strange, considering that Jack's recent triumphs in England should have bestowed great self-assurance upon him, that he should feel a sense of gratitude at the major's call. But this was very much how he felt. And as he made his way towards the group, now watching his approach in a not unwelcoming manner, he found himself eager to find acceptance.

'Henry Lawrence!' The major offered his name and his hand simultaneously.

Jack took the hand and shook it firmly. 'Jack Easton,' he replied curtly, for he was not yet ready to let down his guard.

'Sir Michael has told us something about your story,' the major nodded approvingly with an appraising look in his eyes, 'it seems you're a man who might be useful in a fight! Welcome aboard!'

Jack then found himself passed around the group as each member introduced himself. As usual with Jack, names went in one ear and out the other and it would therefore be some time before he could confidently attach specific names to faces. But what struck Jack immediately was that, despite their differing appearances and build, all six men had the same easy confidence about them.

'They're all selected men,' the major said, as if answering Jack's unspoken question. 'I chose them myself; we've served together before. Some of us are retirees from the British army come to join your fight, and settle when we can find some land.' With this, he waved a hand in the direction of three of the men, middle-aged by appearance, who nodded their acknowledgement. 'And Sergeants Hine, Bryant, and Schluntz here are militia men who served with me in Virginia.'

'Then what brings you to southern Maryland?' Jack asked, puzzled.

'Sir Michael put the word out for professionals,' he answered simply. 'And that's what we do.'

'And the pay is good,' offered the compact Bryant quickly.

'Even though the food is *schweinefutter!*' interjected the lanky Schluntz, and he spat on the ground in an exaggerated act of disgust that raised a chuckle from his companions.

Jack grinned wryly. 'And what makes me doubt that it's going to get any better once we start out? There's not a lot cook can make from the forty sacks of dried beans and corn that I've just had delivered to the quay! Except lashings of lovely gruel! Personally, its my favourite after a hard day's march!' he added, with his tongue firmly in his cheek.

It was during the ensuing laughter that Jack became aware of a presence closing upon him from behind; and judging by the sudden stiffening of their bearing, his new comrades-in-arms had also noticed the approach. Jack turned to find Sir Michael and Lieutenant Colonel Sanderson arriving.

'Ah good,' Sir Michael exclaimed. 'Glad to see you have already become acquainted,' he added unnecessarily. 'Jack, this is Colonel Sanderson.'

'So this is your famous stonemason, Michael?' commented Sanderson without offering Jack his hand. It seemed that Jack was more an article for inspection than engagement, for when Jack thrust out his, the lieutenant colonel appeared taken by surprise.

'Oh!' he exclaimed, and took Jack's hand as if taking hold of something that might bite him.

Returning later to the rear bedroom in the residence at New Hope that had become their temporary quarters, Jack found his wife resting on the bed in her loose underskirt and unlaced bodice, her bare shoulders draped with a knitted woollen shawl of mixed colours. Over the latter, her long dark hair, released from its normal tight restraint, cascaded lustrously like an ebony mane that did not quite conceal the deep cleft between her breasts. She was not asleep, but lay propped up on a pillow, dreamily gazing though the window at the scene outside. The late afternoon weather had settled from its earlier turbulent state, and low sunshine now emblazoned the riverbanks and overhanging trees with gloriously bright colours, which were riven with the darker contrasts of long shadows. In the distance, the newly planted fields had a manicured look, where saplings ruled pale green lines across a textured canvas of ochre soil. The bedroom was relatively spacious, accommodating a wash stand and a table and two chairs, as well as a proper double bed with a down-filled mattress, a luxury that neither Jack nor Rose had ever enjoyed before. And Lady de Burgh had given sharp instructions to the housemaids for the couple to be well attended. On the washstand, a fine china washing bowl and ewer had been provided, and a vase of fresh spring flowers stood upon the table. The fireplace was also kept laid ready for use - although it had been so mild of late that there had been no need to light it. Sunlight streamed in through the open window to join the gentle wafts of country air and the delicate scents of spring blossoms, and the low, beamed ceiling scintillated with watery patterns reflected from the nearby stream. The glittering projection gave the room the distinct feeling of being afloat.

At Jack's entry, Rose turned her head towards him and smiled. The spring held out such a promise of renewal that it had clearly buoyed his wife up, for he had noticed over recent weeks that she had steadily lifted herself out of her earlier gloom.

'Finished for the day?' she asked.

Jack nodded. 'Until Monday!' he said, removing his coat and draping it across the back of the chair, where he now sat to remove his boots. 'We start northwards at midday,' he muttered distractedly, struggling with his laces. When he looked up, he saw her frowning in disapproval and realised instantly why. 'Sorry, Rose; I should have taken them off downstairs; I wasn't thinking,' he said resignedly. He stood, went to the table, poured a little water into the bowl, and washed and dried his face and hands. 'Truth is,' he said over his shoulder as he did so, 'it's all suddenly become rather real – that I'm leaving, I mean. And I've just met Sir Michael's number two - Sanderson. Not someone I'd choose to spend the next few months with if I had a choice.' He turned back, throwing a sort of helpless expression in Rose's direction, then sat himself despondently on the end of the bed. 'We've known about it long enough, I suppose, and I guess there's a need for our going,' he said gloomily, running his hand distractedly around her ankles and up the back of her calves, 'but it's not going to be easy to leave you – especially with things as they are.'

'If the King has sent his regiments to defend us, Jack, then it must be our duty to support him because we benefit from his protection.' Rose said this in a tone that mixed resolution with a hint of residual doubt. It was as if she feared to pose the question that must have been on her mind, for she added a qualification: 'I would feel less positive about it if I felt that this was a mere squabble over territory, for surely there is enough space on this huge continent for us all to share? But since it appears that we must defend ourselves or our fellow colonists from attack, I must be glad that you are going.' This was said lightly, almost off-hand, but it was a statement rather than an endorsement for she let it hang in the air for a moment.

'Anyway, you must not worry about me while you are away,' she continued softly, 'I'll get things put back in order here, and you'll have a new home to return to – and then we can pick up where we left off. I'll be glad to have something to make me think about the future rather than the past.'

Jack smiled fondly at her fortitude. He was so grateful that she had not challenged him on his need to go, and she had not questioned him as he had questioned himself. It was just as well, for he would have had no satisfactory answers. Leaving her would be difficult, but her brave outlook had lightened the leaden weight in his heart, and made him love her the more. 'There are some things after all that cannot bear too much enquiry,' he thought, 'when simple men get swallowed up in the politics of the powerful.'

'There's just one thing I want you to promise me, Jack:' Rose said, her voice turning more emphatic. 'I want you to forget about going after this man, Judd. He can be no further threat to us now, surely! And chasing after him will just keep you away from me the longer - and may be dangerous. Anyway, in the end, what good will it do *us* if you catch him?'

With the preoccupations of his recent duties and his apprehensions of imminent discomfort and reckonable risk of harm, Jack's lust for revenge against Judd had begun to subside. Like Rose, he had also asked himself the question 'what good will it do us?' and wondered if it might be the better part of valour to draw a line under the matter and try to move on. In this he was also not blind to the fact that in bringing the evil of Smyke to a just end, he had unwittingly unleashed other demons to haunt him. Including the escaped Pettigrew and the devious Hayward in his counting, the evil of Smyke had mutated threefold like a cancer into new threats which, in his nightmares, frightened him with their malignancy. And all this had come about directly as a consequence of his original quest. If he had let things lie, had left things undisturbed, had neither moralised nor sought to satisfy the base urges of revenge, then he would not have brought catastrophe upon himself. 'If these consequences had been foretold, would I have gone after Smyke?' he asked himself. 'And might not a new quest to bring Judd to justice multiply the danger yet again?' The genie had been let out of the bottle by his act, so to speak, and he had begun to wonder if the price of righteousness was worth the cost. Perhaps it was indeed safer to turn the other cheek?

In this frame of mind, it was not difficult at this moment of self-doubt to accede to his wife's request. When he raised his eyes, he found hers searching his face while she awaited his reply, and he heard himself answering her question:

'Very well, I promise that I will not go after him, Rose,' he said carefully. 'But what of justice?' he thought at the same time, 'and what if he should come after me?'

Rose smiled and allowed a few seconds to pass before continuing. When she did, her mood had suddenly become much brighter.

'So then, we've a few days to ourselves before you go?' she asked lightly. But the seductive lift in her voice and the impish enquiry in her eyes were unambiguously inviting, and Jack felt a sudden stirring between his loins as if some chemistry within him had been ignited. He had held himself back for so long out of deference to her state, but he had been longing for her signal that she was ready to receive him once again. Now, at last released from this constraint, his passion came at him in a rush like a breaking wave, sweeping before it all other thoughts from his mind. And in an instant, he found himself flushed with such heady desire that it made his flesh tingle in anticipation.

'Then we haven't got a moment to lose,' she said with a playful laugh, and she leant forward and pulled him to her.

Chapter Twelve

Monday dawned so calmly that it seemed incongruous that it should be the beginning of a day that threatened such a great upheaval in Jack's life. He had passed the night in and out of sleep in anticipation of it, tossing and turning in such frequent bouts of fretful wakefulness that it seemed as if he had never slept. The dawn's light had now taken away all hope of finding that blissful oblivion that he had so desperately and so fruitlessly sought. And with a muted groan he gave up the struggle and instead set himself industriously to reshaping his pillow - half-hoping that his frustrated huffing and puffing might wake his partner for the comfort of her company. When she failed to stir, he propped himself up resignedly on the reconstructed mound and turned his desolate and bleary-eyed gaze through the window at the sky. A leaden overcast might have matched his mood better, but instead, rafts of crimson cirrus floated in transparent blue. It was that brief and poignant moment before the sun's incandescence broke the horizon and bring the day in with a gallop; a time of deceptive peace; of pregnant stillness. No breeze yet stirred the branches, nor rippled the slow waters of the river below. It seemed hardly believable that he was actually about to embark upon a soldier's journey to a battlefront on such a peaceful spring day.

Rose slumbered blissfully, her back towards him, curled into her customary coil like a dormouse in its nest, her face all but invisible under the tangle of her long dark hair. Jack felt the warmth of her body across the narrow space between them, radiating like a beacon; it seemed to beckon him closer. He rolled towards her, bringing up his knees to envelope her shape, and draped his free arm around her waist, his hand finding the smoothness of her belly as he pulled himself gently towards her. Already aroused, he felt his manhood press against the rounded softness of her form. She gave out a little murmur - half in sleep, half awakened by his movement - and rolled towards him in that awkward way when movement is restricted by twisting night clothes and crumpled sheets. With a final wrench upwards of her nightdress, she freed herself and moved her thigh across him as he slid his up between her legs and wrapped his arm around her back. And she nestled her head so close that he could feel the moist warmth of her breath upon his cheek. If she had half-opened her eyes during her manoeuvre, then she now closed them again, her face becoming once more serene, her breathing resuming the shallow, regular cadence that it had before, as if she had fallen back asleep. Jack smiled upon her features with both fondness and sadness in his heart. Only a few more hours before he would have to go, he lamented; another parting upon them so soon after his last return; and such agonies as they had suffered, hardly mended! There seemed too much that would be left unsaid; as if neither of them wanted to give expression to their feelings; as if in its articulation, grief best left buried might resurrect itself to sting again. But as he studied the girlish grace of her fair lineaments, he saw the corners of her lips first twitch then stretch into a smile that stole across her face like the dawn's sunlight across a pretty landscape. She opened her eyes slowly, as if knowing that he watched - dark, languid, clear eyes - like deep pools; and so alluring and inviting that he felt as if he were being drawn in, to be as one with her, his flesh as her flesh.

They made love one last time, one last tender time - gently and unrushed - like a parting embrace that neither wanted to end; as if by prolonging its slow and sensual rhythms, by withholding its fulfilment, they might avoid the separation that waited upon them like some dark spectre beyond the bedroom door.

A creak on the timbered stairway and a tentative tap on the door interrupted the couple's lingering moments of tranquil intimacy as they lay dozing later in each other's arms, their legs still entwined.

'At the quay in an hour, Jack, if you please!' came Sir Michael's muffled call through the thick pine planks.

The dozing pair groaned simultaneously, but Jack's head was quickly off the pillow. 'I'll be there,' he managed in a tone that hid the fact that he had been in slumber just moments before.

The sky was clear blue as Jack descended the rolling road to the quay with his bag slung over his shoulder and wearing the hide jacket, boots, and curled felt tricorn adopted by Sir Michael's militia as uniform. The sun's rays penetrated the still sparsely-leafed canopies of the wooded glade to warm his back and light up the misty scene below in shafts of yellow light. Alongside the quay lay a coastal packet barque, her square sails furled on her main and foremast yards, her headsails hanging languidly on their stays like washing on a line. Rafted up outside her, a smaller fore-and-aft-rigged schooner, her two raked masts looking sleek and uncluttered against the bulky spars and heavy rigging of her neighbour. She looked elegant yet purposeful with her long bowsprit and graceful prow and her sails neatly flaked upon their booms. New Hope harbour, a small but deep basin at the entrance to New Hope creek, was connected to the Potomac by a mile of broad and navigable water. It was the loading point for all the New Hope tobacco bound for England via the naval port of entry on the Tobacco River at Charlestown. The surface of the still water was glassy, reflecting the sky and surrounding trees in an almost perfect reverse image. Ships' tenders sat upon their own dark reflections as if suspended in a void, their long slack painters sending little circles of imperfection across the mirrored surface with each light touch. Jack checked his pace as he descended, feeling himself suddenly reluctant to be drawn into this deceptively alluring picture, wishing he could turn about and rush back to Rose, whose arms had held him in brave farewell just minutes before. He slowed further as thoughts of her pulled him back, the gravel grinding under his boots as he came to an abrupt and determined stop. Yet his thoughts whirled in indecision. What options did he have, he wondered, forlornly. Images flooded into his mind of the many times he had rolled the heavy hogsheads of tobacco down this very road towards the quay during his long years of convict slavery. How often had he thought of escape when he had gazed upon this quay? How often had he dreamt of stowing aboard such vessels as now lay before him in a wild and reckless bid for freedom? But now, those vessels lying at such ease below represented capture not escape - for once he stepped aboard he knew he would be bound, if not this time by the manacles of transportation, then by his word. Just for a moment, he toyed with the idea of turning back, but he knew at once that he could not do so without dishonour, without losing the reputation for which he had fought so long and hard to regain. His head was at about the level of the barque's topgallant yard; the dirt track wound gently downwards before him, leading the last hundred yards or so to the quay. And he stood there for some moments longer with his mind caught in a taut equilibrium as these contrary thoughts vied. Then a loud, impatient voice resounded:

'Jack! Jack! Come on!'

Jolted out of his reverie by the shout from below, Jack was spurred to continue his descent. He reached the quay and started across it, negotiating his way through the piled-up casks and boxes that cluttered the open space like an obstacle course. Some fifty yards ahead, Sir Michael waited for him at the gangway, but with these obstructions partially shielding his view, Jack was not inclined to rush. He took this little time to suppress the demons that still tugged at his heart, and prime himself instead to put on the show of dutiful enthusiasm that would be expected. Preparations for departure were clearly at an advanced state with men all around him lifting and carrying boxes and sacks onto the waiting barque, and he felt himself impelled onwards. With a silent sigh of resignation, he let himself be taken by the prospect that now lay before him. It was as if the open door that he had just walked through had closed behind him; the quickest way back, he thought, was to go forwards at full speed! And thus it was that Jack decided to front up to the inevitable – to accept his fate, whatever that might be, and to do his best – for that was what his sense of honour and his self-respect dictated.

Jack saw the schooner's crew already singling up the mooring warps as he drew nearer. Her skipper stood behind the wheel watching his men at work, and from his manner he was clearly impatient to get his vessel underway. Jack stole a quick glance down the creek towards the open water and understood the skipper's haste; the tide was clearly on the ebb. The deep-drafted vessel would have very little water remaining under her keel in the relatively shallow water of the creek and her skipper would be anxious to be away. The shallow-drafted barque, on the other hand, could afford to take her leisure; she would have enough water to make a more ladylike departure in her own good time.

Sir Michael noticed Jack's inspection. 'I have them on a short lease, Jack, and have taken on the skippers and crews so that they'll be at our disposal for as long as we need them. I had quite forgotten your sailing background; good-looking vessels, are they not? '

'Indeed, Sir Michael. But you'd have to agree that the barque looks a bit of a fat cow against the schooner's fine lines!'

'I am glad you like the look of her, Jack,' smiled the older man, 'because you and I will sail ahead on her. I want to be in Georgetown before the main party arrives tomorrow to see that my agent has obtained the supplies that I ordered.'

Jack smiled ambiguously, mindful of the several misunderstandings that had already occurred as a result of his colonel's shaky communication skills. 'A sensible precaution, sir,' he nodded gravely.

'Major Lawrence and his scout platoon will sail with us, and I'll leave Colonel Sanderson to follow on in the barque with the main company when she's completed her loading. And by the way, I shall be calling in at

Charlestown for a brief meeting with Harding this evening if we get there soon enough.'

'Aye, sir,' said Jack, now resigned to his fate, and trying hard to sound engaged. He lingered for a moment longer, not sure if Sir Michael had finished with him, and glanced across the barque's deck to the schooner rafted up outside to see the bearded Major Lawrence on the fore deck surrounded by his scouts. Jack counted seven in the major's platoon, the lanky form of Sergeant Schluntz standing out above the rest, and Bryant and Hine were also there. But of Colonel Sanderson and the main party, there was as yet no sign.

'You'd better get aboard now and stow your gear, Jack. The skipper wants us out of here before we get stuck in the mud!'

As he spoke, the distant tramp of marching feet and the grinding of wagon wheels upon gravel drew the pair's attention up the rolling road.

'Ah! At last!' Sir Michael said with obvious relief. 'I hear Sanderson arriving with the company. You go on; I'll be right behind you once I've had a word with him.' And with that, the colonel turned and made off across the quay to meet his arriving army.

Jack watched him go, and at that same moment saw the company breaking out of the vegetation that had shielded them from his view. In the shafts of sunshine that now caught them, the military phalanx was a splendid sight. But most astonishing of all was the figure at its head: that of Colonel Sanderson in his crisp new uniform, seated upon a white charger of patent pedigree. Jack's face could not hide his amazement at such an ostentatious display of vanity. The man's a buffoon, he thought - it crossing his mind also that such a handsome piece of horseflesh would make its rider a conspicuous target for some French musketeer or Indian arrow.

But his musing on this was interrupted by Sir Michael's rearward shout: 'And by the way, Jack,' the colonel called over his retreating shoulder, 'It's all hands to the boats to tow us out of here – and I've volunteered you and the major's men as oarsmen!' Jack flicked a glance into the treetops where a south westerly breeze now stirred the branches; a fair wind for the sail up the Potomac, he thought. But shielded by surrounding trees, the basin was becalmed - and so with a resigned shrug, he climbed aboard the barque and made his way across the deck towards the waiting schooner. The wind's direction promised a long uninterrupted reach to her first anchorage at the mouth of the Tobacco River, some thirty miles upstream. And, Jack reckoned, the journey would take about six or seven hours if the wind held; leaving enough daylight for Sir Michael to make his call to Charlestown and get back to the ship before darkness fell.

The schooner's departure out of the basin just fifteen minutes later might have looked serene and stately to the militia now assembled on the quay, but for Jack and his fellow oarsmen in the boats, the heavy work of towing such a large vessel was made frenzied by the need to beat the falling tide. It took a further fifteen minutes of hard rowing to reach the deeper water of the river where they and the boats were brought back on board - just as all hands were called to the halyards to hoist the sails. In this, the schooner's fore-and-aft rig offered the great advantage over her square-rigged companion of needing no men aloft. She was therefore soon beating out into the Potomac at a brisk rate of knots with all her canvas taut and resplendent in the now unhindered wind. And after forty more minutes of skilful tacking, she was already rounding St George's Island and setting course up the waterway on a broad reach.

On such an undemanding point of sail, there was little actual sail handling to be done – save for the occasional tweak of the sheets, and the crew might thus have thought that they would be in for an easy time. They were soon disabused of this idle notion! Quick to seize the opportunity of a relatively even keel, the skipper soon had his men scrubbing the decks or set to other chores. By contrast, the embarked platoon of scouts sat about at ease around the wheelhouse in various states of undress, basking in the warmth of the early-summer sun. Major Lawrence and Sir Michael meanwhile leant upon the stern rail locked in conversation, which Jack took to be of some military concern. The schooner had been underway for close on three hours when the square sails of the barque were at last sighted a good ten miles astern emerging from the estuary. The sun's bright rays caught her leaning masts and gave her dowdy canvas radiance in a spectacular Potomac scene. Already twenty-five miles up-stream from the Chesapeake, the river here was still upwards of four miles wide; but due to a dog-leg in its course a few miles astern (the vessel tightening around it onto a exhilarating close reach), the opposite shores of Maryland and Virginia looked so close that a cannon ball might be shot from one side to the other. Wooded headlands on both sides of the river sat low and dark on each horizon, underlined with pale and sandy foreshores. The water, slipping past at gratifying speed and ruffled by the breeze into a slight chop, was a muddy brown when examined from above. But viewed into the distance across the stern, it was as blue and sparkling as a tropical sea.

Jack gazed astern wistfully for a while, his heart caught between the sorrow of a parting and the sense of release that sailing in such pleasant conditions always inspired. And seeking solitude to reconcile the two, he crossed to the starboard rail to watch the Maryland shore glide past. It brought back memories of his last voyage upriver with Ned in the little sailing skiff in which they had nearly been run down by the *Rebecca* in the mist. The recollection was salutary - the near catastrophe had almost brought his mission to an early end, foreshadowing the trials he would later face - it would have been so easy to use the incident as an excuse to give up his quest, he thought. But, thank God, he had persevered. It was a lesson, perhaps, that a fainter heart would never have won him what he sought, even though his victory over Smyke had born a vicious sting in its tail in the shape of Judd's retribution. Rose, with admirable stoicism, had weathered the storms that had lashed her life since being caught up in Smyke's deadly plot. And now she had come through this latest disaster too. She was bruised, certainly, but she had not let herself wallow in self-pity. Instead, with typical fortitude, she had simply put her grief to one side and resolved to make a fresh start. It was this quality in her that he so much admired. She was a partner rather than merely a dependent wife; and she had lessened the burden of their trials rather than added to them with histrionics. Never hasty with glib counsel, she had not dragged him down with recriminations when he had led Judd to their door to deal his evil hand, nor had she protested madly at the questionable mission on which he had now embarked. Jack knew that he had much to be thankful for in their union, a union that had been forged in the discomforts and difficulties that they had both faced. It was as if they had earned each other; two irrepressible souls made in the same mould out of the same stuff. And with her by his side, he knew that they could recapture what they had lost, just as he was confident that he would soon return. With the help of the prize money, their home would be rebuilt, and later, some more land and new comforts and tools would be acquired to make their lives easier than it had been before. And with God's blessing, a child would soon be on the way - to fill the aching void left behind with the cruel death of their son.

From time to time in this introspective reverie, Jack found himself glancing back to the distant bluff that marked the river mouth at New Hope. The barque's bright and leaning sails had cleared the jutting headlands of the eastern shoreline and the vessel was now traversing the dark line of the horizon in a westerly direction. It looked as if she sailed upon the very edge of the world - as if she might fall off with a moment's inattention at the wheel. He wondered whether Rose had waited to watch the barque depart after she had waved him off, and if she might even now be standing on the low ridge above the shoreline watching his sails recede? Or had she turned back towards New Hope soon after he had passed by - back to Ned and Sebi who had bid him farewell with such resignation, and whose existences would now continue as if he had never returned? He felt a sudden pang of emptiness as this thought struck him - as if it were *he* who had been left behind not they. As if in his comings and goings he was a mere perturbation in the steady course of their lives - like the close encounter of a ship passing in the night - a fleeting glimpse of a helmsman's pale face in the binnacle's dim light as the vessel slipped by - to vanish into the darkness astern like some phantom of the sea. Yet Rose's faint call from the river bank, carrying across the water as the schooner had slipped out of the river, had told him that he was more than this. He had heard her voice and had searched the shoreline with frantic eyes lest he should miss a last sighting of her, and had seen her waving her shawl above her head. It had brought a lump to his throat to see her diminutive form standing so alone. She was still waving as he lost sight of her in the distance - as the winds pulled them further and further apart. It would be that image of her that he would hold in his mind to see him through the trials that lay ahead.

Sir Michael returned from his trip to Charlestown to the schooner's anchorage, propelled by a crew of oarsmen who looked as uncoordinated in their oarsmanship as their spirits were high. The echoes of their coming had preceded them along the river by some distance and, attracted by the noise of clashing oars and laughter, Jack had joined others at the rail to watch the approach. Sir Michael was the first up the boarding ladder and he shot the waiting skipper an indignant scowl as he arrived on deck; indeed, the look upon his face might have been fatal had it conveyed as much weight as ferocity. He fumed quietly as the boat's crew tumbled onto the deck behind him, all with silly grins upon their faces, before launching an angry outburst at the skipper for his crew's indiscipline. It appeared that the colonel may have left the boatmen unsupervised in Charlestown for just a little too long, for soon the unmistakable scent of alcohol could be smelt wafting on the river air.

Duly chastised, the oarsmen were banished to the forepeak, followed hotly by the skipper, evidently intent on making them pay for his embarrassment. Sir Michael stood for a moment alone, his face red and all puffed up, glaring about him as if daring anyone to meet his eye. A group of seamen who had been enjoying the entertainment quickly stifled their smirks and took a sudden interest in some item of rigging that seemed to demand attention. And Major Lawrence and his men, sitting in the sternsheets, tactfully averted their gazes, returning quickly to their pipes and idle talk.

By this time, it was already dusk and the schooner swung lazily on her chain in the deep water at the of the Tobacco River mouth, which lay on a sharp bend in the Potomac's narrowing course and was thus protected by rising ground on three sides. On the opposite side of the estuary, the barque could be seen ghosting to a halt with every inch of sail hung out to capture the last vestiges of wind. The distant rush of her cable and the splash of her anchor sounded across the still water like a weary gasp. The familiar landmark of Saint Thomas' Manor looked down from the western slopes; and at that moment, its windows caught the last rays of the setting sun and flared with reflected crimson light - like some fiery-eyed guard indignant at the noisy intrusion.

With his anger spent at last, Sir Michael's form slowly deflated. Then as if struck by some important new thought, he cast his gaze about again. Catching Jack's eye, he beckoned him to follow as he made his way towards a quieter corner of the deck.

'The shipping office was held up last week,' he said in a low voice as Jack caught up with him. 'Harding caught the perpetrator off guard and foiled the attempt, thank God,' he breathed, '- although he got himself injured in the process - fortunately not badly!'

Jack's expression showed his alarm, but he allowed Sir Michael to continue uninterrupted:

'Harding's strong room holds deposits for quite a few of us tobacco traders at this time of year, Jack - receipts are coming in now from our agents' transactions abroad you know – so this is more than a bit worrying for us. And this is the first time such an attempt has been made! I had thought our deposits reasonably secure until now, but this incident makes me very uneasy...'

Jack nodded gravely. 'I would remind you, sir, that Mr Harding also secures *my* deposit!' He interjected this rather testily as if to assert that his stake was every bit as important as his colonel's.

'Hmmm! Yes, of course, Jack. Harding told me; you will be concerned too, I'm sure.' Sir Michael pressed on. 'Anyway, I have spoken with the sheriff, who tells me that your poster sparked off several reports of this man Pettigrew being seen in the area with his fellow escapees. People are panicking about them being on the loose, and I'm sure that some of the reports will prove spurious; but it is quite possible that Pettigrew is behind this, isn't it?'

But by now Jack's thinking was racing ahead on another tack entirely. It had not occurred to him before, but it now seemed likely that when Judd failed to find the prize money at New Hope farm, he would have deduced where it had been left for safekeeping. Judd might be many things but he was not stupid. He must, after all, have followed Jack all the way from the *Miranda,* and therefore he may well have observed his visit to the shipping office on the way through. But Jack could not be sure of this.

'Pettigrew is unlikely to act alone, sir,' he suggested, doubtfully. 'Did Harding tell you what his attacker looked like?'

'The tellers were apparently closing up at the time and the lamps were being put out, so it was difficult for them to see the man clearly. Harding told me that he heard shouting at the front desk and came out of his office with his pistols ready for action just in case. Evidently he didn't get much of a look at the man before the firing started.' Sir Michael was not saying much of any help. 'It appears that the robber had a neckerchief over his face and wore a tricorn hat, so it would have been difficult for Harding to identify him anyway. The only detail that Harding could offer was that the man was of medium height and that he had a bloody scab upon his left cheek, which his neckerchief did not completely conceal.'

If Jack had harboured any doubts that the attempted robbery had been carried out by Judd, then this latter detail disabused him of these immediately. Rose's brave counter-attack with her kitchen knife had provided the evidence! He was now as certain as he could be that it was Judd and not Pettigrew who had been the would-be robber. And, while Harding might have saved the day on this occasion, Jack knew that the former boatswain was the kind of man who would try again. And with his knowledge of tobacco trading, Judd might well be spurred on by the notion that the strong room might contain much more than Jack's sum alone!

'Mr Harding may not have recognised him, sir,' said Jack, gruffly, 'but I am almost certain that this was Judd – and that last detail confirms it in my mind! This was the man responsible for attacking Rose and for burning down my home - and indirectly for the murder of my son! You stopped me going after him, if you remember!' Jack's retort had become a tight-lipped accusation. 'He was the crook that Mr Harding put me aboard the *Rebecca* expressly to ferret out - and I know now that I have paid a heavy price for my success in that endeavour!'

Sir Michael frowned.

'You may not realise it, sir, but you and your fellow plantation owners have been affected by Judd's thieving for some time - although with Mr Harding's somewhat disconnected transatlantic bookkeeping, it would not have been immediately obvious to you. It seems that by putting an end to Judd's game I have rather made an enemy of him, and I believe that he is now determined to get back at me. He followed me all the way to New Hope to get his hands on my money, and now it seems to Charlestown. Yours could well go with it if he tries again! And maybe next time he'll not make such a botch of it?' Jack finished on a level tone, almost as if reconciled to the inevitability of a second attempt. But his apparent calm belied the anger that was rising within him – and the fear, too - that he once again stood to lose the means by which he had hoped to change his life.

'Hmmm!' Sir Michael's expression was both grave and perplexed at the same time. 'The sheriff asked if you could be seconded temporarily to help track down this Pettigrew fellow since apparently you are the only one available who has is acquainted with him. I was inclined not to agree, but now in view of what you say, the situation appears much more threatening than I had first thought, especially since this Judd fellow might still be about. He appears to have no scruples about him either!'

Sir Michael's gaze drifted back up river from whence he had come. Jack could almost hear his mind calculating his own vulnerability as he pondered for a moment in silence. When he next spoke, it was as though he thought out loud:

'Harding assured me that his new night guard would be a sufficient deterrent against any further attempt at robbery, but I now begin to think that it will need more than an old retainer with a blunderbuss.' He paused, then seemed to make up his mind for he spoke more assertively.

'I think that you should help them after all, Jack! It would make me feel a lot more comfortable. None of us will feel secure with these ruffians roaming the county on the loose. All right? I'd give you a note for Harding to make available whatever funds you needed.'

Jack's heart leapt at this suggestion, although he was careful to maintain his sober demeanour as he nodded his agreement, so as not to seem too eager. This new mission was much closer to his instincts and his aptitudes than a ponderous trek to the north as a makeweight militiaman.

'Good man! But remain only as long as it takes, Jack,' Sir Michael added in an emphatic tone. 'As soon as you are satisfied that you have done enough and can be of no further use, then I want you to follow on as quickly as you can. Find a boat to take you up to Georgetown then buy yourself a horse to catch us up – you'll travel much more quickly alone than we shall. I'm intending to rendezvous with General Forbes' provincial forces at Raystown during the late summer, so plan to meet us there. My advice would be for you to follow the Potomac from Georgetown to Fort Frederick then strike northwards up the river valley to Fort Loudon, but speak to Major Lawrence before you disembark to get his view on the fastest route – he knows the terrain better than I.'

'Aye, sir,' said Jack, 'I'll do my best to join you as soon as possible,' he answered somewhat disingenuously, for he knew that he faced a difficult and indeterminate task that might well take more time than Sir Michael imagined. 'But I am glad of the opportunity to see to this matter of unfinished business first. I would not have been a very good soldier with thoughts of Judd and Pettigrew on my mind. And I want to see justice done as well as ensure that our assets are secured.'

Perhaps sensing Jack's equivocation, Sir Michael replied suspiciously: 'Now, Jack, do not let this matter consume you; do what you must, but remember that your duty to me and the King should be your first priority.'

'Of course, sir,' replied Jack robustly. But he did not need to be told where his first priority lay. And suddenly he was impatient to be free of the inhibiting disciplines and sluggish constraints of Sir Michael's corporate bureaucracy. Once he was free to act on his own initiative he would be his own man again, listening to his own assessments and judgements - and obeying his instincts accordingly.

'Well then,' he heard Sir Michael saying, 'I'll have you put ashore at dawn. There'll not be enough time to have you ferried up to Charlestown, so you'll have to make your own way there on foot.'

Chapter Thirteen

After Judd's bungled attempt at robbery at the Charlestown shipping office, the fugitive had retreated the twenty miles to the Brandywine hotel to brood on his ineptitude. He reckoned himself lucky to have escaped at all. Harding had come at him from behind with both pistols raised and taken him by surprise, just as the strong-room came into his view, its iron door tantalisingly ajar so that he could see the contents displayed within. But he had gazed at it an instant too long and was just not quick enough to swing his own weapons before his attacker's first pistol fired. Fortunately, the shot had gone wide of its mark and he had seized the opportunity to loose off a round blindly into the smoke and make a run for it before Harding could fire again. In the gathering darkness outside, he had made his escape before the alarm could be raised, and he was already well outside the town before the ensuing furore erupted. Then, once sure that he was not pursued, he had made his way through the night to reach the hotel in the first light of the dawn, and had climbed through the window of his rented room unseen.

It was now a week since that lamentable event, and he sat despondently over his mug of ale in a quiet corner of the dingy saloon bar pondering his options. It was not for the first time that he had found himself so morose. He took out his purse and fingered its contents, but its weight already told him that time was running out. He had managed to find someone on the Charlestown waterfront to give him a half-decent exchange for the twenty pound note taken from the Easton farm, and the coinage had put a roof above his head and food in his belly ever since. But the money, substantial as it may be, would not last forever. He had not dared to seek work so close to the scenes of his crimes lest questions be asked and connections made; but he would have to do something to replenish his diminishing cache - and soon! He sagged despondently in his chair, let out a weary sigh, and propped up his gloomy face upon his arms. His fingers found the scar and weal upon his cheek and began absently to caress it as if comforting the still raw wound. Perhaps, he thought resignedly, he would have to make his way back to Annapolis to find work aboard a ship. Who knows, with a little cleverness and cunning on his part, he might soon manoeuvre himself into a position from where he could take advantage - and thus haul himself out of this pit of unlucky fortune in which he now found himself. On the other hand, without a boatswain's ticket in his pocket to prove his qualification, he knew it would be impossible to gain employment in any capacity other than as a labouring deck hand – not something that he viewed with particular relish having had enough of it on the *Miranda* on the way over. Moreover, with news of his escape from Cowes undoubtedly abroad, he could not risk enlisting on any English ship – to be spotted by some English deckhand with an eye on a reward! His mind, plagued by such demons and difficulties, was in turmoil, and the prospect of obtaining Jack Easton's money was the single light that beckoned through a fog of desperation. It seemed the solution to all his woes. His thoughts kept returning to it. And he had lain awake night after night scheming the ways in which he might acquire it. With this one abject failure at the shipping office already behind him, he well knew that taking it would not be easy. Yet he had now seen the strong room and had glimpsed the tantalising array of boxes on its shelves, and this had given him an idea. Moreover, the sooner executed the better, he realised, since his bungled stick-up might have alerted Harding to the power of its allure and precautionary measures might soon be put in place. For his plan to succeed, however, he knew straight away that he would need some help. But at least he was now quite certain that there would be enough in the strong room to share.

The Brandywine hotel was located on the turnpike that linked Annapolis with several important settlements and ports in the western part the colony. And with a number of possibilities available for crossing the Potomac further down its route, the road was also a major thoroughfare to Virginia. The bedrooms and dormitories at the hotel most evenings were thus almost always full to capacity, particularly since the establishment was as low in price as it was rustic in its comforts and décor. Like Judd himself, some would sometimes stay for days, perhaps even weeks at a time - for example when work was offered nearby for itinerant tradesmen or seasonal plantation workers. During Judd's stay, a small community of such transient folk had developed, including some who were clearly opportunists and those of doubtful character, to provide a core of habitual users of the saloon during the evening hours. And to these there would be added a regular ebb and flow of visitors of lesser tenure, so that there always seemed to be a bustle about the place. Judd had now been a resident himself at the hotel for several weeks and was thus a familiar face, although it must be said that he had not been overly engaging. Other than to take part occasionally in the gambling games that were a common pastime there, he had kept himself pretty much to himself. Indeed, his reputation for winning at cards seemed to have deterred all but unwitting newcomers from inviting him to their tables. Most evenings, therefore, he had found himself drinking alone in the saloon in a corner that had taken on the nature of a private lair into which only the innocent would enter – and generally only once in their stay.

After his enraged and spiteful setting ablaze of the Easton farm some two months before, Judd had wandered from place to place, living rough and avoiding contact - thinking at first that he might be pursued. Eventually, more out of weariness than any particular plan he had retraced his earlier outbound route to Brandywine, a place with which he had at least a passing familiarity. The hotel was what might be called a doss house, avoided by discriminating travellers who shunned its seedy appearance and the evidently rough nature of its clientele. It had been here that Jack and Matthew had stayed on their way to Charlestown, in company with the good-natured group of itinerant tradesmen, and where Jack had had his encounter with Hayward in which Judd had intervened. And it was also from here that Judd had more recently mounted his hastily contrived attempt on the shipping office having deduced, in a moment of sudden insight, that it was the depository for Jack's money.

From his dingy corner in the saloon, Judd was in the habit surreptitiously of inspecting newcomers as they entered, sizing them up first for any threat but also for the possibility to have cash won from their purses. It was now only perhaps a month short of the summer solstice, and the rays of the late-setting sun shone brightly through the west-facing window, cutting the smoky air like a gleaming sword and spotlighting the door as if signalling some auspicious entrance. Its incandescent trail lit up the swirling airborne particles as if afire, and imprinted a stark crucifix of shady lines upon the door like an aiming reticule projected by the window's frame. Several groups of men had already entered the saloon to find themselves at once dazzled by the light and had retreated, half blinded, to the recesses of the room to find a seat, shunning the few tables still blighted by the illumination. Judd had watched the groups enter from the relative darkness of his corner, shielding his face at each arrival with his mug of ale as a further measure of concealment. He had taken to wearing a bandana under his black tricorn and had trimmed his facial hair from the unruly straggle that it had lately become, to a neat if not dapper appearance. It would thus take more than a casual inspection to reveal his identity (notwithstanding his facial scar that would not frustrate familiar recognition) but he remained cautious nevertheless.

The latch lifted again with a penetrating clack, and Judd's alert glance was at once drawn towards the opening door. Again, he lifted his mug to his mouth and tipped it as if taking a draft, thus concealing his face. Another group of men now entered – Judd counted four of them as they came in one behind the other, the last entering after a noticeable gap in the procession - as if his comrades had been his vanguard. The first three were rather brutish by appearance, having a pugnacious and watchful air about them as if expecting trouble. Judd had studied them closely. Anticipating that the last man in would be out of the same mould, Judd was taken by surprise by his appearance. For a start, he was a good six inches taller than the others and he held his head in a manner that exuded confidence. Although the man's beard and hair had clearly seen no recent professional grooming, and the fit of his clothes was decidedly poor, his face was finely boned; and he had such assuredness of demeanour that he seemed a most unlikely companion to the first three. Yet the four were clearly on intimate terms by the looks that passed between them, and the taller man's authority over the group was quite apparent. Shielding their eyes from the sun's bright incoming rays, the foursome bunched together in some uncertainty at first, hesitating before selecting from the few remaining vacant seats, apparently to let their eyes adjust. They seemed such an unlikely combination of characters that Judd continued to watch them as they seated themselves at one of the brightly sunlit tables, in which light he was able to steal easy glances across the now quite crowded space. The entry of the group had drawn inquisitive stares from others in the saloon, and the loud chattering of voices had dipped momentarily as the scrutiny had run its course. But interest must have quickly waned, for the volume of alcohol-stoked banter in the smoke-filled room soon returned to its earlier tumultuous level.

Eventually, the innkeeper approached the newcomers in his usual off-hand and slovenly manner, treating the arrivals with calculated indifference. But as the man engaged the group, he was seen visibly to stiffen and his manner to become at once attentive if not fawning. It seemed to Judd that something stern had been said, or else perhaps some coinage had been exchanged to effect such a transformation, for thereafter the innkeeper seemed to treat the group with unusual respect. It was during this observed interchange that the first inklings of recognition entered Judd's mind. Something about the tall man in particular set bells ringing in his memory. The apparent leader of the group - let us say 'gentleman', for that was how Judd assessed him - was now seated in such a position at the table that Judd could see the full profile of his face as he addressed the innkeeper. His words could not be heard above the surrounding din but, in view of the hour, it seemed likely that he must be enquiring about accommodation. At first, Judd could not place the hazy recollection of the gentleman's features that hovered just out of reach in his mind. But as the enquiry continued, it began to dawn upon Judd that he was looking at the fugitives from the *Miranda* - last seen from aloft in the yards as he had watched their escape.

In his earlier wanderings about the county, Judd had spotted copies of Jack's sketch posted upon the walls and boards where notices of runaways and felons were customarily displayed. It was a sacred principal amongst landowners that runaways should be hunted down and flogged to show their fellow slaves and servants that flight would not be tolerated. The offer of rewards for recapture was thus not unusual. But that offered for Pettigrew and his group was conspicuously high. At fifty pounds, the sum was at least half their market value and this put a very pretty price upon their heads; and Jack's sketch had made the poster uncommonly eye-catching, for it was rare to show a likeness. Judd found it amusing that in this very saloon, such a poster had been displayed until quite recently when, in a fit of idle malice against its artist, he had removed it, thinking that some use might come of it in due course. But the Pettigrew who now sat so near at hand was not the face portrayed upon the poster. Just as Judd himself had changed his appearance to effect disguise, so had the former transport. And as Judd knew very well, the alterations required to confound recognition by all but the most intimate acquaintances were comparatively slight: a different styling of the hair, the removal or acquisition of a wig, the growth or the trimming of a beard, even the affectation of a simple eye-patch! Any of these would be sufficient when assessed against a likeness drawn from memory – and especially when the facsimile had lost something of its accuracy in its transfer to a printer's engraving block. In Pettigrew's case, the extension of his sideburns to meet the facial hair above and below the lips had made a remarkable alteration to the framing of his face, such as to alter its apparent proportions almost to an unrecognisable degree. But Judd was not fooled, and there was no doubt in his mind that it was Pettigrew whom he now watched with such inquisitive speculation. Clearly the group had also quickly acquired new clothing, for in their prisoner's garb they would not have remained at large for long. But Judd had also noticed that underneath their rough and crumpled topcoats, each had secreted a pistol in his leather belt. And he made a mental note to be similarly armed if he approached them, for it had occurred to him that they may be just the sort of men he was looking for.

With this in mind, Judd continued to steal glances at the group as the evening wore on. Meanwhile, the sun's penetrating rays first turned amber, then dwindled and died, leaving the window through which the rays had shone eventually so black that it became a mirror of the candle-lit activity inside. But Judd had not paid much attention to this as Pettigrew and his companions had consumed their evening meal. It seemed to Judd that most of the discourse at the table appeared to take place without Pettigrew taking much part; or at least if he did so, it was not with his fulsome engagement. There was some ribaldry between the other three that seemed to be predominantly of a coarse nature judging by their gestures and loud guffaws. Their table manners too, left something to be desired, even to Judd's unrefined eye; and their behaviour became coarser yet as the evening passed and as the ale flowed. But throughout all this, Pettigrew was strangely detached and his mind seemed elsewhere; and if he did engage his companions, it was with barely concealed disdain. Despite this aloofness, however, there was no doubt that it was Pettigrew who was in charge of the group for they deferred to him, even in their inebriated state, and it was he who had the attention of the innkeeper, evidenced by the alacrity with which the man attended the table when on several occasions he was summoned.

As cover for his observation, Judd feigned an interest in a game of cards played at an adjacent table while sipping from his mug, the meanwhile contemplating the possible ways by which he might profit from this encounter with the escapees. From those he had considered, he had quickly dismissed the idea of seeking the reward offered for the group's capture. This was not only for the obvious reason of his own possible notoriety, but also because he saw instantly that employing the group might yield a higher return. After all, each might help the other to mutual advantage in a common cause. Like them, he was a fugitive from the law facing an uncertain life of escape and evasion until he could rid himself of pursuit; and so they, like he, might have a similar inclination to gain allies for protection in an unfamiliar land. And perhaps for a small share of the contents of the shipping office strong room, these men could be persuaded to join him in a temporary alliance?

But before he could reach any kind of resolution on this matter, the group stood up and made to depart, evidently with the intention to retire. Pettigrew was the first to get to his feet and his gaze swept the room nonchalantly as he hitched up his breeches and smoothed the wrinkles from his coat with an almost fastidious air. The distracting mannerism appeared innocent enough until Judd found himself suddenly the object of Pettigrew's scrutiny. Judd had been too slow to drop his eyes and for a moment their gazes locked - Pettigrew's: calculating and fiercely appraising; Judd's: startled, like those of a child caught stealing from the pantry. The moment passed in an instant as Judd wrenched his gaze away, trying to disguise his fright with a display of sudden interest in the nearby card game. But he felt his face flush and his heart begin to pound, and it was some time before he could again look back - by which time the group had left the room. It was at this point that he noticed the window's reflections, and it only then occurred to him that while he had been watching Pettigrew, Pettigrew might very well have been watching him, and the thought made him feel distinctly uneasy.

After his uncomfortable moment had passed, Judd did not linger much longer in the saloon and soon made his way out, entering an adjoining corridor through the residents' door. The passageway that then lay before him was so poorly lit (by a single candle flickering on a nearby table) that the dim light penetrated barely half its length. A number of darkly recessed doorways opened off on both sides, like ranks of sentry niches fading into the distant gloom from which the banister of a stairway could just be seen ascending at the far end. In the flickering light, the dark openings seemed to throb with the pulse of living things, giving them an eerie semblance of brooding life, the stuff of childhood nightmares. In comparison with the warm fug of the saloon, the air in the corridor was cold, and Judd pulled his coat around him as a shiver ran up his spine. His mind had not given form to it, but a strange sense of foreboding had begun to dog him. And suddenly eager to reach the safety of his room, he crossed quickly to the table and picked up one of the unlit candleholders waiting there for residents' use. He took a spill and held it in the extant flame, which dimmed alarmingly before flaring as the taper lit. His hand shook as he conveyed the fragile light to his own wick, and in its burgeoning flame, contorted shadows of his form grew upon the nearby wall. He caught the shadowy movement in the corner of his eye and could not stop himself from shuddering as if a hostile presence loomed. The brightness of his candle caused his eyes to narrow so that when he turned from the table, the hallway had grown dimmer yet, and the end of the long corridor had faded from his sight. With rising anxiety, he hurried passed each dark doorway as if some danger lurked within. But the quickness of his passage stirred the air so that his candle flickered and went out and for a moment he was left blinded. The darkest spectres of his imagination now closed in and he found himself in panic and in flight, pacing with hurried tread into the dimness as his sight returned. It was with huge relief that his hand reached the banister, but he did not check his pace and ascended the stairs two treads at a time, feeling the hairs on the back of his neck begin to stand on end. Another candle burned dimly on a table at the top of the stairway and he forced himself to pause there to relight his own; his breathing now was short and rapid from his exertions and his eyes flicked nervously from side to side. His temporary blindness had terrified him and he craved light as desperately as a drowning man craves air. Light was the shield that held back the demons that now manoeuvred at the edge of darkness, and it was thus a great relief to see his wick once more catch alight.

A landing stretched before him into distant gloom. Longer than the one below, it was similarly lined with pairs of recessed doorways opposite each other; but the candlelight did not quite reach his own doorway located at the very end. He proceeded slowly - almost on the balls of his feet - as if to quieten his tread on the bare floorboards, and he held out his candle to gain some view into each doorway before he got too close. He felt suddenly very vulnerable without his pistol to protect him, but he carried his knife in his pocket and his hand almost unconsciously sought it out. It was a comfort when he felt the cool metal of the blade upon his fingers, but the muted echoic noises drifting upwards from the saloon could not drown out the sound of blood thumping in his ears with every heartbeat. The first pair of doorways was empty and so he continued onwards. The second pair was the same. And now the third - empty too. By this time he was beginning to think that his fear had been irrational, that he had made too much of Pettigrew's threatening stare – and that it had been foolish to imagine that the thuggish trio had been sent to lie in wait. Judd continued now less timidly as if bolstered up by the sense of his own argument, but his heartbeat still raced palpably - and as his own doorway neared his pace quickened until his last few strides were almost at a run.

His door was like a blessed sanctuary and, without pausing to look behind, he lifted the latch and bundled himself inside, closing the door behind him and slamming home the bolt. With his movement, the flame of his candle flickered and began to die, and he held himself absolutely still to give the delicate light a chance to stabilise. The flame flickered back to life, its expanding circle of light progressively seeking out the recesses of his room; but it was not until the flame had reached an incandescent whiteness that he became aware that he was not alone.

Pettigrew sat calmly on the bedside chair with his legs casually crossed, his expression apparently one of mild curiosity rather than hostility. But then Judd noticed the pistol resting in the intruder's lap and that his fingers were curled around its butt. Instinctively, Judd's right hand went to his pocket to locate his knife. He pulled it out, but in a flash, strong hands grabbed him from the side, taking hold of his wrist in an iron grip and forcing his arm back and up to an unnatural angle. He struggled, but only briefly, for a warm gust of alcoholic breath assailed him as someone rasped into his ear: 'drop it, or feel this steel rip your guts wide open!' It was said with such vehemence that he was stunned to stillness, and he felt his fingers open as a bolt of piercing pain shot up his tortured upper limb. The knife slipped from his hand onto the floorboards with a clatter, but the pain did not relent. His assailant held him with such force that it was now impossible to resist, and the grip was so powerful that it felt as though his whole arm would be wrenched from its socket. Stifling a cry through gritted teeth, his back arched into a paroxysm as the grip tightened yet further. His limbs set into a grim contortion, his free arm outstretched with the candleholder still locked in an involuntary grip. The candle's wavering light threw ghastly shadows of the spectacle upon the adjacent wall. It was a scene from hell. And then he felt his knees begin to buckle as the light began to dim. Then another pair of hands grabbed him roughly to stop him slumping to the floor, while another deftly relieved him of the candle and held it so close to his face that his eyebrows singed audibly in the searing heat, forcing out another tormented cry. Now held fast at both sides and blinded by the candle's flame, he expected at any moment to feel the first blow to his stomach and he tensed in terrified anticipation.

But instead he heard Pettigrew shout a curt order: 'That will do, gentlemen!' and felt himself at once released from his restraint. Nursing his bruised wrist and shoulder, he glanced quickly left and right. His three molesters had stepped back but hovered menacingly, close enough to make another lunge should he attempt retaliation. But against such overpowering odds it was immediately clear that he would have no hope. The three men eyed him gloatingly, their apparent nonchalance more frightening than any scowl. It was the sheer bulk of their brooding presence that took Judd's breath away so that at first he found it impossible to speak. Instead, he stood rooted to the spot like a rabbit caught in the glare of a lamp, the object of Pettigrew's continuing calm appraisal.

It seemed several long seconds before the seated intruder spoke: 'You were watching me in the saloon,' he said in such a level tone that its lack of any threatening edge took Judd by surprise. 'And I was curious as to your interest. Are we perhaps in any way acquainted?' Pettigrew spoke smoothly, his face an impassive mask save for the lifting of an enquiring eyebrow.

Judd's mind now began to race as he calculated how best to play his part so as to gain advantage. He knew instinctively that equivocation would show weakness, and that in such company, it would be boldness and guile that would win him ground rather than any show of submission.

'I know who *you* are,' he said as plainly as his pounding heart allowed. 'I was a crewman aboard the *Miranda* and watched your escape – you took a father and his son as hostages (the thugs gave out a callous snort at this). And I heard your altercation with Easton. From what was said between you, it seems that we have a common grudge against him - the man seems to have been the cause of both our situations.'

'Was he indeed?' replied Pettigrew, almost with indifference. 'Go on.'

Judd decided to be candid.

'I was previously the boatswain on the ship *Rebecca* on which Jack Easton crossed to England last fall. He tumbled a nice little earner that I had going with some of the cargo that … er, shall we say, got transferred onto my *special* manifest for private sale. Between him and the first officer who I had …' Judd hesitated again, searching for the appropriate word, 'er…*persuaded* to turn a blind eye to my activity, I was led into a trap and found myself apprehended.' He scowled. 'But with some help from outside, I was able to escape and get off the island by finding a berth aboard the *Miranda* as a deck hand. It was not until we had already sailed that I realised that Easton and the same first officer, Goddard, by then promoted the *Miranda's* captain, were both aboard. I had to keep my head down during the voyage, but it now appears that it was a lucky encounter after all.'

'Oh?' uttered Pettigrew in a mildly interested tone, yet with an expression that revealed either indecision or distrust.

Meanwhile his henchmen shuffled their feet as if impatient with the discourse.

Judd continued quickly, feeling the threat of their presence and hoping to say enough to keep them at bay:

'I have discovered the location of a sum of money,' he said, believing that the offer of some bait might be useful at this stage. 'Made up partly of the substantial sum that Easton brought back with him – his share of the prize from a captured French brigantine, from which I ought also to have received a share but was cheated of it!' On this latter point Judd's voice took on a bitter edge. 'But following my recent reconnoitring of the place where it is kept,' he continued, carefully skirting the details of his recent bungled robbery, 'it seems that there might now be considerably more locked up with it. My problem is that it is too well guarded to take it on my own.'

'And you are offering us a cut for our assistance, I assume?' said Pettigrew with a cynical smirk. 'How very generous of you, but we have plans of our own, I'm afraid.' He smiled contemptuously then fell silent for a moment as if in thought before continuing: 'Nevertheless, if you are indeed a seafaring man - bosun of the *Rebecca* no less, we could yet be of use to each other.' Pettigrew had a mysterious air about him as he said this, his eyes throwing a meaningful glance at the nearest of his companions at the same time.

Out of the corner of his eye, Judd noticed the man nod a response. If any of the three henchmen had an ounce of cleverness about them, it was he, Judd thought; the other two seemed as knuckle-headed as prize-fighters, and their dull-eyed leers as moronic. Judd kept his expression carefully neutral, signifying neither interest nor scorn. Something told him that Pettigrew was not finished yet.

Pettigrew pondered for a moment. 'Wait outside,' he said at last, flicking a commanding glance at his companions who responded without question and left the room, closing the door quietly behind them.

'Your name, sir,' asked Pettigrew plainly.

'My name is Judd.'

'Then kindly sit, Mr Judd,' said Pettigrew, waving his hand airily at the only other chair in the room.

Judd was wary. The pistol still sat threateningly in Pettigrew's lap and he could see that his inquisitor remained on his guard. Trying to look more confident than he felt, Judd made his way over to the small writing table on which the candle now flickered lazily in the slight draft from an adjacent window. He took the nearby seat. The two men now faced each from opposite sides of the room with Judd's bed lying squarely in between.

Pettigrew eyed Judd appraisingly, then said at last: 'If I judge your character rightly, Mr Judd, it is possible that you might be open to a proposition.' He took out a folded paper from his jacket pocket and threw it onto the bed with a careless flick of his wrist. 'Take a look at that.'

Judd rose from his chair, retrieved the paper, returned, and unfolded it before him on the table using the candleholder as a paperweight to keep its edge from rolling back. It was a shipping notice: the sort commonly seen on notice boards advertising ships' movements in the advancement of trade. Judd was puzzled by it, but skimmed its contents nevertheless, looking for the clue that would give it the importance that Pettigrew evidently attached to it. The first paragraph gave notice of a vessel departing Annapolis for England with space aboard for passengers and cargo. The second, another bound for the Caribbean offering the same. The third, advertised an inbound vessel to Baltimore laden with metal goods from England that were to be auctioned on the quayside on arrival. Perplexed, Judd glanced across to Pettigrew who seemed to be watching in mild amusement.

'I fail to see...' Judd started to say, becoming mildly irritated at being played with like some dull child in a classroom.

'Read on,' Pettigrew called back.

Judd quickly rescanned what he had already read, wondering if he had missed something, and then continued on, reading now with more deliberation, his brow becoming wrinkled in his concentration in the poor light of the candle. Then he spotted something in the text that immediately caught his attention.

'Announcing the arrival from Dumfries, Va., the Ocean Sailing Vessel, Miranda, in Charlestown on or about 5th June 1758, where she will undergo minor repairs. Shipwrights and Carpenters available for approximately one week's work starting immediately on arrival should apply in person to the shipping agent: Thomas Harding Esq. at the port office...'

Judd wondered how the arrival of the *Miranda* could be of any interest to him, save that of knowing to keep clear of the port to avoid recognition by the crew. He looked up with this question written on his face. Pettigrew still observed him calmly, his eyes speculative, as if waiting for the penny to drop in Judd's deductive reasoning - but apparently he waited in vain.

'Read on, man,' said Pettigrew again; and Judd dropped his eyes once more to the text:

> '...*After completion of works, this reliable and swift Vessel will sail for England. The Ship carries Tobacco from Virginia bound for Cowes, but there remains space aboard at advantageous rates for Charlestown consignments. Enquiries for availability and rates etc to the Agent.*'

Judd looked up again, his blank expression quite devoid of comprehension. 'I don't understand,' he admitted at last, both puzzlement and irritation wrinkling his brow at the same time.

Pettigrew lifted an eyebrow. 'I thought a man of your obvious intelligence would see an opportunity to get even in a flash,' he taunted with an enigmatic smile.

Judd was nonplussed. 'I'm finished with revenge!' he said dismissively. 'I have to turn my attention to something more profitable now! And find safe territory where I will not be hunted down!'

'Quite!' said Pettigrew mysteriously, falling at once silent while his inscrutable gaze searched Judd's face as if awaiting some inkling of bolder thought. This obvious scrutiny seemed to unsettle the seaman, however, and he soon dropped his eyes again to the text, appearing to scrutinise it further. Finally, with a cross puff of exasperation, Judd raised his head and glared at his tormentor angrily.

'Pah! Enough of this,' he rasped impatiently. 'Tell me what *you* have in your mind, and then *I* will tell you what I have in mine.'

Chapter Fourteen

Jack leapt from the prow of the boat and landed with a splash in three inches of Potomac water. He could not have timed his jump more ineptly, for he arrived on the beach at just the same time as the boat's own bow wave. Almost before hitting the water, his legs were in motion, sprinting for the dry ground as if fleeing some mortal enemy rather than merely trying to preserve his boots. He cursed audibly; stamping his feet on the sand to shake the water off, then turned and shouted his thanks to the oarsman, now manoeuvring for his return. The schooner lay beyond, a mere fifty yards out, swinging at anchor in deep dark water. Jack scanned her decks as the oarsman pulled away from the shore and saw the schooner's crew already mustered. Soon, groups of men were at the mizzenmast hauling up the spanker, and at the mainmast raising the mainsail and the jib. The rustle of sails, stirred into life by the gentle morning breeze, joined the rhythmic squealing of halyards in their blocks and the clatter of a capstan taking up the slack; it was the age-old mariners' overture to the dawn. The muted sounds drifted to Jack's ears across the quiet water of the bay that lay so still that it might have been a mirror except for the disturbance of the returning boat. The schooner looked ready to depart. As soon as the oarsman had brought his little vessel alongside, the schooner would weigh anchor and be off.

Jack did not have long to wait to see her go. He raised a hand to shield his dazzled eyes from a rising sun that turned the vessel's sails to gold and saw her head began to swing downwind. The light easterly breeze had caught her jib as her anchor had broken out, and she seemed now to be pivoting almost on the spot. And soon she was on a dead run out into the open water with her mainsail and her mizzen filled, gull-winged, and her foresails flapping lazily in their lee. With her sweeping lines and her tall, slender sails, she made an elegant sight as she quietly slipped away, and Jack could not help but admire her. Sir Michael stood alone at the stern rail with his arms folded in a proprietary manner watching the helmsman at the wheel; Jack half expected a farewell wave from the colonel, or at least an acknowledging glance, but the colonel never looked back. It was while watching for this gesture that the gold letters of the schooner's name, emblazoned on her stern, caught Jack's eye: *'Warrior'*. It was the first time he had noticed it. But as he read the name, he smiled wryly to think that Sir Michael might rather fancy himself labelled thus, standing above the golden characters in his proud pose. Meanwhile, on the opposite side of the estuary, the barque too was already underway, her square sails dropping from her yards and filling with the breeze even as she glided from her anchorage.

It was not long before Jack lost sight of both vessels behind the wooded bluff that shielded their westward courses from his view. And it was only then that he started up the beach, feeling strangely liberated and abandoned at the same time. He was suddenly the lone soul within the sphere of all that he could see, from the endless woodlands that stretched around him to the far watery horizons behind; and he was struck with a sense of his own frailty in this vast and silent space. But for the distant Saint Thomas' Manor high up on the opposite shore, Jack could have been the first settler arriving on American soil.

Happy to be reprieved from military service, at least temporarily, the task to which he had been assigned was still so vague that he could not imagine how he might set about it. The first job would certainly be to make sure that the strong room and his money were protected. But it would take a permanent and substantial armed guard to *guarantee* its security against any serious attempt; a measure that he knew would be neither practical nor sustainable. Harding's old retainer with his blunderbuss was at least both of these, and would have to be enough; he, his blunderbuss, and the safe's iron casing! And as to helping the sheriff track down Judd and Pettigrew (if indeed the latter were even in the area) - well, where on earth would he start? Must he thunder around the county at full gallop in a posse on the off chance of stumbling upon them, he wondered? He derided the thought. At the same time he knew it would be unendurable simply to sit and wait for one or the other to make his move. Yet this was all that occurred to him at the present time. One thing seemed for certain, however, as he struck out along the river path towards the town - he would soon find himself once more pitted against forces that seemed determined to destroy everything that he had built up. And once again, he felt himself profoundly ill equipped for the fight; and he prayed for the Lord's good help that he would somehow be shown the way.

The river path towards Charlestown on the western bank of the Tobacco River passes the customs' port of entry at Neal's Landing about two miles inland from the river mouth. It was here that vessels proceeding to or arriving from overseas ports are required to report to allow their cargoes to be assessed for tax. The landing also represents the furthest point upriver to which large vessels of deep draft can safely navigate. Because of the tall trees on both sides of the riverbank, however, and the quirky or failing winds that frequently result, skippers often find themselves requiring the assistance of boats to draw them into or out of the port. Moreover, the shifting silt banks in the river pose a constant danger of grounding for those who do not know the waters well, and it is prudent therefore for foreign skippers to seek local help. The oarsmen for these sturdy workboats, at other times stevedores or jobbing labouring men at the wharf, supplement their living from such work, and rally for duty when called. And when a vessel's arrival is signalled from the lookout point on Saint Thomas' bluff, the boats will often assemble at the river mouth in the expectation of trade.

As Jack walked the path along the river, he was therefore not surprised to see three such boats being rowed out in some haste, each with a standing coxswain at the tiller and eight oarsmen bent to their oars. Stopping to watch the boats pass, he turned to look back to see what vessel they might be rowing out to meet and he was amazed to catch sight of a splendid three-masted square-rigger at the head of the river, her sails being furled from her yards even as she drifted closer in. The vessel must have approached from the west to have come so near without him seeing her before. He had seen no sail at all as he had stood upon the beach, yet there she was bearing down upon him in all her sunlit glory as if suddenly manifested from the ether. There being no particular reason why he should press on to town with any urgency, Jack decided to wait and watch the spectacle of the vessel's passing. He thus seated himself on a fallen tree trunk from which he was able to gain an elevated view of the river through a gap in the overhanging canopy of branches. He saw the ship's bowlines being lowered to the boats, and then watched as the oarsmen took up the slack so smoothly that it appeared that the vessel never came to a stop. It was as if the rendezvous had been perfectly timed so that the need to drop an anchor might be avoided. It was a fine piece of piloting, thought Jack, for whom the operation was a perfect distraction to his earlier melancholic mood.

The merchantman soon approached Jack's position, and so for the first time he obtained a clear view of her hull, beam-on and pressed towards him in the narrowing confines of the river. The procession glided by soundlessly but for the steady plunge of oars into the water and the thumping beat of their rowlocks, which somehow seemed perfectly synchronised even between the three boats. It was at this point that something made Jack sit up and look closer, for surely the vessel was familiar? The graceful upsweep of her prow; the gun ports forward under the forecastle; the tall raked masts making her look every bit a ship of the line? Jack was now standing on his tree trunk, not quite believing what he saw. He cast a glance to the raised quarterdeck and there was at once no further doubt in his mind, for standing so attentively behind the helmsman stood Philip Goddard in his merchant captain's uniform. It was the *Miranda*! And Jack was struck instantly with the thought that his earlier prayer for help had been answered, for he would now have an ally who would share his interest in Judd's recapture.

Cupping his hands to his mouth, he shouted excitedly: 'Philip!' at the top of his voice. So close by, it was impossible for his friend to miss such a bellowing call from the woody banks, and Jack saw him casting his gaze about. Jack waved both arms, then cupped his hands to his mouth again, and called, lest Goddard should not recognise him from this distance: 'Philip! It's me, Jack!' He waved again. This time it was clear that he had been spotted - and that he had been recognised too, for Goddard returned the wave with equal enthusiasm, then pointed forward as if indicating the landing ahead, which from Jack's elevated position he could now see through the trees. 'I'll see you there!' Jack shouted, leaping from his tree trunk and striding out to get ahead.

Jack was already waiting on the landing as the *Miranda* was brought abeam and turned-about midstream, the boats coaxing her in this manoeuvre as deftly as it was necessary to be with so little room for error. In the peace of the river, there was no wind or tide to take her, and so she turned almost on the spot. Then, with her bowsprit at last pointing determinedly back in the direction from which she had come, she was brought into her allotted berth, closing with such gentleness that her fenders hardly murmured as contact with the quay was made. Jack watched as the vessel was made fast. And he was soon joined by others waiting to go on board, including, not long after, the coxswains of the boats, who were no doubt eager to get their fee. These men, like the noisy crowd of oarsmen congregating alongside their boats already resting on the nearby slip, appeared to be of a certain type: big men, ebullient, uninhibited and boisterous. They reminded Jack of the itinerant tradesmen with whom he had travelled from Annapolis: jobbers who might turn their hand to anything for money. Good men to have on your side, thought Jack, as he sized them up out of the corner of his eye, but men who might have the boots from under your bed otherwise. The *Miranda's* gangway was soon swung into place and, with neither let nor leave, the three coxswains surged forward and up it in a manner that recognised no precedence or earlier claim. It could not even be said that Jack and the others waiting courteously deferred, for they were as nothing to these burly boatmen as they shouldered by. Jack found himself mildly affronted at their rudeness as he followed up the gangway in their wake, trying to think up some apposite sarcasm by way of rebuke. But arriving on deck, the trio immediately veered off towards a ship's officer standing beneath the forecastle companionway with a clipboard under his arm. It was probably a blessing that Jack got no ready chance to give his irritation vent for he would have got back tenfold what he might have given. And diverted by acknowledgements from familiar faces in the crew as he made his way aft, the incident quickly disappeared from his mind.

He reached the companionway to the quarterdeck and began to climb, spotting Goddard at the rail looking down. Their eyes met and both grinned a greeting.

'You were the *last* person I expected to see in Charlestown!' Jack called. 'And just when I needed a friend too! What a fortunate coincidence!' He took Goddard's hand and shook it with such vigour that his friend was visibly taken aback.

'Then the coincidence is undoubtedly more for you, Jack, than for me,' laughed the captain heartily, 'for my itinerary was that I should arrive on the fifth day of June on the rising tide, and it is that day and that tide precisely!' But in an aside, he added with a wry smile: 'I confess my timely arrival was as much by favourable winds as by superior seamanship, Jack; but the crew credit me with the latter nevertheless, and I do not intend to disabuse them of it. Did you not anticipate my arrival then? Surely I told you of my sailing instructions before you left Annapolis, hoping that you might find your way here?'

'Ah!' Jack stuttered. The events of recent weeks had quite displaced the memory of *Miranda's* planned itinerary from his mind. Remembering now, Jack felt somewhat abashed at his forgetfulness but hid it expertly: 'Very well, I admit that I was taken by surprise to see you arriving, Philip, but if I recall correctly, you said you would be here in early summer for your refit, but were no more precise than that. How could I have judged the moment so accurately? Nevertheless, it is a stroke of lucky happenstance that we meet. My business here is of a more serious nature, I am afraid to say, and your arrival is fortuitous.' Jack's tone and demeanour became suddenly earnest at this point, and the beaming smile that still resided on his friend's face vanished just as quickly. 'In any event, I am glad to see you, Philip,' continued Jack, 'but I have some disturbing news to tell you, and as soon as you can be relieved of your duty on deck, we must speak of it urgently.'

'Then wait below in my cabin, Jack, and I will be with you as soon as I am finished here - but surely you can give me some hint of the nature of this news?'

Jack hesitated, about to beg his friend's patience, but then relented. 'Judd's here,' he uttered at last with heavy breath; and with these two words, Goddard's face turned first incredulous then appalled, the colour draining from it even as Jack watched.

It was thus in Goddard's cabin an hour or so later that the pair spoke in private and at length of the events that had befallen Jack since his departure from Annapolis, the discourse finally turning to the matter of Judd at large, which was clearly a potential danger to them both. At first, Jack meant to spare his friend the details of the fire and its tragic aftermath but he yielded to Goddard's innocent appetite to know every particular, ultimately revealing all that had occurred. On this subject, Jack spoke in even tones without emotion, exhibiting a cool detachment that puzzled the captain, who must have wondered if his companion was really as robust as he seemed.

'You speak so lightly of it, Jack,' he interjected, whilst his brow wrinkled in concern. 'And your wife?' he asked tentatively.

'I think that Rose is more hurt than she reveals, but she puts a brave face on it. We have been through so much, the two of us...' he hesitated here, as if choosing his words carefully, '...it seems as if these things have been sent to try us in some way, though for the life of me, I do not know what we have done to deserve such singular treatment. I tell you, Philip, sometimes I feel as if I am being pitched against Lucifer himself! First Smyke, and now Judd – and Pettigrew too who is also apparently still on the loose and almost certainly up to no good!' He sighed heavily, as if to put a stop to such dismal talk. 'But let us not dwell on this further.'

It is in the nature of men to pass over such matters lightly and superficially, and in this deceit the pair became complicit as soon as it was evident to Goddard that he had strayed onto sensitive ground. He shifted in his chair.

'Well, I am sorry for you, Jack – and for your wife, of course,' he said uneasily. 'And I feel myself partly to blame, for it was I who drew you in to my affairs, thus making you Judd's target too.'

'We did each other a service if I remember correctly, Philip;' Jack insisted. You need not blame yourself.'

The pair continued their somewhat fretful discussion on this theme on and off throughout the day, interrupted by Goddard's frequent need to return to the deck to attend to matters requiring his attention. Each interruption left Jack pacing the cabin impatient to resolve a course of action, yet he still had no firm idea of how best he might direct his energies. And each time the captain returned to the cabin, their conversation resumed - often covering the same ground several times - until all possible conjecture as to Judd's likely intentions had been done to death. It was Jack's revelation that Judd had been aboard the *Miranda* on their voyage to Annapolis that had most astonished his friend. The thought of Judd's brooding presence lurking so close and unnoticed throughout the voyage had clearly troubled him deeply since he kept returning to it. But it took some time before he began to piece together the full implications.

'My God, Jack!' Goddard said breathily. 'We both know how suspicious and vindictive he is. He would have taken every opportunity to learn anything that might advantage him. I think we must assume that he now realises that we set him up for capture.' He shook his head in dismay. 'Pah! Our clever plot for his entrapment so carelessly undone.'

'Yes, Philip. Indeed! He most certainly discovered that I carried my prize money with me, for he followed me all the way to New Hope! And his attempt on the shipping office shows that he has deduced where it is now located. And I fear that that will not be the end of it! You can be sure that if he gets wind that you are here, you will become his target too. And so I would advise you to be on your guard!'

'Then what in heaven's name can we do to bring this wretched business to an end?'

'That is precisely what I am asking myself, Philip, and it is the reason that I am on the way to Charlestown. I have been given leave from my military conscription to report to Mr Harding and the sheriff to put myself at their disposal...'

Jack now found himself at once required to recount the nature of his commitment to Sir Michael de Burgh, and the latter's interest in the attempted robbery in Charlestown.

'There have been reports that Pettigrew is in the area, Philip, and everyone has leapt to the conclusion that it must have been he who was behind the attempt. And since I am the only one who would recognise him here, they want me to help them track him down.' Jack shrugged. 'I'm afraid that my drawing is proving to be more a distraction rather than a help,' he confessed. 'For people are seeing him everywhere! Even though he is certain to have changed his appearance, especially if he has seen his likeness scattered around the colony's notice boards! But, as I have already said, I am quite sure that it was Judd and not Pettigrew who tried his luck at the shipping office, and it is on Judd that you and I need to concentrate.'

'I agree, Jack,' Goddard nodded ruefully, 'And I thought we had seen an end of the bla'guard! I want to see him dealt with once and for all, and I will do all that I can while I am here. For a start - you are welcome to have your old cabin if that will be of use.'

'Thank you, Philip; I had not given my accommodation much thought, but now that you mention it, that would be most useful – and it would keep me out of town and out of sight. Following my heroics with Hayward's gang last fall, I am known too well. And there is every reason not to alert Judd to my being here – we don't want to put him on his guard, do we?'

'Hmmm.' Goddard shook his head thoughtfully. 'Yes, Harding and the sheriff can visit you here if they need to, can't they? And I shall instruct my officers to take over the supervision of the work and the loading so that I can be free to be with you. But I'm afraid that I'll have limited time to help, Jack – perhaps a week at the most. As soon as we've taken on our load here and finished the repair work, we must sail for England without further delay - I have a schedule to keep after all!' He raised his eyebrows expectantly. 'So!' he said brightly, 'where shall we start?'

'D'you know, Philip, I haven't got a clue!' Jack laughed. 'Let's get a message to Harding and the sheriff in the morning, shall we? That should get us started. Until then, isn't it time you arranged some supper for us? And I think that we should drink a glass or two of your very excellent wine to celebrate our reunion, don't you?'

It was no coincidence that that same day, another meeting was taking place not twenty miles away in Brandywine. It was at the corner table in a private room of the hotel there, that Pettigrew and his new associate,

Judd, in company with the self-appointed leader of the thuggish henchmen, were now seated as if participating in a sort of rough tribunal. Near to the entrance door, hovered henchmen two and three, their shoulders hunched, their canine faces eyeing the table attentively as if tasty scraps might be thrown from it for them to retrieve. A layer of blue smoke hung in the air like a film of thin silk. No one in the room moved yet the smoke swirled gently as if recently disturbed, and heavy footsteps could be heard retreating in the lobby outside. No one spoke, but the room was charged with expectancy as the seated men gazed thoughtfully at a sheet of paper opened before them. It seemed as if some important consideration were taking place. Breaking the silence, Pettigrew pushed back his chair and breathed a nasal sigh in which were mixed tones of satisfaction and resolve.

'And that was the last of them?' came his proposition at last, although it was more by way of confirmation than query. 'And perhaps only one or two amongst them who have chosen not to join us? The inn-keeper has served us well.'

During preceding days, the innkeeper of this less-than-reputable establishment had carefully spread the word amongst the most likely of his less-than-reputable clientele of a project that might take their interest. As a consequence, the morning had seen a succession of visitations to the tribunal table - a ragbag of belligerent and wary men who had stirred the smoky air, marshalled in and out with rough ceremony by the guardians at the door. These applicants had remained standing at the table just long enough for their qualities to be gauged and their qualifications assessed. This was a necessary process for, as will become clear in due course, the achievement of Pettigrew's audacious objective would demand as much tenacity and skills in the execution as it had demanded brazenness in its conception. The interviews had all followed a similar pattern. Without at first giving too much away, it was suggested that the proposed endeavour would be lucrative but potentially dangerous and require unquestioning obedience. Not all of the men had proceeded with the conversation beyond some initial fencing on these points, for some of the requirements of participation were not to their liking. But the great majority of those attending seemed more than eager for the chance to escape the hand-to-mouth existences in which such sorts often find themselves trapped. Amongst the chosen men, a certain well-spoken individual of patent intelligence and guile could be counted - someone noted by Pettigrew immediately as having potential for leadership within his embryonic organisation. Going by the name of Hayward, the man was neither known nor recognised by any of his interviewers, although unknowingly Judd had, of course, encountered him once before – notably while protecting Jack (and his money belt) from attack outside the very hotel in which he now sat.

By the end of the morning, a score or more candidates had made a pledge of loyalty; and these men between them more or less matched the composition of skills or aptitudes that Pettigrew and Judd had sought. And as for those few who had declined to take part, there would be no great buzz on the streets of Brandywine to give the game away, for there is an understanding amongst communities of this sort that lips remain buttoned when strangers are about. And this would be so even though the opening moves of the carefully planned endeavour were now imminent.

Pettigrew relit his pipe, drew upon it heavily, and exhaled the blue smoke into the air with a satisfied toss of his head.

'Then, gentlemen, I believe that we are ready,' he said calmly.

Judd caught his new associate's eye and nodded a confirmation.

'Aye,' he snorted. 'They'll probably start signing on their workmen first thing tomorrow morning and I'll send some of our new men down to the landing to join the line; I'll have others slipped aboard as the opportunity arises. Most of the crew are on shore leave whilst the repairs are underway, and the ship is taking on cargo at the same time, so there'll be plenty of activity to hide a few extra hands aboard.'

Judd reached into his jacket pocket and produced the shipping notice announcing *Miranda's* arrival and inspected it cursorily.

'Say's here that sailing's planned at the end of the week,' he said, smiling wryly. 'But I suspect that might be subject to some amendment; I still have a few friends on the waterfront who owe me a favour or two, and it's time to call in the debt. Goddard's going to get the surprise of his life!'

Sitting at the table with Judd and Pettigrew, the first henchman grinned conspiratorially, his blackened teeth revealed by increment as Judd's meaning slowly dawned; but henchmen two and three, still hovering at the door uncertainly, showed no apparent inkling of comprehension. While aping their companion's toothy smirk, their brows remained set like clenched fists, and the glances that passed between them were dull. It seemed that their contribution to the coming operation would not be of the intellectual kind, indeed all three may well already have served their purpose as far as Pettigrew was concerned. The latter meanwhile had remained indulgently passive during Judd's short discourse, but he now cleared his throat, drawing the attention of the others immediately upon him:

'Then I will leave the other matters to you, Mr Judd,' he said, enigmatically, and got to his feet.

'I shall retire to my room. When you have finished making your arrangements, perhaps you would be good enough to join me to discuss them.'

Chapter Fifteen

Early the following morning, a trusted messenger was sent from the *Miranda* to inform the sheriff and Mr Harding privately of Jack's arrival, and to extend an invitation for the pair to come aboard for a meeting at their earliest convenience. Jack's time thereafter was thus spent rather aimlessly awaiting their arrival since there was nowhere for him to go without risking recognition and nothing useful in which he might find occupation. By contrast, Goddard was fully engaged in the business of his ship, setting himself to various administrative tasks and to instructing the quartermaster and other officers who would supervise the repair work and the loading of cargo and victuals. While Jack took his ease alone and somewhat listlessly on the quarterdeck, the ship was quickly overtaken with activity, which by degree displaced him to the stern rail where he found himself a perch that seemed not to be in the way. But he was not to spend his time in tranquillity. The loud and coarse hollering of stevedores soon broke out from the holds and derricks as bulging cargo nets began to be swung in from the quay, accompanied by the clatter of rusty winches. Foremen shipwrights and their gangs wandered here and there according to some unknown plan, where they might stand sagely considering some item of damaged superstructure for a while, before setting men to work. Jack watched artisan sorted from apprentice in an obvious pecking order of competence and skills, and it was not long before their hammering and banging added yet more discordance to the growing din. And above all this bustle and industry, great wafts of smoke from the charcoal forge drifted about the decks, mixed with smells of hot rivets and scorched wood, to lend the ship a general air of anarchy.

More hammering and sawing from another group then sprang up nearby to disturb Jack's idle musing, the work this time under the direct eye of the quartermaster as if these men were either new or not entirely trusted. This caught Jack's attention and he too found himself drawn into observation, for these men were clearly of a different type to the others and seemed to work apart. The task that they had been allocated was simple by Jack's estimation – a detail of reinforcement to the quarterdeck rail to be achieved by adding stiffening timbers – but they seemed to be making a meal of it and Jack thought their manner impatient if not belligerent. Indeed, his observation was noticed by one of the group who flashed him a warning glance as if resentful of being watched. Jack quickly looked away, embarrassed to be thought prying, but he wondered at their manner all the same. It was at this point, however, that Goddard's beckoning call from the main deck interrupted his further thinking on the matter, and he responded with alacrity to the captain's call, glad at the prospect of some company at last. Striding to the companionway to join his friend, he left the surly gang behind him, thus not noticing their menacing glances.

It was not until late that afternoon that the sheriff and Thomas Harding arrived at the ship on horseback at a pace that suggested that they had ridden with some urgency. The lithe sheriff leapt from his saddle almost before coming to a halt and made his way up the gangway two treads at a time; Harding, his left arm in a sling, dismounted in some difficulty, assisted by a helpful seaman, and followed up the gangway with some awkwardness. Jack and Goddard had heard the heavy canter of hooves approaching and were thus already at the head of the gangway to greet their visitors as they arrived on deck. The sheriff, an imposing figure of dark complexion, clad in a hide jacket and wearing riding boots, was the first to grasp the hands of the receiving pair, and he did so with such strength that both Goddard and Jack could hardly conceal their discomfort. Harding's gentle grip was thus a relief as he took his turn. Stocky and less flamboyantly dressed than his companion in a sober dark jacket, the older man's face was flushed with exertion, his long silver hair ruffled to unruliness by the buffeting of his ride. Both men were short of breath and, judging by the brusqueness of their manner, evidently intent that no time should be wasted on pleasantries.

'Captain Goddard, good day to you, sir,' said the sheriff shortly. Then without so much even as a courteous smile, he turned to Jack. 'Mr Easton, I am glad to see you back, sir, and I am pleased that Sir Michael has allowed you to return as I requested. He will have informed you, no doubt, as to the circumstances behind my request?' Jack nodded and the sheriff continued almost without a pause: 'Your arrival then is indeed timely for I have today received intelligence that might make your presence necessary sooner than I thought. But first may we retire to the privacy of your cabin, captain, before I speak of it?'

The group retired and the discourse continued below. 'Firstly, may I say that your portrayal of Pettigrew's likeness has been most useful, sir,' the sheriff said, addressing Jack specifically on this point, '- for without it,

Pettigrew and his gang would most likely have got away Scot free, especially since we got no useful information from the wounded convict you left behind in Annapolis. And, I am afraid to tell you that their apprehension has now become a matter of more urgency with dreadful news that has reached me from the sheriff there only this morning. Pettigrew and his cohort are now being hunted for the murder of the two men they took as hostages, a father and his young son, I believe, whose bodies were found washed up on a beach near Point Lookout - with their hands tied behind their backs.'

The sheriff paused briefly as if to underline the gravity of this tragic turn, while Jack and Goddard exchanged glances that were both horrified and appalled. Neither seemed able to find words in response, but the manner of their breathing and the tightening of their features showed their absolute disgust.

'But there is some good news too,' the sheriff continued with a hopeful lift in his voice. ' I was visited this morning by a resident of Brandywine - a stranger to me but trustworthy enough by my estimation – who says that he saw Pettigrew in the hotel there last night. He brought a copy of your poster with him; and there was no doubt in his mind that it was Pettigrew he saw. He tells me that there were others with him well known in the town as being of doubtful character. I suspect that some of these will be on our wanted list too – indeed, you may have encountered one or two of them before, Jack! I speak of Hayward and his gang who I am pretty sure will still be in the area despite your grapple with them on your way through the town last fall.' His face assumed a slightly triumphant expression at this point. 'You know, this could be just the opportunity we have been waiting for! If we can act quickly, we could catch them all in one fell swoop and give our citizens a respite from the constant scourge of petty criminality.' The sheriff was in full flood now, but Jack interjected:

'And there is now likely to be another felon abroad, sheriff! You may already know him: Judd?' The sheriff shook his head doubtfully, and so Jack explained: 'He is a former boatswain of the *Rebecca* who used to call here - but now he is a prisoner on the run, and likely to be at large in this area. Sir Michael may have mentioned my misfortune at New Hope by his hands, which I will not repeat here; but Captain Goddard and I share an urgent interest in seeing him apprehended. He has cast a blight on both our lives.'

Jack now addressed the agent: 'Mr Harding, sir, you will remember that it was he who was apprehended for the embezzlement of cargo from your tobacco consignments.' (Harding nodded here, but frowned as Jack went on). 'Did Sir Michael not tell you of his subsequent escape and flight – and his attack on my homestead?' (To this, Harding shook his head, evidently taken aback by this news). The tightening of Jack's lips was a confirmation if Harding needed one, but Jack continued, hardly pausing in the exchange: 'Perhaps in Sir Michael's mind there was nothing to make the connection; but I am sure that it was Judd and not Pettigrew who held up your office. You may not be acquainted with the latter as I am, and thus may have misidentified him.'

'He wore a scarf over his face, Jack,' said Harding, cradling his left arm with his right, 'but you may well be correct. However, it was not my identification that suggested Pettigrew as the would-be robber but an assumption by others who had seen your poster and who came to this conclusion.' Here, Harding flashed a glance towards the sheriff before continuing. 'Nevertheless, it was not unreasonable in my view since our local felons would have known better than to try, and this man Judd, from your own report, was believed until now to be safely locked up in England.'

'All this is as may be,' resumed the sheriff impatiently; ' but if Pettigrew or Hayward, or any other felon for that matter, is holed up in Brandywine, then we must act quickly to round them up. And if this man Judd is amongst them, then so much the better!'

'And if you need my assistance, sheriff, then I am at your command,' said Jack quickly.

'Well, I propose to send a posse there during this very night so as to catch them unawares as tomorrow's dawn breaks. If you could come with us, Jack, you can confirm identities – if you are acquainted with Pettigrew you will also be familiar with his three co-escapees. And if it comes to a trial later, your evidence will be needed to ensure a conviction.'

Jack nodded his agreement: 'Captain Goddard too is acquainted with all four, having watched them escape from this very ship in the Chesapeake. I am certain that I could identify Pettigrew whatever his disguise, but of his co-escapees I am not so sure - having seen them only briefly and in somewhat stressful circumstances. I suggest, therefore, that the captain should accompany us!'

The sheriff's posse of fifteen men, all regular deputies or paid constables of the town, were already on their way to Brandywine by midnight. They took with them a wagon in anticipation of the several miscreants they hoped to apprehend, and the party proceeded along the road at a trot rather than a canter, commensurate with the vehicle's inability to move at speed. Jack Easton and Captain Goddard rode behind the wagon on mounts requisitioned from the livery according to the sheriff's powers, while the injured Harding, like all except one of the residents of the town, was already sensibly in bed. Only the aged caretaker, rocking his chair at the shipping office with a blunderbuss across his lap, remained awake to hear the nearby church bell striking the hour. If his hearing had been better, he might also have heard scuffling sounds in the alleyway outside.

The sheriff's posse was in position outside the Brandywine Hotel as dawn broke, and its members took up their encircling positions such as to ensure that there would be no escape for the inhabitants. Sitting astride their horses, Jack and Captain Goddard remained a little distance away under the cover of some trees, held back to be brought in later for their appointed task. At the sheriff's signal, the posse closed in: the main group, led by the sheriff himself, proceeding quietly towards the principal entrance, while the others moved to mark possible egress from the building at the rear and sides. Being an establishment serving an itinerant clientele who might come and go at any time, the entrance door was unsecured, and thus the sheriff and his group passed into the lobby without fuss. An oil lamp illuminated this open space with a spluttering flame that made the air heavy with the reek of oil. Giving his instructions by hand signal alone, the senior law-keeper assigned his men their different routes, the larger proportion up the stairway towards the bedrooms above, the rest towards the saloon and parlour.

It was the intention, commencing at a further signal from the sheriff, to cause such mayhem in the building, that its residents would be brought suddenly awake in such fear of their lives that they would flee from their beds in panic into the waiting net. And when the signal came, it was precisely thus. The explosion of noise and clatter created with such enthusiasm by the sheriff's deputies and constables, was followed in short order by a terrible commotion of thumps and bangs, the sound of a multitude of bare feet hitting the floor at great velocity. A torrent of rudely awakened men then rushed crossly from their doors (or climbed from their windows) in a state of undress, some stumbling or hopping in half-donned boots, others hitching up their trousers as they ran. One or two pistol shots punctured the air, though as likely by accident as by aim in the fumbling affray; and there was a great deal of shouting and running about in the gloom of dawn.

The trap was sprung.

The sun rose to illuminate a scene at the front of the hotel that resembled a corner of a cattle market where the runts of the heard are penned separately for sale below the market rate for better specimens. The cohort now held captive there by a girdle of armed constables was indeed as ragged and unappealing in appearance as it was fractious by manner. In due course, Jack and Goddard were summoned to inspect the protesting crowd by a triumphant sheriff expecting that familiar faces would at once be identified. Certain likely candidates had already been corralled off and it was to this group that the arriving pair was first directed. Each of these prime suspects was then brought forth, hands rudely tied, to stand before them. And on each occasion, Jack and his companion shook their heads. This first group at last spent, the sheriff turned his attention to those remaining, now more vocal and yet more fractious in their protests than before, and began the same procedure once again. And once again, Jack and his companion shook their heads as each protesting candidate was brought before them, until finally, all of the captives had been inspected to no obvious avail.

'We'll put them before you again!' called the sheriff, adamantly. He was by now becoming a trifle vexed. 'They may have disguised themselves – look more closely this time; they must be here!' he insisted. And so the procedure was re-run, this time more deliberately and more painstakingly than before. But again it was to no avail; and neither was there even the slightest doubt to raise their fragile hopes.

The same sun that had risen in Brandywine rose that same morning on the distant shipping office in Charlestown to find a very different scene. And when Harding approached the building by way of his customary route along the quay to start his morning's work, he was puzzled to see a throng of clerks and others assembled on the porch. His first thought was that some of his customers must have arrived for early business or otherwise that he had arrived late, and he instinctively checked his pocket watch. But then he realised that the nature of the congregation was not businesslike at all; indeed it had a most solemn air about it that at once alarmed him. He approached closer, now under a premonition of something untoward; and in a state of rising anxiety, he looked more closely, his eyes beginning to dart to and fro in his hunger for some reassuring evidence to quell his sense of foreboding. He could hear the assembly now, and its tone was not at all reassuring but rather doleful in its mutterings. Initially shielded from his view behind the cluster, he now caught sight of the front doors of his office. They hung open at an odd angle as if they had been pulled off their hinges, and several of those nearest appeared to be peering inside in some consternation. But then his eyes were drawn to the sidewall of the building adjacent to the alleyway, which was at that moment lit up by the sun's oblique light. Where once had been pristine painted clapboard was now a charred and gaping hole, at least half the height of a man. Smoke still curled outwards from within. The spectre stopped him in his tracks while he tried to make sense of what he saw.

Noticing Harding standing there, his senior clerk then broke away from the throng and made his way over in some haste.

'They've blown open the strong room and taken everything!' the clerk exclaimed breathlessly, his voice verging on hysterical.

'And the guard?' returned Harding quickly, already fearing the worst.

'Killed in the explosion,' said the clerk, dropping his voice. 'He didn't even get a chance to use his blunderbuss!' this last, uttered in some sorrow. 'Whoever it was, they blew out the wall and got straight in. It appears that they took some horses from the livery to make their escape, for there are several reported missing.'

The wagon travelled back from Brandywine quite empty, accompanied by a sheriff and a posse who hardly spoke throughout the four hours of their doleful journey. Behind them in the hotel, they had left a motley group of travelling men incensed at such rough and unwarranted treatment and an innkeeper who, while outwardly peppery with affront and indignation on their behalf, was highly satisfied with the outcome of his diversionary endeavours. It was late in the afternoon when the posse eventually arrived at the sheriff's office located in the Charlestown square and the day's light was already beginning to fail. Harding had been sent word of their coming and had come to meet them, approaching the dismounting riders in a state of utter distraction. Taken aback by Harding's manner (and not at first understanding the man's distress), the sheriff ushered him into his office, beckoning Jack and Captain Goddard to follow him, and sat the man down to calm himself. The mood was already despondent from the inauspicious raid, but it became utterly despairing as Harding told them of the robbery. (It should perhaps be added here that another robbery had taken place during the same night at Neal's Landing, a mile or so down river, and this would raise even more alarm in due course. But, diverted by the furore that was presently engulfing the town, no one had yet noticed it.)

'A dastardly trick,' swore Jack, resentfully stating a fact that was immediately obvious to all. 'They lured us out to Brandywine to get us out of the way.'

The sheriff looked nonplussed. Goddard shook his head in disbelief.

'This is not Judd's work alone,' said Jack bitterly, his heart plummeting to rock bottom at the thought of losing his precious capital. 'I smell Pettigrew at work in this too. Be warned, gentlemen, dark forces will have conspired here for this to have been pulled off with such audacity. And if Pettigrew and Judd have joined in an alliance, we all have much to fear.' *The master has got himself another puppet,* he thought.

'How much will they have taken?' asked the sheriff, urgently.

Harding did not answer at first, his mind seeming to be elsewhere as his gaze wandered about the room in such bewilderment. The sheriff asked again in a more strident voice that demanded Harding's attention.

'Oh,' the agent uttered in surprise. 'I am so sorry, sheriff; I am made distraught by this terrible event.'

The man is clearly still in shock, Jack thought as Harding continued:

'The loss of my caretaker; poor man - so quick to volunteer himself to guard the strong room following that first attempt upon it,' Harding rambled, distractedly. 'A former militiaman, you know - a brave man, and stronger and fitter than his years might suggest. He would have been a match for any robber. But no one could have anticipated a concerted attack of such magnitude. No one! It is unprecedented in the colony, I am sure.' His voice trailed off to nothing, and there followed a period of uneasy silence in the room with no one seeming to know quite how to respond.

Jack's heart went out to the agent, and he put a consoling hand upon the man's shoulder. 'The sheriff asked how much was taken,' he prompted gently.

'How much taken?' Harding replied, coming to his senses. 'I cannot tell precisely at this moment, for the office books seem to have been destroyed in the blast - but it will be a sizeable sum by any guess. And all in English notes...including your prize money, Jack, I am sorry to say. And also considerable sums held for Sir Michael and other plantation owners on account of their last shipments of tobacco. The payments due on their sales have only recently been received and were not to have been held for long; this robbery could therefore not have occured at a worse time. I keep records of transactions at my home, gentlemen; and so it would be possible to give you a better estimation if I consulted them.'

'Then I suggest we do that straight away,' said the sheriff, firmly. 'If you have details of the denominations or any other means of identifying these notes, I could list them in my report. The sooner we get that information out to trading houses, the more chance there is that we will be alerted of their exchange.'

'Of course,' said Harding. 'Shall we then walk up there together? And since it is now getting late, I suggest that you, Jack, and you, Captain, remain at my house to dine with me and stay the night, for it will be a long walk in darkness if you return to the landing from there tonight. Moreover, your company would be welcome as a palliative for our mutual distress.'

The prospect of a comfortable bed on dry land is always appealing to mariners if damp bedding and narrow bunks are the alternative, and so Jack and his friend accepted the offer readily. The threesome thus set off with Harding forthwith to climb the shallow ridge along which, in company of other distinguished houses of the town, Harding's house was situated. But the mood remained sombre up the winding path as darkness fell; and grew more sombre yet when Harding produced his accounts later in the evening.

'As I said gentlemen,' said he, gazing with some gravity at the paper held before him like an offering, 'a considerable sum. If I make no error in my arithmetic, the total amounts to some twenty thousand pounds!'

At this, the sheriff drew in his breath sharply. 'That is enough to start an army of their own!'

To which Jack added sagely: 'We must send a rider immediately to Georgetown to alert Sir Michael of this calamity. It is of such proportions that his mission to the Ohio might even be affected, and he will certainly wish to know of it before he proceeds further west. It will be up to him how he reacts, but it is at least our duty to inform him.'

'We'll dispatch a messenger first thing in the morning once we have spoken again, Jack,' said the sheriff with an air of finality; and he picked up his hat from the table and dusted it off. 'It is too late to talk further on this tonight, gentlemen,' he added with a note of resignation in his voice. 'We need clearer heads. And after such a day, I do not think it would be fruitful to go galloping off into the darkness on some wild goose chase. The gang will be a good day ahead of us and could have gone off in any direction. And if they have already tricked us once, they will no doubt try to trick us again - so we must not react too hastily. Come down to my office tomorrow morning and we will consider what to do.' And with that, he put on his hat and bid his companions farewell.

But he would be back at Harding's house sooner than that.

Chapter Sixteen

Pettigrew had not taken part in the raid on the shipping office, but from his waiting place, an abandoned barn at the edge of the town chosen for its clear view of the approaching roads, he had watched Judd's group set off and now waited for them to return. And he waited there calmly in the company of the larger remnant of his newly recruited legion as the early hours passed. It would not be until two strikes of the distant town bell that he expected Judd to return.

It was part of Pettigrew's persona to be calm. And if there were ever any uncertainty in his mind about anything, he never allowed himself to show it. He studied calmness, was impressed by it in others, and understood its importance, especially when in command, a position in which he was gratified once again to find himself. He was also quietly content, so far, with the reconstruction of his power. Although there was still some way to go before everything that he had lost would be recouped, he was now at last poised for a new ascendancy. His demise at the hands of Jack Easton and Lieutenant Andrew White in Weymouth had been an irritation, but he had borne it in the certain knowledge that he would rise again. His confidence in this had been unassailable. He had been schooled in a superior way to believe himself above others, and he had inherited the means and the position that gave this belief effect. The loss of all but a hidden fragment of his wealth following his conviction at the Dorchester assizes had been a setback. But he had used his subsequent encounters with the criminal bedfellows of his imprisonment and transportation to best advantage. Even in those trying circumstances, he had found that calmness - and a studied inscrutability - had had the curious effect of rallying these fellows to him. They seemed to crave a figurehead in whom they could believe, a metaphoric rock on which to stand above the fears and uncertainties that threatened men of a certain kind. Even the three brutish accomplices who had aided his escape from the *Rotterdam* had risen to his calculated call, and he had made good use of their particular skills - indeed, his escape could never have been achieved without them.

Now Judd had joined him; and this new fellow, Hayward, too; and the others, many of whom now waited in the barn around him - all selected carefully for attributes that he would soon deploy. Certainly, the promise of a rich reward had been the essential allure that had drawn their initial interest, but all seemed also to have been beguiled by the mysterious quality that he so carefully contrived, and they offered unquestioning obedience in return. It was quite astonishing how easy it was to manipulate greedy men to further one's own aims, he thought. What was this alchemy he seemed to posses, he wondered? A few well-chosen words here; a gesture or two there; a bold objective plainly stated; these were the simple devices which turned a notion into the outcome he desired. It all rested on a web of beliefs that he seemed able to spin in others' minds – the belief that he, and he alone, could lead them to a cherished goal.

And so when Judd returned from his successful raid upon the shipping office, loaded with an unimaginable cache of monetary notes, it was Pettigrew who calmly took the credit for the plan with a deprecating wave of his hand and a patronising smile. He played to a receptive audience. This was the way he engendered belief and bestowed upon himself the mystique that complemented his deception of those he would have follow him. And once again, he had carefully avoided dirtying his own hands with someone else's blood.

The success of the raid demonstrated to his men that he could fulfil the promises he had made. In this respect, he had already learned the importance of incentive and reward - for the promise of a share of the fortune, now visible for all to see, would keep his men content for a long while yet. This was just as well, for the coming stages of Pettigrew's audacious operation would entail some hardships and discomfort.

Still in the middle of this moonlit night, with the hapless sheriff and his unwitting posse sent upon their way to Brandywine with such a simple ruse, Pettigrew now gave the order for the next stage of his plan to commence. He had determined that Judd would lead this stage too, for the former boatswain's experience suited him ideally for it; as indeed his inside knowledge of the shipping office strong room had suited him for the earlier raid. Thus, under the mariner's direction, the whole party set off at once on foot to make their way along the river path in the direction of Neal's Landing. Pettigrew followed some minutes later on horseback accompanied by Hayward, selected by the former as his 'aide de camps', recognising a certain likeness in their characters and an affinity of manners.

From intelligence passed from infiltrated members of the gang already aboard, it was known that loading of the *Miranda* was now complete, and that all provisions necessary for an Atlantic crossing had already been taken on. Indeed it had been this intelligence that had set the timetable of Pettigrew's plan. He was nothing if not thorough, and thoroughness usually paid off. And as he rode down the path in stately procession, attended by his 'aide de camps', there was a certain majesty in his bearing, as if he might be fulfilling some part of his destiny, so outwardly confident was he of his coming triumph.

Circumstances could not have been more opportune if he had planned these too. Intelligence from the ship had furnished information that few workmen remained aboard at night, and it had been seen to that his men already made up all of these. Moreover, the seamen and officers had been granted shore leave for the week due to the disruptive circumstances of the refit. Thus, except for the duty officer and the two men of his harbour watch, the decks were left almost entirely deserted. Some might later say with the benefit of hindsight, that it was rash to leave such a valuable vessel so poorly guarded, but it was routine. And given the long voyage just completed and the long voyage ahead it had seemed to Captain Goddard a wise and enlightened measure at the time, and certainly better than having idle hands grow fractious during an idle wait. Furthermore, that the vessel would be at risk in any way was utterly unthinkable.

The ship was quiet as Judd and his men settled themselves nearby in the shadows of the trees that bordered the quay. Immediately before them lay the open space of the landing platform, bright and bare in the moon's light. And to one side of it, a gravel slip ran down into the river where the sturdy tugboats lay to their painters on the top of the tide. Pettigrew and Hayward pulled their steeds off the track some distance behind the others and positioned themselves in a small clearing from which they had a good view of the quay. The cohort waited thus distributed for nearly thirty minutes, and in such silence and with such stillness that not even a passing roebuck detected their presence. In this stillness, Pettigrew heard the distant bell strike three.

It was at this time precisely, according to his plan, that Pettigrew expected the first movement on the *Miranda's* decks. And he smiled to himself in approval as he watched two dark figures emerge from the forecastle, creep across the main deck, and climb the companionway to the quarterdeck. It was there that the watch officer was on guard, lulled by the quiet night into a complacent slumber. The two men carried out their deft knife work swiftly on the startled man whose limp body was then bundled over the side with such care that no sound reached Pettigrew's ears. The water rippled in the moonlight as the black bundle bobbed and drifted according to the slight outward set of the tide; and for a time the river sparkled with crimson-streaked reflections. But the water was soon still again. A faint whistle was then heard coming from the deck, at which four new dark figures appeared from the forecastle, this time in two pairs, each pair carrying a sagging bundle between them, and each in turn lowered their bundles into the waiting river in similar fashion. There followed more crimson-streaked ripples on the moonlit water and some gentle lapping noises on the slip, which also similarly died away as the all-but-submerged bodies of the murdered harbour watch drifted slowly out of sight.

Pettigrew's mare let out a snort and shook her mane. Perhaps she had also watched the grisly spectacle and was protesting, but her rider pulled sharply on her reins to steady her. Behind him, hidden in the shadows, Hayward remained silent, but had his face been visible, a smirk of satisfaction would have shown upon it at the recent butchery. Both riders then saw a lamp lit on the quarterdeck and waved from side to side. It was the signal for the next stage to begin.

Judd now made his move, walking his men towards the ship in a loose column that might be seen by any casual observer to be disciplined in nature: as a group of seamen might appear. He marched them up the gangway and on to the ship where they joined their comrades already waiting there, and then spread out to take up positions around the decks. Pettigrew counted twenty-five men in all. And from his observation point, he identified Judd and several others, the ex-mariners in his cohort, moving between the groups, where they lingered as if giving instruction. This went on some little time, Pettigrew's view of the activity enhanced by the moon's strong light, until the town's bell struck four.

A stirring in the vegetation and the sound of heavy feet was now heard coming along the path from the direction of the town. Pettigrew and his companion remained silent and still upon their mounts, counting twenty-one men pass by and move towards the ship. Judd was at the starboard rail as the arriving gaggle formed below him on the quayside in a rough circle. Voices drifted on the night air:

'Prompt as usual, Jess.' It was Judd's voice that was first heard.

A rougher voice came back in reply. 'Oh, 'tis you Mr Judd; I didn't recognise you with that beard of your'n! It's a rum time to be called out at such short notice. A sudden change of plan then?'

'Tis that, Jess! But we're finished here and want to take this tide. Our profits are better served by it than stewing any longer in this godforsaken place!'

'Aye. And they'll be some sore heads aboard, no doubt; your crew were in good spirits last night in the saloon; and not one of them in their beds before midnight!' There were some chuckles from the coxswain's crews at this remark.

'Serves 'em right! A bit of sea air will wake 'em up!' said Judd, plausibly.

A slight pause then followed, which might have been a bit suspicious.

'I didn't see you when the ship came in, Mr Judd; where've you been hiding?'

'Just rejoined the ship, Jess. Arrived in Annapolis on the *Rebecca* and came down yesterday.' A further pause ensued. 'Anyway - can't stand here all day in idle conversation. The tide awaits us, Jess, so get your boats into the water now and prepare to take up our lines! Here's your payment.'

There was then a slight disturbance amongst those gathered on the quay as Judd leant over the rail and threw something down into up-reaching hands.

'And there's some extra in the purse for the early call, Jess! Now watch us carefully at the river mouth! We'll set our sails as soon as we get the wind - so don't hang on too long, or you'll find yourselves dragged back to England with us!'

The men laughed and disbursed to the waiting boats and were soon hidden from sight behind *Miranda's* hull as they headed out into the river. It was not until then that the two waiting horsemen broke cover from the trees and made towards the ship at a slow and steady walk.

'Masterly!' said Pettigrew to Judd as he and Hayward came aboard, leaving their stolen mounts to wander as their inclinations drove them, back in the direction of the long grasses under the trees.

Harding and his two visitors had retired to bed in a morose and exhausted state having talked well into the early hours of the robbery and its consequences. Even Harding's excellent Madeira wine, of which perhaps too many glasses had been consumed in the agonised debate, had failed to make them optimistic of the stolen money's recovery. But morose as they had been when they eventually retired, not one of them could have imagined that the coming morning would bring worse news yet. They were awoken rudely from their extended slumber by a loud and impatient banging at the front door just as the hour had turned nine o'clock. The hammering was so vigorous and prolonged that it filled the house with its reverberations, putting Harding's housemaid into a cross temper as she hurried across the hallway to open the door.

'Let me speak to your master!' panted the sheriff, 'Quickly!' He was breathless from his climb up from the town, and his flustered manner silenced the housemaid even before she could open her mouth to vent her irritation.

And neither was there any need for her to climb the stairs to fetch her master, for as she turned to go in that direction, Harding was already on his way down, fumbling with the cords of his dressing gown with his one good hand. And similarly summoned by the commotion, Jack and Goddard had emerged from their rooms and now stood on the mezzanine landing frowning down in some consternation. The sheriff thus at once had the audience that he sought, and striding past the dumbstruck servant into the centre of the hall, he blurted upwards to the mezzanine:

'Your ship is gone, captain! The *Miranda* has gone!' he repeated his message as if to give it emphasis, for, at first, the three men in his audience stared back uncomprehendingly. 'She has been taken!' he said again in a tone of incredulity. 'And she was apparently already underway even before the robbery at the shipping office had been discovered!'

The sheriff paused here, as if waiting for a reaction, while Jack, Goddard, and Harding exchanged glances that ranged from bewilderment to disbelief. Then Goddard called down impatiently:

'Go on man! Complete your report!'

The lawman did as instructed, and as he spoke, his three intent listeners descended the stairs to join him in the hallway; meanwhile the servant scurried for the kitchen in some confusion.

'This man of yours, Judd, is apparently at the centre of this!' The sheriff continued in some haste and still a little breathlessly. 'He had the tug crews called from their beds at an early hour. They were apparently under the impression that he had been transferred to the *Miranda* and so took his orders, as they had done many times before, of course, when he had served aboard the *Rebecca*. They were completely unaware that he was on the run. The lead coxswain thought the sudden departure a bit unusual, but he did not question it too closely and in the darkness he noticed nothing untoward. One of your officers brought this news to me earlier this morning, captain, and I have since verified it and spoken to the coxswain myself.'

'But...' uttered Goddard, whose morning colour had completely disappeared from his face; 'he would need a crew of at least fifty to sail her on a voyage of any duration, perhaps more. My crew numbers upwards of a hundred!'

'The coxswains reported seeing twenty to thirty men on deck when they released her, captain,' came the sheriff's sobering reply.

'Then not all seamen, I'll be bound! Enough for a fair-weather watch perhaps, but they'd struggle in a serious blow, and beating to windward will tax them! Judd must know that. Why, they'd have to work one sail at a time!'

'That's as may be,' said the sheriff, interrupting. 'But there's worse, I'm afraid, captain: your officer of the watch and two of your seamen had their throats cut and their bodies thrown overboard. We found them in the mud this morning within sight of the quay - left there by the outgoing tide.'

Goddard's hand found the back of a nearby chair and he sat himself down on it as if suddenly overcome. 'Revenge indeed,' he gasped, and threw back his head as if in despair.

Jack's hand went to his friend's shoulder. 'We'll catch him!' he said, resolutely. 'He has to sail the length of the Potomac and across the Chesapeake to escape. If we can sail after him and cut him off before he makes the open sea, we'll have him bottled up with nowhere go.'

'They are already a day ahead of you, Jack,' said Harding, gravely shaking his head. 'You'll never catch them. There are anyway no vessels hereabouts that I know of, that would be fast enough for such a chase.'

Jack let out a heavy sigh of frustration, his eyes darting to and fro as if searching for an answer. Then, as if struck by an idea, he strode to the still-open front door and went out onto the veranda, returning a moment later with a brighter expression on his face.

'Just checking the wind,' he said, in explanation. 'It's very light; and what there is of it, is well east of south. And if I recall, it was similar yesterday. Not good for a square-rigger making against it down the Potomac; she won't have got far, especially since each time the tide turned against her, she'd probably make no headway at all. We could ride to Annapolis and commandeer a vessel there, then sail down the Chesapeake to intercept them!'

'But Jack!' retorted Goddard, now recovering his wits, and shaking his head in exasperation, 'any vessel in pursuit would be faced by the same wind! And by the time we got underway we'd be two days behind at least. And once *Miranda's* out into the open water, there's no way we'll find her.'

'Yes,' came Jack's quick reply, 'but if we could find a vessel that's rigged fore and aft, she'd beat to windward at three times the speed...'

Goddard nodded, conceding the point; but then shook his head again. 'Then can you guarantee to find such a vessel, sail-ready and available in Annapolis, Jack!' he taunted, crossly. 'I doubt that it would be that easy, and we have no time to throw away on some fruitless search!'

This angry retort brought Jack's sudden enthusiasm into check, and he sagged as if his argument had been defeated. But then he rallied:

'Sheriff!' he said, turning to the lawman, 'How quickly could we reach Georgetown on horseback?'

The three other men glanced at each other blankly, and then turned their quizzical stares upon Jack, as if he had departed his senses.

'But that's in the opposite direction!' retorted Goddard, derisively.

'Trust me, Philip; I'll explain as we go. How long, Sheriff?' he repeated, crossly.

'Three or four hours, I'd say, Jack. You can take horses from the livery. For a start, you can have the two we found on the quay this morning - the ones Judd stole after his raid on the shipping office.'

'Then we haven't a moment to lose, Philip! Let's get ourselves prepared!' Jack spoke quickly, leaving no room for argument. 'And thank you, sheriff; we'll take you up on that offer.' He turned to the tobacco agent. 'Mr Harding, sir, can you get a message urgently to Ned Holder at my farm at New Hope? Explain what has happened. Tell him to keep a lookout for the *Miranda* between Piney Point and Point Lookout. He will remember the *Rebecca* – tell him the *Miranda* is her sister ship, so that he'll know what to look for. And tell him also to look out for a twin-masted schooner by the name of *Warrior* making down the Potomac in hot pursuit over the next day or so. If he sees her, he should sail out to meet her as she approaches, bringing any information he has of the *Miranda's* passing, and particularly of her heading as she enters the Chesapeake.'

Harding nodded. 'He'll get the message before the day is out,' he said, resolutely. 'Indeed, I'll deliver the message myself! I can manage the trap with my one good hand!'

'Then you can help him keep a lookout too, for you will certainly know one ship from another! But one more thing,' said Jack. 'Tell him that he must not on any account approach the *Miranda*, or alert her of his interest. We do not want Judd to know he is being tracked.'

'We also ought to get word to Annapolis, Jack,' added Goddard quickly. 'The *Rebecca* should be there by now if she has stuck to her itinerary. She might yet be of some help. If this *Warrior* of yours can catch the *Miranda* and slow her down, the *Rebecca's* arrival on the scene could prove decisive. I'll brief my officers before we set off and tell them to get the crew on their way there immediately – perhaps you could help transport them, Sheriff?'

Calling by the Centennial Hotel to pass his orders to the crew, Goddard extracted the first officer, the boatswain, and half-a-dozen of his best crewmen from the complement to accompany him and Jack to Georgetown. It was some thirty miles by dirt road on a route that would have been direct but for the dogleg to find the ford across the Anacostia River, which lay squarely in their path. This, and the one or two moments of navigational uncertainty brought on by a paucity of signposts and the disorientating woodland, meant that the party took rather longer than they had anticipated to reach their destination. But they rode with such determination that it was not yet mid-afternoon as the grim-faced party entered the outskirts of the town.

Georgetown, the furthest point upstream to which ocean-going vessels could navigate the Potomac, was a relatively new settlement, and it looked like it. There was much new building in evidence to the two riders as they rode along the rutted main street in the direction of the quay. It had been only seven years before that the town was established on sixty acres of private land purchased by the Maryland Legislature, but since then it had expanded rapidly to become a thriving commercial port. Like Neal's Landing and its neighbouring Charlestown on the Tobacco River, the Georgetown site began merely as a tobacco warehouse and inspection point that served as an embarkation port for produce of the area to be shipped overseas. But it was not long before wharves were extended, and the chandleries, the smithies, the shipwrights and the like were founded to service this burgeoning activity. And around all this new industry, a flourishing little community soon grew.

When Jack first caught sight of the busy waterfront, it reminded him of Weymouth harbour by the sheer intensity of waterborne activity that filled the river, and it took a moment or two to identify the two vessels for which he searched amongst the confusion of masts and rigging which met his gaze. Pulling his mount to a halt even as his eyes still swept the harbour, the others came alongside, their flushed faces equally intent on searching but not quite sure of what they looked for.

'Ah, over there!' Jack said at last, pointing to the far end of the quay where the Sir Michael's barque and schooner lay rafted up alongside. Goddard's glance followed Jack's, and he raised a hand to shield his eyes from the sun.

'She looks fast, Jack,' said Goddard. 'I'd say we'd have a chance to catch the *Miranda*, if we can have her.'

'Don't worry about that, Philip - Sir Michael will see to it. With so much of his own money at stake, we'll have to rein him back! Mark my words, if I've not completely misjudged the man, we'll be underway before nightfall.'

Chapter Seventeen

As Jack had predicted, Sir Michael was galvanised into immediate action by the shocking news that he and Goddard so abruptly conveyed.

'Then you'll have to take command, Captain Goddard! And you'll have to train your men to sail her,' said Sir Michael firmly. 'I dismissed the crew for their drunkenness at Charlestown the moment we docked, and I laid the skipper off until I had something useful for him to do – no sense in paying the man to sit around and twiddle his fingers, is there? And there's no time to recall him now!'

Goddard caught Jack's glance, a twinkle coming into both men's eyes despite the general sobriety of their features otherwise. 'I am reminded of our teamwork on *L'hermine*, Jack,' said Goddard with a confident air, as he appraised the schooner's rig. 'Between us, I think we should be able to manage her, Sir Michael'

Jack nodded his agreement. 'She'll be a damn sight easier to sail than *L'hermine* with that stunted jury rig of hers, I'd say, Philip!'

Goddard smiled tightly, then turned to his first officer. 'Number one, take the bosun and the men and drill them on the rigging and sailing procedures as best you can. Then get her ready for departure.'

It was fortunate that Sir Michael's militia were somewhat behind schedule in sorting their provisions and equipment into the order necessary for their northward march. The delay was due, it appeared, to a misunderstanding of some of the colonel's advance instructions by the resident agent, who consequently had some hasty requisitioning to do (and disposals to make) before the stores could be loaded in the proper configuration onto the waiting wagons. Whoever was to blame for the resulting hiatus need not concern us, but it was helpful to the new arrivals that most of the stores were still on the quay rather than on the road, as they should have been by now. Captain Goddard, Sir Michael and Jack were therefore able to select from this splendid array whatever they were inclined to take. Thus, not only were sufficient victuals for an extended voyage quickly put on board, but also as much gunpowder and weaponry as might be needed to lay siege. (It will already be clear that this new mission of Sir Michael's had been abruptly elevated to a higher priority than the militia's original objective – for which the inventory would now need yet further attention.)

'Jack, I've been thinking,' said Sir Michael a little later in the afternoon as the loading of the schooner neared completion, 'and I've decided to take Major Lawrence and his scout platoon with us. They won't be needed until the militia enters hostile territory, and they'll be invaluable to us if we get into a scrap. I've already informed Colonel Sanderson of my decision, and once he's sorted out the logistics he'll lead the militia northwards and wait for us in Raystown. My guess is, whether our chase is successful or not, we'll be back here within the week, so we won't be far behind. If we haven't caught up with the *Miranda* within a few days we're never going to!'

'I agree, sir. If Judd's got as many men as were reported, we're going to need some expert firepower - we've not only got to catch him, we've got to stop him too!'

'Good point, Jack, good point,' said Sir Michael, who seemed suddenly to have lost the aloofness of recent months.

Warrior slipped from her berth with at least three hours of midsummer daylight remaining, and it was the group's intention to sail as far down river as the light and the south-by-southeast wind permitted. With the sun's elevation declining, however, it was not long before the wind began to back and decrease, a trend that continued progressively as the evening wore on. While this diurnal shift gave the schooner a long and, at first, swift and easy reach down the narrow upper river for the best part of ten miles, her speed soon after began to fail, until eventually only the evening zephyrs and the river's slow drift propelled them.

The helmsman soon began to struggle with an ineffective wheel.

'Losing steerage, sir,' he called over his shoulder.

'Have a boat lowered, number one,' said Goddard with a resigned sigh. 'Leave the heads'ls up for the present to capture any last breaths, but get the mains'l down. We'll row her down river for a bit; we've got an hour or more of twilight left and can't afford to lose it.'

'According to the tables, captain, moonrise is at ten,' returned the mate, helpfully. 'If we can get her another five miles downstream before nightfall to where the channel widens, we may be able to pilot her by moonlight without too much worry of running aground.'

Goddard called Jack and Sir Michael to his side and briefed them on his intentions, then in a louder voice, directed aft at the stern rail where

Lawrence's platoon stood about in idle conversation, he added: 'Any of your men fancy some evening exercise, major?'

And so, once again, Jack found himself coxswain of a boat. But this time he had a most uncommon eight-man crew. With Major Lawrence in stroke position to set the pace, Sergeants Schluntz, Hine and Bryant were oarsmen two, three, and four to starboard, with the four other scouts seated on the larboard side. Jack mused at the twist of fates that now put him in command of this professional soldiering group. These were men more used to the close confines of the forest than the open water, but they had taken to this new element like schoolboys on a new adventure, and were putting their bare backs into it without complaint. The bearded Lawrence, his features weather worn and slightly wild, seemed lost in his thoughts as he rowed, his lips moving almost imperceptibly as if counting the steady beat. Behind him, the gaunt German, Schluntz, his lanky height elevating his shaven head a good six inches above the rest, the muscles under his taut skin drawn like an anatomical diagram, pulsing with the effort of each stroke. Next came Bryant, short dark hair, stocky proportions, thickset and densely built, carrying the concentrated power of a prize bull. Finally, at the bow, came Hine, medium height, a neatly trimmed goatee, and thinning, greying hair, now made into a wispy halo in the last of the day's light. These four middle-aged men, and the four others like them sitting alongside, shared something that Jack instinctively liked and trusted. He wondered what it was that drew him to them: was it their quiet confidence, their imperturbability, their boyish delight in the new? He tried to define it, for he admired these qualities, perhaps because he saw something of himself in them? Was it simply that they were at ease with themselves and each other, having proved themselves in battle and earned each other's respect? Or was it something deeper? Then in the eyes of each of them he saw it, even as the dusk's light dwindled; certainly there was self-sufficiency and individuality there, but there was something else. For all their reputed skills, and bravery, and military derring-do, they were humble men with no demands or expectations but that of loyalty to each other and honour in the deed jointly undertaken. If Jack could have had his pick of men to be with him on this uncertain mission, he could not have hoped to find better than these.

'Nice and steady now, major,' called Jack, smiling. 'You'll wear your boys out at that pace. I've a feeling it's going to be a long night!'

The night remained mostly calm, but with a few illusive breezes that seemed to spring up from nowhere, live a short and tantalising life, and then die away again almost before the schooner's night watch could sheet in the feeble power. These zephyrs, fleeting as they were, gave occasional relief to the eight men who, for a few moments, felt their oars lighten, saw their towrope slacken, and heard the fragile ripple of the schooner's bow wave as she surged. Each time, there was hope that their long slog was over, and each time there were sighs of weary resignation as the gentle flurry passed. The night passed thus, punctuated by these moments and short breaks for refreshment and rest, as Jack and his uncomplaining oarsmen ploughed the silvered path laid down by the moon, until the early summer dawn.

Soon after the sun's arrival came the first breezes of the day, and the boatmen and boat were brought aboard just as the huge mainsail, raised in anticipation, began to rustle into life once more. And only two hours later, with the shadow of her tall main sail still long upon the water, the schooner was already rounding the last of the major river bends - passing the shingled beach at the entrance to the Tobacco River where Jack had stood just five days before.

It was also at this same point that the pirated *Miranda* would have cast off her tugboats and set sail, putting her a full forty-eight hours' ahead of her pursuer. With the wind holding in the south-east, however, the schooner's rig would now give her a huge advantage over the square-rigger, for on each tack she could sail thirty degrees closer to the wind. Even so, *Warrior* still faced a forty-five mile beat to windward down the widening Potomac to the Chesapeake, and then a further fifty-five mile south-by-south-east beat to reach the open sea: a hundred miles against the wind with the *Miranda* perhaps already as much as fifty miles ahead.

'We could still catch her,' said Goddard, almost talking to himself, yet by now he had been joined at the stern-rail by Jack and Major Lawrence and several of his men who listened intently to the captain's words. 'Close-hauled, our progress along track could be three or four times as fast as a square-rigger, maybe more against Judd's inexpert crew. If they have made a mile down river per hour on average over the past two days, I would be surprised. They'll almost certainly still be in the Potomac even now, Jack.'

'Then that could put them within sight of the New Hope shoreline, Philip! Harding and Ned Holder could be looking at the *Miranda* even as we speak!'

'Indeed, Jack.' A thoughtful pause followed. 'Number one!' Goddard called, 'get a lookout up to the crosstrees with a glass to scan ahead. I doubt that we shall be so lucky to as to see the Miranda's sails from here, but its worth a try.'

The first officer barked an order and a seaman was seen immediately to spring up from the deck and make for the windward shrouds. Clambering upwards as nimbly as a monkey up a vine, he was soon straddling the spreaders, where he took out his glass. The group at the stern rail watched in hushed expectancy as the lookout levelled his instrument and adjusted its focus. Jack also scanned ahead; no sails could be seen down river from his eye level, but the lookout's extra elevation would give him an extended view of craft hidden by Jack's horizon.

'Distant sails ahead, cap'n!' shouted the lookout from his lofty perch. 'But only the mastheads are visible, sir, so I cannot make them out or judge their course.'

'Thank you, Number one; get the man down,' said Goddard. 'It is possible that the *Miranda* is one of them, I suppose,' he added doubtfully to the cluster of companions around him. 'From that height, the lookout could spy a sail-top twenty or so miles ahead on a clear day like this. But I very much doubt that she is that near – and even if she were, it would still take us a full day's sailing to catch her.'

The major raised his eyebrows at this remark. 'Then it looks like we'll be manning the boat again tonight, captain!' he said in a tone that combined stoicism with resignation, his woolly face soon puckering into a withered smile as several groans erupted from the men behind his back.

'You must have noticed how much we enjoyed our little *wasserfest* last night!' quipped Schluntz, with uncharacteristic irony.

'You did so well!' rejoined the captain lightly with a smile. 'But yes; I am afraid that it may come to that, major – so you and your men should get some food inside you, and rest up during the day. I'll call you if and when I need you.'

It took as little as the mere mention of food to turn the several expressions of weary resignation into ones of plucky cheerfulness once more; and seizing the moment, the major led his men below.

'You too, Jack,' said Goddard, firmly. 'The first officer and I will split the crew and take turns on watch, and you had better get some rest while you can. We have a long haul in front of us without let-up; we must not let *Warrior* rest tonight if we are to catch the *Miranda*. Once she's into the Chesapeake, she'll have an easier point of sail and our closing speed may well reduce. By my reckoning, it will be a close run thing - even assuming we can identify her in time out of all the other ships afloat in the Chesapeake. Why, we could so easily chase the wrong damned sail if we're not careful! And even if we catch her, we still have to get ahead and find a way to turn her before she makes the Atlantic, for once she's on a dead run in open water, she'll fly before the wind. That's where a square-rigger with the sail area of the *Miranda* would beat us hands down!'

'Turning her will be another matter entirely, Philip; she must be three times our size. And don't forget that she has eight cannon in her bow - and that Judd knows very well how to use them.'

'I had not forgotten, Jack. But let us first catch her before we worry about that.'

It was mid-afternoon when Jack ascended the companionway to see Goddard again on watch with Sir Michael at his side. Both stood close behind the helmsman at the wheel where they could brace themselves against the mizzen-sheet horse, which spanned the after-deck. The schooner was heeling on a starboard tack in a good stiff breeze, quite close into the eastern shore and making good way, her galloping progress made audible by the roar and gush of speeding water slamming against her hull. There was a moderate chop on the surface and the breeze whipped the little crests into sparkling foam, throwing up a spray from time to time that stung the eyes and wet the deck. Jack made his way aft along the windward walkway, swinging himself hand-over-hand along the bulwark to steady himself. At first, it seemed strange that neither Goddard nor Sir Michael caught his eye as he progressed so awkwardly towards them. But then he realised that their gazes were cast forward, beyond him, as if watching something of great interest ahead. Several of the scouts, Major Lawrence amongst them, had wedged themselves under the stern rail against the vessel's frisky motion, and their interest too had been captured. Jack followed their gazes and saw, not a mile ahead, the sails of a small skiff set to a broad reach; the little boat was closing on the schooner at some speed, tossed about like some toy boat in the waves. On a premonition, Jack flashed a glance towards the eastern shoreline looking for features that he might recognise and saw at once that they were already approaching the waters off New Hope. There, on the larboard bow, was St George's Island and the familiar estuary behind; and there, two points off the starboard bow, was the opening into the Chesapeake, so boundless on the horizon that it looked like open ocean. His focus returned to the little boat now fast approaching.

'Your glass, Philip?' asked Jack quickly as he joined them on their perch; and without waiting for an answer, he took the instrument from its holder on the binnacle and held it up to his eye. With its aid, he could now see two figures in the approaching boat, one large, the other small, both sitting on the windward side and leaning out to keep the boat on an even keel. There was then no further doubt in his mind.

'It is my boat from New Hope, Philip; with Ned and Matthew sailing it. We shall need to heave to.'

Amidst the sudden flurry of sails and the clatter of tackle that followed the captain's curt order, *Warrior's* bow was brought through the wind, her headsails thus forced to back - while her main and mizzen swung across the deck to be immediately freed off, if not quite completely; this slowed her to a walking pace almost as quickly as the manoeuvre had been performed, and held her in a steady equilibrium across the wind, pointing towards the western shore. And as the crewmen played the main and mizzen sheets to trim her point of balance, the approaching craft closed in and sailed into the calmer waters of her lee, Ned deftly dropping the jib as they came alongside.

'Tie up there and come aboard, Ned!' shouted Jack over the larboard rail, pointing at the boarding ladder which had been wound down amidships. And he watched anxiously while Ned and Matthew tied up then dropped the gaff onto the thwarts and lashed it down. Although sheltered from the worst of the chop and the breeze in the shelter of the schooner's freeboard, the little boat still bucked and bounced against the hull as if straining to pull free, knocking the wind-blown pair off balance several times as they worked. Eventually, they finished and clambered up the ladder, their rosy faces grinning from ear to ear in evident satisfaction to have accomplished such a tricky rendezvous with such panache. And their skill deserved the approving comments they got from the crew as they were helped aboard.

'I got your message, Jack,' beamed Ned, breathlessly as he arrived on deck. 'The *Miranda* was off St George's about this time yesterday. Mr Hardin' and I spotted her from the headland at New Hope - then we kept her in sight until we lost her over the horizon; we followed her a little distance by trap along the coast road towards Point Lookout. Mr Hardin' was in no doubt that it was she - and she was definitely makin' for the sea for she was trackin' sou' sou' east when we last had sight of her.' He paused for breath as his eyes darted for the horizon. 'Over there,' he said pointing to the low headland on the distant Virginian shoreline; 'That's where she was as dusk fell last night.'

'And how was she sailing, Ned?' asked Jack, quickly interjecting.

'I'd say a bit clumsy and slow, Jack. And she seemed to be turning the long way round each time she changed course on her beat to windward - and losin' ground badly at each turn – wearin', I think you call it? I don't know that she had all her sails set either - and she took a long time to sheet them in for they were a long time flappin' about.'

'Only twenty-four hours or so behind then - we have caught up a lot, Jack! I am grateful, sir, for your help,' said Goddard; and reaching for Ned's hand, he grasped it and shook it warmly in clear appreciation of the useful report. 'And to you also, Matthew,' he added taking the boy's hand in turn. 'But, I am afraid that we have no time to dally here if we are to catch our prey. So I must ask you please to be off; we shall reset our sails as soon as you have moved clear.'

'But...' both Ned and Matthew expostulated in unison, both strangling their utterances simultaneously as each caught the other's eye. The young man, however, immediately deferred to his elder, leaving Ned to continue alone:

'I had hoped, sir,' he ventured somewhat tentatively, 'that we might be permitted to remain aboard to render any assistance as you may require from us.' He spoke using his best vocabulary.

In the hesitation that followed, Matthew leapt in:

'Experienced ship's boys and musket-loaders are scarce come by in these waters, captain!' He said this with an audacious smile. 'And you know my credentials well, sir!'

'And you will get to know mine, if you allow us to come with you,' burst out Ned, with a disarming chuckle.

The captain threw a glance at Jack and raised an eyebrow – to which Jack responded with the slightest of nods.

'Bring the skiff aboard!' called Goddard to his boatswain, 'and find these new recruits a place to hang their hammocks – not that they'll spend much time in them!'

Unable to sail a more direct southerly course towards the opening to the ocean because of the persisting wind from the south, the *Miranda* was by early evening that same day half way across the Chesapeake on an east-by-south-easterly course. At this latitude, the eastern edge of safe navigation for larger vessels in the Chesapeake is marked by a line of low-lying islands, which rise from a submarine spit that might at one time in its history have been exposed to the air, parallel to the extant peninsular that bounded the waterway to seaward. It was fortunate for the fugitive vessel that her course was as it was, for had she been sailing just a few miles north of her current track, she would have come to a mysterious yet abrupt halt surrounded by what might have appeared to be open water. That she had avoided this premature end to her scurrying escape was entirely due to circumstances rather than any judgement on Judd's part, for while he could name every part of the ship from stem to stern and knew from experience how she should be sailed, he had never been schooled in the art of navigation. It was true that he was able to take a bearing, and draw a line on a chart, and measure it in nautical miles and degrees; and having done all this he could then give instructions as to the course for the helmsman to steer. But in appreciating those little but sometimes critical details such as the range and flow of the tide or magnetic variation, and of the skills required to obtain a running fix, even assuming that he could identify a landmark from a chart, he was as clueless as a ship's cook. Moreover, while he was sure that the diminutive numbers that appeared all over the chart of the Chesapeake represented depth and not some other maritime parameter, he was not exactly sure of their units or of the ship's draught, either loaded or unloaded. And so, having given himself a headache pondering the matter, he had quietly decided to ignore the unfathomable code, preferring instead to trust his visual observations and the occasional heave of the lead line to keep him out of trouble.

The captain's cabin, now used principally by Pettigrew as his private quarters, also served as a navigation and planning room since it was there that the chart table and all the ship's charts and almanacs were located. Judd had been on deck since passing into the Chesapeake and he had watched the Virginian shore recede behind him until it was lost from his view. For a time thereafter, no feature had appeared within the watery circle of his horizon to provide any point of reference. Yet the vessel had ploughed steadily eastwards in a stiffening breeze, the helmsman being under strict instructions to sail by the wind, close-hauled, so that progress down the waterway would be at its maximum rate. But having recently noted a group of low-lying islands some two miles to the north, Judd had returned to the captain's cabin to consult his chart. Correctly as it happens on this occasion, he was able to identify the islands, marked on the chart some halfway across the twenty-five miles of open water that separated the two coastlines at this point of the Chesapeake. Alongside the depiction of the islands on his chart, the word *'Tangier'* had been scrawled in a shaky hand; though why such an exotic and colourful name should be attached to such desolate mud flats was beyond him. Judd now picked up his marker and rule and carefully drew in his estimated position and course, the latter lying towards the southern entrance of a wide Sound labelled *'Pocomoke'* on his chart. It would have been evident to any observer that this task had taken Judd's utmost concentration not only by his finicky manner but also by the skewed set of his jaw. He now bent over the chart and examined his markings thoughtfully, wondering how far along his line he could proceed safely before taking up his next tack. Pettigrew sat beside the table looking somewhat bored, his head propped upon his hand, and gazing through the wide stern windows at a despondently yellow and darkening sky. Hayward sat nearby, slumped in an armchair, his legs outstretched. But if the latter's pose suggested slumber, the man's sharp eyes belied this, since they were at this moment fixed on Judd's bent form with a sceptical cast.

Since taking up this tack some two hours before, the vessel had maintained a steady course. And it was Judd's intention as deputed master, to whom Pettigrew, perhaps unwisely now deferred on matters of seamanship, to sail the complete width of the major seaway before wearing to the south-west. By making his tacks so long, he aimed to reduce the number of turning manoeuvres required, and thus reduce the amount of sail work asked of his clumsy and inexpert crew. In the narrower confines of the Potomac, much time had already been lost in the shambolic frenzies that had characterised each tack so far, where, to the exasperation of the former seamen in the group, new blunders seemed to compound old confusions, causing the vessel to miss stays and fall off the wind frequently on her early attempts to tack. He had quickly realised that this was not a manoeuvre to be risked; especially in confined waters, where falling off the wind might drive them aground before regaining steerageway. He now preferred instead to wear the ship around when required to come onto the other tack, bringing the stern through the wind rather than the bow. Such a manoeuvre might be inefficient, but at least it did not demand sail handling skills and coordination beyond the attainment of his men. But now that the ship had entered the more open waters of the Chesapeake, Judd hoped that these frustrations should at least become less frequent. Here, as has been said, the Chesapeake was some twenty-five miles wide, thus there remained approximately ten to twelve miles more to run on the present course before turning. Judd sighed wearily; another two hours remaining on this tack, he estimated; another two hours for the old salts amongst his crew to instruct the others on handling the sails. Who knows, he thought, they may make seamen of them yet. But in his heart, he knew this to be a forlorn hope; some had fallen seasick as soon as the *Miranda* began her gentle pitching and heaving in open water, and the rest were to a large extent disinclined to learn the arts of seamanship.

Thinking thus, he turned his thoughts once more to the chart with some sufferance in his manner. The next tack would achieve a more favourable south westerly course and take the vessel diagonally back across the Chesapeake towards the Virginian shore. Estimating the ship's probable new heading from earlier tacks in the Potomac, Judd judged that a course could be achieved that would put the vessel south of the Rappahannock estuary at the end of the next leg, representing good progress along the intended track line at last. He took up his straight edge and marker again and, with the same deliberation, he drew in the line carefully, placing crosses at the planned turning points at each end. When he had done this he scribbled some calculations in the margin of a logbook lying open to the side, and then straightened and stretched his back.

Attracted by Judd's movement, Pettigrew turned his idle gaze towards the man and instantly, almost as if at the turn of a switch, adopted an impatient and quizzical air.

'Well?' he challenged in a manner clearly calculated to maintain the upper hand.

'This wind's not helping us,' sighed Judd, shaking his head at the zigzag lines drawn on his chart. 'But four more tacks should see us able to plot a clear course directly into the Atlantic.'

'How long?'

'Even under-canvassed and with our bungling sail-handling, we have averaged eight knots when we've had the wind,' said Judd, looking once more at the chart and shaking his head as if remembering some insufferable display of ineptitude. 'If we were able to sail a direct course, it would be fifty or so miles to the ocean, but with all this tacking, it will be more than twice that.'

'Another half a day, then?'

'If the wind holds, perhaps; but, if tonight's anything like the last two nights, the wind will drop at dusk and we'll make hardly any headway overnight. And we've also got the foul tides to contend with…'

'Yes, yes,' said Pettigrew, irritated now not to have his answer. 'Then what is your best estimate, man!'

Judd shifted his weight uneasily and looked a little bruised by Pettigrew's demand, like a teacher might look when tripped up by the challenge of a persistent and clever pupil.

'Mr Pettigrew,' he said testily. 'This plotting requires some skill, you know,' he added as if offering this very quality. 'It is a complicated procedure that needs to be conducted with great precision, and it is wise not to rush it while the safety of the ship is carried upon my shoulders.'

Judd had decided not to reveal that this was the first time he had ever practiced it. And by puffing himself up in this manner, he was reacting to his instinct for self-preservation, for he had begun to feel uneasy about a future so clearly in the hands of this manipulative man. Pettigrew raised an eyebrow. If he was not completely taken in by Judd's assertion as to competence, then this was the only sign.

'I ask only when we shall reach the open sea, Mr Judd' he said, shortly, 'bowing, of course, to your superior skill in this matter.'

Judd nodded his acceptance of Pettigrew's apparently more respectful tone, deaf to the hidden sarcasm, picked up his rule, and set himself once more to his chart as if engaged in some weighty calculation. Unseen by Judd, Pettigrew took the opportunity to glance across the cabin towards Hayward, still recumbent in his chair, and rolled his eyes. And from his chair, Hayward responded with an audible sigh and a look of mild amusement.

In due course, Judd finished his protracted fussing with his rule and lifted his head with an expression that asserted confidence. 'I'd say about this time tomorrow - taking everything into account - and assuming the wind direction does not become even less favourable than it is,' he said, not able to resist the qualification.

'Then it is as well that we are not being pursued,' replied Pettigrew, as if holding Judd to account for the wind, 'for we would be vulnerable whilst we remain in such confined waters and with such slow progress towards the open sea!'

'No one could catch us now,' insisted Judd, bravely. 'We must have at least a day or two's lead on any who might have tried to follow – and they'd have to tack just the same as us.' Here he spoke from the standpoint of one who had never sailed an American schooner, nor even paused to consider that such a vessel could now be steadily overhauling them unseen on the other side of the waterway. And neither could he know that his former ship, *Rebecca*, was also joining the chase from Annapolis with *Miranda's* crew aboard.

Hayward cleared his throat. 'Then perhaps it is time for Mr Judd to know our intentions once we have broken out of these constraints?' He threw in this remark languidly from his chair, without changing his position even so much as a glance towards the table.

Pettigrew was silent for a few seconds. 'To head northwards,' he said at last, as if the admission had been forced from him with some reluctance.

'We'll not find sanctuary there,' retorted Judd, quickly. 'Word of us will soon be spread throughout the thirteen colonies. We'll not be secure anywhere on the east coast.'

'Then look at your chart of the Atlantic, Mr Judd,' said Pettigrew in the tone of a master admonishing a tardy apprentice. 'And estimate for me, if you please, how many days it will take us to reach the St Lawrence with a favourable wind.'

At this Hayward pulled himself up in his chair to a more attentive posture.

'French territory!' the 'aide de camps' said, in a tone that might have been admiring. 'Clever, eh Judd? The French will pay handsomely for a vessel like this, and there'll be traders who'll give us a good price for our tobacco and then ship it to France at a profit.'

'And for those of us who wish,' continued Pettigrew, smoothly, 'a passage across the Atlantic too. Which is precisely what I have in mind - to procure a small estate for myself somewhere on the Loire with my share of the money.'

Judd had remained silent for a while, but the frown on his forehead showed some disquiet.

'I had not reckoned on selling out to the enemy,' he asserted. He became quite surly now. 'And I would have no wish to settle in an enemy country.'

'Oh!' puffed Pettigrew in mock surprise. 'Such principles from an upstanding citizen of England! You have come too far for that, I am afraid, Mr Judd - England is our enemy now. But horizons are far wider than France for a wealthy man such as you will be, and I am sure that such a man could find land and a position to suit him in due course - perhaps in Spain or in its colonies?'

Judd was silenced by this riposte, and he made no response for several seconds; but when the tense lines of his features melted, it seemed to signal a sort of grudging assent. 'You speak of share,' he then said, roughly. 'What would your reckoning be on this, then? It is as well to be clear!'

'Half for me and a quarter each for you, gentlemen,' Pettigrew said with a face that revealed no trace of hesitation or fear of challenge - as if it were his right to take the lion's share. 'Twenty thousand in notes,' he said, patting the bulging leather saddlebags that lay upon the table. '...and upwards of twenty thousand each for the ship and for her load, gentlemen. That makes at least fifteen thousand pounds for each of you - enough for you two to set yourselves up for life. And my share will restore to me some of what I have lost!'

'Are you not forgetting the others?' It was Hayward who said this from his armchair in a tone that was curious rather than critical.

'No, I am not forgetting the others, Hayward;' said Pettigrew carefully, 'but it is unlikely that they will have much use for money once they find themselves in French hands!'

Judd and Hayward exchanged glances at this reply, but their expressions remained cautiously neutral.

Chapter Eighteen

The wind strength would diminish but not die completely throughout that evening and night, and so there would be no need to deploy *Warrior's* boat to tow her, much to the relief of Major Lawrence and his scouts. Goddard had seen a change in the weather coming, heralded by a yellowing sky at dusk and the approach of high cloud from the west. He had watched the cloud thicken and lower progressively as dusk had passed to night, and now he noticed a veering of the wind too.

'Hmmm! All the signs of a change of air on the way, I think;' he muttered, 'it could be to our advantage on this side of the seaway, Jack; we're now making ten degrees more southerly on this tack than we were.'

The two men stood with their backs to the mizzen-horse, using it as a prop to steady themselves against the ship's light motion, and scanned ahead along the path of glittering reflections laid down by a low moon in the south-east. The schooner had just been put about and was now once more on a starboard tack. The dark outline of low ground, a mile or so off the starboard quarter, half-astern, marked the Virginian shore. It was as close as they had dared to come in the darkness. Three lookouts now remained on watch: one each at the starboard and larboard rails, and one in the bow. The rest of the crew had been stood down, and Sir Michael and Major Lawrence's platoon had retired to their hammocks below. Ned and Matthew had been found space in the crowded cabins too; while on the deck, their little skiff had been strapped down, company for the ship's boat, her mast and sails neatly stowed beneath her upturned hull.

'We'll lose the moon behind that cloud soon, Jack, and my guess is that we'll see some sort of precipitation later as the cloud base lowers. Warmer air approaching is my calculation - and that usually brings drizzle and sea mists for a while as it rides up the colder air in front of it. I fear that by the morning, our chances of seeing the *Miranda* will be pretty slim,' Goddard continued gloomily. 'It's anyway like looking for a needle in a haystack now that we have the full width of the Chesapeake to search. They could be anywhere.'

Jack glanced upwards to scan the sky.

'Another hour of moonlight?'

'Probably less by the rate that cloud is moving, Jack; the wind speed will probably pick up by morning too, if my experience is anything to go by. Yet in all my years at sea, I cannot say that my expertise at forecasting has become any more accurate. It is a black art which I have yet to master.'

Both scanned the horizon in silence for a while longer, each in thoughtful mood, as *Warrior* ploughed on through the night, the gentle ramming of her hull through silver water sounding soft and even to their ears, while their hearts, in contrast, began to beat a little faster at the prospect of the confrontation that both hoped would soon take place.

'Better look at the chart,' said Goddard. 'Helmsman! Steer her by the wind to keep her close-hauled, and call me if your heading approaches one-seven-zero; we do not want to come too close to land in this darkness.'

And both men went below.

Warrior's navigation 'cabin' was little more than an alcove within the glazed companionway combing that was the only construction, other than the low bulwarks, that protruded above the schooner's otherwise flat deck. It thus enjoyed the benefit of an outside view in several sectors (except where obstructed by equipment and items stowed on deck), and so the navigator could often take his bearings without moving from his station. But cluttered with chart tubes, equipment, and other navigation paraphernalia, meticulously shipshape as they were kept, it was a tight space in which to work, with room enough only for two. The two men reached it by stepping up from the companionway, and then sliding themselves into the built-in seats that lay along each side of the table. Even with the slight motion of the schooner, it was an awkward manoeuvre dressed in their thick jackets, but once wedged in, a man would stay put in any sea. Goddard turned up the wick of the lantern and surveyed the chart in its amber light. Below them, in the dark cabin, hammocks swayed gently on quietly creaking timbers, amidst the sounds of men in slumber.

'We were here an hour ago, Jack,' Goddard said, placing the point of his finger on the chart. 'And we made a steady eight knots over the past hour on our south-westerly tack.' He picked up a rule, placed it down and oriented it by reference to the compass rose annotated on the chart. 'We're tacking down this line now – south-by-south-easterly – see?'

Jack nodded.

'So now, we'll be ...' Goddard picked up a set of dividers, adjusted the width between its points against the longitude scale at the edge of his chart, and then walked the implement down his line. '...here!' he said with some satisfaction. 'Now, with this shifting wind, I do not want to move too far eastwards or we could find ourselves pressed onto the eastern shore. I'll beat down the western side, like this.' Goddard now ran his finger in a zigzag down the chart. 'If the wind swings into the south-west, our course could become more of a reach, which will suit us very well.'

'Where shall we be at dawn?' asked Jack.

'Hmmm! Good question.' Goddard bent over the chart and moved his rule in a series of zigzags, each time marking off a distance with his dividers and making a feint line. 'Dawn in, say, four hours? That would put us about there;' he said, pointing, 'and, if the wind continues to veer, we should be at the cape by mid-morning.'

'Unless we see the *Miranda* first!'

'She'll be having a hard time with this shift of wind, Jack. My guess is that we'll already have passed her by dawn. Our best bet, in the reducing visibility, will be to wait for her at the Cape. Here,' he said, placing his finger again on the chart. 'She'll want to cut it as close as she can to put herself quickly onto a run or a reach to put some distance behind her. If we await her there, we'll have every chance of catching her off guard. She'll certainly not expect a threat from forward of her position, so that'll give us an advantage.'

'What's the tide doing?'

Goddard glanced at the moon through the glazing and then at the ships clock, while his right hand felt along a nearby bookshelf as if it had a will of its own. Even without looking, he located what he sought – a small leather-bound booklet that had clearly seen considerable use, judging by its dog-eared cover.

'I found this earlier: *Warrior's* handy little almanac for the Chesapeake.'

He flicked quickly through its pages and then spread the booklet open before him, lowering his head to read a table of small figures that lay written on the page.

'Still on the flood at the moment;' he muttered as he read further, 'low water in about an hour; high water at about eight. A range of just three feet.'

'Shouldn't trouble us too much, then.'

'We shall need to be careful, nevertheless. As we saw with the *Rotterdam* when we came in, Jack, there is a lot of shallow water in the Chesapeake, and three feet could make a big difference in terms of how close we could safely come to the shore. Many a good seaman has come to grief by not paying attention to the soundings on the chart. Look here...' Goddard ran his finger down the eastern shore towards the cape, evidently deriving satisfaction in his adopted role as tutor. '... even with our draught, we could run aground as much as two miles out. And see these shoals here littering the entrance to the Chesapeake around the Cape. With the draught of the *Miranda*, fully loaded as she is with tobacco, Judd could easily come a cropper if he's not careful. But while grounding may hinder his escape, it won't do us any favours; a grounded vessel becomes very vulnerable if a sea gets up especially in an onshore wind, and I would rather like to have my ship back in one piece, if you please!'

The officer of the off-going watch, to whom Goddard had handed over in the middle of the night, shook the young captain awake at eight o'clock the following morning.

'Nothing out of the ordinary to report, sir,' said the officer. 'I've brought the plot up to date. Visibility has fallen to about two miles in drizzle in the last hour, but I managed a sighting of the Virginian shoreline before our last tack - so I know our longitude is reasonably accurate. And I think I got a decent latitude off Polaris at dawn before the cloud rolled in, which I transferred using track, speed, and the tidal vector to hazard a running fix. I'm fairly confident, all in all, that our present course should take us directly to the Cape. We're on starboard, full and by, making ten knots. ETA: late morning if the wind holds. All written down in the log, sir.'

'Thank you, number one. Is my watch on deck?'

'Just taken over, sir, and posted to lookout positions; mine is stood down. Mr Easton has taken over. Sir Michael, Major Lawrence and the others - all at breakfast, sir.'

'Good man! You and the bosun get some rest now; I'll call you when I need you.'

It was to greet a grey and murky morning that Captain Goddard later came up on deck to find Jack taking his turn at the helm. With a good southerly breeze, *Warrior* heeled ten degrees to larboard, and was prancing through the slight swell like a filly given her head. Goddard made his way aft, using the backstays and shrouds to steady him as he went, and took up his customary position on the mizzen-sheet horse. The sea was a featureless grey disc of indistinct radius under an equally featureless grey dome of low cloud. There was no discernable horizon. At the edges of view in every direction, the sea simply merged into the sky in a transition that seemed to have no beginning and no end, so that the only indication of attitude came from the ship's deck itself – this and the pull of gravity, which, with the variable angle of heel and pitch, were often in some conflict with each other. Because of the potential disorientation, Jack was paying more than usual attention to the compass and did not notice Goddard's approach.

'Morning, Jack,' said Goddard, grimly shaking his head. 'We'd have to be on a collision course to see her in this!'

'Oh, morning, Philip!' said Jack, a little startled by his friend's sudden appearance at his side. 'At least it'll be just as bad for the *Miranda*. How good is Judd's navigation, by the way?'

'I wouldn't know, Jack. But probably worse than yours!' The captain smiled wryly.

'Doomed then!' Jack replied, laconically.

'Perhaps you'll show me your plot, Mr Judd?' asked Pettigrew with a yawn, having arisen from his bunk and stretched himself awake. 'I may not be a mariner, but I would like to know how well we are progressing - if it is possible for a mere land-lubber to understand such intricacy.'

He stretched again, approached the table and bent over the chart. Then, with squinting eyes, he minutely examined the myriad of markings annotated thereon in Judd's hand. Evidently he found them difficult to understand, for the frown on his forehead persisted.

'What are these crossings out and erasures?' asked Pettigrew, shortly.

With no one to whom Judd was prepared to hand over the watch during a long and uncertain night as the *Miranda* had ploughed blindly down the Chesapeake in almost total darkness, he had allowed himself no sleep. Drained of his reserves, he therefore found himself somewhat on the defensive at Pettigrew's sudden inquisition.

'Ah! Recalculations,' offered Judd, shaking his head dismissively, as if to say that errors and corrections were of little consequence. 'In the poor light, I...'

But Pettigrew cut him off. 'Then where are we now? It is difficult to tell from this...this cat's cradle of lines and scrawls!' he said, derisively.

Judd swallowed. He picked up has dividers with slow deliberation, and, closing them carefully to a point, brought them down on to the chart.

'Here,' he said, confidently enough, but his eyes seemed to suggest that he was somewhat wary, as if he already anticipated a challenge.

'What, still some ten miles north of the cape? How did you reckon our speed, then?'

'With the log-line and timing glass, sir, in the normal manner,' Judd retorted, almost in affront. 'We have made eight knots throughout the night - while you slept peacefully in your bunk!' A hint of pique now crept into Judd's tone with this reply.

'And how did you account for the tide?' Pettigrew persisted, like a prosecutor in cross-examination, his tone hardening.

'The ebb and flow should average out over the period...so I have not reckoned it...' replied Judd, but less confidently this time.

'You think that wise?' cut in Pettigrew, raising his eyebrows; 'And you took leeway into account, of course?' This was Pettigrew the former ship-owner talking now - a man who knew the terms and principles of navigation if not the methods - and someone who could recognise sloppy chart work when he saw it.

'I did indeed, sir!' puffed Judd indignantly, although his conviction seemed to be waning quickly in the face of Pettigrew's critical enquiry. 'Although – ' he hedged, 'leeway cannot be accurately calculated without a suitable landmark and a knowledge of the tidal flow. I made an allowance of course...'

'Did you indeed? Then how confident are you of our position?'

Hayward approached the table at this point, having risen from the armchair in which he had slept overnight, giving Judd a withering glance as he arrived at Pettigrew's side.

'It's difficult to be completely confident in such conditions,' Judd hedged. 'And with the darkness and the poor visibility... we've not had sight of land since before midnight. How could anyone be sure!' Judd's voice tailed off; he was now in full flight, an experience that he was not at all accustomed to.

'You mean that you have tacked down the Chesapeake all night, without sight of land on either side!'

Judd seemed to take Pettigrew's remark as a direct attack, for his eyes flared in anger.

'Yes! While you two have been fast asleep, and I and the good old salts amongst our pathetic band of idle lubbers have been working all night without a break!'

Judd's resentment had been brewing up since the previous evening's unsettling conversation and now it found voice.

'Where would you be now without me?' he sneered. 'Back in Brandywine festering in that rat-infested hotel dreaming up grandiose schemes that could not possibly work without someone like me to lead you by the hand. It was I who got the money!' (As he said this, he could not seem to stop himself casting a glance towards Pettigrew's bunk where he had seen the bulging saddlebags stowed the previous night – but he brought his eyes back quickly). 'And it was I who took possession of this ship and put her under my command! While you just sat about and watched! And now you have the gall to claim half the proceeds! This is unfinished business as far as I'm concerned! I have not agreed to the share-out that you propose! And you had just better watch out, Mr Pettigrew,' he spat out vehemently, ' - the men respond to my orders now! Even your thugs would take my orders if I told them what you had planned for them in the St Lawrence!'

Judd recognised at once that this last was idle rhetoric, used instinctively to reassert himself after Pettigrew's bruising interrogation, and he instantly knew that that he had gone too far. It had been a mistake to reveal his feelings, and he realised it at once, but having said what he had said, he now had no choice now but to brazen it out.

Pettigrew showed no reaction to Judd's outburst, but instead stood calmly watching, as if noting the behaviour of some interesting specimen in a laboratory.

'I think that Mr Judd is getting a little above himself, Mr Hayward, don't you?' he said at last to his 'aide de camps' hovering at his shoulder, the menace in his voice made starker by the coolness with which he spoke. 'Perhaps I should remind you, Mr Judd, that it is I who give the orders here, and you would be wise not to forget it! I should not try to rally those men against me if I were you. Do you think that they would take your word over mine? You would find them resistant, I assure you. You are perhaps forgetting that I have the means to control them, just as you were yourself... shall we say 'persuaded' at the hotel by my companions. They at least know where their loyalties lie.'

With this, he smirked dismissively, exchanging a conspiratorial glance with Hayward, who still stood at his side. And Hayward's eyes narrowed as he swung a mocking gaze back in Judd's direction. There was no doubting where Hayward's loyalties lay, thought Judd, dismally.

The silence that then fell in the cabin became electric as the colour of Judd's face flushed, even as his expression changed from defiance to defeat. But there then came a shout from the deck that saved him from an inevitable and humiliating climb down:

'Five fathoms, and the bottom sandy!'

With a pugnacious pout, Judd excused himself defiantly and made for the door in some fluster, leaving the cabin without so much as a word or rearward glance. The two men left behind looked slightly bemused.

'I think that he has taken the point, Mr Hayward, don't you?' said Pettigrew evenly. 'But I am afraid that we shall have to be a little more careful with him from now on. However, we could not reach our destination without him, and so we shall need to humour him a little longer.'

'A *little* longer,' echoed Hayward in reply. But just as he said this, the ship was felt to swing with a motion that was so wild that it threw both men against the table - while on the deck above their heads, the sounds of running feet and the clatter of machinery resounded.

Chapter Nineteen

'So much for my weather forecast!' lamented Goddard from his navigation table to Jack standing abrace the wheel. 'We seem to have the worst of both worlds now - can't see much more than a mile in front of our faces and the wind is dropping - just when we needed to be quick on our feet!' He returned his attentions to his chart for a few moments and then called again: 'Oh, and keep the leadsman at his soundings, Jack, I'm using them to judge our distance off – we must be quite close now. What's our speed doing, d'you think?'

'Decreasing, Philip; I'd say about three knots through the water; no idea what the tide is – I've got no fixed marks to judge it by.'

'Still on the ebb, Jack, and will be for some time yet if these tables are correct. If you maintain the heading I gave you, it should be taken into account. We'll find out soon enough - if we ever get a landfall!'

During the past few hours, *Warrior* had been sailing steadily on what should be her final starboard tack across the Chesapeake on a heading estimated to make a landfall at Cape Charles, the northern rim of the neck opening into the Atlantic Ocean. The long, broadening peninsular stretching a hundred and forty miles northwards from the Cape formed the eastern boundary of the Chesapeake. On Goddard's chart, its periphery was made ragged by the many fissures and low islands that characterised the entire shoreline; and adjacent waters were dotted with hundreeds of shallow soundings, which continued the pattern, as if these too might at one time have been land, long since submerged. A channel through this labyrinth of shoals was also marked on the chart - although a navigator unfamiliar with these waters might prudently use a deeper, more southerly route instead - albeit incurring additional mileage. It was Goddard's hunch, however, that in the prevailing headwind, Judd would be tempted to use the northerly route to save several hours of tacking; or else he would be entirely oblivious of the hazard and thus simply plot to round the Cape close by, as the shortest course out into the open sea. Goddard had therefore decided to lay in wait for the *Miranda* where the northern channel came closest to the Cape, just outside a small horseshoe-shaped island located at its tip.

If the lookouts' anxious, sweeping gazes could magically have penetrated the mist, it would have been seen at once that *Warrior* was indeed approaching the intended position from the northwest. But not gifted with such faculties, not one of them had yet called the sight of land - although there had been some darkening of the mist to leeward from time to time that had brought the larboard lookout within a breath of it. Goddard was navigating his craft blind to any helpful reference, entirely by dead reckoning - plotting track and distance according to compass, log, and an estimate of tidal flow - accurate enough in the open sea but in such close proximity to potential hazard, it was nerve-wracking to say the least. These were treacherous waters in which to be unsure of one's position, and an apprehensive quiet had thus descended upon the ship's complement. The muted rippling of the bow wave and the sombre creaking of rigging and timbers heightened the pervading sense of expectancy and made the silence yet more poignant. *Warrior* had become a ghost ship drifting through a grey haze, and her occupants had been frozen in their poses as they gazed so intently about. The regular cast of lead into the water from the bow and the leadsman's lonely calls were the only sounds of life.

Below, the cabin had been cleared for action. Only Matthew and Ned remained there, both sitting at the mess table bent to their allotted tasks: filling powder flasks and shot canisters and laying them out in trays. The *Miranda* might be spotted at any moment, and everything must be prepared to swing instantly into the attack. The group might only get one chance and they would have to make it count. Muskets and pistols had thus already been broken out and charged by Major Lawrence and his men, and the weapons had been placed in racks aside the companionway, ready to be passed up should action stations be called. Sir Michael's regimental stores in Georgetown had been so severely plundered in preparation for this chase, that every man aboard would have at least half a dozen charged weapons ready to hand. The cabin had been transformed into a veritable armoury. If *Warrior* would hardly rate as a man of war, she could count herself a marauder, for she carried enough firepower to start a minor insurrection. And if she could get close enough to her quarry - avoiding the firing line of any of *Miranda's* cannon that might be brought to bear - she had the means to savage her enemy's decks with a barrage of blistering proportions.

'By the mark, six, sir!' came the call from the larboard bow.

'The island should be directly ahead, Jack!' called Goddard from his navigation cubicle. 'If we're on course, that depth should put us about two miles off the Cape, just entering the approach to the North Channel. Any sign of land?'

'Nothing yet, Philip!'

'Number one! I am intending to drop anchor at four fathoms, or sooner if we see land. Are the anchor watch prepared?'

'They will be, captain,' replied the first officer. 'Everyone's on deck with their eyes peeled for the *Miranda*! By the way, sir, there are eddies in the water off the larboard quarter that suggest there's quite a current running – north to south.'

'Thank you, number one. We're probably just entering the narrow channel between two major shoals; they'll be acting as a funnel,' replied Goddard by way of explanation. 'The tide's on its way out now at full ebb. Come larboard a bit, Jack, to compensate for the drift – say zero six zero – I don't want to be pressed too far down.'

'Zero six zero it is!' called Jack, turning the wheel a spoke or two to larboard.

'By the mark, five and half five!' came the call from the larboard rail.

'Depth decreasing, five and a half!' called Jack into the hatch so as to ensure that Goddard received the linesman's sounding.

'At four and a half, Jack, I shall want you to bring her head northerly into the current.' A brief pause followed, then Goddard called out: 'Number one?'

'Aye sir!' came the first officer's brisk reply.

'I'll want the main and mizzen scandalised as we anchor, rather than dropped – if the crew can manage that short-handed - so as to be ready for a quick get-away if and when we sight the *Miranda*. The extra windage should not be a problem in this light wind - the current will push us back as the cable is laid out. Flake out twelve fathoms on the fore deck; that should be enough to hold her; I do not expect to be here long. Get the major and his men to lend a hand!'

'Aye, sir,' shot back the first officer who, hardly pausing for breath, relayed the captain's orders forward to the boatswain, already seen garnering his crewmen about him on the main deck, evidently anticipating the command. 'And Major Lawrence, sir!' he added; 'You and your men will join me on the foredeck, if you please! - And Sir Michael too, if you wish, sir, – we shall have some heavy work to do shortly!'

Some minutes now passed with much industry on deck as groups of men were set to their different duties; and when these had been accomplished to the boatswain's critical satisfaction, they stood about with an uneasy watchfulness about them, as if the fearful imminence of hostilities had suddenly struck home.

'Land ahoy!' came a call from the bow at long last; and all heads turned in that direction. 'Two miles on the starboard bow!'

'Land ahead, Philip,' Jack relayed through the hatch. 'Looks like the island – sandy beach; low lying.'

At this, Goddard slid himself out from beside the navigation table and clambered up the few steps to join Jack and the first officer at the wheel.

'That'll do us,' he said. 'Head her up stream, Jack; and come to anchoring drill if you please, number one! Watch your bearings against the shore and let go as we come to a relative stop. I'll give my orders to the bosun from here.'

The next few minutes saw some frantic action as *Warrior's* head was brought up into the current, a manoeuvre that put the wind almost directly behind her stern. Still driven through the water by her sail power, the vessel maintained her steerageway, but her speed relative to the seabed five fathoms below her keel decreased to a crawl.

'Proceed bosun, if you please!' called the captain calmly when all appeared in prepared.

Urged on by the staccato orders of the boatswain, two groups of men now simultaneously heaved down on the main and mizzen boom toping lifts, letting go the sheet tackle at the same time to free off some slack. With each concerted heave, the heavy main and mizzen booms were thus inched upwards, their canvases folding and bunching roughly between spar and mast as the angle increased, until at last the booms pointed some seventy degrees above the deck. The headsails still pulled gamely, but with the two larger sails effectively taken out of action, or scandalised, as the procedure was known, the schooner began to slow. And eventually a point in her continuing deceleration was reached where her speed over the seabed (as measured so finely by the first officer's steady bearing on the nearby shore) came to zero. It was at this precise moment that the order was given for the anchor to be let go. It was a tricky operation that would have been difficult in a stronger wind, but it had the advantage of making the sails more readily available if needed in a hurry, for the booms need only to be dropped for power to be regained.

'Stopped, sir! Anchor away!' came the shout from the first officer at the bow.

There was a mighty splash as the anchor plummeted from the cathead and hit the water. And it dragged thirty feet of heavy cable through the hawsehole after it at very high speed – until its escape checked abruptly.

'Anchor's on the bottom, sir! Drop back when you are ready!' came the call from the bow.

'Thank you, number one. Bosun! Let fly the heads'ls!'

More frenzied activity erupted on the foredeck now as the captain's order was relayed, and several men leapt to release the headsail sheets from their cleats. And one by one, the three slender sails on the bowsprit were freed from harness to flap lazily in the following breeze. With no more than mere windage now to drive her, the vessel began slowly to be pushed backwards by the current, and with this movement, the remaining seven fathoms of anchor cable, already flaked out on the deck, were further drawn out. To those who watched the cable slide, it was as if it had a will of its own - like some monstrous snake making a slithering dash through the hawsehole. But its tail snapped taut as the restraining friction of the capstan bit and stopped the reptile's accelerating race for freedom with a yank; and with this, the ship's rearward movement was checked.

'Holding fast, sir!' came the call from the bow some several seconds later, as a sudden calm descended upon the deck, the men previously so intent upon their tasks made at once redundant.

'Keep your eyes peeled everyone,' shouted Goddard. 'If the *Miranda* intends to take the North Channel, we shall see her first on the larboard bow.'

'And what if she doesn't?' queried Jack, as he stepped back from the wheel to join his friend now perched upon the mizzen horse.

'Then you and Sir Michael have lost your money and I have lost my ship, Jack – and probably my career with it, I am afraid to say,' replied Goddard gloomily, as his eyes searched the grey and indistinct horizon. 'But let us hope that it does not come to that.'

Judd stood upon *Miranda's* quarterdeck brooding sullenly as the ship ploughed on, the satisfaction of his fugitive command diminished by two gnawing anxieties, both of which now mixed together in his stomach to make a bitter brew that had quite put him off his food. The first of these was his growing uneasiness at being saddled with Pettigrew and his unctuous companion, Hayward, both of whom he had begun to despise as well as mistrust. Indeed, dogged with resentment and humiliation from his last encounter with the pair earlier that morning, his mind had already begun to scheme the ways by which he could be rid of them. Like others in the delinquent crew, he carried a pistol and a knife in his belt, and in his imagination he had already seen himself slitting both their throats and throwing their bodies into the sea. And but for his fear of retribution from Pettigrew's loyal thugs and others of the fickle crew who might see it in their interests to join them, his murderous thoughts might have already been turned into action. Judd had also not been slow to realise that he would become vulnerable once he was no longer useful to the pair, just as would the rest of the crew, as Pettigrew had revealed. While the *Miranda* remained at sea, therefore, Judd would be safe, but he would have to watch his back once the voyage had been completed. The question he now pondered was thus not whether, but when and how to strike, for should he leave it too late or botch it in some way, he knew he or his cherished prize could be lost.

The second anxiety, however, rapidly gaining potency in his gut as time had passed, now quite suddenly took over all his thoughts... With the wind having veered into the southwest, the *Miranda's* course had turned more favourable for the Cape. Moreover the tidal flow was now aiding the vessel's progress down the Chesapeake rather than hindering it. It had thus seemed entirely possible when Judd had taken up the present tack, that this would be the final leg out into the open sea. But if his last plot had been accurate, he now reasoned anxiously, surely the eastern shore would be visible by now? That he had not seen it may have been due to the deteriorating visibility, but it could equally have been because he had made a miscalculation of some sort. All kinds of demons now began to haunt him as he searched the misty horizon in vain for some helpful signpost as to his whereabouts. He had hoped to gain visual contact with the peninsular just north of the Cape so as to guide his entry into the deep middle channel and so take up a safe course out into the Atlantic. But now he wondered if he had perhaps come too far south - that he had already missed the Cape and was proceeding blindly into an area on the chart that was littered with warnings of shallow water! This posed a dilemma: Should he wear now, and set himself upon a new tack to the west, turning away from his objective, thus losing much time as well as compounding the uncertainty of his position? Or should he press on?

It was his dithering on this, rather than any conviction one way or the other, that kept him on his present course; and it was this failure of good captaincy that would soon put his vessel into jeopardy. At this crucial moment, even as Judd could have taken belated action and thus have saved the day, Pettigrew and Hayward arrived on the quarterdeck and took up a position behind him at the stern rail. It was perhaps because of the earlier heated exchange between them that Judd failed to acknowledge the arrival of the pair or meet their silent glances as they passed him by. Instead, he held his gaze steadfastly upon the horizon - intensely conscious of their presence, yet contriving not to show it. It was the presence of these two that undermined what little confidence he had left, so that he found himself suddenly self-conscious and inhibited; the fear of being seen to make the wrong decision preventing him from making any decision at all.

And so when the call came at last:

'Land ahoy, one mile and a half off the larboard bow!' his relief was real and manifest. But this was at once tempered by the awful fear that, in the shallow waters of the eastern Chesapeake, the coast could be much too close for safety. It was only now that he realised that it had been far too long since he had received a call of depth from his leadsman - his mind had dwelled too long on other things when he should have been concentrating on navigation. At once he flashed a reproving glance towards the foredeck seeking the object of his disapproval, and puffed himself up ready to bawl the man out for his tardiness. He spied the crewman lounging on the bulwark idly twiddling the lead line in his hand, engaged in some jocular chitchat with men nearby. Judd seethed at the man's culpable neglect.

'Depth! You bla'gard!' he swore in exasperation, 'I'll have your guts for garters!'

But he was cross with himself for his inattention too. With visions of imminent grounding springing into his mind, he only just overcame a sudden urge to leap at the wheel and turn the ship to starboard, away from the danger. It was as well he controlled himself, for to have attempted to come about would certainly have put the vessel into stays and set her drifting closer to the shore. It was perhaps this realisation that checked him.

'Five fathoms!' came the linesman's insolent call after a delay that seemed inordinately long.

'Not much more than six feet under the keel!' Judd reckoned quickly in his mind. 'My God, we cannot risk coming any closer in!'

Yet if he attempted to wear the ship to larboard, he knew the manoeuvre would have the effect of doing exactly that. Besides, his crew were not prepared.

'Too late' he thought, grimly. He could turn neither left nor right - he had got himself into a nasty corner from which only providence could extricate him. Judd felt his heart begin to race as prickles of sweat tickled his brow, but he forced himself to take stock. With the wind now south-by-southwest, the present course appeared to be approximately parallel to the shore rather than converging upon it to any great degree; but it was in the lap of the Gods as to whether he would stay afloat or run aground. He could only hope that the bottom contour would save him, for he could not bring his course more to windward without stalling the sails.

'Hold her steady helmsman, as tight as you can on the wind,' he whispered hoarsely in the helmsman's ear; and then shouted more robustly at some men gathered on the main deck:

'You men there! Tighten those mains'l braces and sheet in the heads'ls as tight as you can!'

With this, he hoped to claw himself out of his predicament. But although mortified at the thought of having run his ship into near catastrophe, he showed no outward sign of his distress. That reaction might come later, but for now neither of his two critical observers nor the majority of the crew seemed aware of the peril. Only a few of the former seaman amongst those assembled on the main deck looked back at him anxiously.

And then came an agitated shout from the lookout at the bow: 'Vessel dead ahead!'

'Ship ahead, captain!' called at least two of *Warrior's* lookouts almost simultaneously; and all eyes at once turned in response. About one mile forward of the bow, a square-rigger bore down upon the schooner's anchorage, her taut canvases barely visible against a grey and misty background. Goddard took out his glass and held the instrument briefly to his eye.

'By heaven's blessing! She's the *Miranda!*' he breathed almost incredulously, after taking a few extra seconds of inspection to be sure. 'Delivered to us on a plate, by God!'

Goddard was exultant. He snapped his telescope shut and stood thoughtfully for a moment while assessing the oncoming vessel's progress; she was closing slowly and steadily but was still some way off. 'Well gentlemen!' he continued calmly, 'time for action, I think. Sir Michael and Major Lawrence, sirs: take your men below and arm yourselves, but do not come up on deck until I call you.'

At this, Major Lawrence led his men quickly down the companionway, with Sir Michael following in train. Ned and Matthew's excited voices were heard to ring out up the hatchway as the party reached the lower deck; the pair had remained in the cabin to finish off their munitions work and had evidently been taken by surprise by the sudden call to arms. This left Goddard and Jack on deck with the ship's officers and crew.

'Jack: you take the wheel. Bosun: have the anchor cable taken in half so that we're just holding the ground. And when you've done that, secure the heads'l sheets so that the heads'ls draw, then stand by to drop the main and mizzen booms - I want to be ready to sail at an instant's notice if we have to!' Goddard flashed a calculating glance at the closing vessel, then beckoned his first officer closer.

'Bring up a box of pistols from Ned's armoury and place them here on deck ready for our use, just in case we need them.'

He took out his telescope again, extending it and raising it to his eye in one slick motion; but this time he held it there while he spoke: 'She's the *Miranda* all right, Jack,' he said, muttering under his squinting eye, his words muffled by his upheld arms, '- sailing well sheeted and braced, very tight on the wind.' He fell into a thoughtful silence while continuing to observe. 'Hmmm! Not very well either − her helmsman's pinching like mad. Judd's got himself on a lee shore - he probably knows how close he is to grounding and is trying to get off. How in hell's name did he allow himself to get so close?'

The *Miranda* sailed ever closer. She was now some eight cables off, just over three-quarters of a nautical mile, and closing on a steady bearing from the schooner's bow.

'She's coming directly at us, Philip,' called Jack from the wheel; he held the wheel's spokes tightly as if steering, yet the schooner remained stationary at anchor. 'It'll be a near miss unless she's able to claw herself into deeper water − there can't be enough depth for her to pass to our landward.'

'And she'll draw a good fathom more than we do, Jack,' agreed Goddard, 'there won't be enough depth for her anywhere here. Try the helm to larboard! I've got an idea.'

Jack spun the wheel half to larboard. Although the vessel remained at anchor, the continuing outgoing tidal flow still provided some steerageway. Deflecting the rudder, therefore, caused the schooner's stern to swing and her head to pivot on the anchor cable where it came in through the hawsehole - like a kite on a line. *Warrior* now took up a heading askew the stream, pointing at an angle away from the shore and into deeper water. With this shift of heading, the headsails billowed gently and began to pull the vessel forward on her cable.

'Good!' called Goddard. 'Hold her there, Jack. By holding us across her path, I'm trying to force her to come about. And it'll give us a good purchase on the wind when we drop the main and mizzen.'

The *Miranda* had now closed to about five cables.

'Major! Sir Michael!' Goddard called down through the hatch. 'Standby for my call! And when you come up, go straight to the bulwarks. Stay low and keep your weapons out of sight.'

'They could be training their glasses on us, Philip,' Jack warned, pulling his cap well down over his forehead. Goddard took the hint and followed suit. If *Warrior* herself would not yet appear to pose the threat of armed attack, recognition of her crew would give away the surprise she held in store.

'Head further out, man!' blurted Pettigrew. 'You'll hit her at this rate!'

Judd heard the irascible remark from behind his back but preferred to ignore it. There was anyway nothing he could do to change the Miranda's course. Except to leeward, he thought - quite the last thing he would want to do at present as the vessel ploughed her narrow path between the devil of the shoals on one side and the siren call of deep water on the other!

'She's changing course!' shouted the lookout from the bow.

Judd saw the schooner begin to swing. At this distance and in the poor visibility, he had not yet seen the schooner's anchor cable, and thus when he saw the vessel's change of heading, he leapt to the assumption that she would soon pull out of the way.

'We'll pass behind her!' he said dismissively over his shoulder to his two critical observers, as if to say: 'I know what I am doing, so leave me to it!' But his heart was racing just the same.

It is in such circumstances that the brain can play tricks on human sensibility, especially a brain as fatigued and flustered as Judd's was at this moment. The schooner's aspect elongated as she swung further, and with her headsails apparently drawing, she did indeed appear to move clear. Without a clear horizon behind her and against a grey and featureless sea, there was no reference by which to judge. But the few degrees by which the distracted helmsman had inadvertently eased the pressure on his wheel contributed to the illusion. Judd should have been watching his compass rather than depending upon his eyes to inform him. Had he been more attentive, he would have seen that his heavy-laden cargo ship was now converging with the shore. The illusion persisted only a little longer than a minute while Judd's misguided hope triumphed over reality; but it was long enough.

The bottom contours so far from the shore lay in a pattern of smooth undulations varying in height by only a few inches, a variation produced by the action of waves and tidal flow on sand and muddy sediment. The first contact of the Miranda's keel with the bottom was at such a shallow grazing angle that it created only the slightest jar. One or two crews' heads turned inquisitively towards the helm, but most aboard, including Pettigrew and Hayward, seemed unaware of the glancing blow. Only Judd realised what had happened and he threw himself at once at the wheel, sending the helmsman flying in the process, and spun it hard over to starboard.

'Helm-a-lee!' he shouted at the top of his voice. 'Coming about! Quickly with those sheets and braces you bla'guards, or we'll be here for the night!'

The *Miranda* was sprightly in a stiff blow, but in lower wind strengths such as that pertaining, her response was rather more sluggish. Even an experienced crew would have difficulty bringing her though the wind. But Judd had the devil's choice between attempting it or running firmly aground, bow first. He held the wheel hard over, hoping desperately that the ship's momentum would be enough to carry her through. The bowsprit traced a lethargic arc around the hazy horizon; forty degrees off the wind, then thirty, then twenty as the bow swung further. But the swing was slowing. He could see the rate declining rapidly as the main sails snapped full astern, acting as huge air brakes. Ten degrees to go!

'Get those damned braces swung over!' he cursed angrily. If he could spill some wind the rearward drag would be reduced.

Responding to Judd's expletives, more orders were bellowed on the main deck, and the crew were raced from one side of the vessel to the other. At last the yards were swung. If Judd could get the bow to point up just a little further with the little way he had left, he might yet be able to back the foresails to pull the *Miranda* onto the other tack. She was slowing rapidly but she was still turning. Only five degrees to go!

'Back the heads'ls!' he shouted. He could wait no longer; and his voice was shrill.

Half a dozen crew now hurried forward to pull in the larboard headsail sheets. The headsails, until then fluttering lazily in the headwind, were at once tightened with the wind aback. At first it looked as if they might bite and push the bow through the wind's eye. Only a few more degrees to go and they would achieve it! But the drag of great square canvasses was just too much. Billowing back now in the dead-on headwind, they pressed into the shrouds with such a mighty force that the foresails' puny fight was made futile as the *Miranda* was brought to a complete stop. The rudder was now a useless plank in still water.

For several seconds, the bowsprit hovered in the balance, moving neither one way nor the other. Judd hung onto the wheel; the crew hung on to their rope ends; all frozen like statues into fearful poses. All watched the headsails still clawing on the wind, but every man jack of them knew in their hearts that the fight was already lost.

'She's going astern!' someone shouted from the foredeck as the headsails suddenly lost their grip and broke into a flapping frenzy.

Having come to a halt in its clockwise sweep, the bowsprit now began to swing back as rearward way picked up. Judd threw an anxious glance astern, briefly catching the frightened looks of his two companions as he did so, and spun the wheel hard to larboard. Even in such dire circumstances, he was apparently still thinking clearly. With the rudder now hard over in the opposite direction, the rearward way might help to slow the swing. In his mind was the thought that he must keep his ship from going aground bow first, for she would be the devil to get off in the prevailing wind. In this instinctive if desperate measure he was successful, for a moment later the floundering vessel slid stern first into the mud and shuddered to a halt.

'Drop the heads'ls; furl the mains!' Judd shouted with resignation in a hoarse voice; and he watched the men rallied out of their confused state and driven into action once more.

'Impressive!' came Pettigrew's sneering tones from behind Judd's back. 'Now what, Mr Judd?'

But Judd ignored the remark, and instead let his eyes seek out the one former seaman he had learned to trust as second-in-command on those few occasions heretofore when he had gone below. Catching the man's eye, Judd beckoned him come closer.

'See to it that everything's squared away, mister, then get three boats over the side and run a couple of kedges out from the bow to stabilise her. With luck, we'll be able to winch ourselves off the mud on the next tide.'

Chapter Twenty

'Delivered, plucked, and ready for a roasting, I'd say, Philip!' said Jack from underneath his telescope. 'She won't be going anywhere for a while!'

'Hmmm! Seems that way, Jack,' said Goddard, looking extremely pleased with himself. 'Wheel amidships, and time for a conference, I think.'

Leaving the lookouts and crew on anchor watch, Jack and the captain now retired to the cabin to find Sir Michael and the militia armed to the teeth hovering at the foot of the companionway. With their blood up and impatient to join battle, there were frowns of puzzlement on their faces when they were ushered back into the cabin to allow the arriving pair space. And this turned into consternation at Goddard's inscrutable smile.

'Well, gentlemen,' he said with barely concealed delight, 'the *Miranda's* gone aground barely half-a-mile in front of our bow! She's just sitting there with her sails flapping! And probably within the musket range of your marksmen, major!'

He waited for the ripple of astonishment to peter out before continuing:

'But she went aground not long before low water, so there's every chance that she'll re-float within the next few hours, depending upon how hard she's driven herself into the mud.'

He beckoned Jack, Sir Michael, and Major Lawrence to the table, and indicated that the others seat themselves on the wooden benches along the cabin bulkheads. Sergeants Schluntz and Bryant chose instead to hover near the galley stove on which a large cauldron of some steaming substance gave off an enticing aroma of meat and potato broth – Ned's recipe, left to simmer following an earlier culinary initiative. The assembly fell into an expectant silence while they waited for Goddard to take his seat at the table.

'If she's within musket range, captain,' said Lawrence, sagely stroking his beard, 'then we've got her. We could pick off her crew one by one, or at least stop anyone moving about on deck – so she could never get herself underway again.'

Sir Michael shook his head. 'No, no,' he interjected. 'That would simply create a siege situation. They would take cover and return fire. Why, she'd become a fortress - they could hold us off indefinitely.'

'Or they'd wait for nightfall and slip away in the darkness,' chipped in Jack.

There were murmurs of agreement at these contributions, and thus encouraged, Jack continued:

'I'd say that our best bet may be to wait awhile and not give the game away. Judd cannot yet know who we are – and as long as the captain and I - and young Matthew here - don't get recognised we'll maintain the initiative. Judd will need to lay a kedge or two into deeper water in order to winch the *Miranda* off the mud. And that means that he'll have to put at least half his crew in the boats - that's when they'll be at their most vulnerable. And that will be the moment that we should make our move, and not before. If we take a boat down to her then, say, under the guise of offering assistance, we'll only have the remnant of the crew aboard to deal with. With any luck, we'll catch Judd off guard.'

Major Lawrence nodded. 'It might work,' he said, carefully. 'My boys and I could go down looking like a regular crew, get ourselves aboard somehow, and ...well, by the time their boats got back to the ship, they'd find a new captain in charge!'

'Excellent idea!' exclaimed Sir Michael, slapping his thigh.

Goddard grinned. 'And they'd have saved us the trouble of laying out the kedges ourselves! Very helpful of them, I must say!'

'Right! Well then, you'd better get yourselves prepared, gentlemen!' said Jack emphatically. 'I'll set up watch topside while you get the boats in the water, Philip?'

'Agreed;' said Goddard, 'but, Jack, for heaven's sake keep your cap down!' Then, turning to his first officer: 'Number One: get the boats in the water and signal "We are rendering assistance", - which they are going to get whether they like it or not!'

When Jack climbed back up the companionway and stuck his head above the hatch, he saw immediately that the tide had turned, for *Warrior* had swung completely about on her anchor to face into the now incoming current. The *Miranda* thus now lay astern rather than ahead - although, held fast in the clinging mud, her beam-on orientation had not altered. Picking up the telescope from its holder, Jack made his way aft - casually, in the manner of a seaman, just in case he might be under observation from the merchantman's decks - and took up a position behind the stern rail where he could watch the *Miranda* unobtrusively. He extended the glass and levelled it at the Miranda's quarterdeck where he spied a group of figures engaged in some sort of animated discussion. What he saw surprised him.

'Well, well,' he muttered to himself as he scanned the faces in the group. 'Looks like Pettigrew is there too!' he called over his shoulder to Goddard. 'The master puppeteer!' he thought grimly, 'I might have guessed it! I'll wager that it was he who dreamt this up, and that Judd found himself manoeuvred to serve his wretched purpose - whatever that may be? Judd would not have had the imagination to think of it himself!'

He swung his view quickly to locate the former boatswain. On first sweep, Jack did not identify him for his shaven head and beard. Only when he looked again, this time examining the eyes more carefully, did he find him; his appearance was quite unexpected despite Harding's description, but there was no doubt.

Suddenly, without warning, a musket shot rang out behind him and he threw a startled glance over his shoulder in consternation. But even as his pulse began to race, he saw at once that there was no cause for alarm.

'Just to attract their attention,' laughed Goddard from behind the main mast as the signal flags were run up the halyard. 'Looks like it got yours too!'

Jack grimaced and returned to his observation, the tingling in his fingers subsiding as he once more levelled his glass. Aboard the Miranda, the shot had had the effect of turning faces towards him, just as intended, and he took the opportunity of studying them more closely. There was Pettigrew again – he looked as smooth and as complacent as ever with his condescending gaze redirected now at Judd to whom he appeared, by his remonstrative manner, to be saying something of a critical nature. Jack swung his view, and felt his pulse begin to thump as he watched Judd mouth a pugnacious retort. A wave of loathing engulfed him as he studied the man's hated features; he looked as surly and as shifty as Jack remembered him despite his attempts at disguise. If Jack had held a musket in his hands at that very instant, he may well have been tempted to blow the man's head off. In his mind's eye, he saw the lead ball hit Judd squarely in the face, renting it to smithereens - and wiping the sneer off his lips forever. But it would be too much of a risk to try; he could easily miss at this range. Jack would have to bide his time, but he revelled in the idea that his time for revenge was nigh.

Through his narrow field of view, Jack watched Judd then move away from the group; he seemed to be shouting orders into the yards where a few men could be seen still bundling up the sails. Perhaps reacting to Judd's call, some started down the ratlines, and Jack followed them as they descended to the main deck. The *Miranda* lay beam on with her bowsprit pointing out across the Bay; three boats had now been lowered over the near side and were lying tied up in a line along the hull. Men were beginning to clamber down the boarding ladders into the leading two; the last, unused for the present time, had been left to drift towards the stern on a long painter. Jack swung the glass back to the quarterdeck where he spied a crewman at the flag halyard hanking on some flags.

'Signal from the *Miranda* being prepared, Philip!' he shouted over his shoulder. 'They seem to be manning their boats - it looks like they are doing exactly what we predicted.'

He swept his view along the vessel's full length and refocused on the foredeck. 'Yes - I see two kedge anchors being shackled up on the foredeck. Is the major ready for his little outing?'

There was a pause, while the captain checked over the schooner's starboard side. 'Yes, Jack - a veritable raiding party - armed to the teeth, but managing to look like butter wouldn't melt in their mouths!' he called back.

'Good,' returned Jack, quickly. 'Tell him that Pettigrew's also aboard so he knows to watch out for him as well as Judd - and that I want them both alive if at all possible – I've got a score to settle with both of them! But don't let the major set off until I say so, Philip; I want to see the *Miranda's* boats well clear before we let them go.'

He returned his scan to the group on the *Miranda's* quarterdeck. Judd had a glass to his eye now - pointed in his direction - and Jack instinctively ducked out of sight behind a stanchion. 'We're under inspection, Philip,' he warned.

'They're signalling, Jack!' called the captain. 'They're sending "We do not require assistance"; but I think we'll ignore it, don't you?' It was a rhetorical remark. 'The way we're lying, the major's boat won't be seen until he's underway.'

Jack ventured another inspection from behind his stanchion. Judd had left the quarterdeck and was now making his way forward along the larboard rail, towards the foredeck. A gaggle of men had accumulated there. Some were inching the two kedges down into the boats with tackle from the catheads; others were flaking out further cable on the deck ready to be paid out. Judd had reached the mainmast shrouds now; he looked curiously unruffled for a grounded skipper, for his walk was unhurried. Jack watched him pause and lean over the bulwarks. He appeared to be checking something along the hull, but Jack was not sure what might have drawn his attention; only a single empty boat now lay alongside. Judd then straightened and continued to the foredeck and took up a supervisory stance with his arms folded; he appeared to be barking some orders. Jack continued to observe through his glass while the work proceeded - it was like watching a mime, for no sound of the activity reached his ears. There appeared to be some difficulty at first settling the kedges into the boats; although relatively small compared with the main bowers, these small anchors were still clearly heavy and unwieldy; and the clumsy movements of the oarsmen more than once threatened to tip the boats over. It was quite evident that the crews were not particularly skilful in their boatmanship.

But eventually Jack saw the boats move clear of the *Miranda's* bow, splaying out at an angle to each other as they rowed into the deeper water, the anchor cables being paid out both from the boats and through the *Miranda's* hawseholes as each craft moved away. It was apparently an increasing struggle for the eight oarsmen in each boat, for the vessels sat markedly stern-down in the water. The flat iron flukes of the kedges protruded well above the boats' transoms, neither of which was more than a foot out of the water under the weight; and either would have been quickly swamped if the sea had been less kind.

'Their boats are clear, Philip! Wish the major and his men good luck and send them on their way!' Jack called.

Jack returned to his scrutiny of the group on the quarterdeck. Now only two men remained there: Pettigrew and another who Jack at first did not recognise. But as he studied the second man's face, recognition slowly dawned; it was Hayward.

'So!' he exclaimed under his breath, 'the triumvirate of all my torments! Three snakes in a basket – if I had *Rebecca's* rear-facing cannon, I could blow them all out of the water here and now...'

Aboard the *Miranda*, the angry arguments and recriminations that had broken out on the quarterdeck after the vessel had gone aground were soon replaced by a fuming silence. Pettigrew was furious at Judd's incompetence and had flown into an uncharacteristic rage, which Judd had borne insolently. He had since escaped to the foredeck to direct the laying out of the kedges, and was now supervising the anchor party paying out the cables as the two boats pulled away. However, the operation was proving even more difficult and laborious than he had thought. Against the flood of the incoming tide, the boats were struggling to maintain their course at the required angle to the bow - important if sufficient purchase were to be obtained. If this were not achieved, the whole lengthy procedure might need to be repeated from the start - against the unrelenting ticking of the tidal clock. The increasing drag and weight of the cables as they lengthened were further impediments to progress. To offset the increasing weight, Judd had already instructed his party to attach floats to the lines as they paid them out. Otherwise they threatened to drag the boats down at the stern and stop them altogether, or even sink them.

With the boats' crews and the foredeck party thus engaged and preoccupied, only Pettigrew and Hayward were alert to the quiet advance of Major Lawrence's craft.

'I thought we had signalled that we did not require assistance?' queried Pettigrew crossly.

'They appear to come, nevertheless,' replied Hayward languidly. 'Perhaps we could use some extra hands?'

'I think better not, Hayward,' asserted Pettigrew, shortly. 'I don't want any further complications, and our boatswain seems at last to have things under control.' He rolled his eyes. 'You go to meet them, Hayward; I would prefer my face not to be seen – one never knows who might recognise me from Easton's damned poster! When the boat comes alongside, decline their offer; but be civil in case we should require help after all – it is still possible that we might need them to pull us off the mud if this plan of Judd's fails to work.'

The major's boat pulled alongside *Miranda's* hull and her bow oarsman, the stocky Bryant, made the painter fast. Major Lawrence now stood up on his thwart and reached out to grab the boarding ladder to pull in the stern. He was about to clamber up the ladder when a voice issued from the rail above his head.

'And a very good afternoon to you, gentlemen.' The speaker was Hayward, standing at the bulwarks with a bland expression on his face.

'Good afternoon, sir,' was Major Lawrence's polite reply as he paused in his progression, one foot remaining on the ladder, the other still on the thwart.

'Perhaps your captain did not see our signal? We seem to have things under control at present and so do not require assistance, thank you. But send our thanks to your captain all the same.'

'I'm glad to hear it, sir,' said the major, casting his eyes left and right in a casual manner, but actually to determine if he were being observed from elsewhere. And then seeing that this was not the case, he continued:

'Well then, I'll bid you farewell!' in a jaunty voice and offered up his hand. It was a bit of a stretch for Hayward to reach it, but it was an instinct born of breeding as well as the desire to be civil, as instructed, that made him try. However, as soon as Lawrence felt Hayward's grip close around his, his face altered from one of courteous farewell to one of outright menace, and his fingers tightened so that Hayward was unable to pull away. At the same instant, Lawrence pulled his pistol from the back of his belt with his other hand and thrust the muzzle sharply under Hayward's chin.

'One sound of alarm on your part, sir, and your scattered brains will bloody that natty suit of yours!' he growled so vehemently that Hayward's eyes bulged in alarm. 'And now you will help me up, sir!' Lawrence ordered.

Pettigrew had watched his companion go to the rail to meet the arriving boat and had caught Hayward's words in the subsequent intercourse. And lulled into thinking that the visitors would soon be sent on their way, he had allowed his attention to be drawn to a further bout of shouting from the foredeck crew as instructions to the boats were conveyed. When he returned his gaze to Hayward, he was somewhat annoyed to see him apparently assisting a bearded stranger onto the deck. But with Hayward's retreating back obscuring his view, Pettigrew was not able to see the weapon at his companion's throat, nor at that moment did he notice the scouts stealing onto the deck behind them. By the time he realised that something was seriously untoward, Pettigrew found himself looking down the muzzles of several pistols with their firing arms already cocked to strike.

The lanky Sergeant Schluntz threw the former ship-owner a warning glance as he leaped silently up the companionway onto the quarterdeck, his pistol unwavering in his hand. In the shock of utter dismay, Pettigrew backed away, shaking his head as the shaven-headed German approached, seemingly too dumbstruck to think of escape. He was thus quickly overpowered by Schluntz's towering frame and put into an arm lock with a pistol muzzle shoved painfully into the small of his back. It had taken just thirty seconds for the two men to be subdued. And, partially obscured by the clutter of the intervening deck and rigging, the capture remained unnoticed by the distant foredeck party who were still heavily preoccupied with their task.

'They're on board, Philip,' Jack called from his observation point. 'And they've taken Pettigrew and Hayward. Judd's on the foredeck, but he doesn't seem to have noticed.'

He continued to watch as the major and his scouts made short work of restraining the two captives and bundled them below. From Jack's distant perspective, it had all seemed almost too easy - like a stage production of some speechless drama, the moves so well rehearsed and silent that it had taken on a surreal, almost artificial quality. But this playlet was real enough, and the terrified looks on the two captives' faces made Jack rejoice in the sweet malice of retribution.

'That's two of them in the bag, Philip,' Jack continued, eye still to glass. 'I guess the major reckons to let Judd and his anchor detail finish off our work for us; and we don't want to interrupt their endeavours, do we? So now, if Ned has got the skiff ready, Philip, I think that it is our turn for an outing!'

Judd was annoyed to see the little sailing skiff approaching, for he himself had ordered the signal flags raised to refuse the schooner's offer of assistance and had thought the matter closed. But he had then been diverted by the activity on the foredeck, and this had so taken his attention that he not been aware of Major Lawrence's earlier arrival. Flashing a glance aft to the quarterdeck, he was surprised and irritated to see that neither Pettigrew nor Hayward was there to ward off the craft. He cursed under his breath.

'The idle pair have gone below,' he thought, crossly; 'a pleasant lunch over a glass of wine no doubt - while I do all the work as usual!'

And with this vexing thought uppermost his mind, he left the foredeck in some dudgeon and made towards the main deck, ready to rebuff the skiff's crew in no uncertain manner. But as he made his way along the larboard walkway, he was surprised to see an unfamiliar boat already tied up alongside, ahead of the *Miranda's* own that he had checked so carefully before. Judd knew at once that visitors from the schooner must already have boarded, and he was therefore puzzled not to see them on deck. It was completely beyond Judd's current reckoning that such an arrival represented any kind of threat, for the thought that the *Miranda* might have been pursued had not entered his mind since they had left the Potomac. Surmising thus that the visitors had been invited below, he imagined some meeting taking place with Pettigrew and Hayward in the captain's cabin. Someone with less damaged self-esteem might well have gone there directly to see what was going on, but Judd began to think instead that he might deliberately have been left out. Instantly suspicious and resentful, he halted and, not wanting to appear irresolute, he feigned interest in some item of the nearby rigging in case he might be observed. Then with studied determination, as if seized by some idea, he turned about and made his way to the forecastle companion, through which he disappeared without looking back.

As we already know from descriptions of his last voyage aboard the *Miranda* when he masqueraded as a simple seaman, Judd knew every inch of his ship like the palm of his hand. His curiosity now aroused, he thus determined to make his way aft below decks to the stern where he might be able to discover whatever might be taking place without giving his presence away. In his mounting paranoia, he would not have put it past Pettigrew and Hayward to be working something out with the visitors that would enable them to dispense with his services, and thus gain a greater share of the spoils for themselves. If he had begun to distrust them before the vessel went aground, he felt even more vulnerable to betrayal now.

Descending quickly to the orlop, he proceeded with some stealth into the familiar cargo hold. Here, noises of the anchor cable being run out along the foredeck, reverberated through the ship's timbers, sounding like an old man's moans. In the darkness, he found himself put on edge by the sounds, becoming suddenly apprehensive of what he might find ahead. He thus wound his way with some nervousness through the dingy passages that led between the high stacks of tobacco, until he reached the familiar, little-used companionway to the officers' mess deck. He had used this place for his observations before, and arriving there he settled on the steps where he knew he would best overhear any conversation taking place above. He waited some minutes in silence. But hearing only the continuing dragging sounds of the distant cable and the beat of his own pulse coursing through his ears, his disquiet increased. Perhaps some mischief is afoot, he began to wonder? And the enduring silence then began to concern him more; it felt almost as if the carcass of the ship was holding its breath in expectation of some imminent event.

The sudden thump and clatter of a boat coming alongside startled Judd almost out of his wits, and his heart leapt into his throat. He realised at once, however, that this must be the skiff arriving, and chastised himself for having forgotten its approach. He waited and listened. At first he heard no movement, but then came the sound of footfalls on the boarding ladder and across the deck, light as if stealthily trod, yet swiftly too. Alarm now overcame him, and he decided to risk raising his head above the lip of the hatch so that he could gain a view. The messing area into which his head was thus tentatively inserted served also as an antechamber off which the doors of several cabins opened, including the captain's. The hatches through the hull had been left closed, and so the only light came from the companion leading through a small storage space towards the main deck. Judd waited as his eyes adjusted to the dim light, alert for any sound or movement. Everything seemed strangely still at first, but as he peered into the gloom, he became aware of shifting shadows at the far end of the companion. It appeared that a meeting of some sort was taking place there, but curiously, he could hear no sound of voices. Confident that he would not be seen in the dim light, he thus ascended into the area and moved closer, hiding himself behind a bulkhead where he might bring himself within hearing range. Only now did he hear the mutterings that passed within the group; they seemed urgent and clipped, as if some plot were being hatched. Judd's heart began to pound and he felt the prickle of fear break out on his forehead. Suddenly it dawned that the ship was about to be taken, just when it was at its most vulnerable with the crew split, distracted, and unarmed. And he realised at once that it would not take many intruders to overpower them now. Not for the first time on this calamitous day, his thoughts fell to flight. Indeed he had begun to prepare for it with the launching of the third boat in case escape became opportune. Now, however, with the arrival of a sailing skiff, he might have a swifter means of escape.

'But what of my money?' he wondered. He had come too far to flee without that!

With bated breath, Judd started across the antechamber towards the captain's cabin. Before him stood the mess table, and he skirted around this carefully on the balls of his feet so as to make no noise. He need not have been quite so careful; the creaking of timbers and the sounds of lapping of water in the slight sea would have masked all but the clump of heavy boots. He reached the cabin door and pushed it open; strangely it had been left ajar. He went inside, quickly pushing the door to behind him, and leant against the doorpost, his heart thumping in his chest from fear that he might have been observed. But there was no sign of any reaction from the companion. Daylight streamed in through the stern windows of the cabin. He gathered his wits and looked about; and his eyes encountered a most unexpected and awful sight. On the cabin floor, lay the bodies of Pettigrew and Hayward, trussed up in such a way that their wrists and ankles met behind their backs, their arched spines bent like bows. And tied at the back of their heads was a thick cord that ran the full circumference of jaw and neck across their gaping mouths like a gag that was pulled so tight that their faces had been stretched as if set into a scream. Judd's hand went to his mouth in horror, for the sight was both grotesque and frightening. He thought at first that they were dead; but then he saw their eyes and heads moving to and fro in urgent movements, as if pleading to be released. Driven by rising panic, Judd dropped to his knees instantly and began to loosen Pettigrew's ropes, glancing repeatedly over his shoulder at the door as if expecting it to be thrown open at any moment. The knots were tightly tied; his fumbling fingers began to ache with the strain, yet he seemed to be making no progress. And then he stopped and sat back on his heels, letting his hands fall to his sides.

Pettigrew's eyes flashed the question that he could not speak, and he jerked his head wildly as if urging Judd to continue. But Judd did not respond; instead his face broke into a self-satisfied expression - as if he were reminded of an amusing notion. Pettigrew now yanked against his restraint and tried to cry out - but the gag reduced his angry shout to a strangled gurgle. Hayward did the same; and for a while both bodies writhed on the cabin floor, struggling desperately to get free. But Judd did not respond. Instead he simply turned away, indifferent to their enraged glances, and with a smug leer upon his face, he rose and moved across the cabin towards Pettigrew's bunk. He found what he sought straight away...

Chapter Twenty-One

Jack slipped from *Warrior's* lee and sailed the skiff down tide and down wind, taking a course that approached the grounded vessel from the rear. With him, all armed and keyed up for a fight, were Sir Michael, Ned, and Captain Goddard. They left behind the first officer, his crew, and Matthew to guard against the possibility of retaliation once fighting broke out; while the unarmed boatmen of *Miranda's* anchor party might not pose much of a threat against *Warrior's* musket power, nothing was being left to chance. Heading up and dropping the gaff in one slick manoeuvre, Jack brought the skiff neatly alongside and tied up, then led his group quietly up the boarding ladder and onto *Miranda's* deck. Although there was still a lot of activity on the foredeck, all the attention there seemed focussed on the boats to seaward, and the main and quarterdecks were thus eerily quiet. For a moment, Jack wondered what next to do, but then he saw Major Lawrence beckoning from the companion doorway underneath the quarterdeck, and made immediately towards him.

'In here!' whispered the major urgently, holding the door open for the group as they approached, and pushing it closed quickly behind them.

The arrivals now found themselves in the gloomy storage area that was also the passageway that led to the officer's quarters further aft. When their eyes had adjusted to the dim light, they saw that they were crowded in the narrow space by the scouts, all bristling with muskets and pistols. The area was dusty and cluttered with shelves, full to overflowing with ropes and other paraphernalia; the atmosphere smelled of unwashed clothes, sweat, and damp timber.

'We've got the two who were on the quarterdeck tied up in the captain's cabin,' said the major, sweeping his glances around the new arrivals' enquiring faces. 'Hopefully they are the two you wanted, Jack? And as you see, the crew are still so occupied with all that thrashing about in the boats that they seem not to have noticed our arrival.' Then to Goddard: 'I thought we may as well wait for them to finish our work for us, captain; I was certainly not going to volunteer to row another damned boat for you if I could avoid it!'

Jack moved to the door, pulled it ajar and peeped through the gap.

'You said you had two of them tied up, major?' he asked, shortly. 'There was a third – bearded - the one who was in charge of the foredeck party when I last observed him through my glass - but I don't see him now.'

'I saw someone go into the fo'csle as you were approaching, Jack – possibly the one you're talking about – I haven't seen him come out yet, so he's still in there.'

'Hmmm,' muttered Jack doubtfully as he continued to scan the decks through the gap. The major had not known that there would be three in charge, for he and his militia were already underway when Jack had first spied Hayward. Jack felt a sudden shiver of alarm to think that Judd was at large somewhere on the ship. He scanned the milling crowd of seamen on the foredeck once again. It was difficult from this distance to be sure that Judd was not amongst them for some were as bearded and swarthy as he. Wherever he is, Jack thought, let's hope that he is still unaware of our presence... But his thoughts were interrupted by some loud shouting from the foredeck, and he saw one of the crewmen climb onto the spit and draw a hand across his throat in an exaggerated manner a number of times – a clear signal that the boats had at last reached a position where they could drop their anchors.

'The signal's been given,' whispered Jack urgently to the assembly pressed up behind him in the dark. 'And that means that the boats will be on their way back very soon. We'll need to have the foredeck party rounded up before they approach otherwise there'll be too many of them for us to cope with all at once. There's still that one in the fo'csle – almost certainly Judd himself, and probably the most dangerous of them all. If he doesn't already know we're here, he'll know as soon as we make our move – and he could cause us trouble if he's armed himself, so we'll need to watch our backs!'

It took some minutes for the kedges to be released from the boats, for they were awkward to manhandle over the transoms. There is always a risk of capsize or hull puncture when levering such heavy, unwieldy objects into the water from small and relatively unstable vessels, and the coordination and balancing required seemed at first quite beyond their crews. It was necessary too for some of the flotation buoys to be cut off the cable to allow it to sink to the bottom and take up the proper line. All this resulted in a degree of chaos in the boats, and at least one man went overboard in the process - much to the amusement of the observers on the foredeck who had nothing for the moment to do, except enjoy the entertainment!

At last the boats completed their tasks and started to return, while the foredeck crew now put heir backs to the capstan bars to take up the slack. This was accompanied by much grunting and wheezing from the men, for it was heavy work, spurred on by coarse encouragement from the former seamen who well knew the procedure from past experience. The lines wound in turn by turn and eventually both went quite taught, lifting themselves clear out of the water at the bow. More effort was now required of the men sweating at the bars as the tension in the lines increased, the wringing fibres groaning and creaking under the tremendous strain put upon them. And suddenly, there was a distinct lurch of the *Miranda's* decks as her head began to respond. It was at this point that new orders would normally be expected, since on the rising tide, the *Miranda* might start to slip off the mud bank at any moment. Several heads thus turned towards the quarterdeck in anticipation of such instruction. But one by one, the men fell silent as they came to see the row of raised muskets that now faced them. The looks upon their faces became suddenly so full of dismay, that in other circumstances some sympathy might have been evoked. But it must have been at once obvious to all that the game was up, for not one moved from his position nor even let out a single syllable of protest.

'Leave me two men, major,' said Captain Goddard, 'these bla'guards seem so good at capstan work, they may as well continue!'

The captives stood at the capstan bars, transfixed, as the captain and two scouts now climbed onto the foredeck with their weapons raised.

'Right, gentlemen, put your backs into it!' And although there may have been some surly looks, the cohort had little choice but to comply.

With the foredeck now under Goddard's strict command, Jack called the remainder of the party around him

'Sir Michael,' he said, quickly, 'We shall be safer holding off the returning boatmen, rather than attempting to round them up as they come aboard. A shot or two across their bows might convey the message, I think?'

'They'd otherwise be quite a handful,' nodded Sir Michael. 'Even though they're not armed, I wouldn't trust them all on deck. We'll make them row against the current for a while to wear them out. The schooner's crew will send them packing if they think of boarding her, so they'll have no choice eventually but to row ashore!' He flashed a glance towards the shoreline in the mist, and then smirked: 'At least that'll get them out of our hair for a bit while we figure out what to do.'

'If they go ashore there,' smirked Jack, following Sir Michael's glance across the shallow water, 'they'll be marooned; that's the island!'

'Even better,' Sir Michael laughed maliciously, rubbing his hands.

But Jack became more serious at once. 'One problem solved, maybe, but Judd's still on the loose below,' he said. 'I'll take Ned and sweep below decks from stem to stern and try to flush him out. You put a couple of the militia under the quarterdeck to ambush him if he comes aft. But get them first to check that our two captives are still secure – we don't want them up and about complicating matters even further.'

Jack stepped aside as Sir Michael, the major, and his group of scouts deployed accordingly, then beckoned Ned to follow him towards the forecastle. 'You and I have work to do,' he said grimly as they walked.

Ned flashed his companion a meaningful look. 'Now we'll get the bastard!' he sneered, pulling the two pistols from his belt.

It was not an easy task to check the holds and the several levels of deck and interconnecting companionways that made up the dingy labyrinths below. Moreover, the lanterns that they carried proved a liability rather than a help and were quickly discarded, for they blinded the eye to anything outside the dim circle of light thrown from the flames. Jack realised too, that Judd would need no better warning of their stealthy advance than to see the loom approaching. They reconciled themselves thus to depend upon their ears rather than their eyes; but this meant agonisingly slow progress - and careful cover of each other's backs. Judd lurked in every recess, his shadow behind every turn, the rustle of his clothing imagined with every slight movement of the ship as the capstan turned and the ship inched her way slowly off the mud. Silently, the pair proceeded; crouching here in silence on bottled breath; flattened there against some bulkhead - expecting Judd to be waiting just beyond. And Jack and Ned's pulses were not steadied by the shots that rang out from Sir Michael's muskets in such tense moments. But Judd was nowhere to be found for all their searching. Yet even as they passed the last hatchway, the creepy feeling haunted them that Judd still watched from some concealment in the cavernous gloom that brooded behind their backs.

They found Schluntz and Hine waiting for them in the messing area when they ascended the stern companionway from the orlop. The space was now illuminated by daylight coming from an open hatch on the starboard side.

'He's not up here, Jack,' said Schluntz, shrugging, the contours of his shaven head glinting in the oblique light. 'We've been through all the cabins, and there is no sign of him.'

Jack was stumped.

'But the other two are still awaiting the pleasure of your company in the captain's cabin - gift-wrapped!' said Hine, mysteriously.

'Hmmm! Thank you, gentlemen.' Jack lifted his eyebrow in curiosity. 'You two head back to the deck now; Sir Michael may need a hand with his turkey shoot! Ned: you stay here and keep a lookout; I'll check the captain's cabin!'

Jack knew at once what Hine had meant when he stepped into Goddard's cabin to find Pettigrew and Hayward trussed up on the floor.

'Frontier expertise!' he thought, admiring the efficient rope work. And for all his revulsion of the bound figures, especially of the former ship-owner from Weymouth who had cost him so dear, he could not help himself snort triumphantly at the sight of these hated men, made to look ridiculous and impotent.

'You'll not get away so easily this time, Pettigrew,' he sneered, dropping onto one knee alongside the contorted form. Then, taking out his pistol, he thrust it under Pettigrew's chin with such force that the man's head flinched backwards with a jerk.

'In fact, I may just deal with you now!' he added, cocking it.

Pettigrew squirmed and whimpered - his eyes bulging as if about to burst. He tried to scream a protest, but it came out as a muted moan, his lips lathering where his distorted mouth chafed upon the rope. Jack bent over the prostrate figure threateningly, bringing his face so close that he could smell the man's fear, and he leered maliciously.

'But I'd rather watch you hang, you bastard!' he rasped through gritted teeth; then threw a careless glance towards the other form lying inertly alongside. 'And you too, Hayward!' he growled. But Jack had no time to dally further; his search for Judd was certainly more pressing than idle taunting.

Getting to his feet, he scanned the clutter in the cabin for anything that might provide a clue. The thought of his money flashed into his mind as his gaze roamed.

'If it is anywhere aboard, then this is where it would be hidden,' he thought.

But there was no time to dally with Judd still on the loose and so he made to leave. Then some activity in the water outside drew his eye astern, through the glazing. Stepping closer to the windows, he saw the ship's two boats heading off to landward in an unexpected hurry. Evidently Sir Michael's muskets had done the trick and the oarsmen had given up trying to get back on board. Their strokes, however, were in some disarray as they pulled for the distant beach amidst a flurry of splashing, and they rowed with such apparent frenzy that it seemed almost as if they were pursued. Yet what could be pursuing them, Jack could neither see nor guess. But then he began to wonder if instead the boats were pursuers rather than pursued, for something in the water ahead of the splashing oars then drew his gaze. In his scan of the cabin earlier, he had noticed an eyeglass on the table, and he now returned to pick it up. Extending and levelling the instrument to his eye, he focussed upon the distant object. At first he had some difficulty in making out its shape for the flurry of spray in the foreshortened foreground that obscured it. But then he realised what it was. It was the gaff rig of his own skiff that he saw; the useful little vessel that he had left so carelessly left tied up alongside when he had boarded. And there hunched over the tiller, was Judd.

His heart sank. 'And my money with him!' he thought bitterly.

Chapter Twenty-Two

'Judd's taken the skiff!' Jack shouted at his friend as he raced through the lobby on his way back to the deck; and Ned was not slow to follow. But in their blind haste, it was not until the pair reached Sir Michael and the scouts standing at the starboard rail that they became aware that another vessel had appeared upon the scene. The sight of her large and majestic form so close at hand was both astonishing and impressive. Little more than a hundred yards off the starboard bow, ghosting to a stop against the current in the deeper water of the channel, *Miranda's* sister ship, *Rebecca*, dropped anchor with a tremendous splash. While at her stern, three of her boats were already underway, each with a full complement of oarsmen bent energetically to their oars. And it was clear that the three craft had pursuit very much in mind, for in their bows stood several men with muskets raised in the direction of the fugitives, now disappearing fast towards the shore.

Jack was astonished at the sight.

'By God, *Miranda's* crew must have galloped non-stop the whole way to Annapolis! Nor could they have lost a single minute before getting the *Rebecca* underway. They have done well!' said Jack, surveying the handsome craft with his telescope. 'And I see some familiar faces of our crew in the boats too!'

At this moment, Captain Goddard came running down the gangway from the forecastle, out of breath.

'We're afloat and swinging to anchor,' he said in some relief. 'Now we'll have them!' He flicked a glance at the pursuit astern and grinned. 'Sergeant Hine: you and four of your men stay on board to guard our captives there,' he ordered, cocking a thumb at the foredeck crew who now slumped on the capstan bars exhausted from their labours. 'Everybody else: I suggest you grab your weapons and follow me! We'll join the chase! We've got a score to settle!'

And so it was that the *Miranda's* remaining boat was soon cast off and pulled away under six oars. And with Sir Michael, Captain Goddard, and Major Lawrence rowing on the starboard side, she had a determined crew; with Ned, and Sergeants Schluntz and Bryant to larboard making it formidable. In the prow was stashed as much weaponry as they had been able to carry down the boarding ladder, while at the helm, in his customary position, stood Jack.

A gull's-eye view of the pursuit would now have seen three vessels being pursued by four, the latter comprising three from the *Rebecca* in line abreast, with Jack's boat bringing up the rear. The three pursued boats, forming an inverted 'V' formation with Judd's sailing skiff at its acute apex, were somewhat more dispersed. Judd, leading the others by some three hundred yards, was probably as intent upon out-distancing his former comrades as those who followed on behind, for he had no intention of being caught-up by any of them – either on sea or land. As far as he was concerned, the *Miranda* exploit was an enforced complication in his scheme to get rich. And since he now had the money, he needed none of them any more. However, although Pettigrew and Hayward could be counted as out of the picture for good, the scum who followed him so closely might still pose a threat, especially if they were to catch him with the saddlebags. His intention had been to slip away from the *Miranda* unseen and run the skiff ashore, and then make his way northwards on foot to find some unsuspecting community where he might settle. But the arrival of the *Rebecca* on the scene and the flight of his former comrades now forced him to re-assess his plan, for even though he would beat his pursuers to the beach, they would be breathing down his neck once on land. The beach was now only half a mile ahead; it was time for a decision.

Our gulls squawking overhead would now see the skiff turn sharply northwards, to run parallel with the beach instead of directly for it. At first, the two fugitive boats behind continued steadily on their courses, but soon they too began to turn, although there seemed to be some uncertainty in their manoeuvres. It was the starboard boat that was the more decisive and the quicker to react, while the larboard vessel seemed to hesitate before commencing the turn - one might imagine some disagreement amongst the crews who would by now most certainly have been tiring. Because of the difference in their rates of turn, however, the paths of the two craft now began to converge - slowly but surely. And this seemed to go unnoticed by the distracted helmsman as the vessels closed. Until at last the oars of the two craft began to overlap. More experienced coxswains could even now have made a change of course that would have pulled them clear, but alarmed by the near collision, at least one oarsman panicked and pulled too hard, causing his oar to slip out of its rowlock. With the sudden loss of purchase on the ensuing stroke, he lost his balance and toppled backwards into the oar of the man behind. This was the trigger for a chain reaction, for within seconds, all the nearside oars of both boats were enmeshed, askew, or floating in the water, accompanied by the resounding clatter of wood upon wood. From an airborne perspective, the two craft, from height resembling a pair of lovelorn hexapods locked in some mating embrace, came to an abrupt stop, the water around them whipped to foam by floundering oars. And while they struggled to push themselves apart, they were surrounded by their pursuers arriving at the scene.

Judd must have thought himself blessed when he glanced astern to see his former comrades in such a pickle, and he watched in triumph as they were encircled by the *Rebecca's* boats. But he had not yet seen Jack's boat hidden in their wake.

Judd's earlier sharp turn presented Jack with a corner to cut, and he now steered his boat to take up an intercepting course. At his urging, his gallant crew increased their pace, digging deeper and bending further with each stroke so that the *piano* melody of the wave playing on the bow as it parted the rippled water rose to a boisterous *fortissimo*. The boat now fairly leapt along, and at first seemed to be closing on the skiff. Judd was clearly within musket range now, but it would be a long shot from an unsteady platform.

'Better come closer before we try,' thought Jack.

But the wind, unlike Jack's oarsmen, was tireless, and under its gentle caress the skiff accelerated on her new point of sail – now a reach rather than a run. Jack shouted encouragement to his flagging crew, but he knew they were nearly spent. It was Sir Michael and Captain Goddard who by their evident distress and laboured breathing were closest to exhaustion. The supremely fit major, in stroke position, maintained a punishing pace, but even he was tiring - as were his fellow scouts. And despite the initial benefit presented by the skiff's turn, the sailing craft still led by several hundred yards - and the range was now no longer closing.

Reluctantly, Jack conceded.

'Easy now, boys,' he said, resignedly, 'we'll never catch him now. Rest your oars.'

And the boat came quickly to a stop, the resting oars acting like brakes in the water. Several of the oarsmen threw back their heads and gasped for air, others slumped over their oars; but in all their flushed and sweating faces was the acknowledgement of defeat. Despite their valiant effort they had lost, and there is no worse punishment for such men than failure.

But Jack had not yet given up. He clambered across the thwarts using the shoulders of his doubled-over crew as props to reach the stash of muskets in the prow. He pulled one up, cocked it, and raised it to his shoulder. The skiff was a good three hundred yards away and moving swiftly across his line of sight. It would be a difficult shot, he thought - and one made more difficult by the unsteadiness of the boat! He stilled his breathing and took aim. His target was a mere speck above his foresight, which wavered unpredictably with the motion of the boat - sometimes by so much that his shot might be thrown off target by tens of yards. He would have to average it, he decided, elevating for range and taking wind and rate of crossing into account as best he could. It was pure guesswork, and in his heart he knew that it would be a miracle even to come close. He squeezed the trigger, and out of the corner of his sighting eye he saw the flintlock swing over and slam down with a spark. But the charge did not ignite.

'Wet!' he swore volubly and threw the weapon down, and rummaged in fury amongst the stash to select another. Once more he took aim and squeezed the trigger. This time the charge ignited with a splutter, and half a second later the musket fired. But the recoil was unexpectedly fierce, and with his stance made awkward by the confines of the prow, the kick blew him sprawling rearwards onto the bent backs of Sir Michael and Ned sitting directly behind. They yelled an irritated protest but turned to help him up. Jack struggled to his feet muttering oaths under his breath as though the whole world conspired to thwart him. He picked out another musket and raised it to his shoulder. The skiff sailed on across his sights. His first shot had clearly missed its mark; but he had no idea where it had fallen and so had no basis on which to adjust his aim. He made a random guess and fired again.

Another miss!

Behind him, his crew were now beginning to stir - shifting in their seats to get a view - and the boat began to rock unsteadily with their movement.

'Stay still!' he shouted, and pulled a fourth musket from the stash.

Jack braced himself upon the gunwale as the rocking subsided and then impatiently took aim again. But he could not steady his weapon. A surge of desperation ran through his veins; his target was diminishing with each second lost and he was beginning to lose hope. But just as he was about to fire again, there came a thundering retort that shook the air. He ducked instinctively; and almost instantaneously the air was rent by a whining shriek that zipped overhead at sonic speed. Two seconds later the shriek terminated in a great plume of water that shot twenty feet into the air, not a hundred yards beyond. Jack glanced behind to see a waft of smoke curl around the Rebecca's bow; and as it cleared, the four gaping mouths of her larboard gun ports were revealed.

'Jesus! A bit more elevation, if you please!' he shouted at the vessel in some pique, and he jerked a finger towards the sky as if signalling to some observing telescope. Then with a triumphant laugh he shouted:

'The game's back on, boys! Sir Michael, you take the helm and steer for the skiff!' With this he levered the exhausted and un-protesting colonel from his seat and took up the abandoned oar as Sir Michael stumbled aft to take the tiller. Meanwhile, his comrades, reinvigorated by the action, straightened their backs and took their oars once more into their grip.

Ned was now Jack's new companion on the bow thwart - he caught his friend's eye and winked conspiratorially as they strained with their first stroke. 'We'll get our money yet!' he grunted.

'Set the pace, major!' Jack shouted. 'But keep it slow and steady. We don't want to come too close until the firing's over.'

'How the devil are they bringing their guns to bear whilst still at anchor?' muttered Ned as the stroke rate took a marked step up.

'Steerageway in the current,' answered Goddard from the seat immediately in front, 'But they won't have that much azimuth control.'

Another thundering retort now split the air; and another plume of water shot into the sky - this time so close to the fleeing skiff that Judd might have got a drenching. Sir Michael, seated at the tiller, had the best view. 'That's the idea!' he shouted gleefully, appearing to have recovered from his earlier fatigue. 'Up a notch, and it'll hole her!'

'As long as she doesn't take our money to the bottom with her, I'll be happy with that!' panted Jack in between his strokes.

Ned grunted his agreement.

'Wait! He's turning for the shore!' shouted Sir Michael.

'Trying to get out of range,' said Goddard.

'He'd have a better chance if he stayed on his line,' said Jack, sagely.

And just as he said this, the *Rebecca* fired again, and again the shot went screaming overhead. This time, Jack could not resist craning his head at the back of his next stroke to catch a glimpse of where the shot would land; and he was disappointed to see the plume erupt some twenty yards beyond Judd's fleeing craft.

'Close!' called Sir Michael, from the helm.

'Not close enough!' said Jack, craning again to catch glimpses of their target at the back of each alternate stroke.

But when he caught sight of the skiff next time he looked, something about the set of the skiff's main sail had changed. At first it was not clear what had happened, but with a second glimpse he saw at once that the tall gaff had been severed just above the masthead. The shattered remnant, along with the entire upper half of the main sail, had thus collapsed, making an untidy and ineffectual heap of the canvas that almost completely enshrouded the rear half of the boat. There might be a little residual windage from this heap in the following wind, but now only the small jib would make any real contribution to her propulsion.

'Her main's gone!' Jack shouted triumphantly. 'The shot must have clipped her gaff! We've got her now!'

'Don't speak to soon; Judd's taking out his oars!' called Sir Michael from the helm. 'He's not giving up!'

'Up the pace, major!' called Jack. 'Let's give it everything we've got!'

Jack took another glance over his shoulder. Even at the distance, Judd's dark figure could be seen manhandling his long oars into position and pushing aside the debris to make a place to sit. With all the clutter around him, the boat would be awkward to row, but his oars were soon seen splashing in the water as he bent his back to the task. In the meanwhile, the range between the skiff and her pursuer had closed, and was reducing markedly each time Jack stole another glance. But even though the skiff's speed was now a fraction of what it had been, she still made steady progress towards the beach, and Jack soon realised that they would not beat her to it. Sir Michael clearly had the same concern:

'If he gets into those dunes, we could lose him!' he cautioned from the stern seat.

The major now glanced over his shoulder towards the skiff and the fast approaching beach. He glanced again several times between his powerful strokes, clearly making some assessment with his calculating eyes. And with each glance he saw both vessels coming closer to each other and to the shore; but while the skiff had perhaps a hundred yards to go, Sir Michael's boat had at least two.

'Steer directly for the beach, Sir Michael,' said the major, 'Give us a stable footing before he finds cover and I'll wager an extra week's pay we'll bring him down!'

'You bring him down, major, and there's two weeks extra pay for the whole of your platoon!' replied Sir Michael, emphatically.

The skiff's long keel hit the beach with a shudder. Judd leapt over the gunwales into a foot of water and waded quickly ashore. In his belt he carried two pistols. Draped across his chest, he carried a bandolier of shot and powder; and over his shoulder he carried the two saddlebags containing close on twenty thousand pounds. A glance to seaward showed him that he was a little less than one hundred yards ahead of the fast approaching boat. A glance towards the dunes revealed an equal distance to reach cover. It took an instant to calculate his chances of reaching it before his pursuers arrived upon the beach, for if he could not, his back would be exposed to the volley of musket fire that would surely follow.

It was at once clear what he must do; the lucky canon shot had reduced his lead to too slender a margin, and he must try to buy more time. Pulling out a pistol, he levelled it at his pursuers. His target was now eighty yards from the shore and closing quickly.

Stifling an almost overpowering urge to fire and run, he forced himself to wait; with only two shots at his immediate disposal, he must ensure that each would count.

The range closed to sixty yards!

The broad backs of the two front rowers in the approaching prow now straddled his foresight; but they were still not close enough.

Forty yards!

Either back would serve as aiming point, he thought, for he could not distinguish between them at that range and could not see that one of them was Jack.

Thirty yards!

He made his choice, steadied his aim, and squeezed the trigger. The firing arm swung and the pistol fired. Immediately, he took out his second pistol, levelled it through the lingering smoke, and fired again. Then, without waiting to see if his shots had struck home, he turned, stuffing his weapons into his belt, and scrambled headlong up the beach as fast as his legs would carry him.

Only Sir Michael was facing forward as the boat approached the shore, but the six men that rowed before him with such fervour, partially obscured his view. Over their heads, he saw the skiff's stunted mast come suddenly to a halt, and between their straining shoulders, he saw Judd leap into the water and start up the beach. His view was cut into glimpses by his oarsmen's rhythms. It was not until he heard the first report that Sir Michael realised that Judd had not fled up the beach as he had expected but had made a stand; and it took him quite by surprise. So much so indeed, that a second shot was to ring out before he would react.

Too late he swung the tiller over to throw off the shooter's aim, and even as he did so, he saw the starboard bow oar drop into the water as Jack let out a grunt of pain and fell forward in his seat. Time seemed suddenly to slow then, and he saw the unfolding sequence as if each fraction of a second extended a hundredfold. The yaw of the rudder and the loss of starboard thrust now summed to turn the boat sharply. Despite the swing, the rowing rhythm, driven by inertia, did not at first falter. Thus, on the succeeding stroke, the two starboard oars collided with Jack's, and were deflected deep into the still fast-moving water. The oars thereby were driven to pivot about their rowlocks with such impetus that their rowers were yanked bodily from their seats. The resulting shift of balance now caused the boat to roll, lifting the larboard oars abruptly clear of the water at the peak propulsive moment, when the rowers' backs were strained to the maximum degree. The sudden loss of purchase at an instant of such high torque threw all three oarsmen sprawling backwards, and their oars fell about them in disarray. The boat thus slewed to a sudden and untidy stop some ten yards from the beach. And all this had occurred within a few seconds of Judd's last shot.

It took a few seconds more before several dazed heads raised themselves above the gunwales to take stock. Ned's first instinct was immediately to attend to his fallen friend, and within moments he was at his side, probing the nature of his wound. Sir Michael and Captain Goddard were also drawn to Jack's condition, as the water that slopped around their feet now turned scarlet with his blood. Major Lawrence, however, had other priorities on his mind; and it took only a glance at his two scouts and the firm set of his jaw to convey his command. Without so much as a murmur passing between them, he and his two companions were over the side and wading ashore, carrying their long muskets at shoulder height. And already in their sights was Judd, who by this time was half way up the beach, still racing flat out for the sanctuary of the dunes. The sand was clearly soft underfoot, for his stride was both frantic and irregular. And he could be seen glancing over his shoulder with every half-dozen steps. The major and his men moved without haste as they came onto the firm sand just above the water line, walking with their weapons levelled to their aiming eyes. Behind them the boat drifted in, askew, borne by the lapping swell, with Ned and Goddard still bent over their wounded comrade; while only Sir Michael stood upright to watch the coming execution.

No sooner had the military trio reached the shore than all three dropped down onto one knee in a line, taking up their firing positions with such symmetry and order that it must have been well rehearsed. A few more seconds passed as Judd scrambled further up the beach; but there seemed still no haste about the marksmen's careful aim. Indeed, to Sir Michael's anxious gaze, it looked as if they were leaving it too late.

'You first, major,' said Schluntz calmly from under his stock; and a second later, the major's musket fired.

There was no need for a second shot.

As the smoke cleared, Judd's distant form could be seen lying prostrate on the sand not ten yards from the dunes he had failed to reach.

And so it seemed that with the major's deadly aim, Jack's fight with Judd was ended as he had wished. But Judd's last shot had also met its mark. Now Jack's life hung in the balance as he lay dazed and bleeding in the boat; and for him, another fight had only just begun.

Chapter Twenty-Three

It was now three days since Ned and Matthew had sailed the skiff out to meet Jack in the Potomac to convey the important news of the *Miranda's* passing. Harding and Rose had watched them set off from the bluff at the mouth of the river and had seen their rendezvous and subsequent departure. And it had not been any surprise that Ned and his young companion had remained aboard, for both had professed an eagerness to join Jack in the chase – Matthew most enthusiastically. Having watched them go, Rose and Harding had then been driven back to New Hope by Sebi, who might have pressed to go aboard the schooner too had he been twenty years younger. But the injuries from his fight with Judd had also affected him; even so long after the event, he still complained of headaches and walked with a slight limp – and it was sadly beginning to look as if his age was catching up, for he had lost his former ebullience.

Harding had been quick to relate the nature of the mission upon which the New Hope men were now embarked, and therefore no one, least of all Rose, underestimated its dangers. The days of waiting for the schooner's return had thus passed anxiously for those who had remained behind. Indeed, such was the level of fretfulness, particularly for the two women who had perhaps the greatest at stake, that Lady de Burgh suggested that it might be therapeutic if a lookout were maintained in the hope of an early sighting. A sort of informal roster had thus been drawn up that sent Rose accompanied by Mr Harding, or Lady de Burgh accompanied by Sebi, to make the short journey to the bluff from which a distant view of the Chesapeake could be gained. And between these visits, those not so occupied could return to some semblance of normal routine.

It was the second such visit of the third day, during the late morning to be more precise, when Rose and Harding reached the bluff on foot, both having been quite keen for the exercise as a distraction. Harding was first to spot a distant sail resembling the schooner's rig entering the Potomac; and he was at once certain that it was she. They waited patiently as she progressed towards them on a steady reach, but it was not until some two hours later that the vessel finally rounded the bluff, coming at that time just close enough for them to recognise the forms of some of those aboard. Goddard's first officer was at the helm. And there was Sir Michael, and Ned, and young Matthew on the afterdeck, with others who neither Rose nor Harding recognised. But they could not see Jack's profile amongst the group as the vessel passed abeam and headed for the creek.

At first, Jack's absence did not alarm them, for he could well have been below. But there was a strange solemnity about the group that was unexpected and immediately worrying. A successful outcome to the mission would surely have produced more celebration or levity in their behaviour? Harding and Rose followed her along the path in thoughtful silence. Their hearts were telling them that something was amiss, yet neither wished to voice their intuition. The vessel turned into the creek before them. It was nigh on high water, so she had a clear run in and was able to use the last of her residual momentum to come alongside the quay, even as the encircling trees took her wind. She was expertly piloted to a stop.

The pair continued along the path, which now led around the southern perimeter of the basin on the side opposite to the quay where the schooner now lay. Here they stopped and watched as her warps were made fast – it was the closest they could come from their direction without the long walk round. They might have stood within thirty yards of her, yet apparently they had not been seen through the greenery that must have shielded them from view. Impatient for news of the pursuit, Harding strode out onto the gravel beach and hailed across the water:

'Sir Michael,' he shouted in a half-hopeful tone, cupping his hands to his mouth. 'Did you catch her?' His voice echoed in the enclosure.

Sir Michael looked across the glassy water and lifted a hand in recognition.

'Yes! We got her,' he shouted back. But his voice was weary, not one which signalled any triumph or elation.

Rose frowned. 'Something is wrong,' she whispered to herself, her innermost fears at last given expression. 'Why has Jack not come on deck?' And with this thought she stepped forward onto the beach to stand at Harding's side.

'Is that you Rose?' Sir Michael shouted in some surprise. 'I'm sorry, I did not see you, my dear.'

'Where's Jack?' she returned, anxiously.

Sir Michael paused only the slightest moment before replying, but his evident consternation was enough to confirm Rose's fears.

'Where's Jack?' she demanded again, this time with some apprehension in her voice.

Harding took her arm, for he too feared the news that was to come.

'You are not to worry, Rose,' called back Sir Michael in a consoling voice. 'He has been hurt, I'm afraid, but...' He faltered, as if unable to speak the lie of false hope; and then repeated rather lamely: 'You're not to worry, now; we shall bring him to the house directly.' Then in a commanding voice directed at the agent: 'Harding: you must take Rose and go there at once, and have the doctor sent for without delay.'

Rose raised her hand to her mouth and let out a little gasp of distress, but she leant on Harding's arm and let him lead her away.

An array of anxious faces greeted Sir Michael's procession as it came within sight of the house along the track up from the quay. Lady de Burgh stood out prominently amongst the cluster of servants hurriedly called to the front door to await it. They were ready for any contingency. In her customary manner, the Lady had taken charge, relegating Rose to the role of observer in a medical reception that looked almost more military in its nature than it looked sympathetic. This may have been just as well, for in such circumstances, the cool head of Sir Michael's good wife was exactly what was required. Thus, no sooner had Harding conveyed the news of the emergency, had the preparation of a sick-bed for Jack been ordered, a rider to fetch the doctor dispatched, and several pots of water put upon the stove.

Jack came into view recumbent on a flat handcart, bundled in blankets, secured by several leather straps, and drawn in a sort of silent, almost funereal, reverence by Major Lawrence's militia. Sir Michael, walking at a brisker pace had got ahead, and Ned and Matthew were not far behind him.

Rose broke ranks from the reception party and ran along the track towards the procession as quickly as her skirts permitted, barely acknowledging Sir Michael's expectant glance as she passed him by. But Ned blocked her path as she came upon him and he caught her in his arms.

'He's hurt bad, Rose,' he said urgently as he restrained her. 'Shot in the back by Judd.'

She gave out a little cry. 'Oh Ned, let me go to him!'

'He's unconscious, Rose. They stopped the bleedin' aboard the *Rebecca* but could not get the bullet out. Jack went into a fever last night as we sailed for home as fast as we could, but he's gone terrible cold and pale now. He's lost a lot of blood.'

By this time the cart and its guard had caught up and Rose swung a wide-eyed gaze towards it. In some desperation, she broke from Ned's grip and rushed to Jack's side, Major Lawrence making space for her as she approached. But the cart continued on.

'I've seen worse, ma'am,' the major consoled gently as he took up step beside her. 'If we can get a proper surgeon to him quickly to get that bullet out, we'll pull him through.'

But Rose was not to be so readily soothed.

'Jack!' she gasped, reaching her hand tentatively across her husband's still form, removing the blanket from his face. 'Oh Jack!' she cried to see the ashen greyness of his features and the smearing of dried blood revealed upon his cheek and neck. 'What a mess they have made of you,' she thought. 'Oh, my poor Jack!'

'Took it in the shoulder, ma'am,' said the major, 'but the charge must have been light, for the bullet does not appear to have gone too deep; and I don't think that the bone has been penetrated by it.'

As soon as the cart arrived at the house, eager hands were at once at the buckles of the straps to release Jack from his restraint.

'Be careful now!' cautioned Lady de Burgh. 'Ned! Major Lawrence! Bring over that stretcher,' she ordered, casting her gaze about. 'You men: get your arms under him like a cradle! Gently now! And lift him...carefully!'

Jack's limp, unconscious body was now borne up by six strong militia arms from one side of the cart while a stretcher was slid underneath from the other. He was then lowered upon it with such infinite care that it seemed his bearers thought he might be shattered by the slightest jar. Now, with Ned taking the handles at the front and the major at the rear, the stretcher was lifted clear.

'Right,' ordered Lady de Burgh as if she had been leading a military charge, 'follow me!' And the whole party followed her obediently into the house.

The doctor arrived from nearby Leonardtown an hour later, and he raced to Jack's bedside to find Rose and Lady de Burgh hovering uncertainly nearby.

'I came as quickly as I could, Caroline,' he said, slightly out of breath. 'A bullet wound I hear. Let me have a look at him.'

The doctor was a short, bespectacled man whose young face made it difficult to believe that he could be old enough to be a qualified medical practitioner with an Edinburgh degree. But he clearly had the full confidence of Lady de Burgh who had greeted him like a friend. He strode to Jack's bedside and pulled back his sheets. Jack lay on his side with his wounded left shoulder uppermost; it was the sight of the bloody bandages that covered the wound so roughly that greeted the doctor's examining eyes. The doctor's face remained expressionless in the manner of one hardened to such gruesome sights. He picked the bandages away and stooped to survey the glistening wound so closely that one might have thought him a little short-sighted. The edges of the wound were blackened with congealed blood, and the flesh surrounding it was torn, evidence of some clumsy attempt to extract the projectile still lying deep within. Bloody hand marks and fingerprints covered the entire shoulder and breast.

'Hmmm! The bullet's still inside,' he said, straightening. He raised his hand to Jack's neck where it searched for a pulse, and he brought his ear closer to Jack's half-open mouth as if listening for breath. 'Hmmm. Breathing shallow; pulse a little weak,' he muttered almost to himself as Rose and Lady de Burgh anxiously looked on.

'I have some laudanum, but I do not believe that he will benefit from it in his current state,' he continued. 'Indeed a modicum of pain, if he can feel it, may arouse him from his stupor.' The doctor rummaged in his bag, brought out a small wooden box, and selected from it a number of metal instruments, which he then placed in an enamelled dish.

'Here, take these and boil them well in water, then put the instruments in the dish to carry them back,' he said. 'And do not on any account touch the instruments once you have boiled them - fish them out with this hook - I have a theory that that is how infection will spread.' He flashed the lady a meaningful glance. 'And I will also need a large bowl of cooled, boiled water to bathe the wound and some freshly laundered linen to use as swabs and bandages.'

Lady de Burgh took the instruments and hurried towards the door.

'You will have some rum in the house, Caroline, no doubt,' the doctor called to her retreating back, 'I shall need a bottle of your very finest – and not for my consumption either!'

The doctor had managed this levity just as the door was closing, but the tautness of his instructions revealed an underlying apprehension that Rose was quick to detect. The doctor returned to his examination at once, and in the silence that ensued, she felt her hopes falter as she began to contemplate the possibility of the worst of outcomes. In this mood, and in the very room in which she had miscarried their son not many weeks before, her head began to swim with terrible phantoms of utter desolation - as if Jack had already been lost. Her hand went out behind her seeking the back of a nearby chair. She found it and seated herself, and sat for a few moments quite motionless with her hands clasped in her lap, staring forlornly at the doctor's stooping form, praying that he could bring her husband back to life.

The doctor straightened and turned towards her. 'You must be the man's wife?' he asked in a kindly voice, as if sensing her distress.

Rose cleared her throat nervously;

'Yes,' she said, almost in a whisper.

'Good; then you will be my assistant,' he said with an authority that was immediately reassuring. 'Firstly, I shall need as much light as I can get to illuminate my work as dusk will be upon us before long. Fetch me more candles or lamps and arrange them here at the bedside. Then bring some hot water, soap, and clean towels for us to wash our hands. And get yourself a clean pinafore to wear!'

Rose stood, smiled tensely, and wiped the corner of her eye with her hand. She was happy to have something to do.

'Will he be all right, doctor?' she ventured as she made to go. But he had returned to his examination and appeared not to hear her.

The congregation that had assembled in the hallway after Jack's transportation by stretcher to the room above had since thinned out, leaving only Sir Michael, Ned, Matthew, Major Lawrence, and Mr Harding behind. The rest of the scouts had returned to the ship, evidently not wanting to be in the way; and Sebi, having seen Jack taken upstairs had returned to the farmstead with instructions for Matthew to come for him when there was news.

Little had since been said in the hallway. The men had waited uncertainly and in a sort of uncomfortable silence, lost in their own thoughts; and when at last the doctor had arrived, he had paused only long enough for the barest of details of Jack's injury to be conveyed before hurrying up the stairs. The men's fretful stares had watched him go, and the uneasy silence had again fallen like a cloak around them. It had been apparent to all that their presence was now superfluous, but not one of them had been able to bring himself to leave. Instead, holding quite still as the doctor's tread creaked upon the floorboards above their heads, each had pricked up his ears and strained to understand the muffled voices heard spoken at Jack's bedside.

Lady de Burgh and then Rose descended the stairway on their missions for the doctor, but they passed through the hallway distractedly, casting only worried glances at the men's enquiries that met them on the way. The two women returned some minutes later with a laden housemaid in their wake, cutting a path through the assembly with the same fluster and the same determined reticence as before. Again, the group fell quiet as the procession disappeared up the stairway.

Eventually, perhaps eased by this evidence that Jack was in good hands, the atmosphere in the hall became less strained. Thomas Harding was the first to venture conversation; curious to hear about the *Miranda's* recapture, he now pressed his companions for information. The story of the *Miranda's* pursuit into the Chesapeake, the lying in wait at the Cape, and the subsequent taking of the ship and capture of her fugitive crew was thus related, with each contributor adding his own perspective of events. At first, the voices were rather flat and distracted, but fuelled perhaps by Harding's encouraging, sometimes astonished retorts, the tale began to take on something of the nature of an entertainment. It was only when describing Jack's shooting that the tone became more sombre, but the telling recovered its enthusiastic buoyancy as subsequent events were described:

'It was a perfect shot,' said the major, smiling crookedly. 'Over fifty yards!' He got a nod of agreement on this point from Sir Michael. 'And Judd was probably dead before he hit the sand! We'd have dug a grave for him there and then, but with Jack in such a state, we had to leave him where he was. We just grabbed the saddlebags and ran back to the boat.'

Sir Michael interjected as if by way of explanation: 'The main priority was to get Jack back to the *Rebecca* with every possible haste since this was where we would find medical assistance. I must admit that it felt strange to leave Judd's body just lying on the empty beach, but there it is; he was then the least of our concerns! Anyway, Goddard told us he would send a detail back later to deal with him.'

The story continued thus: Jack had been barely conscious as the boat had been hooked on and winched aboard the *Rebecca*, his limp body still cradled in Ned's arms on the forward thwart where he had slumped after being hit. He had then been lifted from the boat and laid out on the deck where the ship's cook-cum-surgeon had at once set to work. The man had done his best to stem the bleeding and clean the wound, but had soon professed that he had neither the skill nor the confidence to attempt the removal of the projectile. It seemed that the bullet had gone so deep into the shoulder that its extraction risked rupturing a major artery.

'And so I insisted at once that Jack be ferried back to the schooner,' said Sir Michael, rather grandiosely, 'in order to sail us back to New Hope as quickly as possible. At least I knew that I could provide a competent doctor here! And Captain Goddard helpfully assigned us the same crew to sail the schooner back – with his first officer as our captain. They, by the way, will sail us up river once we're ready to leave, where they'll wait for the *Miranda* to return to Charlestown to clear her cargo through customs. Apparently, Captain Goddard is obliged to do this before setting off across the Atlantic.'

'Hmmm. As I expected,' replied Harding. 'There will also be some formalities to attend to regarding his murdered crew, I am afraid! The sheriff will want the captain's evidence for his report before he leaves. But what of Pettigrew and Hayward?'

'They and the few fugitives we left aboard the *Miranda* were being transferred to the *Rebecca* just as we departed – where they would join the others rounded up by her boats,' Sir Michael said. 'No doubt the sheriff in Annapolis will know what to do with them when they're handed over!'

Harding nodded sagely. 'They'll need to be made an example of, that's quite certain!'

Sir Michael resumed his story-telling: The schooner had set sail soon after Jack had been brought on board, leaving *Miranda* and *Rebecca* still at anchor off the Cape. With prisoners to secure and the *Miranda's* crew to take possession of their re-captured ship, he opined that both vessels would most likely remain at anchor overnight.

'At any rate, they were still there at dusk when we lost sight of 'em,' chipped in Ned. 'By then we were reachin' up the Chesapeake like a rabbit with a ferret nippin' at its backside!' He chuckled briefly, then checked himself, throwing a guilty glance towards the ceiling.

Sir Michael continued the story, with occasional contributions from the others: The sea distance from the Cape to New Hope measured some eighty miles, and with a fresh breeze steady from the southwest, *Warrior* maintained a good five knots. Jack lapsed in and out of fevered consciousness into the early hours, with ship's rum being liberally administered as disinfectant as well as anaesthetic. But as time had passed, it had become clear to all who took turns to nurse him that he would not survive the brutal regimen for long. By dawn, his brow had begun to cool, his face had turned by degree from bright scarlet to pale grey as his periods of wakefulness had shortened. His body had fought the poison in his blood bravely, but the struggle had apparently drained away his strength.

'For those last few hours before we berthed, it was touch an' go,' said Ned. 'It seemed as if he was jus' slipping away. We jus' prayed we could get back in time.'

And with these words, the tale seemed to come to an end, and there followed a long silence as each of the participants sat back reflectively.

Harding's sigh eventually interrupted it.

'Quite a story,' he breathed at last. 'Let's hope it doesn't end there. Jack deserves to know his victory!'

It would be well past midnight before any news of Jack's progress would be brought down from above. And by this time, the men had moved from the hallway and had distributed themselves around the adjoining living room - a richly furnished space with wood-panelled walls adorned with fine paintings in gilt frames. It now, however, looked somewhat worse for their occupation. An oval rosewood table in one corner was littered with the detritus of an informal buffet of some sort, and there were plates and mugs untidily deposited in various unlikely places around the room. Matthew, Ned, and Major Lawrence lazed in their rough attire incongruously on classic period chairs, while Sir Michael and Mr Harding stood contemplating a detail on the stone fireplace that was the room's impressive focal point - Sir Michael's family coat of arms, which, it might be remembered, Jack had carved some years before.

'This fireplace was Jack's first stonework here,' Sir Michael explained. 'I suppose that you could say that it was this project that marked the beginning of his rehabilitation from convict to freeman – even before he proved his innocence.'

'And it appears that he won it at considerable cost, Sir Michael;' said Harding. 'I wonder if he would now say that it has been worth it?'

'I think...' Sir Michael hesitated. 'I think that with his dying breath, he would confirm it. Only by accompanying him on this last exploit, did I begin to get his full measure. He is a man of such strong principle, Harding, that he is almost reckless in pursuit of it. And his tenacity has served us both very well, has it not?'

Harding nodded but said nothing for several moments while he leant forward to examine Jack's carving more closely.

'Fine work,' he said at last, rubbing his finger over the relief.

'Indeed,' replied Sir Michael, thoughtfully.

There was then the sound of whispered voices from the stairway, and footfalls were heard descending. All five men were instantly alert to the approach, and as the doctor and Lady de Burgh entered the living room from the hall, all eyes were already upon them. There was a moment's hesitation before anything was said, during which the doctor's eyes were seen to flash towards his companion's as if seeking permission to be the first to speak. The Lady nodded with a tense smile.

'The bullet is extracted,' said the doctor, holding up the article between his fingers for all to see, 'and I have sutured, disinfected, and dressed the wound. Just as I had hoped, the surgery proved a stimulus to restoring the balance of his humours, and his circulation seems to have rallied as a result of it.'

The doctor spoke coolly, without emotion, as if describing the repair of some machine, rather than of human flesh and blood.

'He has now gone back into a fever, which I am confident is an indication that the body has once more taken up the fight to heal the poison of the penetration. I have left his wife with him to keep him as comfortable as possible and to re-hydrate his body with a special infusion that I have used before to the great benefit of my patients.' The doctor paused here as if wondering whether there was anything further to add.

'I cannot say that the danger is over, gentlemen, but I can say that we have done everything that is possible to save him.'

The doctor's audience had stood stationary with bated breath as he had spoken, but now they let out a collective sigh of relief.

Upstairs, Jack's fight for life would continue for some hours yet, his fever coming and going, his consciousness ebbing and flooding like the regular turn of the tide. At each crest of fever, his face flushed, his brow poured with sweat, and he swung his gaze about wildly and unseeingly, muttering and mumbling uncomprehendingly. And with each subsequent trough, he subsided again into fitful sleep. When he slept, Rose slumbered in the nearby chair; when the fever raged again, she was back at his side - cooling his brow with a damp flannel and spooning the doctor's special potion into his mouth. Eventually, the fever reached its peak and then broke almost in an instant; and Jack's eyes seemed all at once aware of his candlelit room and his constant attendant.

'I thought I would lose you,' said Rose, tenderly, as she smoothed away the sweaty locks of hair upon his brow.

Jack smiled weakly, and breathed: 'We Portlanders are not so easy to be rid of, are we Rose?' And he gave out a little grunt that would have sounded defiant if he had not been so exhausted.

Then, quite abruptly, there followed a strange moment of seriousness during which Jack appeared to be battling with his thoughts, his face suddenly becoming beset with consternation as if trying to make sense of some mystery. No words were spoken. Perhaps he hadn't the strength? But he searched his wife's concerned gaze for a full half minute as if looking for some explanation to whatever phantoms that had plagued his fevered dreams.

'What is it, Jack?'

'I'm not sure, Rose. I can't seem to get hold of the idea again. Just a bad dream, I suppose.'

And then, with a half-resigned, half-contented sigh, he fell into a peaceful sleep.

Rose was sleeping too as the first light of dawn arrived at the window, and she was not disturbed by a gentle tapping at the door. It was opened by Ned carrying a small tray upon which a few items of refreshment were laid; and he placed it on the table and retreated quietly, leaving both inhabitants to their slumber. He came again a few hours later, this time with Matthew in train. There was again no answer to his soft knock, and so he opened the door quietly as he had done before and peaked around its edge. Matthew craned in tentatively behind him. The sight that met their eyes astonished both, for there, on the bed before them, lay Jack and Rose – he: sitting up, his left arm and shoulder bandaged in a tight sling, ruffled and baggy-eyed but cheerfully aware of their presence at the door; she: sprawled upon the bed at his side, fast asleep.

'What? You two got no work to attend to?' said Jack, wryly.

And so it would appear that Jack would live to fight another day. And fight he would, for after a short period of convalescence, made shorter by his impatience at being treated as an invalid, his duty to Sir Michael and his militia would call again.

But then, that is another story…

OTHER BOOKS BY RON BURROWS

An American Exile
ISBN 978-1-84549-217-5

Available through Amazon and good bookshops

Lightning Source UK Ltd.
Milton Keynes UK
UKOW050912110512

192371UK00001B/7/P